JAMES E. GURLEY is a 61-year old writer of science fiction and horror born in Corinth, Mississippi, but now living in the deserts of Tucson, AZ., with his wife, Kim, and two cats, Coco and Shoes. An avid musician, he plays rock and roll with local area bands when not writing or doing research for his novels. His great loves as writers figure from Lovecraft to Faulkner to King. His life in the medical field, an oil field worker, demolition, a musician, and as an Atlanta chef plays a large part in his writing. He is an active member in the Horror Writer's Association, the Society of Southwestern Writers, and the Baja-Arizona Southern Science Fiction Association.

I dedicate this novel is to my mother, Pearl Irene Kellum Gurley. She was and always will be an inspiration to me.

First Montag Press E-Book and Paperback Original Edition April 2016

Montag Press
ISBN: 978-1-940233-33-8
Cover art © 2015 Dwight Clark
Cover, layout, & e-book © 2015 Blush Book Design

Montag Press Team:
Project Editor – Mara Hodges
Managing Director – Charlie Franco

A Montag Press Book
www.montagpress.com
Montag Press
1066 47th Ave. Unit #9
Oakland CA 94601 USA

Montag Press, the burning book with the hatchet cover, the skewed word mark and the portrayal of the long-suffering fireman mascot are trademarks of Montag Press.

Printed & Digitally Originated in the United States of America
10 9 8 7 6 5 4 3 2 1

THE
POOLS
OF YARAH

A NOVEL BY

JE GURLEY

HRAMACK OF NINGCHA

THE SEARING HEAT OF THE AFTERNOON SUN BEAT FULLY DOWN UPON Hramack's broad, bronzed back as he wandered up and down the steep stone paths of the village. His anthracite eyes carefully searched the village for signs of Kaffa, the Village Elder. He had much on his troubled mind and felt he must speak with his old friend. He wore only loose-fitting trousers and a leather vest in spite of the sun's fury, his arms and shoulders well protected by the oil rubbed into his skin. His thick shock of long, black hair braided atop his head like a burnoose protected it as effectively as the customary leather hat most village men wore.

As Hramack came in turn upon each of the three village cisterns carved deep into the red sandstone rock of the cliffs, he found long lines of women awaiting their daily ration of precious water. He searched eagerly for Teela among them, hoping to speak with her, but she was not there. He assumed she was tending to the children while the other women visited the cisterns. Each woman's haggard face bore the unmistakable signs of strain and something Hramack had never seen on any villager's face – fear.

Like his, their clothing bore innumerable stains from lack of washing. Water was too precious a commodity these days to waste on clean clothing. Dirty clothes were the new badge of honor. He heard none of the good-natured bantering and idle chatter that usually accompanied such gatherings of women. Each woman wordlessly accepted her sadly reduced water ration and returned directly to her home. Soon, he feared, quick anger and resentment would replace silent complacency. Many of the women drank sparingly themselves that the children might have more. Their selfless sacrifice would prove of little avail when the end came, for the children could not survive long without the adults, but he admired their courage and devotion.

He, too, had passed his daily ration back into the cistern many times during the past few weeks. He was young and strong and could tolerate long periods without water. Kena had taught him that. Thoughts of his father brought home the uncertainty of Kena's prolonged absence. Hramack feared for his father and longed for his return from the Burning Lands. Soon, conditions would worsen, and people driven to the limits of their endurance could turn on each other. The village would sorely need his father's skills as Healer then.

Hramack was painfully aware of his own limitations in such situations. Often, the ill or injured hid their pain or the cause of their misery for fear of judgment by others. Kena could ferret out the root cause of their discomfort and heal their wounds. Hramack's inability in this area came from no lack of empathy. He truly wanted to be a Healer, to follow in his father's example, yet the skills of Healing eluded him like water cupped in an open hand. He suspected that he would never become the Healer his father wished him to become.

He glanced across the narrow canyon to the empty Pools of Yarah at the base of the dry springs. The annual return of the springs was three long months overdue, and the water supply in the underground cisterns was running dangerously low. Never in the long history of Ningcha had the water been as late in its return. Soon, the newly planted crops would wither and die in spite of the shade netting strung across the valley to protect them from the searing sun. He feared the sorghum, the puny chickpeas, the flax, and the sadly undersized squash in the fields below would be inadequate for their needs. If the yields were too small, it might become necessary to eat the seed needed for the next year's crop. *If there was a next year.*

The animals grew thinner and weaker daily. Many of the females were no longer producing milk, forcing the villagers to slaughter them for meat. Already the larders were full to overflowing with smoked *goatelope* meat. The hybrid cross between hardy southwestern mountain goats and Gobi Addex antelopes were low-maintenance foragers well suited for the desert climate, and provided both meat and wool. Hanging beside the haunches of goatelope meat were links of spiced sausages made from javalinas, a domesticated peccary. The lack of water was especially hard on the chickens, causing them to lay fewer eggs, but they would outlast the grazing animals. Sadly, starvation would not be the villagers' demise: thirst would.

Dark thoughts such as these plagued Hramack's mind as he spotted Kaffa sitting under the shade of a great *Yar* tree at the foot of the path leading down to the springs.

"Greetings, Elder," he cried as he entered the shade provided by the spreading branches of the massive tree, older than the village itself; the difference in temperature was dramatic. Though not cool by any means, it was a spot often sought out for relief from the searing sun. Hramack noticed that even the great *Yar* was not immune to the lack of water. A carpet of purple heart-shaped leaves covered the ground, crunching beneath the weight of his booted feet.

"Peace and prosperity to you, Hramack," Kaffa responded politely, his voice brittle with age, but still bearing traces of a once-powerful orator's voice.

Hramack bridled slightly at the Elder's jubilant greeting. The *Words of Greeting*, used for hundreds of years, seemed to have lost their meaning lately. Neither spoke for several long minutes, as Hramack settled himself comfortably on one of the many exposed roots polished smooth by countless generations of backsides, and Kaffa shooed away several of the younger children playing loudly beneath the shade of the tree's spreading limbs. Neither heat nor drought slowed the young in their pursuit of amusement. Hramack's eyes followed them as they ran away playing a game of tag. He wished he too could return to the joys of youth, the days when running and play were his only concerns, and lessons and chores the only tragedies. The mantle of coming manhood sat tightly about his neck like a worrisome yoke, choking out memories of his youth and reminding him painfully of the duties and labors of adulthood.

Kaffa noticed the look of dire concentration on his face and broke the silence. "You look troubled, my son. Please unburden yourself. You cannot carry the problems of the entire village upon your back, though a strong, broad back it is."

He offered Hramack a piece of *pori* fruit. In spite of his mental turmoil, Hramack smiled at the gesture. Kaffa could always defuse a troublesome situation. He took the piece of fruit and bit into it, enjoying its cool, moist flesh and delicate taste. The pear-shaped *pori's* burgundy-hued skin was thicker to seal in the moisture. Once peeled, the fruit itself was juicier but had only a single small seed in its center. This made it difficult to reproduce; thus, *pori* was always in short supply.

Kaffa returned Hramack's smile and said, "Our forefathers developed the *pori* fruit from the pear, genetically altering it centuries ago when such manipulation was possible."

Hramack nodded. He had read all of the books in the village's meager library many times over. Many such modified fruits and vegetables graced their tables, designed by plant geneticists centuries ago to adapt to the growing harsh, dry climate. Such things were no longer possible.

"Thank you, Elder," he responded. "Your words always place things in their proper perspective." Hramack nodded at the half-eaten fruit in his hand. "There are few of these left."

"Yarah will see us through these harsh times," replied the old man. "But tell me, what brings you to me with such weariness written in your young eyes?"

Hramack examined Kaffa with his eyes, noticed the slump in the old man's shoulders, the once-brilliant eyes withdrawn into their sockets, the deep wrinkles furrowing his weathered brow. As Elder, Kaffa was a fount of wisdom to the villagers, but as village Precept, conscience of the Council, he took on the additional burden of leadership. His voice had been the one the villagers heard calling for the rationing of water and food, his face the one the people associated with their misery. The responsibility the old man bore was tremendous. Hramack hated that he must add more stones to that weighty burden.

Hramack stood and began to pace back and forth beneath the canopy of the *Yar*, trying to collect his scattered thoughts. He had much he wanted to say, but he had not bothered to organize his speech. Instead, he would speak from his heart.

"Our people grow weaker each day," he began. "Soon, there will not be enough water for both the crops and the herd animals. We cannot survive the loss of either."

Kaffa stood, wearily leaning on his great staff: a delicately carved branch of the *Yar* tree, its polished multi-colored wood topped by a silver orb, and placed a gnarled hand on Hramack's shoulder to stop his restless pacing. He forced Hramack back down to the root and stood facing him, leaning forward slightly to stare at him. Hramack suspected the Elder's eyesight was failing.

"Long ago, our world was green and fertile, and water fell from the skies. Our people grew greedy and destroyed their world. In anger, the sun became hot and boiled dry the great oceans. Most of our people scattered to other worlds among the stars. Yet, some remained, refusing to abandon the land of their birth. They had faith in the future, in their God. When the last of the great domed cities fell centuries ago, Yarah led us here where *He* has allowed us to flourish." He added with a twinkle in his eye, "Do you think *He* would abandon us now? Do not abandon *Him* so quickly."

Hramack sighed. He had heard the same familiar words many times from his father, but belief didn't come easily when your world, your friends were suffering. To avoid offending the Elder, he chose his words carefully.

"I have read the *Teachings of Nuama*, Elder, but with my own two eyes I have seen the great dry salt sea far to the south. Beyond it, the oceans once spread farther than the eye could see. With my father, I have walked in the Burning Lands that surround our sheltered valley. I have even ventured into the fringe of the Empty Lands near the mountains where only sand fleas and predatory beasts live. I do not dispute from where we have come, Elder, or that we have had Yarah's help in surviving thus far. I wish only to know where we are going now. What of tomorrow?"

Kaffa slowly shook his head. "You are truly your father's son. Kena is a great Healer, the greatest in generations, but he too is an impatient man. Our people desperately need him now, but he has been absent a fortnight, gone into the Burning Lands searching for herbs and medicines." Kaffa closed his eyes and lowered his head for a moment in thought, then raised a hand and made a flicking motion. "More likely, he is searching for the ruins of the old cities. It is best to let dead things lie."

"We will all be dead things lying soon enough," Hramack shot back at Kaffa.

Defending the actions of his father had become a full-time job lately. The entire village questioned Kena's wisdom in leaving. He immediately regretted snapping at the Elder. He knew Kaffa only worried about his father.

His father had gone into the Burning Lands two weeks ago in search of *pei*, a small shrub that produced a pungent sap used to treat fevers. Its bark could be ground into a powder to produce a tea that relieved the swelling in joints, while its aromatic leaves seasoned food. He had been gone days longer than usual. His father was an excellent shot with the bow, but Yarah only knew what beasts roamed the Burning Lands or the treacherous Empty Lands that lay beyond.

Kaffa ignored Hramack's impertinent outburst. "Nuama tells us that Kane called to Yarah for guidance when the Dome fell, and Yarah led him and his followers here. Yarah struck the rocks with his power, and water poured forth. Our village has been here ever since, carved into these cliffs overlooking the canyon, protected from the scouring winds that blow across the Burning Lands and sheltered from the full fury of the sun. There are no other civilized people on the face of the world. Remember, Ningcha is the last refuge of Mankind."

With these words, Kaffa turned and hobbled slowly down the path to the Temple of Yarah situated beside the empty pools. Hramack noticed that the Elder leaned heavily on his staff and wondered if he had been drinking his daily water ration. *Probably not*, he decided. The Elder was a stubborn man, but he was selfless in his devotion to the welfare of the villagers. Hramack regretted making him angry. The Elder was trying to hold the village together in this time of crisis, and he was not making Kaffa's job any easier.

Hramack looked around, surveying the only home that he had ever known. Few people roamed the paths or sat on the stone benches in the heat of the day. Most were in their homes, praying or hiding from the sun. Even the children had returned to the shelter of the caves or to their homes.

The village of Ningcha perched on the western side of a narrow canyon protected by a large, overhanging cliff. The stone houses' bright white adobe walls embedded with tiny flakes of mica shone like jewels, as the sun rose each day. Most of the village was carved deep into the cliff face itself, utilizing the density of the stone to cool the homes during the hottest part of the year when the temperatures could reach 55° Centigrade.

There was no longer a winter. For almost a thousand years, since the time of the Great Migration, winter had been absent from the face of the Earth. Snow appeared only on the highest peaks of the Earth. Even there, most of it evaporated before it could melt and reach lower altitudes. The seas were barely thirty percent of their original size and so concentrated with salt that life could no longer exist in them. The very earth had trembled during the Upheaval, as if trying to shake off its unruly children. Freed of their watery burden, the ocean beds rose, dramatically shifting the continental shorelines. Earthquakes toppled cities already abandoned by a star-bound population. The planet had become a desert, and only those things able to adapt to harsh desert conditions had survived.

Humanity, those few people remaining after the Great Migration outward, had survived using remnants of technology. When at last, even that technology had failed and the domes fell, mankind had clung to life solely through tenacity and the strong will to survive. Hramack feared that even strong will would no longer suffice.

Above the village along the rim of the canyon, the gracefully curved blades of a lone wind turbine spun slowly in the light breeze, generating power to light the village and to run the few remaining machines. The rusted trunks of three similar windmills slowly crumbled into the sand. The banks of solar panels surrounding the lone windmill were growing old and were often unreliable. The meager remains of a once vast, planet-spanning technological base were slowly breaking down. Soon, the village would be at the complete mercy of the hostile environment. The last millennium-and-a-half of technological advancement would be lost forever.

Hramack gazed across the canyon. A long, wooden suspension bridge spanned the canyon, providing access to the grain storehouses, the pens for the animals, the workshops, and his home, which also served as his father's infirmary. A narrow path led along the cliff face to the small crevice from which the springs normally emerged. Now, the springs were dry. Where sparkling waters once tumbled into the pools below, dust blew. A broad, winding path led down to the bottom of the canyon, where the animals foraged on the wild plants growing there or ate the fodder provided to them. Stacked-stone walls kept the animals from the newly planted crops. It was the middle of the day, and the animals were in their pens protected from the sun's full fury.

Hramack looked up expectantly toward the cliff top and the path down which his father would come on his return, but saw no sign of his long-overdue father. He prayed Kena was all right. Fourteen days and nights was a long time to be alone in the Burning Lands, even for one as inured to the harsh landscape as Kena. His father could carry enough water for only six days, and the water caches that they had previously established held only enough for three or four days more. His father knew which plants held water hidden in their roots. Even so, two weeks was much too long a time to be gone. Many of the villagers made the Sign of the Bereaved as Hramack passed, believing Kena surely dead.

The village could ill afford to lose its only Healer. Try as he might, Hramack did not have the knack for healing that his father possessed. True, he knew the herbs and ointments and how to find the plants that rendered them, but he did not have the gift of empathy that allowed his father to discern the source of his patient's ailments or to ease their troubled minds. Perhaps it was because he had never felt pain. Not knowing pain, he was unable to cure it. The only pain he had ever faced was the loss of his mother, a pain of the heart and mind, not of the body. Kena was indispensable to the village; Hramack knew he was not. He sighed, realizing that he had made his decision.

Later, when the sun had set, he would venture into the Burning Lands in search of his father. He knew what areas his father frequented to forage for *pei* and *leche* root. He would try there first. If, as Kaffa believed, Kena had left to search for the ruined city, Hramack might never find him. His father worked only from small clues, which he had gleaned over the years. The Burning Lands presented a vast area to search, a seemingly impossible task. He drove that negative thought from his mind.

Thoughts create reality. Kena was alive. Hramack knew it. He did not know how he knew this thing, but the bond between father and son was very strong. He often knew Kena's words before he spoke them, or knew where in the village Kena was, though he had not seen him go there. Such bonds were a gift from Yarah, Kaffa had said. It meant father and son were destined for great things together. Hramack was not as certain, not if greatness meant popularity.

His mother had died ten years earlier when she had fallen from the wooden bridge spanning the canyon during a sudden summer sandstorm, a *haboob*. Though custom dictated that Kena remarry, he had chosen not to. Hramack held his father in high esteem but never more than when he had chosen to honor the memory of Allana, his deceased wife, over custom. This action had turned many of the people against Kena, especially Chu Li, whose daughter Megan would have been Kena's new bride. Chu Li, the High Priest of Yarah, now spoke out openly against Kena and his attempts to find the ruined city, calling it a blasphemy against Yarah. Most villagers ignored the High Priest because Kena was necessary to the welfare of the village. More to the point, they did not want a return to the old, harsh religious laws that Chu Li advocated.

Now, with Kena's prolonged absence and the springs so late in their return, many were beginning to heed the High Priest's words more closely. They felt abandoned by both their Healer and by their God. A return to the old ways seemed a likely solution to those seeking Yarah's approval.

Hramack knew he must go in search of his father. Though many of the villagers his own age would gladly accompany him, it would only draw down upon them the wrath of the Council. He would go alone. It would be better to expose only himself to the risks of the Burning Lands. He would carry only enough water for three days. The village could spare no more. He too knew how to find the water root plants if necessary. He would leave that night after dark, when the moon had risen above the canyon rim, telling no one lest they attempt to stop him. Inept as he was, he was the only other Healer the village had, and they would challenge his leaving. He could not even tell Teela, for she would insist on going with him, and he would not risk her safety.

Teela! Hramack's heart skipped a beat when he thought of her. Teela's parents had been lost in a great sandstorm when she was a little girl, leaving Kaffa, her maternal grandfather, to raise her. Hramack's parents had arranged his marriage to Teela in early childhood. Unlike many such arranged marriages, both he and Teela were delighted at the prospect. To Hramack's young, lovesick eyes, she was the most beautiful girl in the village. However, she did not let her beauty overshadow her exuberant personality or hide her intelligence. Her nimble mind grasped things he could not fathom, and her selfless devotion to the village amazed him. She saw things in him he found difficult to believe. Her faith in him frightened him sometimes. She had once confided to him that she sensed greatness in him, like her grandfather. He sensed only a gnawing fear in the pit of his stomach.

He feared the Burning Lands, even with his father beside him. They were wild and relentless, hungry, like the creatures that stalked their sun-parched sands. Death waited patiently for the slightest misstep, a moment of weakness. To go alone into the desert ... He chilled at the very thought, but he feared worse to admit his fear to Teela. *Perhaps*, he mused, *facing fear is one of the rights of passage into adulthood*. There seemed to be too many such rites to keep track of. It sometimes became confusing. He wished Kena were there now to talk to when he needed him most.

As night settled upon the village, and the oppressive heat of the day released its death grip on the land, the people began to stir. Hramack gathered his small bundle of food and water, his staff, and his hunting knife, and set out for the Burning Lands. He remembered one of his father's maps and tucked it safely in his pack. Many paths were dangerous, and Kena had charted most of them. He walked quietly up the path towards the canyon rim, stealthily bypassing the motion detectors placed on the path to warn of the approach of any large predatory beasts. He paused for a short while to look back out over the canyon and the comforting glow of the lights in the houses below. He felt a brief pang of anguish for leaving them with no Healer, but he had to find his father. Time was running out.

Readjusting his pack, he tried to summon the courage to continue. He had never before gone into the Burning Lands alone, and in spite of his youthful blustering, he was afraid. Unlike his father, he saw no beauty in the Burning Lands, only the many dangers that lurked there. Before, Kena always had been there with his trusty bow and keen eye. Now, he would be alone. His survival would rely on his limited skills and his decisions. He swallowed his fears, reached down to touch the hunting knife in his belt reassuringly, and started forward. He wished he had a bow, but sadly, the skill of its use, like Healing, still eluded him. It would have been useless weight for the journey.

He had taken no more than a dozen steps when a rustling of something large in the brush nearby startled him. He quietly pulled his knife from his belt and laid his staff on the ground at his feet. Trembling with fear, he braced himself for an attack. Puma were a constant threat to the flocks. Even the larger nightstalkers sometimes haunted the canyon rim hoping for a stray animal. They were the deadliest of creatures. He prayed no nightstalker was stalking him.

To his relief, the branches of the mesquite thicket parted, and Teela stepped suddenly from the brush. She stood staring at him, hands on her hips. "Boo!" she shouted, laughing laughed when she saw his knife out and ready. Then she noticed his startled expression and asked, "Did I scare you?"

"It's not funny," he stammered. "You could have been hurt." Hramack replaced his knife and picked up his staff. "What are you doing here, anyway?" He tried to sound angry but was secretly pleased to see her.

"Why, following you, stupid. Did you think you could leave without me? I know you're worried about your father. I figured you would go after him." She walked back into the brush and re-emerged carrying a large water skin and a bundle of food. She held them up for his inspection. "See. I came prepared. I notice you carry very little. Will you drink sand and eat lizard meat?" Then, more seriously, she pleaded, "Please let me go with you, Hramack. I can walk as fast as you can, and I, too, am worried about Kena. I don't want you to go alone into those accursed lands. Don't leave me here to weep if you don't return."

Hramack knew at that moment, more than at any other time, that he truly loved Teela. She feared for his life, was willing to share the danger with him, and he treasured her concern for him. He swept her into his arms and kissed her long and hard on her soft lips. She melted into his embrace, became a part of him. Holding her, his fears evaporated. Her long brown hair still bore traces of the scent of the jojoba shampoo she used to wash it, though it had been many days since she had done so. He inhaled her sweet scent hungrily, knowing it would be quite some time before he would see her again.

They embraced for thirty heartbeats before Hramack reluctantly broke away. He held her soft hands in his and stared into her eyes. Her pupils, enlarged by the darkness, were twin, deep voids into which he tumbled. Unable to distinguish the color of her eyes in the dark, his memory provided their bright sky blue color for him, searing them into his brain so that he would not forget.

"I love you very much, Teela, but you cannot go with me. The way is dangerous, and I risk the wrath of the Council by leaving. If you go, your grandfather will be in a bad position as Village Precept and member of the Council. Chu Li will use it as an excuse to excommunicate my father and me, maybe even you. If I can return with my father, he can do nothing but grumble."

A voice came out of the darkness in answer. "You are very wise for one so young, Hramack, and I thank you for your concern for my granddaughter's safety, as well as for my position."

Hramack recognized the voice of Kaffa before the old man stepped out into the moonlight. He moved assuredly in spite of his age, gliding across the crusted earth with hardly a sound. His white hair and beard glowed in the moon's pallid light, reinforcing his aura of authority. He carried his staff in one hand and a small leather pouch in the other. He softly admonished his granddaughter.

"Teela, Hramack is right. You must return with me. It is far too dangerous out there for you. Hramack cannot watch your back and his own. This task falls to him alone." Seeing Hramack's small pack, he added, "Carry both water skins and all the food. You will need them." Hramack began a protest, but Kaffa stopped him with the wave of his staff. "We have saved this water for you over the past few days. Teela was certain you would attempt this journey eventually." He glanced at his granddaughter and winked. "Teela knows you better than you think, my son. You will need this also." He handed Hramack the pouch. "If your father has truly gone in search of the ruined city, this map will help. Here, also, is a compass in case the sands blow and you cannot see the stars."

Hramack gratefully accepted the gift of the compass. He opened the pouch, removed the compass in its carved ebony case inlaid with bits of turquoise, and watched the silver needle slowly spin, and then return to point to true north. His own crude homemade device resembled a child's toy in comparison to the fine craftsmanship of the centuries-old navigation tool. He placed it back into the pouch and tied it to his belt.

"I thank you, Kaffa, both for your gifts and for your discretion. I'm afraid I didn't plan my secret sojourn as well as you have planned it for me." He stood silent for a moment trying to curb the emotion in his voice. "I will return with my father. This I pledge to Yarah." He kissed the tips of his pointer and index fingers and placed them to his forehead as a sign of his pledge.

He turned to Teela, who had begun to sob quietly. "Don't weep, Teela. If I haven't returned in seven days, then you can sing the Song of Bereavement." He smiled to show her that he was jesting. "I will return to you. This, too, I pledge."

She wiped her tears and forced a half-smile to her lips. He picked up the extra water skin and food and walked straight into the night, resisting the urge to turn and look back at her, knowing that the sight of her receding would slow his steps. In the silence, Hramack could hear the Teela and her grandfather's footsteps as they picked their way down the rocky path to the village below. He sighed and marched boldly and alone into the Burning Lands.

2

The Burning Lands

Like a fiery Sword of Damocles, the glaring yellow sun dangled high above the Burning Lands, taunting the tormented earth with its awesome power to deliver death and destruction. Its fierce heat had long ago stripped the land until only parched sand and hard-baked earth remained. Kena lifted his arm to shield his eyes from the burning glare, his eyeshades and hat long lost somewhere behind him. The skin of his forehead and his cheeks was blistered and peeling, burning as if from the sting of a scorpion. The distant horizon ebbed and flowed like the long-vanished ocean's waves, mocking him with its promise of liquid relief. However, there was no respite from the ever-present wrath of the sun.

As a Healer, Kena knew he was slowly succumbing to heat exhaustion. With every fiber of his being, he could feel the symptoms he knew all too well – extreme thirst, weakness, fatigue, anxiety, and the tingling of the limbs. His poor judgment had spurred him to press on when he should have rested until sunset, and now he was stumbling and falling more often, a sure sign of incoordination. If he checked his blood, he was sure he would find a high concentration of nitrogen wastes as his kidneys began to shut down. Add to that mixture a nagging thirst, his gnawing hunger, and physical exhaustion, and he knew he would make a very bad patient with a poor probability of recovery.

Next came psychosis, if indeed it was not now already upon him. The whispering would not leave him be. The relentless power of the blazing sun above him had wrung all traces of life-giving moisture from his body. He tried to lick his parched, swollen lips but felt only searing pain as his dry tongue rasped across the blisters clustered there. The heat-shimmering landscape danced endless and unmerciful before him, his path blurred by tearless eyes, leaving him stumbling onward.

Heedless of the agony each slow step produced, ignorant of the damage he was inflicting on his ravaged body, a single thought drove Kena – to reach Ningcha. His overwhelming fatigue scoured all other thoughts from his mind. He attempted to focus on this one last task with the blind determination he once thought his greatest asset. His resolve had served him well in the past. He had survived shorter encounters with the Burning Lands. At each of those times, he had also thought each moment would be his last, but he had made it home.

He had survived the death of Allana, his wife. Surely, the pain that had consumed him then paled to this mere physical agony where only muscle, bone, flesh, and sinew were involved. The agony that had struck him then, at her death, had threatened his soul as well as his mind. Only the infinite love and care of his son had enabled his survival. He had come to terms with the will of Yarah then, though he professed no great understanding of His ways. Yarah had not forsaken him during those times. He would not forsake him now.

Kena moved his body forward one small step at a time.

"Hramack!" he cried hoarsely into the empty wastes, though the effort caused his punished lips to crack and bleed. He willed his voice to carry the many leagues to Ningcha, to his son. His water long gone, he longed for one single drop of moisture with which to wet his parched lips. Only by sucking out the precious moisture hoarded in the roots of scarce water root plants had he survived this long. Now, he could find no more of those remarkable desert plants. Even his vast store of desert knowledge was of no use. The grilling orb of searing gases overhead that had ultimately given life to this very desert was slowly draining the last of his strength and killing him. The muscles in his legs protested with each awkward step, and his head ached with each fragmented thought. His breath came in ragged gasps that brought pains to his chest.

He must get back to Ningcha and Hramack. He must.

Summoning what strength and will remained in his parched and broken body, Kena plodded forward, step by grueling step. His tall frame bowed by his effort, he clung to his bow as if it alone could bring him home. By his fevered reckoning, he was still three days' march from the village, but he would never make it in the full heat of the sun. It was doubtful he could have made it even in the relative coolness of night in his drained and battered condition. His feet were raw and bleeding, blistered by the hot sand filling his boots, and his lungs were full of fine particles of burning alkali dust, making each breath a battle.

For all he knew, his body had absorbed more radiation than he could possibly survive. It had been many years since a large solar flare had illuminated the skies of the desert southwest in a display of the aurora borealis. By his measurements, as crude as they were, the solar radiation levels had been steadily declining for many years, but that did not mean it was safe for prolonged exposure.

"Foolish to worry about radiation now," he laughed. "I have a host of choices in dying."

He doubted that Chu Li would regret his failure to return. As if opposite poles of a magnet, the two men, Healer and High Priest, were markedly different in manner and deed. Reconciliation seemed impossible. The enmity between the two had divided the small village at a time when unity was essential. The Pools of Yarah were empty. His people could no longer survive on their meager supply of hoarded water. Chu Li, as High Priest, dutifully prayed to Yarah, and the people wailed out their fears and concerns, but Kena knew the water would not return unless someone ventured north to locate the source of the water. He had found information that could help. If only he could get back with his find.

He was a man of medicine, a Healer, yet he did not cast aside the need for hope or faith in his belief in the sciences. He had faith in Yarah, but he did not believe Yarah required men to sit idly by and wait for divine deliverance, as the High Priest Chu Li preached. Yarah helped those who were bold enough to help themselves. It was thus his duty to find the answer to the water shortage. None other would try.

Finally, even blind determination must eventually succumb to nature's indomitable iron will. He could push his worn body no further. He felt the cold fingers of Death closing around him and was almost relieved for even this small respite from the ever-present heat. If Death must take him, the least Death could do was offer its victim a small degree of cool comfort in exchange for the soul it was receiving.

With trembling hands, Kena scribbled a last, hurried message on a scrap of paper in the slim hope of someone finding it, stuck it tightly in his belt, and, giving in to the fatigue that enveloped his body, collapsed onto the sand. If anyone found the message, it would surely be his son. Only Hramack would ever venture deep into the desert searching for him. Son had accompanied father into the Burning Lands many times searching for herbs. They had also hunted the horned lizards and feasted on their sweet, moist flesh. Now, Kena mused, lizards would probably dine on him.

He could find no substantial shade from the deadly sun, and not wishing to die in the open, dragged his body under the meager protection of a dead, dried-out thorn bush, scraped out a shallow depression in the sand, and placing himself in Yarah's hands, settled down to await the arrival of Death. He could do no more.

The voices returned. Around him, the heat hammered at the seared earth, raising towering dust devils that pranced around him, whispering their secrets to him as he lay there. Whether it was the voice of the wind or the voice of Yarah, Kena could stand no more.

"Taunt me no more," he croaked from his shallow open grave, his throat tight from disuse. The parched skin around his mouth again split and bled, but he could no longer feel the pain.

Still the voices whispered; a litany of voices spanning the centuries of Mankind's last days, telling him of great domed cities and starships and the almost magical science of his ancestors. These were just whispers now, memories only to those who had died, or to those who still cared, such as Kena and his son. In his heat-ravaged mind, a small portion of remaining intellect knew that psychosis was upon him, but the voices persisted.

"Leave me to die! I can go no farther!" No tears accompanied his outburst. His tear ducts were dry.

"*Your job is not yet finished,*" they chided him from the cool safety of his mind.

"I am finished," he yelled, knowing in his mind he was speaking only to that place within himself that still urged him onward.

"*No,*" they whispered, enticing him with visions of lakes of cool water, sparkling like crystal in the sun.

"No," he whimpered. "I am dead." Ignoring the voices he knew were only in his mind, he shut his eyes tightly and succumbed to his fatigue. To Kena's relief, the voices remained as silent as the desert around him.

3

ALONE

H RAMACK PUSHED HIMSELF TO THE EDGE OF EXHAUSTION, MARCHING steadily until near dawn before stopping to rest. The ruddy sky to the east presaged a blistering day. After a quick meal of amaranth bread and dried fruit, washed down with a few swallows of tepid water flavored with lemon juice, he resumed his journey. As the sun rose, dissolving the desert shadows like ice on a hot griddle, the temperature steadily mounted. Already it was almost 40°C, 104 on the old Fahrenheit scale, and the sun was merely a finger's width above the horizon. At noon, it would reach 50°C or more. He would have to find shelter soon. He remembered a nearby rocky outcropping containing a small cave he and his father had used many times in the past.

He was exhausted by the time he reached the shelter of the cave, really just a shallow horizontal gap in the outcropping where a layer of sedimentary rock had crumbled away and time and wind had removed it. He eagerly collapsed against the wall. He took one sip of water, laid his head on his backpack, and slept.

Awaking a few short hours later, he drank more of his precious water and ate sparingly. He searched the sandy floor of the shallow depression cave and found indications that his father had been there, but the signs were at least ten days old. Kena had probably rested there on his outward journey. Hramack had seen no other sign of his father's passing all night.

Outside the cave, the desert broiled. Nothing moved, not even the wind. Most desert creatures had the intelligence to seek shelter from the full heat of the sun. Hramack shared his small cave with a tiny desert kangaroo mouse huddling quietly in a dark corner, as if fearing to attract Hramack's attention. Its large pink ears appeared oversized for the diminutive creature, but they allowed the mouse to cool himself more efficiently. Its large dark eyes stared at him, searching for any sudden threatening movement.

Hramack broke off a small piece of bread, dipped it into the water, and laid it where the mouse could see it. The mouse, like most desert creatures, quickly caught the scent of precious water and cautiously hopped over to the offering. Hramack did not move for fear of frightening his new cave companion.

Satisfied that its giant roommate offered no threat, the mouse leaped upon the bread, grasped it between its two front paws, and gobbled it down. He squeaked a few times as if offering thanks and hopped back into the corner of the cave, methodically preening his whiskers for any last morsel of food or drop of water. It lay down in the sand, curling its long tufted, tail around its body. Hramack wondered if his father had also fed the tiny mouse. The long-eared hoppers often led Kena to patches of *pei*. The mice liked to burrow into the soil at the plant's roots and feed on the tiny, nutrient-rich nodules that grew on them.

Hramack whiled away the daylight hours napping and trying to complete the carvings on his staff. Not overly adept as an artisan, he still managed to carve a reasonable facsimile of a rare desert hawk.

He admired the graceful bird with its great wingspan and its ability to soar almost effortlessly above the desert and canyons. A hawk could have covered Hramack's night march in minutes.

He had been working diligently on the staff for almost two years, ever since Kaffa had first given him the long, straight piece of cottonwood, a rare find. Familiar animals and those gleaned from books he had read graced its curved surface. He had left a spot for Teela's likeness near the top, but felt his talents were still inadequate to capture her grace and beauty.

Finally, the sun began to drop behind the western peaks, casting a pale, rosy glow across the landscape. Twilight lasted only for a short while in the desert. Long shadows gathered into dark pools beneath the mountains and raced toward him like a long vanished monsoon flood. Darkness descended rapidly. Hramack gathered his belongings and resumed his journey. Between twilight and the rising of the moon, he could still see well enough to navigate the uneven terrain. Heat radiating from the desert floor caused the quartz crystals and mica flakes in the sand to become softly iridescent, outlining plants and rocks. He looked behind him and noticed his boots left glowing tracks in the sand. He frowned.

Nightstalkers hunted mainly by scent, but they would easily be able to see his glowing footprints from a great distance. Bred from mountain lion stock and genetically enhanced through careful manipulation of jaguar DNA to propagate a dying species, nightstalkers had further mutated from exposure to excessive solar radiation, becoming larger and more deadly. They were fearless hunters, tenacious trackers, and Alpha predators commanding the top rung of the food chain in the Burning Lands. All creatures feared them, even man. Hramack would have to be on guard at all times. He tried to stay on hard rock whenever possible, but he still left oddly glowing tracks. He trudged across the endless sands, watching every shadow lest a nightstalker leap upon him unawares.

Hramack had watched once from a distance as a smaller, female nightstalker attacked a large horned lizard, quickly devouring it after slashing it nearly in half with her razor-sharp claws. A large nightstalker would show no qualms in attacking a man. Kena had made Hramack's backpack from the skin of a nightstalker that had attacked him on one of his trips into the Burning Lands. Kena had survived only because of the warning call of a desert hawk and his excellent marksmanship with his bow.

Soon, the faint sliver of the waning moon appeared over the horizon and Hramack relaxed slightly. At least in the moonlight, surprise became more difficult. He began a sweeping zigzagging path across the desert floor, searching for signs of his father's passage. There had been no great winds for days to cover the tracks in the slowly changing desert. Still, he saw nothing.

He climbed a low rise and scanned his surroundings. The night air was clear and crisp. He could see for kilometers. Nothing moved on the desert floor. The night was strangely still. No sound reached his ears, not even that of the wind. Overhead, the stars twinkled almost mockingly. Somewhere out there, if the old stories were believable, the Scattered Ones lived and prospered in their new home, while those they had abandoned might be the dying remnants of humankind, one lone village remaining from a population that once reached fourteen billion. He could barely fathom such a large number. The hundred or so people of his village were nearly too many to count.

If the water did not return soon, Mankind's birth world could become no more than an ancient memory – a dried-up, desiccated planet devoid of life.

He pushed himself hard, continuing until dawn, halting only long enough to eat and drink sparingly from his supplies. As the first rays of the sun bathed the eastern peaks, he discovered a large outcropping of sandstone that would offer shelter from the sun and lay out his sleeping roll beneath it. In spite of his fatigue, he had difficulty in falling asleep. A vague premonition of danger troubled him, but he could not pinpoint its source.

He decided to make a signal fire atop the outcropping. If his father were nearby, the fire would serve as a beacon. Gathering small pieces of dried wood with which to kindle the fire and dried animal dung to keep it going was easier than finding green plants that would produce smoke. He settled on a small creosote plant whose sap produced a dark, pungent smoke.

After seeing that the fire would burn for a while, Hramack tried to force himself into the sleep his body needed to rest his weary muscles for the remainder of his journey. He closed his eyes and concentrated on Teela's features, conjuring up a mental image before him. Her high cheekbones, slim frame, and short stature belied her inner strength and determination. Even as a child, Teela had been afraid of nothing and would not hesitate to attack anyone larger than herself for the slightest tease. Her beauty and strength of character placed her above the other girls of the village, but she seemed oddly unaware of the effect she had on men.

Her piercing blue eyes saw more in Hramack than he could see in himself. She had told him once that he was destined for greatness and intended to be always by his side. Though he doubted the wisdom of her words, he felt pride that she would choose him. He wished he could be with her now, to hear her sweet voice as she sang, to feel the soft touch of her caress. He felt complete when with her. They were soul mates in every sense of the word. Only the search for his father could have pulled him away from her. He made a solemn vow never to leave her side again.

He fell asleep with her name on his lips.

Hramack awoke hours before sunset, feeling an urgency that would not let him wait until the sun had dipped below the horizon to depart. He knew it was unwise to leave before sunset, but he was certain speed was of the essence. Drinking the last of the water from his first water skin, he was again thankful for Teela's gift. He tucked the empty skin in his pack, slung the large skin she had provided over his shoulder, and started out.

He had traveled only a dozen kilometers before the blazing sun began to take its toll. Already he was becoming tired and lightheaded. He forced himself to drink sparingly from his remaining water skin. The water-filled skin cooled through evaporation, leaving a cool spot in the middle of his back as a constant reminder of its liquid promise. He rested often, but by nightfall, he was exhausted from the heat and famished from hunger. He stopped and built a small fire, and then prepared a simple posole stew from his meager supply of vegetables, amaranth flour, and preserved meat. His small, portable pressure cooker prevented the loss of water through evaporation by redirecting the steam through a series of tightly looped coils, which used the relatively cooler surrounding air to condense it, forcing flavor and moisture deep into the food. He used only a small amount of water, making the stew thick and creamy, like a casserole. To save space in his pack, he had brought no herbs and only salt and dried chilies to flavor it. It was a very plain dish, but it satisfied his hunger.

The warm stew filled his belly and sent renewed strength surging into his limbs. He broke his self-imposed rule and drank deeply from the water skin. He felt refreshed for the first time in days. It was his third night in the Burning Lands. He had seen only the old signs in the cave of his father's passing, but he would not give up hope. His father was alive. He knew it. He knew his father's death would leave a void that he would be able to feel in his heart. The bond between them went deep: a bond shared by few in the village. Only Kaffa seemed to understand it almost as well as Hramack.

"Some spirits unite beyond the boundaries of time and space," he had once told Hramack. "This bond joins two people with one heart and one mind."

He believed he and Teela also shared such a bond. Her absence tugged at him like a tether urging him to return. Though betrothed as children by their families, it would not be binding if either found another, more suitable mate. He could not fathom such a thing happening. In extreme cases, the High Priest could arrange or deny a marriage if deemed in the best interest of the village, but such an instance had not occurred for a hundred years.

He rested a few hours longer and continued his journey at the rising of the moon, realizing how unwise it had been to walk in the heat of the sun. He had deeply depleted his water supply and had covered only a short distance. Such mistakes could kill. He would have to be more careful if he were to be of any use to his father. Still, he could tell by landmarks he recognized that he was nearing the Singing Caves and, hopefully, his father.

The Singing Caves were a series of caverns carved into a red sandstone mesa high above the valley floor by the relentless desert winds. He and his father had discovered the caves a few years earlier while chasing a wounded antelope. Custom and hunger dictated that they track down and dispatch the beast to end its suffering. The hunt had led them to the caves. Wind blowing through the interconnecting caverns caused them to sing a low, mournful tune. Hramack believed they were ghost voices lamenting the damage done to Earth during the Upheaval. Kena had found artifacts dating from before the fall of Denver Dome – a flashlight that worked perfectly when he removed the old, corroded power cell and replaced it with a fresh one; a collapsible telescope with a broken lens; and, more importantly, a map. Delicately traced on a thin piece of non-corrosive metal, the map showed the location of the old city of Taos and Santa Fe, New Mexico.

Taos, New Mexico, had been one of the last cities abandoned during the migration into Denver Dome. Its few remaining inhabitants were mostly Diné Indians who had steadfastly refused to leave their homeland of nearly 2000 years. Many returned to their ancestral ways and moved deeper into the desert rather than live in one of the domed cities. It was unlikely that they had survived the intervening centuries.

Taos or Santa Fe could still hold many things that would be useful to the villagers of Ningcha. Metals were always in short supply, as were parts for machinery, like the pumps and wind generators. Perhaps they could find even more of the precious power cells. From material readily available, they could construct crude batteries to store electricity from the solar cells and wind generator, but power cells demanded high-tech, precision manufacturing techniques and required materials difficult to find and even more difficult to manipulate. Hundreds of layers of one-molecule-thick lead foil were sandwiched between equally thin layers of nano-gold crystal fibers impregnated with lithium ions, vacuum-sealed under extreme pressure, and then coated with a non-conductive carbon-fiber shell. Power cells produced electricity at a variable rate, were durable, easily rechargeable, and stored power almost indefinitely.

These though were just excuses for his father's wanderlust. Kena wished to look upon the ruins of one of man's accomplishments. It would put his own life into proper perspective to see the achievements of his ancestors. Kena had confided in Hramack his suspicions that humankind was slowly losing its hold on civilization.

"Soon, we'll be worshiping fire and wearing animal skins like our ancient ancestors," he had said. Sometimes Hramack agreed.

The moon cast a feeble light to aid in Hramack's trek through the Red Valley. The soil's reddish color was the result of extensive copper mining in the past. The soil was too laden with heavy metal tailings for plants or animals to thrive. The fine dust raised by his footsteps burned his nostrils. He wrapped his scarf around his face and mouth to keep out the acrid powder. The dust made his exposed skin itch. Each step was a struggle. The loose sand sucked at his boots like dry quicksand. At times, he plunged knee deep into dust-filled depressions, crawling out on his hands and knees. No pack animal or wheeled vehicle could traverse the Red Valley. It was difficult enough for a human on foot.

Here, the Elder's compass came to Hramack's aid. Dust clouds kicked up by a sudden light wind covered the moon and stars, making it impossible for him to use them as a guide, and the close high bluffs hid the distant mountain peaks from his sight. The compass needle unfailingly pointed the way for him. Without it, he could easily stumble over the edge of the kilometers' wide chasm, the great ragged scar in the earth of the vast open pit mine. After a few hours, he emerged from the hills and valleys of the red earth and found himself on a narrow, flat plain skirting the cliffs of Singing Caves.

Here, unlike the red dirt region, the plain was alive with the sounds of animals. Birds called to mates, and lizards hissed from their burrows at his approach. Having encountered few humans, the creatures did not recognize man as a predator, but only as competition for the meager supply of available food. Occasionally, he heard the sounds of a scuffle as some predator caught and devoured its hapless meal in the dark. He became more cautious lest he too became something's dinner.

At a slight rustle in the underbrush, too large for a hare or lizard, he tightened his grip on his staff and planted his feet for balance just as his father had taught him. This time it would not be Teela. He forced his anxiety behind him and fought to calm his racing heart. Minutes passed. He began to think he had imagined the noise and relaxed; then, his nostrils caught the heady, musky scent of a nightstalker, and his resolve quavered. Fear gripped him, coiling around his heart like a cold slithering serpent, not his earlier dread of the unknown, but the terror of imminent death. Of all the threats the Burning Lands presented, and they were myriad, nightstalkers were the most deadly. One could seek shelter from the sun or a sandstorm, carry water and food, but the desert cats were intelligent, cunning, and superbly suited for their environment.

He had no place on the flat plain to seek cover. His attacker could come as silently as the night itself from any quarter. He licked his lips suddenly gone dry, and stared into the darkness. He saw the nightstalker leap from beneath a shrub beside him just in time to throw himself flat on the sand. The beast overshot its mark and sailed over his prostrate body. It made no sound as it twisted its supple body in midair to land facing him, undaunted by his narrow escape. Its hunger had driven it to leap too early.

In a desperate land where skill was the thin margin between life and death, she had made few such mistakes. Hramack leaped to his feet and faced his quarry. Luckily, the beast, a juvenile female, was only slightly larger than he was, less than a meter and a half from her flaring nose to the tip of her swishing tail. Luck, and his quick reflexes, had saved him. If his courage held, he might survive.

The wary creature inched forward, head held low. Hramack swung his staff. The whistle of the staff as it swept before the creature's eyes forced the nightstalker to shift slightly, but she did not back up. She eyed Hramack and his staff with respect, circling him just outside the staff's reach. At intervals, she raised her head and let out a piercing scream, calling out to her nearby mate. He could delay no longer. He could not face two such beasts. He summoned his courage and leapt at the nightstalker, delivering a flurry of blows with his staff. She was unprepared for prey that fought back. Several blows found their mark before the beast could scamper away. She retreated a few paces and stood licking her wounds, waiting for her mate.

Knowing that time was of the essence, Hramack slipped his knife from its sheath and held it in one hand. Then he renewed his attack with his staff with one hand. She met the thrusts with swipes of her large, sharp claws, her powerful forelimbs almost knocking the staff from his hand. Hramack forced her to back up slowly, and then, as she glanced backwards to secure her footing on a patch of loose rock, he pushed her head aside with his staff and lunged with his knife, flinging his entire body at her. It was a desperate move, one that would leave him helpless on the ground. He held his breath, expecting the nightstalker's sharp teeth to sink into his flesh at any moment. The blade entered the beast's left shoulder just above her ribcage. The blow was not fatal, but it inflicted great pain. Howling in rage and fury, she limped away into the night.

Hramack could savor his victory only for a moment. He knew the larger male was nearby, and he had no strength left to fight it off. He glanced to the east. The sky was already turning a ruddy hue. It would soon be dawn. He had to reach the cliffs quickly, or the full fury of the sun would catch him on open ground. Because he had severely injured its mate, the male would not seek shelter at dawn as they usually did. It would stalk him until it had caught and killed him. He had only one chance. Dropping all his belongings except his water skin, his staff, and his knife, he raced as fast as he could toward the cliffs.

The cliffs were only a couple of kilometers distant, but he doubted that he could make it. He had at best a slim chance, but any chance beat dying. The nightstalker could run much faster than he could and could sustain that speed over much longer distances. He could not face the beast on open ground with only a knife for protection.

Hramack ran for his life. His strong leg muscles acted as pistons, propelling his body forward, but as strong as his legs were, the fight with the nightstalker had drained him. The loose sand gripped his boots, slowing him as if in league with the creature. He ignored the growing pain in his calves and the burning ache in his chest as his vision began to swim. The sun rose and seemed to draw his life out through the top of his head. He was running headlong into the rising sun, and he stumbled several times over objects lost in the bright glare.

Soon, too soon, exhausted and nearly blinded by the rising sun, he could go no farther. The cliffs were tantalizingly close but much too far away to reach in time. He realized that he stood no chance against a large male, but better to die fighting than struck down from behind while on his knees. His labored breath drowned out all other sounds around him. His heart pounded in his ears. It was as if all the Burning Lands held its breath, waiting to see who would be the victor of the coming battle.

Hramack turned and faced the direction from which he felt certain the attack would come. To his dismay, he saw the male nightstalker loping toward him, not bothering to hide or to circle its prey. Less than a hundred meters separated them. Hramack dropped his water skin and took a firm grip on his knife, bracing himself for its attack. Large predator cats were grapplers, using their mass to subdue their prey while steel-trap jaws crushed windpipes or razor-sharp claws disemboweled. If he did not kill it with his first blow, he knew he would not get another chance. Once within reach of its massive clutching forepaws, his life would be measured in seconds. He must aim for the creature's heart, protected by layers of muscle and bone. His aim had to be true.

"Yarah, guide my hand," he prayed aloud.

Only fifty meters separated them now. He could see the fire of rage in the creature's golden eyes. Sound returned in a rush, as if to taunt him. The crunch of the sand beneath its churning paws as they ate up the distance between them was thunder. However, the cat made no sound. Only ten meters away now. The nightstalker was gigantic, almost two and a half meters long and double Hramack's 80-kilogram weight. Its paws were as large as Hramack's head, tipped by twelve-centimeter daggers, longer than the blade of his knife. Hhe hoped the beast could not smell his fear.

I do not want to die today, he thought. *I will not die today. I promised Teela I would return to her.*

Enraged, the nightstalker did not slow its pace as it raced toward him. It was not hunting for food. He had wounded its mate. It was intent on the kill. Unlike Hramack, it had no fear and sensed an easy kill. When only a few meters away, it put on an extra burst of speed, its paws barely touching the ground. For a death machine, it was hauntingly graceful. The massive muscles bunched beneath the nightstalker's ginger-colored fur as it sprang at him. Hramack raised his meager weapon and lowered his head.

To Hramack's astonishment, the beast suddenly yelped in pain and twisted wildly in midair. It landed beside him with a thud, clawing frantically at its belly, scattering sand in a wide arc as its massive hind legs propelled it in a circle in the sand. Hramack backed away out of reach of the creature's death spasms. The feathers of two arrows protruded from its blood-soaked abdomen like a bouquet of flowers. The nightstalker thrashed noisily on the ground a few moments more, then died. Hramack dropped his knife in the sand and fell to his knees dumbfounded, his heart pounding in his chest. He breathed deeply, drawing in great lungfuls of scorching air. His vision swam. He watched numbly as a shadowy figure walked slowly toward him, the blazing sun at its back.

At first, he did not recognize his savior, but then a broad smile came to his parched lips.

"Father, thank Yarah I have found you, or rather, that you have found me. I thought myself breakfast for this stalker." He nodded at the dead beast. Already, small, furry scavengers were scurrying around the animal, fighting for a place in line for such a grand feast.

Kena stood unsteadily on his feet, as if pulling the bow he held had used up the last of his strength. He reached out to help Hramack from the ground and succeeded only in losing his own balance. Hramack reached out his hand to help steady his father.

"Come. We can talk later," Kena whispered to him. "We must leave this place before the carcass attracts larger scavengers." He pointed to Hramack's water skin. "Give me a sip of your water, and we can help each other to the Singing Caves."

Kena raised the skin and took a long drink of water, careful to allow none of it to escape, wincing as it touched his swollen, cracked lips. Hramack noticed his father's badly sunburned and blistered face and his bleeding hands. A strip of his shirt wound around his head to replace his lost hat. Clearly, he was on his last legs. Putting his arm around his father's waist for support, they headed for the shelter of the caves in the nearby cliffs.

The cooler darkness of the caves and the remainder of the water helped revitalize both father and son. Some dried fruit Hramack had stuffed into his pocket became their meager breakfast. After resting for a short while, Kena recounted his journey and his discovery.

"And I would be dead now if not for a desert mouse," he concluded. "As I lay near death and without hope, a small hopper chanced by me carrying a water root in its mouth. I summoned my strength and reached to grab it. I missed and had to crawl after it. When it disappeared down its burrow, I dug and found its larder of water roots. I sucked the moisture from them all save one, which I left for the hopper. Then, I saw smoke on the horizon. I suspected it was you, searching for me.

"I was still too weak to travel far. I rested and ate the water root stems for strength. I figured you would try to reach the Singing Caves and decided to intercept you. I saw you only a few moments before I saw the nightstalker. I was not sure I had enough strength left to make the shot. I prayed to Yarah for help and strung two arrows, hoping one would find its mark." He added, "Many times as I stumbled along, I thought of dropping the bow as useless weight, but something told me to hold on to it. Perhaps Yarah was helping all along."

"It would seem Yarah had His hands full watching after the two of us," Hramack joked. "I suspect Chu Li would admonish us for calling on Yarah only when in need." Hramack toyed with a small piece of metal he had picked up from the sand on the floor of the cave. It was twisted and broken but not rusted. It was yet another example of the artistry of humans before the Upheaval.

Kena was staring out the mouth of the cave into the desert beyond. "We must return to where you left your pack. We will need the food. I have a cache of water jugs buried near here that will see us home if we conserve it, but we must leave at sunset. Can you walk?"

Hramack nodded, smiling at his father's concern for his condition. It was typical of him to ignore his own exhaustion. "Perhaps we should rest a short while longer," Hramack suggested. He rolled over and made himself comfortable on the sandy floor of the cave. Soon, the sound of the wind blowing through the entrance lulled him to sleep with its low, soft mournful song.

HIGH PRIEST CHU LI

C HU LI, HIGH PRIEST OF YARAH, REPEATEDLY BANGED HIS GREAT WOODEN staff on the stone floor of the Council Chambers like a gavel. Its metal-shod heel echoed loudly in the enclosed space. All eyes turned to him. Although almost fifteen centimeters shorter than either man, his demeanor and position as High Priest stopped the lively discussion-turned-argument between Kaffa and Madras, the stone carver. He motioned for them to retake their seats.

"Enough, both of you," he said forcefully but quietly. "For all we know, Kena is dead. It has been almost three weeks since his departure. You, Kaffa." He turned to stare down at Kaffa, a position that delighted him. "You foolishly allowed his son to go off searching for him. Now, we have neither Healer nor Healer's apprentice. If, by the grace of Yarah, they return safely, we cannot allow them to wander the Burning Lands again. It is a blasphemous thing to dig into the past. Yarah destroyed the past so that we, His chosen, could work towards a future free of the past's follies and mistakes. If, in the future, Kena must go in search of his herbs and roots for tonics and poultices, we must appoint a guard to accompany him to assure his prompt return to his duties. We each must do our part to ensure the survival of our village."

Secretly, he would not be disappointed if Kena did not return to the village, but keeping him under thumb if he did would be equally pleasurable.Kaffa stood and addressed the Council. "I admit my guilt in allowing Hramack to search for his father, but felt it was necessary. The love between father and son is a bond not easily broken and one far stronger than any chains or shackles or constraint that could be placed upon him by order of this Council."

Chu Li was glad to hear a few quiet mutterings at this last statement.

"Fellow Council members, Kena means no disrespect to our village or to Yarah. Of this, I am certain. He is our Healer, yes, but he also repairs most of our machines. The same machines that make our lives tolerable here in this land of desolation are slowly breaking down. Yarah has blessed Kena with deft fingers and a nimble mind. His sojourns into the Burning Lands are not for his own pleasures alone. He seeks both medicines for his Healing craft and parts with which to keep our slowly dying machinery running. Without electricity, we would have to pump water up from the floor of the canyon by hand, a long and laborious task. We would have to post guards to protect our village from marauding beasts rather than use the motion detectors. We would have to search far for wood to burn to cook our food instead of using the induction ovens. No, my friends, Kena is a true son of Ningcha."

Madras, still angered by the argument earlier with Kaffa, rose. Kaffa's quick wit and logical mind had bested him, and all present knew it. Slow-witted and a poor speaker, he chose volume over substance.

"Perhaps Kena is a true son," he bellowed, "but Hramack is neither a true son of Ningcha nor a true son to Kena. His thoughts are always of how things were, not how things are. He corrupts my son with his talk. Hramack will be our Healer when Kena dies, yet he treats his duties as no more than a joke. I say he should be punished for his sins and should never be allowed to leave the confines of the canyon again." He slammed his heavy fist onto the wooden table, punctuating his statement.

There was some mumbling as other members of the Council reluctantly agreed with Madras. They, too, thought Hramack too slack in his duties in spite of his past contributions. Only recently, Juresh, Madras' youngest son, had left the flock untended at Hramack's request to help Hramack repair the windmill. Jorah, Juresh's elder brother, had rounded up the scattered flock and threatened both Hramack and Juresh with a severe beating. Only Kaffa's swift intervention had prevented open conflict.

"This discussion is moot unless they return from the Burning Lands," interjected Chu Li. "Roagneau, you will take your two sons and set out tomorrow night in search of them. Go only as far as the first terrace level of the valley, no further. Return before dawn, with or without them. Let no one say we did not offer all the assistance we could. I will risk no one else in the Burning Lands. If they are indeed dead, we must choose a new Healer and begin his training."

Kaffa exploded. "They are not dead. This talk of choosing another Healer is premature."

"How do you know this?" Chu Li asked.

"I feel its truth," Kaffa replied softly, "here." He touched his heart.

Several people snickered. Chu Li smiled. Such statements from Kaffa's own lips served his purpose.

"We cannot conduct our lives on your *feelings*, Kaffa." His emphasis on the last word conveyed his contempt for Kaffa's conviction. "If they have not returned by nightfall tomorrow, we must choose another to study the Healing arts. Aparu, son of Roagneau has shown an interest in such matters. Let him begin the study."

Chu Li had not suggested Aparu for his ability, for he was slow and lazy, but to bind Roagneau, one of the few Council members who supported Kena, to him. Chu Li's rapidly growing band of supporters could soon convince the villagers to dismiss Kena's large list of contributions to the village and punish him and Hramack for their excursions into the Burning Lands. By doing so, he would be eroding Kaffa's power to sway the villagers. Even the Elder's age and wisdom would not prevail against the word of the High Priest and the will of Yarah.

"If the Council wishes it," Roagneau said with head bowed to hide his smile.

Kaffa was furious at the tone of the meeting. "You show a discouraging lack of faith by planning Hramack's replacement. If neither returns, with whom do you think Aparu will apprentice. Hramack has been gone only a few days. He carried supplies for a week's journey. Give him time."

Chu Li pounced. "You accuse me of a lack of faith. I am the High Priest of Yarah. I have devoted my life in service and faith to Him and to this village. In this time of scarcity of water, Hramack carried enough water for a week? That was ... " He paused to allow others to fill in their choice before finishing, "unwise."

"He carried only enough for three days. I provided him more from my allotment."

Chu Li had trouble hiding his smile. Kaffa was digging his own grave. "You met him? You were a party to his stealthy departure? As Village Precept, is not your duty to your village stronger than your friendship to Hramack or Kena?"

"Upon Hramack's shoulders rest the future of our village. Around him, the threads of the past and the future intertwine, weaving infinite possibilities."

"Now you are a seer." Chu Li shook his head. "Your affection for Hramack has clouded your mind. You have allowed his betrothal to your granddaughter sway you. It is unbecoming of your position of authority." He searched the faces of the others around the table, delighted to see that many agreed. "Now let us pray to Yarah for guidance in this matter and return to our homes."

After the others had left, Chu Li stood and looked around the empty Council Chambers with its polished carved stone table and seven chairs. He breathed in the heady air of power that permeated the room along with that of candle smoke and let it fill his lungs with the wisdom of those who had gone before him. As High Priest, he was in charge of the village's spiritual guidance, but he longed for more worldly control. Now that it was within his grasp, he would not allow that old fool Kaffa take it from him, even if it meant Kaffa's death.

Of the five remaining Council members, three were securely under his control: Madras, the stone carver; Harred, the miller; and Sevrin, the baker. All were important men in the village and their families were large. Roagneau was a friend of and kinsman to Kena, but he would submit to Chu Li's will if his son became the new Healer's apprentice. Kaffa would never support him. That left only Mitsu in opposition. The quiet herder also enjoyed hunting in the Burning Lands. In this way, he was much like Kena, strong and determined. However, unlike Kena, Mitsu held closely to the old teachings. If it came down to backing Kena in spite of a charge of blasphemy, Mitsu would follow the lead of the High Priest. Each day the waters did not flow, Mitsu sat and watched his herds slowly grow weaker and their numbers dwindle. No. He would be no problem.

Chu Li did not worry. As a servant of Yarah, what had he to fear from Kena or Hramack, his son? Kena's stubborn insistence upon delving into the past troubled many of the villagers. Chu Li played upon those fears. The failure of the springs to return had frightened even him, but he was quick to use this evil omen to his own advantage in his attempt to usurp control of Ningcha from the Council. Kaffa's close ties to Kena played directly into his hands. If Kaffa defended Kena too vigorously, he would alienate many of the Council members. In spite of his wisdom, people would begin to think he spoke only out of love for his granddaughter and her betrothal to Hramack.

Chu Li absentmindedly stroked his pointed beard. Wisps of gray were beginning to show in it. He was no longer the young, energetic priest he once was. He had clawed his way to the top, all for the sake of his family. He would not let one man destroy that hard work. If Kena returned, he would never accept the constraints placed upon him by the Council. He was too obstinate for that. That stubbornness could play easily into Chu Li's hands. He would see to it that Kena had no choice but to defy the Council openly. By doing this, Kena would be eliminating Kaffa as well as himself as an obstacle to power.

Chu Li chuckled at the irony and poured himself a small glass of *kalquat*, strong liquor made from fermented sorghum. As High Priest, he did not drink. As a man, what he did in private was no one's business. He raised his glass in a mock toast to his adversary.

"May the best man win," he whispered, as he poured the fiery liquid down his throat.

As the Council left the building, Kaffa slowly scanned the cliff face but saw no sign of the returning father and son. Teela was waiting for him, eager for news.

"What did they say, Grandfather?" she asked. She knew of the anger in the village over Kena's prolonged absence. The Council could not ignore the people's sentiments.

Kaffa recounted the discussions of the meeting to his granddaughter and waited for her reaction. As he knew she would, she exploded.

"What do they expect to do, lock them in chains? What harm have they caused? Is everyone close-minded to our past? What of the springs? Is our dying of thirst not enough to concern the Council that they must also lock up our Healer and his son?"

Kaffa waited for her outburst of anger to subside, and then spoke quietly. "Not everyone agrees with Chu Li and Madras. They are just afraid to speak up. If it comes to a vote, I think they will be safe.

It would be better if they would not go off exploring for a while, though."

Teela took her grandfather's hand and walked with her to their home overlooking the canyon floor.

"I am worried about Hramack."

"I, too, little one."

"Why must he be so stubborn?"

"Kena?" he asked in jest. He knew she had meant Hramack.

"No. Oooh! You did that on purpose." Teela wrinkled her nose and shook her head at Kaffa, who laughed.

"You worry too much, granddaughter. They will be back soon. Hramack knows his future, as does Kena."

Teela stopped and stared at her grandfather intensely. "Have you seen this?" she asked.

He nodded. "Yes. This and more. The solution to our problems does not lie here in this village. Kena and his son must seek it out."

A look of horror crossed Teela's face. "You mean Hramack must leave again. Oh, grandfather, you must be wrong. He can't leave me again." She began to sob.

Kaffa knew he should not have spoken about his dreams, but it was too late to take it back now. He hugged Teela tightly and let her sob into his shoulder. He knew how she felt. She and Hramack had known each other all their lives. He had watched childhood devotion grow into love. Now, she could lose Hramack because he must choose his future, and that future could lie away from Ningcha.

"He is all I have," she sobbed.

"Sometimes a man, even a young man, must accept the challenge that comes his way. Yarah has much in store for Hramack and his father. Even the stars say so."

"The stars?" she asked, wiping a tear from the corner of her eye.

"In my dreams I see the stars coming to their aid. They will save Ningcha, have no fear of that." He spoke with as much confidence as he could summon. He did not tell her that his dreams also told of death and betrayal. These things were in the hands of Yarah and nothing he or she could do would make a difference.

"Fire hardens the steel to make it stronger," he added. "Hramack must face the fire."

NINGCHA

THE RETURN JOURNEY TO NINGCHA WAS LONG AND ARDUOUS, BUT BOTH father and son marched side-by-side without complaint, resting at sunrise, and reaching the village shortly before dawn of Hramack's seventh day out. After his long desert ordeal, Kena's exhaustion forced him to lean on his son's shoulder on the steep path leading down from the canyon's edge. The village dogs awakened to greet them, but stopped their barking as soon as they recognized the villagers' familiar scents. Too tired to cook, Kena and Hramack ate a quick, cold meal and went to their separate rooms to sleep. Kaffa and Teela, who had been awake all night watching for their return, interrupted their attempt at sleep only minutes later.

Barely awake, Hramack answered the persistent knock at the door. "Teela. Elder. Good to see you again," he said, grabbing Teela, who surprised him by leaping into his arms and almost smothering him with her enthusiastic kisses. Moments later, she realized how unladylike she was being and pushed away.

"Come in, please," he said grinning at her. He held the door and ushered them into the house.

The two entered and seated themselves before the small fire Kena had started in the fireplace, an oddity in the village since most cooked using electric induction ovens. Although he was at heart a scientist and the village ombudsman for all things mechanical, Kena preferred his independence from the overburdened electrical grid. More than anyone, he knew how fragile the thin line between technological man and primitive man was. He collected the dried dung from the herd animals and used it for fuel. Often, his root extractions required the slow, low heat only a fire could provide.

Teela was grinning, too excited to sit still, happy to see Hramack alive. Kaffa was more somber. His staff rested solidly across his lap as he sat, like a vise locking him in place. Hramack wondered at the Elder's dour expression.

Kena entered the room still yawning, visibly thinner from his adventures in the Burning Lands. He walked gingerly on blistered feet, greeted the Elder and Teela warmly, and took a seat on a bench by the table.

"Hramack, brew some tea for our guests," he suggested.

No one spoke for the few minutes it took Hramack to put water on the fire to heat. To avoid water loss from evaporation, he topped the kettle with a reclaimer, a coil of tubing designed to condense the steam and add it back to the kettle, similar to the pressure cooker he carried into the desert. He allowed the mixture of ground *ephedra* twigs, sagebrush leaves, chicory, and a few flakes of dried red pepper to steep for several minutes. The warm, aromatic tea soothed digestion and invoked a sense of serenity. The serving of tea was a ritual that promoted friendship and strengthened communal bonds. The slow pace of the ritual allowed the participants to gather their thoughts and for anger to cool.

Hramack poured the tea into cups and served it. Teela's hands grasped his as he handed her a cup. Her eyes held such love and devotion for him, he wanted to hold her, forget the others in the room, and show her how much he loved her, but the ritual came first.

As the guest, Kaffa broke the silence. He set his cup aside after only two sips. His voice was full of regret. "I hope you found what you sought, Healer. The price you pay may be high. The Council is very troubled by your abandonment of the village's needs these past three weeks. Chu Li will not treat this offense lightly. Prepare yourself well. They have learned of your return and the full Council meets tonight. They require your presence." He looked over at Hramack. "Your son's also."

The sharpness of Kaffa's voice and the curtness of his speech disturbed Hramack. He almost choked on his tea. "Do you vote against us, Elder?" he asked warily.

Kaffa's shoulders slumped as he sighed. "I do not vote. Because of my affection for the two of you, I have resigned as Village Precept. It was the only thing I could do to show my support." Kaffa did not look up at Hramack. He idly stirred the ashes of the fire with the tip of his staff. No longer a staff of office, it was now merely a cane to support the weight of an old man made weary by his years of service.

Kaffa's admission shook Hramack deeply. Kaffa was no longer Precept – things had gone too far. The village sorely needed the guidance of the Elder, especially now. Chu Li and the Council would tighten their hold on the villagers until no free will remained. Anger surged in his young body, washing away his fatigue.

He could barely control the quaver in his voice as he burst out, "Elder, I'm sorry for what we've brought upon you, but we cannot hide here in our village and expect Yarah to see to all our needs. The springs do not return in their annual flow. We must find out why. The answer lies out there," he waved vaguely at the cliff above them, "in the Burning Lands. The water must come from somewhere. We must find its source. My father and I know the Burning Lands better than anyone here." He looked at Kena, who nodded his agreement. "It must be we who attempt this search."

Hramack and Kena had discussed the mystery of the source of the springs on their return journey, but Hramack surprised himself with his suggestion that they search for it. It sounded like something his father would suggest. Teela, startled by his words, bounded from her seat, knocking over the jar of prickly pear fruit syrup used to sweeten the tea. She ignored the thick liquid oozing across the floor and stared at Hramack in stunned silence, forcing him to look away.

"You promised you would never again leave me." Her anguished face bore a mixture of anger and fear.

Touched by here raw emotion, it broke Hramack's heart to say, "For all our sakes, I must break that promise."

Kena slowly stood on battered feet, holding on to the edge of the table for a moment to steady himself, and walked to the stone mantle of the fireplace, his weariness visible in each tired step. He picked up a charcoal drawing of Allana, his wife, and held it for a moment before setting it back in place. The drawing was an excellent likeness. It caught her ready smile and the curve of her lips, but the black and white rendering could not capture the soft azure of her eyes or her gentle laughter. Those, he kept in his heart. He leaned on the cool stone of the great mantle and cleared his throat.

"I found something in the Burning Lands that I must bring before the Council – a map showing the location of the old city of Denver. Denver Dome was built south and east of the ancient city on a vast plain. It may be that the answer to all our problems lies there in the ruins of Denver Dome."

Kaffa spoke up. "You tread on a dangerous path, my friend." He stood and paced the room nervously as he spoke. He peered out the window as if to make certain they were not overheard. "Few here want to remember our past. Fewer still want to revive it. What we need and what we want are separate issues. I ask you, no, I beg you – do not bring this matter before the Council."

Kaffa's vehemence surprised Kena. He shook his head vigorously. "We can ill afford to revert slowly to savagery. We must try to reestablish at least some of the technology of our past. What little we have is wearing out in spite of our best efforts to maintain it. Each year our numbers grow fewer. Children are stillborn and our villagers die from illnesses I cannot cure. We have more young men than women." Kena's voice rose as he spoke. Hramack knew his father became angry when he thought of the deaths he could not prevent. "We must go to Denver Dome. I, at least, must go. The map shows our valley was once part of a great river whose source was in the mountains to the north. I propose to follow it. Along the way, I'm sure I will find the source of the spring and some means to restore the flow."

Kaffa closed his eyes and raised his staff high in the air. He brought the tip back down to strike the floor, but only tapped it gently. "Nuama tells us Yarah struck a rock with his power and the spring burst forth," Kaffa quoted from the *Teachings*. To Hramack's ears, the words rang hollow in the stillness of the room.

"Even so, the water does not appear here magically. It comes from somewhere. Even Yarah does not manifest water simply for our pleasure."

Kena paced in front of the fireplace as he spoke, trying to think things through. His gait was unsteady. Kena believed deeply in Yarah and the *Teachings*. When that belief conflicted with his knowledge of how things worked, as it did now, it troubled him. He knew the inconsistency was due to his lack of understanding and not Yarah's failure. Kaffa shuffled toward the door. "Tonight you can speak your mind, but I warn you, you will raise few allies. Few will go against Chu Li now. He and Madras have formed a strong alliance. People are afraid because the springs do not return. Fear causes people to cling to their religion. Chu Li believes you will raise old ghosts. The people are apprehensive that you will abandon them once again and leave no replacement to see to their needs." He looked pointedly at Hramack. "Many see that Hramack's heart does not lie in Healing." He waved his hand in dismissal. "My voice is weak and few will listen to me."

With these final words, he walked out the door, closing it quietly behind him. Teela remained behind, staring silently at the spilled syrup on the floor at her feet. Kena made an excuse to leave the two alone.

"I must see to the new herbs I brought back from the Burning Lands." As he walked to the rear of the house, leaving the two young ones alone, he mumbled, "Water. Water is what we need, not more prayers."

Teela was overjoyed at seeing Hramack alive and well but feared for his future. His insistence on following in his father's footsteps would cause dissension in the village. Still, she loved him deeply. Embarrassed by her earlier outburst, she dropped to her knees beside the broken jar of syrup.

"Bring me a towel and I will clean up my clumsy mess."

Hramack drew her to her feet and sat her beside him on the couch. "Forget the mess."

She gazed at him: dirty, exhausted, and blistered. She tried hard to imagine what hell he had gone through. She laid her head on his shoulder. His was a strong shoulder and eased her worries with its solid comfort.

"Hramack, I was crazy with concern while you were gone these seven days. Why must you leave me for the Burning Lands?" She raised her head and reached out to stroke his cheek. The stubble of beard felt rough to her fingers. He winced as she touched a blister. Even the few days he had been gone had left him looking frail and thinner.

"I do not wish to cause you pain, my love, but I had to find my father." She was surprised at how weak Hramack's voice had become. The past few days had been hard on him, harder than he would ever admit to her. Part of his strength was hiding his weaknesses so that he might lend a portion of that strength to others. "We are on the verge of collapsing, but few will see it. I must stand with him. It is my duty as his son. Would you have me do otherwise?"

Yes! her mind screamed at him. *Marry me and stay beside me. I am almost a woman who wants the family and future all such women desire.* In her heart, she knew he was right to stand with his father, but it placed them squarely against what most of the villagers believed. The Burning Lands were death. Only in the village was there life. The past should remain forgotten. Even she feared the past, but knew that Kena was right. Unless someone did something soon, the village would die. The women did not speak of it aloud, but that did not make it go away. She knew that Hramack was destined either to lead their people to greatness or to go away forever. Kaffa had seen both endings in his dreams. Would she go with him if he asked? She didn't know. She knew only that he was here now, and that was enough for her.

"I truly believe your father is right," she answered. "Death walks close by each of us these days. People are afraid. Chu Li has so long railed against your father, blaming his delving into the past for our present troubles that people are beginning to listen. I hear them stop talking when I approach. They know of my love for you and of Kaffa's deep respect for your father. Each day their prayers to Yarah grow longer and more fervent."

She looked deeply into Hramack's eyes and spoke quietly, as if afraid that speaking the words aloud would make them true. "There has even been talk of sacrificing one of the herd animals." She was horrified at the thought. It sounded barbaric. "Can you believe that? We will lose most of them soon enough if we do not get water."

She could see that Hramack, too, was aghast at this revelation. Like her, he had thought most of the villagers were too intelligent, too resilient, to revert to the old ways. Now, he had a clearer grasp of Kaffa's concern. She knew things would not improve on their own, no matter how much they prayed to Yarah. Hramack saw this as well. Why couldn't the rest of the village?

She could understand Chu Li. His motivation was simple. He held a grudge against Kena and used him as a pawn to increase his control of power in the village. She did not know why Roagneau, Meelier, and Mitsu heeded him. They were, or had been, close friends and supporters of Kena in the past. Hramack knew their sons well, considered them close friends. Would they turn on him now when he needed their support most?

Hramack reached out and pulled her to him, running his fingers through her long, silky hair. His touch thrilled her. She had feared for his life out there among the creatures that haunt the Burning Lands. She caught a whiff of Hramack's pungent body odor and pulled back sharply. She could smell the feline muskiness of a nightstalker even above the flinty odor of the sand and the acrid dried sweat. *What ordeals had he endured out there?* She would probably never learn.

When she pulled back, Hramack guessed the reason. He laughed.

"Teela. I must wash this desert stink off me and sleep before the meeting tonight. Promise me that no matter what happens, you will not speak out against Chu Li."

Teela glared at him. "I will not be silent."

"Chu Li is a dangerous man. He desires power and will stop at nothing to gain it. His devotion to Yarah is second only to his lust for control. No matter what the Council decides, my father and I must leave Ningcha. We must find the source of the springs soon, or we will all die. If you speak too openly in my defense, Chu Li or the Council could take steps to punish you."

Teela's eyes blazed with anger. "I am not afraid of Chu Li. Let them try to silence me."

Hramack shook his head. "I do not think you would like it if you were forced to marry one of Madras' sons, perhaps Anseer?"

Her heart skipped a beat. As High Priest, Chu Li could invoke an ancient rule that governed marriages by the needs of the village, a way to broaden the tiny gene pool. "He would never ... I would never ..." She trembled at the thought.

Hramack touched her lips with his finger to silence her. "He would stop at nothing to consolidate power. He needs Madras as an ally. Just the threat would force Kaffa to keep silent about what he knows. He would do anything to protect you."

"Even Chu Li would not do such a despicable thing," she said. "The people would not stand for it." As she spoke, she wondered if it was true. Many things had changed lately. She looked at Hramack. He seemed poised to speak but uncertain whether he should.

"What else?" she asked to prompt him.

"My father suspects Chu Li in the death of Herat, the old High Priest. He has said nothing to the Council for lack of proof, but his reasoning seems sound. If Chu Li is capable of murder, or even of letting Herat die unaided, of what else might he be capable?"

"Murder? No villager has ever murdered another, not in nearly 300 years. How ..." The words would not form. "How do you know this?"

"The medicine my father made for Herat was missing when he found the body. Herat needed it for his heart and kept it nearby at all times. Only Chu Li could have removed it."

"If what you say is true, you and your father are the ones in danger, not I. He could bind me to another, that is his right as High Priest, but no man would touch me against my will and live. You are a threat to Chu Li, and he would not hesitate to kill you."

She saw in his eyes that Hramack was just now grasping the real threat of Chu Li – not his attempt to control the village, but his ability to control Kena through his son.

"You're right. My father must be warned." Hramack stood. "Go now, before others see you here. My father and I must prepare for tonight."

He pulled her to him and kissed her as if it were the last time he would taste her lips. She prayed that it would not be so. He pulled away and strode quickly into the back of the house. She stood silently for a moment, wiping the tears forming in her eyes with her hand, and followed Kaffa.

✳

Kaffa walked slowly to allow his granddaughter to catch up with him. He read her disappointment in her eyes. "Hramack cares deeply for you. He is torn between loyalty to his father and his love for you."

"He doesn't show it," she replied.

"He faces choices his young heart does not wish to make. Sometimes, the most difficult choice is the right one."

"You agree that he should leave with his father?"

A flash of light high in the night sky caught Kaffa's eye. A second and a third followed, long flashes of brilliant white light that streaked across the sky. Kaffa had seen meteors before, but these were not the streaks caused by a meteor's incineration in the atmosphere. The angle was wrong. The flashes seemed brighter: more intense, almost like the beam of a powerful flashlight. He continued to watch as he walked, but the event did not repeat itself. The image stirred the memory of his recent dreams.

"The decision is beyond his control," he replied.

6

LONG JOHN BALDRY

*L*ONG *JOHN BALDRY* SLID SILENTLY OUT OF THE EMPTINESS OF SKIP SPACE AND into the complex gravity fields of the moons, moonlets, and swirls of dust just outside the orbit of the fifth planet of the star system. A momentary flash of light and a burst of gravity waves accompanied the ship's transition into real space. Lieutenant Cathi Lorst hurriedly shook off the disorienting effects of Skipping, looked out the bridge view screen at the planet below with its faint rings of ice and dust, and saw beauty. If the ancient navigation charts were correct, the planet, a colorful gas giant, was Jupiter, and the star beyond it was Sol, Homeworld's sun. After an absence of nearly a thousand years, mankind had at last come home. Tightness formed in her chest at the enormity of their accomplishment.

She compared the spectrometer readings with those provided by the crumbling old star chart. They matched within tolerable limits – mass: 1.9×10^{27} kg. The distance was good – just over 778 million kilometers from the primary. The bands of gases surrounding the planet still swirled with gigantic storms, though the Great Red Spot was no longer there. According to the records, it had lasted at least five hundred years. She wondered why it had finally disappeared.

Next, she focused the ship's powerful imager on the third planet. It was not as blue as the ancient charts had indicated, but that was understandable. Planets change and humans had pretty much used up Homeworld's resources before abandoning it a millennium earlier. She detected no electromagnetic emissions on any frequency other than those of natural origin. Earth appeared to be a dead world. Closer inspection revealed signs of massive geologic upheavals and areas devastated by what must have been weapons of mass destruction. She saw only small, shallow seas where once waters had reached depths of nearly eleven kilometers. She found no trace of the legendary domed cities, but she could see only one side of the planet.

Cathi was not certain what she felt. She had hoped that there would be some sign of life: some proof that those left behind had survived the long centuries of massive solar flares and deadly bursts of radiation, had survived the dense cloud cover and incessant storms caused by evaporation of the seas. To think that after all this time and their long journey here, there would be no welcoming committee, was a bitter disappointment. She sighed. Such a valiant effort to survive the threats from the unstable sun wasted because the worst threat had ultimately come from Man himself. A deep sense of loss now tempered her thrill at finally locating Homeworld.

Growing up a dirt grubber on a tiny agricultural world frequented often by ships of the Traders Guild, Cathi had heard all the tales about Homeworld. Every bar in a hundred worlds had one old spacer, who for the price of a drink, would spin yarns filled with half-truths, lies, and fantasies. Her favorite was the great domed cities filled with great riches and technologies far beyond anything one could imagine. Legends of Homeworld had merged with the *Tales of the Arabian Nights* and the myth of *El Dorado* rolled into one to hundreds of millions of poor working-class citizens in the remnants of the old empires. She had vowed to find Homeworld, to walk the streets of her ancestors, and to bring home the treasures left lying about – precious jewels, ancient statues, and priceless paintings: things deemed unessential to a race reaching for the stars, the things that connected the human race to its roots.

When a Traders Guild Merchant ship arrived the day of her eighteenth birthday, she had considered it a sign, a portent of things to come. She so impressed the captain with her resourcefulness and willingness to learn that he had agreed to allow her to work her way to their next port of call. Two years later, she had won a permanent berth aboard the *Baldry,* moving from land grubber to gypsy. Now, eight years later, she was an officer.

Reluctant to take her gaze from Earth, she turned her instruments on the fourth planet. This world did show signs of human habitation. Oxygen and greenhouse gases were abundant in the atmosphere. It was no longer the cold, dead world of old as indicated by the charts. Lakes and rivers dotted its surface. She detected small cities and an impressive network of roads. She also picked up radio signals. Her heart beat faster. Someone lived there. Perhaps a remnant of Earthers had survived after all.

She turned to her captain, Angus Cyril Moore, as he quietly stared out the view screen at the nearby gas giant, watching the bands of clouds swirl around the planet. His long, red beard ended in three jewel-tipped braids, and his prominent gold bicuspid gleamed brightly when he smiled, lending him the aspect of a modern day pirate, a façade he cultivated to its maximum effect. Instead of his captain's uniform, he wore a pair of brightly colored shorts, an equally flamboyant pullover, and sandals. He sipped coffee from a large mug. A smile broke across his ruddy face as she handed him her report.

"Captain, it looks like we did it. Sol. I would not have given us a chance in a million of finding it with that outdated chart you picked up at Tau Ceti Delta. Hell, I thought Homeworld was just a myth. But there it is, less than four hours away."

Captain Moore looked mildly amused by her excited outburst, but she guessed what he was thinking. If they came away from Homeworld with a hold full of trade goods, he could refit the old *Baldry* and maybe buy another ship. He quickly scanned Lorst's report.

"Good job, lieutenant. Set a course for the fourth planet. Mars is its name, if I remember my history correctly, named after a god of war. I see that it is inhabited. Well, good and better. We'll need supplies and fresh vegetables." He jerked his thumb aft toward the rear of the ship and the cargo holds. "Maybe we can trade some of this gol-fricking mining equipment we've been hauling across half the galaxy. Hmm," he added. "Mars. Let's hope the name isn't a bad omen."

He turned to the rear of the bridge and yelled, "Helmsman, make for the fourth planet at one half speed. Comm, see if you can raise anyone. Sweep all frequencies." He turned back to Cathi. "We'll announce our presence. We don't want to alarm them. They probably haven't had visitors in quite some time."

"Yes, a thousand years," she replied. "A thousand years – ten centuries."

The centuries of expansion by the colonists from Earth had been both haphazard and, in many cases, undocumented. Freed from the confining central governments of Earth during the Scattering, new colonists felt no ties to old political bodies or religious philosophies. Some simply vanished into the Void, concealing their passage from those who might follow. Others moved from world to world and from sun to sun, blithely stripping them of their resources as they had done to Earth.

Homeworld! Names changed and legends grew, eventually shrouding Earth's exact location in mystery. Many planets laid claim to the title and profited from its memory, but none could produce proof to substantiate the validity of such a claim. Gradually, as planets became embroiled in wars and the fight for survival, old records were lost or destroyed. Memories became legends and legends fairy tales. Slowly, over the centuries, humankind had expanded across the galaxy until all ties with the past, and each other, were lost. Some remained isolated either by desire or by distance. Empires, kingdoms, democratic hegemonies, republics, and religious empires – all came and went with little or no effect on the galaxy as a whole. Warlords, despots, and religious zealots rose and fell in the hundreds. Finally, small groups of worlds developed trade agreements among themselves and financed a fleet of ships to seek out new partners, the beginnings of the Traders Guild. Slowly, the scattered remnants of worlds began to meld once more into some semblance of order.

Traders were a group unto their own, owing allegiance only to the tenants of the Guild, seeking trade wherever and whenever possible. Their homes were their ships, and their crews were their families. They seldom stayed in one place very long, preferring the vast emptiness between worlds. They were the peddlers and tinkers of the modern era. All worlds, even those ruled by right of force, recognized the sanctity of the Traders Guild and abided by its tenets. All worlds granted Guild vessels safe passage and the right of free trade wherever they went.

Over time, the Traders Guild, through shrewd trade agreements, often coerced worlds to grant new rights and freedoms to its citizens, thereby becoming a political force in the galaxy. In the nearly half a millennium since its inception, over a hundred worlds had opened to free trade.

Long John Baldry slowly turned away from Jupiter and toward Mars. A C-Class Merchant Freighter of the Traders Guild, she carried a crew of twenty-six, including seven children. The long trip out from Tau Ceti had been difficult for the crew and hard on the ship. The twenty-Skip voyage required weeks of idle time to retune the engines, and the side effects of Skip technology, the harnessing of gravity from micro black holes to Skip along the edges of curved space-time, played havoc with the human body. If not for the suppression drugs, long Skips would be almost unbearable. Everyone now looked forward to some well-deserved shore leave, especially the children.

Kal Anderson, the ship's communications officer, called out to the captain from his console. His voice was, as always, even and precise. Cathi had never heard him excited or flustered in the eight years she had known him. "Sir, I'm picking up a request for identification and destination, at least I think it's a request for ID and D. The language seems to be Standard English, but the dialect's a little strange. I'm having trouble translating some of the words."

"I'm sure they haven't heard your thick Brosnian accent before either, Anderson," Cathi quipped with a smile.

"Answer their request, Mr. Anderson," Captain Moore replied.

Anderson spoke into his microphone. "This is the Traders Guild Merchant ship *Long John Baldry*. Our port of call is Epsilon III, outbound from Tau Ceti Delta. We come to trade as representatives of the Traders Guild. We wish coordinates for landing, please." He listened as a bemused voice on the other end answered. By the odd look on Anderson's face, Cathi perceived there was a problem.

"Sir, they don't believe us. They think it's some kind of joke."

Captain Moore laughed at Anderson's confusion. "We've been gone a thousand years, man. Of course, they don't believe you." He grabbed the microphone from the startled Anderson's hand. "Listen, you micro-brained, desk-bound, hollow-eyed, thumb-sucking cretin, this is the captain of the *Long John Baldry*, Angus Moore of the Traders Guild. We're here for trade. Find us a place to land, or I'll drop my ship in your lap."

They either understood the words or correctly interpreted his tone, for landing coordinates quickly followed. Minutes later, another voice came on the radio. The speaker spoke very slowly, as if carefully choosing his words.

"Captain Moore, this is President Anjiro. This is a moment of historical significance. We welcome you to our planet. I am most certain that a mutually satisfying agreement for free trade can be ..."

"Yeah, yeah," Moore said, interrupting the president's speech. "We can deal with that later. I'm busy landing my ship now." He switched off the microphone. To Cathi's look of astonishment, he said, "Bureaucrats! They love the sound of their own voice. Let him squirm a while."

After a few minutes had passed, he spoke into the mic again. "Mr. President, we are eager to visit Homeworld, Earth. Can you arrange this?" Cathi and Captain Moore stared at one another as the silence lengthened. "Must be having a quick confab," he said.

Finally, President Anjiro returned. His voice was no longer jubilant, but petulant, as if reprimanding a child. "I advise you, captain, do not visit Earth. None of our ships that have ventured there have returned. Earth is a dead and dangerous world. Very bad. All that remains of humankind in this system is here on Mars and the asteroid mining colonies in the Belt. We welcome you and your crew to our planet with open arms and greatly desire to trade with you. Please, land and meet with us. We will celebrate this auspicious occasion with a state banquet."

Captain Moore looked at his bridge crew and frowned, but replied, "Aye, a good meal would be nice. We'll send representatives." He closed communications again. "They're probably stripping Earth bare of its resources and salvage and don't want us interfering with their operation. Until we know more about them, we proceed slowly."

He turned to Cathi. "Lieutenant Lorst, take Anderson and two others and pay a little visit to Earth in the shuttle. See what you can find out. Be careful. We don't know how well armed they are." He stroked his red beard in thought before adding, "Take a portable laser with you, just in case."

The portable laser's primary use was in mining, but it could be a formidable weapon in the right hands. The *Baldry* carried two much larger lasers and a missile launcher, but they were fixed to the hull and nearly useless on the ground. The ship would be a sitting duck.

Having the small laser in the shuttle in case the *Baldry* needed rescuing seemed a sensible precaution.

She was eager to see Earth, to feel its soil beneath her feet. It would be the culmination of a lifetime's dream. "Yes sir, captain," she answered, unable to keep the smile from her lips.

She picked her crew carefully. Because of the inherent dangers involved, she chose no one in a monogamous relationship or with children. She eliminated anyone essential to the welfare of the ship – hydroponics, Skip Drive technicians, or navigation. If anything happened, she wanted to ensure the survival of her ship, her family. Ten minutes later, she, Kal Anderson, Tai Whitehall, and Ialin Pegari boarded the *Baldry's* shuttle. Using Mars' largest moon, Phobos, to shield their departure, she kept power at a minimum until she was certain that prying eyes on Mars could not track them. She chose a longer, elliptical orbit instead of a more direct path to allow them the opportunity to scan both Earth and some of the larger asteroid colonies in more detail.

The colonies were small-scale affairs, often extended families, carved deep into the bodies of asteroids as they removed the ore. They refined the metals on-site and transported them to Mars. She detected a few ice-rich comets towed by powerful little tugs for delivery to Mars to replace atmosphere lost through attenuation due to its low gravity. None of the colonies appeared threatening.

The long-range scans of Earth continued to show no signs of advanced life. Small forests and grasslands dotted the upper Temperate Zones, but vast expanses of desert covered most of North and South America, Africa, parts of Central Asia, and almost all of Australia – the entire Equatorial and Tropical Zones. Minimal ice caps dotted the Polar Regions. A two-thousand-kilometer-wide sea was now all that separated the continents of Africa and South America. No large herds of animals roamed the grasslands. No schools of fish swam the seas. No cities broadcast on the E-M bands. Earth appeared to be a dead world. She held out little hope for survivors, but continued to peer through the telescope for any signs of a remaining civilization.

As the distance diminished, she distinguished signs of massive destruction that upon first glance she mistook for natural disasters. Closer examination revealed converging roadways that ended abruptly in deep craters. Straight, kilometers-long scars across the terrain gave testament to the power of space-based lasers. She counted the ruins of seven great domes in the hemisphere visible to them. There was not a single sign of any surviving advanced culture – no maintained roads, no radio signals, and no airborne traffic.

"They wiped themselves out," she relayed to Anderson, who sat in the seat beside her. He merely nodded and remained intent on his own console. She couldn't understand why he wasn't as dejected as she was by the lack of communication. They had come a long way to find Earth, and yet he displayed neither excitement nor gloom.

As they approached Earth's moon, she detected old settlements and bases on its scarred gray surface, but they, too, were silent. She was surprised to find no orbiting stations around Earth from the construction of the Migration fleet, but then remembered that a thousand years was a long time to maintain an orbit, especially with increased solar winds from the raging sun.

Ten thousand kilometers from Earth, Anderson called out, "I'm picking up something on the scanner just ahead of us, maybe a thousand clicks distant."

She peered at his screen. "I don't see anything."

"It comes and goes, but it's there. It's small, cold, and metallic. See. There it is."

She watched as an object flashed into existence, and then disappeared again. "Keep an eye on it," she advised. "Try for a visual."

A few minutes later, Anderson piped up, "It's a satellite. I'm not getting any readings from it though. It appears to be a derelict." He paused, then added with growing puzzlement, "No, wait. I'm getting something now."

Through the viewport, Cathi watched the satellite slowly began to unfold two large solar panels like angel's wings, *or dragon's wings*, she thought with a sudden chill.

"I'm getting a large energy spike. It's powering up and scanning us," Anderson called out. "It's an automated defense satellite."

As she noted the near panic in Anderson's normally controlled voice, she throttled the shuttle's engines to full power and began a tight curve away from the now fully active satellite, but the compact ion engine was designed for power, not speed. The lasers from the defense satellites would be powerful enough to destroy any approaching ship unable to supply the proper recognition code, which they could not.

"Pegari! Power up the laser and target that satellite. I'm getting us out of here. Fire if the satellite shows any sign of targeting us."

She fought the controls to swing the shuttle in a tight turn not recommended by the manufacturers. She fired all attitude thrusters on one side to help facilitate the turn. Pegari grunted as she slammed into a bulkhead. Over her shoulder, Cathi saw Pegari shake it off and scramble to slam her helmet over her curly brown locks. They had mounted the laser in the airlock, meaning Pegari would have to evacuate the airlock and open the outer door to fire it.

When they reached a distance of one hundred kilometers from the satellite, it began to show definite signs of hostility by sweeping the shuttle with a powerful magnetic resonance beam. Without the proper shielding, the beam would have shorted out the shuttle's electrical power. Still, alarms began to sound all over the ship. Now, the satellite was actively targeting them.

"Pegari," she yelled.

A brilliant beam of light shot from the shuttle and disintegrated one of the large solar panels of the satellite. A cloud of debris and gas expanded away from the satellite.

"Got it," Pegari yelled in triumph over the intercom, her young voice shrill with excitement.

"Don't dance yet, Pegari," Anderson cautioned. "It's still active."

Almost as if to prove Anderson correct, the satellite fired a laser burst, missing the shuttle by mere meters. Cathi flinched as the beam shot across their bow, scorching the shuttle's paint. In her worst nightmares, she had never imagined being under attack by a fully awakened defense satellite. If this was what had destroyed the Martian ships, perhaps they should have heeded the president's warning after all.

"Anderson, send a message to the *Baldry*. Warn them about the automated defense satellite while I try to get us out of here." Another laser burst sliced through space just behind them. The satellite was getting closer with each shot. One more shot and the satellite would have them targeted. Luckily for them, the satellite was dormant when they arrived. If it had been at one-hundred-percent power as they approached, she doubted they could have survived this long.

"Pegari, shoot that damn thing," she screamed into her headset.

"I'm trying," Pegari snapped. "I can't get a good lock on it. The damn shuttle's shaking to pieces. Try to hold it steady."

The G-forces Cathi was putting the shuttle through in her wild maneuvers could indeed shake it to pieces, but that was the least of her worries. She glanced at the distance indicator hoping they were out of range. If she could only get another few hundred kilometers ... The shuttle shuddered and bucked as the satellite zeroed in on them. Its powerful laser sliced through the aft section of the hull, rupturing one fuel tank, an oxygen tank, and damaging the main engine. The hiss of escaping gases spewing into the vacuum of space was deafening. Their luck had run out. One more such hit and they were finished. She slammed down the faceplate of her helmet. Dense black smoke poured through the aft door and curls of flame licked the ceiling.

"Whitehall. Put out that fire." She tried to keep the rising panic from her voice while she barked out orders.

Whitehall unstrapped and directed a stream of fire-retardant foam at the door, but the fuel-fed fire burned too fiercely for the extinguisher. He emptied the extinguisher and looked at her hopelessly. There was only one thing left to try.

"Everyone drop your face shields and be sure you're on suit oxygen. I'm purging the cabin."

Anderson gave her a warning glare, which she promptly ignored. He dropped his face shield. She touched the purge icon on the console panel screen. It turned red, indicating the ship was venting its atmosphere. Within seconds, the fire was out, as was their cabin air. The suits held less than six hours of life-giving oxygen, and their main oxygen supply was gone. With no main engine and their fuel tanks ruptured, they had no hope of returning to the *Baldry* before they were breathing vacuum. *Or of outrunning the next laser blast*, she mused silently.

Then, as if by a miracle, their luck changed. The expanding cloud of frozen atmosphere she had just vented provided cover for the damaged shuttle. The satellite's targeting laser, scattered by the expanding cloud of ice crystals, could not obtain a clear lock. The shuttle's targeting alert went silent. Its sudden silence lifted a weight from her shoulders, allowing her to think clearly.

"Thank the stars, we now have a chance," she whispered.

Acting quickly, she turned the shuttle directly into the planet's atmosphere, hoping the thickening blanket of air rushing at them would absorb at least some of the laser's energy once it managed to reacquire the shuttle. They plummeted toward the planet like a rock, the ceramic skin of the shuttle burning away in layers. They plunged toward the ground out of control.

As she hoped, the next laser hit did only minor damage to the aft section. The thickening atmosphere had diffused most of the satellite's laser energy. It normally operated in the vacuum of space as a defensive screen for the larger laser platforms that had destroyed much of Earth's surface. In spite of its limitations, it had delivered a deathblow to the shuttle and likely doomed them. They were entering Earth's atmosphere at an alarming speed, and the main engine was gone. The shuttle had only the small maneuvering thrusters left to slow them. She checked her navigation screen.

Twelve percent off optimal glide path. Damn!

A quick check on the computer told her that the thrusters would not be enough. The shuttle would either become a flaming beacon to light up the night sky, or add one more crater to the many that pockmarked the ground. Neither prospect boded well for their immediate survival. If she could level the shuttle just a little, the aerodynamics of the shuttle itself, designed to operate in an atmosphere, would work for them. A long, steep glide could slow them enough to prevent incineration. Landing was another matter. If she used all the remaining fuel to decrease their angle of descent, there would be none left for landing. In the dark, with no way to choose a landing site, it mattered very little anyway. She chose to tackle one problem at a time.

Firing the forward maneuvering thrusters, using all her strength to pull back on the almost frozen control yoke, she managed to reduce their angle of descent a few degrees, just enough to gain limited control of the plummeting shuttle. Then, the remaining fuel tank emptied, and the thrusters sputtered and went silent. Now, the shuttle had become a very fast, very heavy glider.

Six percent off optimal glide path. It was the best she could do. She would have to trust the shuttle's exterior to handle the extra heat. Cabin temperature soared another ten degrees Celsius. Even with her suit's air conditioning, she was perspiring heavily. A proper landing was out of the question. Gravity would choose their location for them. It appeared they would hit somewhere in the vast broken plains just east of what had once been Denver Dome. Perhaps that was providential. Denver Dome, unlike most of the other domes they had scanned, appeared mostly intact. It was, however, radio silent. If they survived the crash, the odds were low that they would find help there, but it was their only choice.

At 25,000 meters, an atmospheric microburst slammed into the shuttle with a hammer blow, shaking the contents of the cabin like a cocktail shaker and rattling her teeth so hard she bit her tongue. The shuttle abruptly dropped two thousand meters as wind fell away from the underside of the airfoils. At the same time, the wind shear tried to flip the shuttle onto its side. She fought the controls to bring up the nose and keep the deadweight craft level. Gradually, the nose lifted, but it was too little too late. They would never make Denver Dome.

They passed over a long, deep scar in the earth that had once been a mighty river. The faint light of the moon picked out the rusted hulks of ships littering the bottom, and the rubble of a collapsed bridge, which divided two short sections of cracked and pitted highway. Beyond the river, a series of wide craters whose bottoms remained deeply shadowed scarred the landscape. They skimmed over the desolation at a height of less than two thousand meters, trailing a stream of molten metal and burning ceramic tiles lighting the dark terrain beneath them.

Finally, she could do no more. Gravity, the Big Attractor, was winning. She fired the landing thrusters, hoping for just a few seconds of power to gain altitude. The engines sputtered for a mere four seconds before shuddering to silence. *Was it enough to raise the nose and level them out?* Now, she was no longer the pilot. She was a passenger. She did not bother dropping the landing gear. The uneven ground beneath them would have ripped the gear away instantly.

The shuttle struck the ground with a bone-jarring thud at a speed of over three hundred kilometers per hour and bounced back into the air like a stone skipped on a pond. The impact jerked her forward in her harness, and then slammed her head back into her seat hard enough to blur her vision. Only the adrenaline rush from the danger kept her from passing out. Her chest ached where the restraints bit into her flesh.

The shuttle landed heavily on its starboard side six hundred meters from first impact. The starboard airfoil crumpled from the impact. A series of metal-wrenching shorter bounds slowed them to one-hundred-eighty kph. Pieces of the shuttle's ceramosteel alloy hull peeled away, like carving flesh with a chef's knife, leaving bone-like naked support struts. A five-meter section of the fuselage and deck sheared away, taking Whitehall's seat with it. She watched the look of sheer terror in his eyes as he disappeared in a cloud of dust.

The shuttle once again righted itself as the nose began plowing into the dirt. The seven-centimeter thick, triple-layered aluminum-silicate forward window shattered, spraying the cabin with slivers of glass. An arm-length, knife-edged piece penetrated the seat just above her head. A shower of dirt and rocks poured into the cabin through the shattered window intent on burying them alive. Friction with the ground, acting like sandpaper on the shuttle's keel, gradually slowed them. Finally, the shuttle skewed to the right and flipped onto its damaged starboard side. The noise was deafening, a groaning of earth and metal. The shuttle came to rest only meters from a deep ravine.

Inside the crashed shuttle, nothing stirred.

For many long minutes, the only sounds coming from the demolished hulk of the shuttle were the popping of red hot metal cooling and the groaning of sagging structural supports. That *ping, ping, ping* sound of cooling metal was what finally brought Lieutenant Cathi back to reality. Loosening her shoulder harness, she fell hard out of her tilted command chair and landed on her hands and knees in the dirt covering the crumpled wall of the cabin, which had now become the deck. She pushed to her feet to check on the condition of her crew. The only light came from an overhead panel wrenched from the ceiling, swinging hypnotically from its wiring. She fumbled for the flashlight at her belt and played it around the demolished cabin.

Pegari was dead. A piece of steel torn loose by the impact had plunged through her upper torso, pinning her to the half-open inner airlock door. Her helmet faceplate was smashed. Cathi didn't know if she had died from her injury or from lack of oxygen. Either way, she had lost a dear friend and comrade. Pegari, two years younger than her, looked up to her. She and Pegari had often taken shore leave together. She would miss her.

The laser that had saved their lives had broken free of its securing mounts and now lay in a smashed heap inside the airlock, its power cell crushed beneath it.

Anderson was conscious but dazed. A trickle of blood ran down his dark cheek from a small cut on his forehead. He stared at her in disbelief, shaking his head to silence the ringing in his ears. He noticed Pegari's dead body and quickly began checking himself for injuries. He probed the cut on his head and moved his extremities experimentally, but satisfied he would live, nodded at Lorst's order to check on communications. After unbuckling his harness, he removed his helmet and picked his way through the maze of wreckage and debris towards the main communications panel in what remained of the aft bulkhead. She watched him for a moment to make sure he was all right, and then continued her inspection of the shuttle.

Whitehall was missing, as was a section of the starboard side of the shuttle, sheared away by the impact. She eyed the moonlit landscape in which they had crashed through the gap in the fuselage. It was an inhospitable terrain – scorched, blasted, and lifeless – offering no refuge for the survivors. In spite of the darkness, a river of searing, hot air poured in through the rent hull. Concentrating on their immediate needs, she gathered what medical supplies and foodstuffs she could salvage and carried them to the hole in the hull. To her eyes, they presented a pitifully small pile. Anderson returned looking more aware of his surroundings, but still dangerously close to shock.

"Report, Anderson," she barked at him, hoping to snap him out of his growing dismay.

Anderson shook his head slowly and looked up at her. "All communication equipment, except for two short-range hand-held units, is gone. Irreparable. I couldn't even find some of the components. Our automatic transponder is working. They can locate us, but if the *Baldry* comes after us, that satellite will destroy it too. I debated shutting it down."

"No, leave it on," she answered. "Hopefully our warning got through. In the meantime, we survive. We have to search for Whitehall. It won't be easy in the dark." She glanced at Pegari's body. Strangely, she felt no sadness at her death, only guilt. She assumed sorrow would come later to replace the numbness after she had time to absorb the consequences of her decisions. "Then, we bury Ialin."

She noticed that her voice had suddenly ranged higher. Anderson stared at her questioningly.

"It's the helium coolant from the Craddock fusion reactor," she realized. "The reactor automatically went off-line in the crash, but the coolant lines ruptured. We can't stay here. I've gathered some supplies. Grab anything else you think we might need and meet me outside the ship. Hurry."

Her faceplate had cracked during the crash. She ripped off the useless helmet and flung it to the ground in anger, then stripped off the heavy vacuum suit. She barely remembered to trigger the survivor transponder clipped to her belt to let the *Baldry* know that someone was still alive. The helium gas expanded as it warmed, filling the entire ship. Without her suit oxygen, breathing became more difficult. She took one last look around the wreckage before climbing out through the rip in the starboard side.

She had thought the inside of the shuttle was stifling. Outside, the heat struck her a physical blow. Hot air rose from the sun-baked earth in waves. Each breath was a struggle, feeling as if it was searing her lungs. She looked around for the missing section of the ship and Whitehall, but she could see nothing in the darkness. She went back into the shuttle to retrieve her cap and one for Whitehall and Anderson. When the sun rose, they would need all the protection they could find. Then, she joined Anderson.

She pressed her finger to a spot on her neck just above her sternum to activate the communicator embedded just beneath the flesh. Each crewmember had the implant for shipboard communication. "Cathi to Whitehall. Come in Whitehall."

She waited a few moments but received no response. She fought the growing panic that Whitehall was dead: another life lost that had been her responsibility.

"Whitehall, answer me if you can hear me," she said, almost pleading for a reply.

"The communicators are short-range, "Anderson reminded her. He still wore his vacuum suit, but he had removed his helmet and gloves. He tried his communicator, frowning at the silence. "Maybe he's unconscious," he suggested. He tactfully avoided mentioning the more obvious conclusion, that Whitehall was dead.

"Yeah, maybe," she replied.

"The atmosphere is full of ions," he said. "They could be interfering."

"We'll find him the old fashioned way," she said.

As they walked away from the shuttle, she realized just how lucky they had been. The rough landing had ripped away the tiles and had torn away large sections of the hull, strewing twisted metal and melted tiles like confetti along a trail over a kilometer in length. A deep gash ground into the earth indicated how the shuttle had lost velocity. They had passed within meters of a stony outcropping that would have smashed them to pieces. It was by a miracle more than her piloting skills that anyone had survived. Had they slid another fifteen meters, they would have plunged into a ravine over twenty-five meters deep.

They searched using handheld flashlights, meandering along their flight path calling Whitehall's name, searching through pieces of debris, and dreading to find his corpse beneath each one. Finally, they heard a faint reply to their calls. Cathi's heart leaped with joy.

They found Tai Whitehall strapped to his seat, still bolted to a section of the hull torn free on impact. It had slid for thirty meters before coming to rest in an upright position. Whitehall would have gotten off without a scratch if not for one, lone, scrubby tree. His makeshift sled ground to a stop just as he rammed into the tree's single branch, pinning him to his seat.

After carefully releasing him from his seat and removing his helmet, Cathi examined him with the handheld medical scanner. She quickly discovered that he had suffered at least two broken ribs, but had difficulty determining if there were any further internal injuries. The scanner had suffered damage in the crash, and the readings were inaccurate. They freed him from his seat and helped him back to the shuttle.

She insisted they all eat, though she didn't have much of an appetite.

"We'll remain near the shuttle for the time being. The *Baldry* is bound to have picked up our distress call, and will mount a rescue mission."

She didn't add that they had nowhere to go and that Whitehall was in no condition for a journey, or the fact that if no help came within a few days, they were probably on their own. By Anderson's glum expression, he had already arrived at the same conclusion. He removed the rest of his vacuum suit, leaving only his sweat-soaked jumpsuit. Always neat, he folded the suit and laid it beside his sleeping bag. He lay down and closed his eyes, but Cathi doubted he was asleep.

Whitehall had drifted to sleep immediately after their meal. His breathing sounded labored, and he moaned whenever he moved. Cathi was concerned for him. The medical kit was limited in scope, and her knowledge of first aid was limited to shipside minor wounds. He needed real medical help, but help seemed unlikely in their present situation.

She was exhausted and wanted to sleep, but her mind roiled with doubts about her ability to lead. She paced around the crashed ship replaying every minute of their flight and the battle with the defense satellite. She saw no obvious mistakes she had made, but she couldn't argue with the outcome. They were on a seemingly hostile planet with little food or water and only a slim chance of rescue.

If help didn't come soon, she could think of no option but trying to reach the ruins of Denver Dome. It would be a long, grueling hike, especially for Whitehall, but it was also the nearest sign of civilization. Even though the scans indicated it long abandoned, perhaps they would stumble across help along the way. She could not accept that everyone on Earth was dead. Even if her ancestors had left the planet a thousand years ago, Earth was still the Mother World – Homeworld. It couldn't be dead. It just couldn't.

At the first hint of dawn, they buried Ialin Pegari on a small rise beside the shuttle. Using pieces of metal from the shuttle as digging tools, she and Anderson barely managed to scrape a hole in the hard-packed soil deep enough to accept Pegari's petite body. They wrapped her body in a piece of insulation and reverently placed it in the hole. She dutifully read from her officer's manual the words for the dead, but mere words seemed inadequate for the heart-wrenching sense of loss she felt. She had never lost a friend to death before. She had also never lost someone under her command.

"I'm so sorry, Ialin," she whispered to the small grave as she drove a piece of metal into the grave to serve as a marker. She laid Pegari's ID bracelet over it. "You came all this way only to die on Homeworld without a proper ceremony."

She turned away and swiped at the tear in her eye. She had shipped with Pegari for nearly four years. She had been quiet and solitary aboard ship, but always ready with a joke at a moment's notice. On shore leave, she submerged herself in whatever culture she encountered, living each day to its fullest. She had helped Cathi study for her officer's exam. Her death would leave a large hole in the ship's company and in Lorst's heart.

The sun rose hot and merciless. She had never been on a world where the sun beat down on the land as hard. Within an hour, the heat became unbearable, baking her through the thin material of her jumpsuit. They needed shelter. The helium had cleared from the shuttle. She deemed it safe to return to its relative comfort out of the relentless heat of the sun. Whitehall didn't complain, but she knew he was in pain in spite of the sedatives. She had bound his damaged ribs as best she could the previous night and administered antibiotics and anti-inflammatory drugs, but she knew he needed better care than she could provide. He insisted on helping with the daily chores – cooking, operating the small water still, and searching through the wrecked shuttle for useful items – but she could see him wince whenever he bent over or pushed himself too hard.

The malfunctioning medical scanner indicated that his ribs had aligned properly and would mend with time and care, but it provided little reliable information beyond that. He steadily grew weaker throughout the day, and the color drained from his face. She was concerned about internal bleeding, but they could do little about that eventuality.

The days passed with no sign of rescue. Food and water were beginning to run low. The portable water still, sufficient for recovering moisture from ship's air or from the atmospheres of most worlds, struggled to wring moisture from Earth's bone-dry air. It already showed signs of failure. She decided it was time to leave.

A part of her could not face the fact that they were now on their own. She was not ready to command the small group of survivors. She was not sure if she was up to the challenge. On the ship, the captain was always there for advice. His word was law. She was great at carrying out orders, but she doubted her ability to lead. In the present situation, that could prove fatal. She could not afford to show her doubts to her comrades.

On the evening of the fourth day, she informed them of her decision. "They're not coming, and we can't stay here waiting for them. We're running out of supplies. Our only chance is to head for the ruins of Denver Dome. Maybe we can find a way to contact the ship or at least find some help for Whitehall."

Anderson merely nodded his head. She could not read his face or know how he felt about the situation. Since the crash, he had become even more taciturn than usual. Whitehall said nothing, but she guessed his thoughts. It would be tough going for even the hardiest group. It would be especially challenging for him. Waiting until sunset, they gathered their meager remaining supplies and headed west. *What lay there?* She wondered. *Possible rescue or just empty buildings long abandoned.* Either way, they could no longer remain where they were, hoping for a rescue that might never come. Looking back over her shoulder at the ruined wreck of her lost command, a pile of shattered metal littering the landscape, she felt pangs of anguish. She glanced at the unfamiliar constellations overhead. Once again, she wished for the familiar polished steel corridors and comforting, close confines of the *Long John Baldry*, her home for nearly eight years. The vast, open spaces around her made her feel vulnerable and alone.

They relied on their flashlights until the moon rose behind them, a mere sliver of light but bright enough to illuminate their path. Much of the terrain around them bore indications of high-energy laser blasts – razor-sharp shards, heat-fused surfaces, and silica glass beads. Her hands bled from numerous small cuts and abrasions incurred while scrambling over jumbled piles of shattered rock or glass-smooth inclines. Her jogging had not prepared her for traversing such obstacles. After travelling less than ten kilometers, the muscles in her legs ached to the point of tears, but she refused to show any signs of weakness to her companions. They needed her strength and guidance if they were to survive.

She heard Anderson and Whitehall puffing and groaning behind her. Neither was in great physical condition, and Whitehall was weak from his injuries. She hated to push them hard; however, she knew their time was limited. They could not travel in the heat of the day, but the darkness held its own dangers. Twice, she barely managed to avoid sliding down steep slopes into the black, unknown depths below. She kicked herself mentally for failing to bring some wiring to use as a rope. She was sure other such failures would slow their journey.

At last, shattered rock gave way to a flat, featureless plain. Walking became easier. She increased their pace. They badly needed rest, but she was afraid that once stopped, it would be too difficult to continue. Overhead, the faint glowing edge of the familiar Milky Way brought her some comfort. *One of those bright dots*, she thought, *is my home world*. Then she remembered that it was over a hundred light years away. She searched the sky for some sign of the *Baldry* but saw nothing. She despaired that they were ever coming.

A sound like a baby's rattle stopped her in her tracks. She shined her light about and almost stepped on the sound's source. A coiled serpent struck at her boots with such force that she felt the impact of its fangs through their tough, leather sides. She jumped back, pulled out her laser, and fired without thinking. The snake sizzled as the beam sliced its two-meter length neatly in half.

Anderson immediately checked her leg. "It didn't penetrate," he said with relief.

"What was it?" She stared at the snake still writhing on the ground. She knew about serpents, having encountered them on her home world, but this one was different. It showed no fear of man.

Anderson picked up the piece with the head and examined it closely. "It looks like a pit viper. We had them on Brosnia, though not as big. It's most likely poisonous." He kicked the tail with his boot, making it rattle. "The tail rattle probably serves as a warning for things too big to eat. It didn't want to waste venom or energy on you until you almost stepped on it." He looked at Cathi and smiled, his first since the crash. "You're too big to swallow."

She shuddered. "I hope there aren't more around."

Anderson tossed the snake to the ground. "Too bad. We might have eaten it."

She didn't know if Anderson was joking, but had no desire to taste snake. She wasn't quite hungry enough to eat meat of any kind, especially serpents.

"Let's go," she said, carefully avoiding the two halves of the dead rattler.

The remainder of the night passed without incident. As the first light of the sun peeked over the horizon behind them, the temperature soared, forcing them to seek shelter from its withering rays. Anderson found a small crevice between two large boulders, barely space enough in which the three of them could lie down. After first carefully inspecting the crevice for another snake, the trio made camp.

Though she had been on Earth for almost a week, the fury of the sun when it crested the horizon always caught her by surprise. It was like the blast of an ion engine raking across the planet. The temperature soared twenty degrees in less than half an hour. During the night, she had heard sounds in the distance – insects, birds, maybe even more snakes, but as the sun reclaimed the land, all sounds ceased. Every creature sought refuge from the relentless heat. Without the shelter of the domes, she wondered how man could have survived on this hostile world. No water, no animals, no crops – what would they eat? If they encountered any survivors, they would assuredly be different from those who had remained during the Scattering. How could anyone survive the death of their world without being fundamentally changed?

She rationed their meager water supply, a few swallows each, and handed out tasteless but nutritious ration bars to conserve their rapidly diminishing food supply. As it was, they were expending far more calories than they were consuming. They could not continue long at that rate.

"Get some sleep," she ordered, but saw that Whitehall was already soundly asleep. Anderson ran the scanner over Whitehall's body and frowned.

"His fever is getting worse," he said. "He's weak. This pace will kill him."

She understood Anderson's concern, but couldn't give in to her impulse to allow him more time to heal. "We have a week's worth of rations left and very little water. If we remain here, we die." She looked toward Denver Dome. "If we have any chance of surviving and getting home, it's out there. We have to keep going."

He nodded his head in reluctant agreement, too tired to argue. She was glad she couldn't see the accusation in his eyes. He joined Whitehall and was soon asleep. She kept watch for a while, trying hard not to dwell on the futility of the situation, but weariness overcame her, and she too succumbed to sleep.

7

UNDER HOUSE ARREST

JUST AS KAFFA HAD PREDICTED, THE COUNCIL DID NOT LOOK KINDLY ON Kena's prolonged absence. To worsen matters, Kena insisted on telling of his discovery of the map to Denver Dome. Upon hearing this, Chu Li erupted in fury. The light of the burning braziers used to illuminate the room cast his shadow against the stone wall behind him, augmenting his menacing façade. "This is blasphemous! Denver Dome is an evil place full of the unclean and the impure. Your place is here as our Healer. Yarah will punish us all severely if you persist in your blasphemy."

Madras stood and echoed Chu Li's sentiments. "It is because of your sins our water has not returned. The Pools of Yarah are dry because you insist upon your unholy crusade to return us to the old days." His finger trembled as he pointed it at Kena like a knife.

Pandemonium erupted as various Council members tossed insults at one another. Chu Li stamped his staff upon the floor to return order. Hramack could tell by the High Priest's smile that he was enjoying the melee.

Kena raised his voice. "The old ways are dead. We will all soon be dead if we do not attempt to locate the source of the water. We need parts for our failing machinery. We need knowledge of what lies around us. We cannot learn these things by hiding in our valley and pulling the sand over our heads."

Of the entire Council, only Roagneau stood by Kena. Kena suspected Roagneau's show of support was more out of respect for Kena's dead wife, a kinsman, than actual support for Kena's purpose.

"Kena has spent his life serving others," Roagneau said. "Some of what he says is apparent. Our machines slowly deteriorate. True, we can continue without them, but only at great cost. If what Kena says is true, I say let him search." More voices rose at these words. Roagneau raised his hands into the air and shouted, "Hear me!" When the room quieted, he continued. "Kena should go, but Hramack must not. We must have a Healer. He is all we have if Kena insists upon this reckless search."

He sat down and lowered his gaze to the table, unable to look at Hramack's stunned face. Mitsu supported Kena's reasons for exploring, but feared the wrath of Yarah. His lackluster plea for tolerance moved no one. In the end, he too was shouted down. Kaffa sat silently at the rear of the room, voiceless. His presence was all the support he could show for Kena and Hramack. It was proving to be not enough.

After hours of yelling and screaming mingled with fervent prayers to Yarah, the six-man Council finally reached a decision. Chu Li rose to announce the Council's decision.

"Kena, you are our only Healer. Ningcha needs you and your craft. From this day forward, you will go into the Burning Lands only to collect herbs as needed and only when accompanied by two others to prevent you wandering. Hramack, since he shows no respect for the Healing arts, will no longer study medicine under you. Aparu, eldest son of Roagneau, will become your new apprentice. Hramack will tend the flocks with the children. Perhaps this will help him to grow into a responsible member of our village. He, too, cannot leave Ningcha. If either of you breaks this edict, Hramack will forfeit his life. Both of you will be held prisoner for ten days in one of the grain silos, only being released to tend to the sick. This is deemed fitting punishment for your transgressions and will serve as a reminder to others that the Council works solely for the benefit of the people of Ningcha. This punishment may seem harsh, but these are harsh times. The Council has spoken." Chu Li slammed the heel of his staff onto the rock floor with a resounding thud.

Chu Li's pronouncement stunned Hramack. He had expected a warning at most. As a mere herder, he could not marry Teela. Herding was a job left to children not yet deemed of marrying age. The High Priest's threat of death as a punishment for further transgressions was unheard of. Chu Li had grown too strong. No one could stop him now.

Ningcha had held no one prisoner in its long history. It had never been necessary. This move was Chu Li's personal notice to Kena that things were changing. The Council, under Chu Li's leadership, was now in charge. Without Kaffa's wisdom and guidance on the Council, Chu Li now could forbid any attempt to seek the materials to repair the rapidly failing equipment. In addition, Kaffa had lost power by supporting Kena. Those who would have sided with him would now be afraid of opposing the High Priest. It was too much for Hramack to comprehend.

Unless the springs began to flow soon, all would die. Would Chu Li be willing to sacrifice a life to appease Yarah, as in the old days? Hramack did not doubt it, and probably with himself as the first sacrifice. He could not bear facing Teela with the news of the Council's decision. She would hear of it soon enough from Kaffa. Kaffa would not stop Hramack from seeing Teela, but Chu Li would. He would force her to marry another of his choosing to consolidate his power.

It was clear that Chu Li desired complete control of every aspect of village life and a return to the days of ignorance and unquestioning obedience to Yarah and Yarah's earthly representative, the High Priest. He had even cleverly refused to appoint a second priest to prevent a rival to his power. Hramack could not let this happen, but he could think of no way to stop it. More importantly, would Kena abide by the wishes of the Council and give up his quest for Denver Dome? It seemed unlikely. He had watched his father become angrier and more frustrate throughout the meeting. His outbursts did nothing to sway his detractors. Kena, a man of reason, could not understand that frightened men could forgo reason and instead cling to old beliefs. Hramack was sure Kena would not stay, but would he leave Hramack alone to face the wrath of the Council?

His answer came sooner than he expected. After Chu Li's shocking proposal, he and his father were dismissed so the Council could hold a closed-door session. Kena stormed out of the building. He followed his father down the trail to the springs, wondering what his father had in mind. He turned abruptly and faced Hramack.

"I cannot remain in Ningcha and watch all we have fought for over the years crumble into dust. I must attempt to find Denver Dome. I must find the source of our water." Kena's vehemence surprised Hramack. "I cannot leave you behind to face the wrath of Chu Li alone. The man is mad with power. Will you come with me?"

Hramack appreciated his father's dilemma. He feared for his son's safety but was reluctant to expose him to the dangers of the journey. Hramack feared more the dangers of remaining behind.

"Of course I will go with you, father. I wouldn't let you go without me. You are still weak from your last journey."

Kena wrapped his arms around Hramack, and then smiled at his son. "Good. I am proud of you. I need your courage beside me. Go gather our supplies quietly. We must leave now before Chu Li can enforce his edict. Take only those things that we will need and can carry – weapons, food, medicines, extra clothing. I will fetch water for ten days only. The village can spare no more."

Hramack realized that if they did not find the source of the springs, they could not return to the village. They would either become nomads or die in the Burning Lands. He turned to leave and took only a few steps before Madras and Eithan, Madras' cousin, stepped out of the shadows, one armed with a spear, and one with a crossbow. Madras wore a wicked smile on his face.

"The Council sent us to enforce your punishment, Kena. You will follow us to your place of confinement."

Hramack sighed. They were too late. Chu Li had moved too fast.

Kena spoke up. "I must see to my plants, or they will be lost. We will go with you later." He made as if to brush by them.

"Now," Madras said, his voice filled with determination. He motioned to Eithan, who raised his spear and pointed it at Kena. Eithan looked ashamed at his actions, but Hramack knew he would obey Madras.

"Very well," Kena conceded.

Hramack felt humiliated as they were marched into an empty silo, stood against the wall, and searched. Madras secured the door behind them with an ancient padlock and chain, almost as old as the village. Until now, there had been no need for locks. Eithan winced and turned away as the wooden door slammed unable to look the pair in the eyes. Only a narrow slit in the door used to check on the amount of food allowed moonlight into the room. Their prison would become unbearable in the heat of the day. Hramack was certain this would please Chu Li.

Hramack walked around the small room and examined their makeshift prison cell. The roof was made only of thatch, but the walls, composed of finely placed stones, made the ten-meter climb to reach it almost impossible.

"What do we do, now?" he asked in exasperation. Already the small space was bothering him. How could he last ten days in such confinement?

"We wait," Kena said as he slid to the floor with his back against the wall, "and we heal."

As he paced the small space of the silo, Hramack's humiliation and growing uneasiness turned to anger. He became irate at his father's seeming lack of anger. Finally, tired of pacing, he plopped down opposite his father.

"Do you have a plan?" he asked gruffly.

"For what?"

"To get us out of here," Hramack snapped.

Kena seemed unmoved by Hramack's anger. "Yarah will provide a way."

"Yarah! It seems Yarah now works for Chu Li."

His father looked up at him sternly. "Do not think such thoughts. Chu Li has forgotten the true meaning of the *Teachings of Nuama*, but Yarah has not forgotten us."

Having no means of venting his frustration and anger, Hramack followed his father's lead and tried to relax. Even with his eyes closed, he could feel the confined space closing in on him, stealing the air from the room. He fought to drive the sensation from his mind. He made a mental survey of their problems. The village was without water and slowly losing vestiges of civilization. Chu Li had won control of the Council and confined them to prison. He had condemned Hramack to death if either left the village. Teela would wed another, and Kaffa had lost all power in the Council. The problems seemed insurmountable, yet Kena sat calmly as if taking an afternoon nap. Finally, the exhaustion incurred by the past few days' efforts erased the tensions and problems, and he fell asleep with his back against the cool stones of the wall.

The creak of the door opening woke him with a start. He looked up to see Eithan standing in the doorway with a jug of water and a bowl of bread and fruit. He quietly set them down and turned to leave.

"Why do you help Chu Li?" Kena asked him. "Surely you see the wisdom in my words?"

Eithan glanced uneasily at his two wards. Almost in a whisper, he said, "I cannot go against the Council or my cousin's wishes. If I do, my son will not become apprentice to the metal smith as he wishes. Without a trade, he cannot marry."

Hramack knew Eithan's son, Mica. He was younger than Hramack but intelligent and patient. They had often played together as children. Hramack was sure Mica would apprentice well as a metal smith, but right now, he did not care. His anger boiled up, and he exploded.

"You sell your village's life for your son's future," he shot at Eithan. "What good is securing Mica's future if he is dead, if we are all dead?" he was prepared to say more, but the look of condemnation in Kena's eyes silenced him.

Kena spoke softly, trying to ignore Hramack's outburst. "I understand your problem, Eithan, but doing nothing solves nothing."

Eithan pondered Kena's words before replying. "Chu Li promises water soon. The Pools will soon fill. Yarah has promised it," he ended with hope in his voice.

Kena merely nodded. "Trust in Yarah, but be wary of Chu Li."

"He is the High Priest," Eithan shot back, shocked by Kena's words.

"Yet you can read Yarah's words in the *Teachings*. Where does it say the High Priest controls the village? It is not right. The Council rules."

"The Council rules now."

"Your cousin Madras sells his vote for his sons. You obey him for the sake of your son. What have the others received for their votes? Kaffa's removal from the Council is because of his opposition to Chu Li. Do you think Kaffa a fool?"

Quietly, he answered, "No, he is a wise man."

"Then speak to Kaffa. Hear his thoughts. Then follow your heart."

Eithan looked as if he were going to speak, but then changed his mind and left, securely locking the door behind him.

"Will he help?" Hramack asked. Eithan's troubled face spoke of the conflict within him. Hramack felt a surge of renewed hope.

"We will see," Kena answered.

Day came, and the heat in the close room increased quickly. Its thick stone walls were not constructed to keep out the heat but to keep the crops dry and safe from the animals. If not for the slight upward ventilation caused by the rising heat, the air would have been suffocating. Even so, it was difficult to move about. Hramack lay on the floor and drank sparingly of their water. He knew there would be no more that day. Occasionally, by staring through the slit in the door, he could see men and women, once friends, walking back and forth in the village going about their daily chores. None dared glance his way for fear of Chu Li's wrath.

All except Teela.

He twice caught a glimpse of her standing defiantly near the bridge watching the silo prison. He wished he could talk to her, but of course, the Council had forbidden them visitors. He watched Kaffa, walking more wearily than ever, going to their home, perhaps to water the herbs Kena used in his medicines. The old man looked tired and defeated, each step carefully placed before the next, his staff bearing the greater portion of his weight. Kaffa had spent his entire life caring for the people of Ningcha. Now, he was almost an outcast because of Chu Li. Hramack visualized an enticing image of his hands wrapped around Chu Li's throat, but could not hold it for long because of the stifling heat.

He was glad to see the sun slip slowly over the western edge of the canyon on its journey across the once immense Pacific Ocean. The stars twinkled overhead as the light disappeared over the horizon, oblivious to the petty politics and human suffering below. If only he could get out of his prison, even for an hour, just for the freedom to walk about and enjoy the fresh, cooler air of the evening.

For three days, they remained confined to their prison. Hramack paced the five steps from wall to wall until he had trod a furrow in the dirt floor. Still, Kena seemed undisturbed by their predicament. The days brought renewed strength to his father. Eithan had finally acceded to Hramack's plea to fetch an ointment from the infirmary for his father's sunburn. Hramack could see the improvement in his father's face. His blistered skin peeled and flaked away, revealing pink healthy skin beneath it. His feet, cracked, blistered, and bleeding after his return from the desert, healed more slowly, but by the third day, he began to exercise in the coolness of the evening. He spent the heat of the day sitting quietly with his eyes closed in meditation. Hramack suspected he was dreaming of the Burning Lands and the freedom they offered.

"Yarah will provide a way," he replied each time Hramack's anger and frustration erupted.

Darkness collapsed around them like a heavy blanket on their forth night of captivity. Hramack longed for a candle or a lamp and one of the books in his father's library to pass the long hours. A few minutes after Eithan had in his accustomed silence delivered their jug of water, bowl of bread, fruit, and a small piece of dried and salted goat meat, Hramack once again heard the lock moving. When the door opened, he was surprised to see Kaffa.

"I cannot allow such things to happen in Yarah's name," Kaffa said. "You must flee, now, tonight." He turned and walked off into the night.

"Where did you get the key?" Kena asked.

They heard his whispered response from the shadows. "Eithan spoke to me as you asked. He gave me the key." Then he was gone.

"Come, quickly but quietly," Kena whispered to Hramack. "I will fetch water. You gather our supplies."

Kena left for the cisterns, using the shadows to conceal his movements He crouched low as he sprinted across the bridge. Hramack went to their home to collect their packs without alerting anyone who might have been watching. It took only fifteen minutes to fill the packs with all the food and supplies they could each carry. The packs were heavy, but they would become dangerously lighter with each passing day. He waited on the path for his father's return.

Kaffa came upon him without warning. The old man's silent tread constantly amazed him.

"I spoke with your father, and I ask only that you take care and return quickly. I showed your father a secret path few know about. Chu Li has ordered all others closely watched. Roagneau stands guard above the canyon rim. He has moved quickly. For years, we have survived because of the annual return of the springs. The legends of our arrival here are only partially true." He reached into his robe and withdrew a tightly bound book, words etched onto thin metal leaves. The book was extremely old, an artifact from the Ancient Days.

"Here is the true account of the exodus from Denver Dome after its fall and the journey to Ningcha in Arun Kane's own words. Perhaps it will guide you in your quest. Remember, if you are caught, you will be put to death." Kaffa presented the volume to Hramack and embraced him. "Go with Yarah, son of Kena." With those last words, he turned and left, looking wearier than Hramack had ever seen him before.

Soon after, Kena returned with two large water skins and more supplies and weapons.

"I see you have said your farewells to Kaffa." He nodded at the book in Hramack's hand. "Kaffa told me he was giving us something to help. Is that it?"

Hramack nodded as he placed the book inside his pack. He wanted more than anything to see Teela, but he knew it would be better if he did not. He was not sure he could leave if she asked him to stay. His heart felt tight, stretched in two directions. His duty lay with his father, but his love was rooted in Teela. He feared leaving her at the mercy of the High Priest, though, in reality, he could do little for her now. He swore to return to her quickly.

To his surprise, Kena led him along the ascending path to the mouth of the springs rather than the trail to the rim of the canyon. The springs poured their nourishing waters from a crack in the cliff face high above the canyon floor. At least it did when the springs were running. Now, the crack looked like a sad, twisted mouth in the darkness above them. The path led to a small ledge used for the ceremonial collection of the first jug of water each time the springs burst forth. An intricate system of aqueducts and stone pipes collected the water and carried it to the cisterns dug into the rock of the cliff side where the village lay.

Now, the aqueducts were bone dry.

Kena spoke softly as they walked. "Kaffa told me to crawl through the mouth of the springs, and I would find a larger cavern beyond. A tunnel travels northward for kilometers under the Burning Lands. When the water runs, it is impassable. Kaffa once followed the tunnel for several days." He smiled at Hramack's look of astonishment. "This was long ago when he was young. Did you think he was always old?" Kena continued, "It has been years. Much could have changed. He said there were several places where the sky was visible from the tunnel. We should be able to gain access to the surface through one of these openings many kilometers from here. The Council will not know what has happened to us until it is too late. They will not be able to track us, but they will search for us nevertheless. We must go now. I brought torches and the last electric lanterns and power cells. They should see us through."

Hramack hoped so. He did not relish the idea of stumbling around blindly in a dark tunnel beneath the earth.

"Here," Kena said, pulling Hramack's floppy, sweat stained, linen hat out of his pack and placing it on his son's head. "You will need this. We go deep into the Burning Lands." Kena donned his own hat, letting the cloth sunscreen attached to the back brim drape over his shoulders.

They slipped through the crack in the cliff and found the cavern beyond just as Kaffa had described. It was four meters high and twice as wide. The rock had been worn smooth over the centuries by running water. The tunnel beyond opened up before them, a black mouth ready to swallow them whole. Hramack shuddered at the mental image. The tunnel was slightly smaller than the cavern, but spacious enough for men to walk two abreast. Kena carried the lantern to light the way, but shielded it with his body to prevent its light from shining through the spring's mouth and betraying their presence.

The tunnel meandered considerably, hiding its dark secrets beyond every turn. Various hues of red, pink, buff, and gray streaked the smooth walls, created as the water cut through the different sedimentary layers that composed the area – sandstone, limestone, and shale. Crystals of all colors and sizes grew from the ceiling and walls. The light of the lantern caused the walls to glow with a life of their own. In spite of his fear of small spaces, the spectacle fascinated Hramack.

They hiked for hours before coming upon the first opening in the ceiling. A section of the tunnel's roof had collapsed at some time in the past. It would be difficult to reach the lip of the opening some fifteen meters above them but not impossible. Kena decided that they were still too close to the village and suggested they stay with the tunnel a while longer, just to be safe. After another four hours, they halted to eat and rest. It was early morning above. Kena lit one of the torches to save the electric lantern. By its dim, flickering orange light, they ate a quiet meal and drank sparingly from the water skins. They had been walking for nearly a day, and Hramack was exhausted. His father seemed energized by the journey, the thoughts of what lay behind them forgotten.

"At least the tunnel is much cooler than the Burning Lands above," Hramack said as they ate, trying to convince himself that the tunnel was a godsend. "At this rate, the water should last much longer, and we will be able to travel by day as well as night. Kaffa has saved us much time and torture with his secret way."

After his meal, he decided to open the book Kaffa had given him. The dim light made reading difficult. Kena asked Hramack to read aloud, as he leaned against the wall slowly chewing a piece of dried pori fruit.

8

Deadly Pursuit

"**G**ONE? WHAT DO YOU MEAN THEY ARE GONE?" CHU LI SCREAMED AS Madras stood beside Chu Li's bed. The distraught and obviously intoxicated Madras had just roused him from a restful sleep, and the unpleasant news did not improve his disposition.

Madras' words burst forth between gasps for breath, panting hard after his long run from the makeshift prison. "The door ... is open ... and they ... have fled. I went to check on them ... before first light." He did not add that he had not slept but had instead spent the entire evening swilling *kalquat*.

Chu Li shrugged off his sleepiness and gathered his thoughts. Suddenly, his eyes narrowed to mere slits in the feeble candlelight. "It was your cousin, Eithan," he yelled as he threw off the covers. "He had the only key."

"He would not do such a thing against my wishes," Madras protested, taking two steps backwards to avoid Chu Li and almost tripping over a nightstand.

Chu Li sniffed the air and frowned at the smell of liquor. "I saw him speaking with Kaffa earlier last evening. I should have suspected something. The fool listened to the old man's twisted lies." With Kena and Hramack gone, people would question his ability to lead. He had to act quickly. "Bring Eithan to me, now."

Madras saw the cold, dark look in Chu Li's eyes. "No. He is not to be hurt. He is my cousin."

Chu Li grabbed Madras by his cloak and pulled him closer. "Listen, you drunken fool," he spat. "If Kena escapes, people will think he is beyond the punishment of Yarah. They will begin to question other things he has said. If I lose control of the village, you will fall with me. By Eithan's sacrifice, Kena will become forever outcast. Then, no one will stand against us. You will have your revenge." He looked pointedly at Madras, trembling with fright in the dim light of the candle. "Do not forget what secrets I possess. If Kena were to learn ..."

Madras blanched. "All right, but no one must know."

"Only you and I, and if either speaks it will mean both our deaths."

Madras bowed his head and said nothing.

"And do not think to hold this thing over my head," Chu Li warned. "The villagers will heed my word over yours. Bring him quietly back to the silo," he cautioned. "None must see."

When Madras left, Chu Li cursed his luck. He had placed too much faith in Eithan's ties to Madras, and the candle maker had let him down. Chu Li threw on his sacramental robe over his sleeping clothes and picked up his dagger from the bedside table. He looked at his reflection in the polished steel of the blade by the flickering candle. All was in order.

"By such sacrifice is order kept," he whispered to himself as he slipped the knife into the robe's sash. He repeated the phrase several times on his journey to the silo.

✳

"Alarm! Alarm!" Madras cried as he stood before the open door of the silo prison for the second time that morning. "The prisoners have escaped!"

People slowly began to rouse from their homes at his cries and crossed the bridge to the grain silos. Many gasped when they saw the body of Eithan lying before the open door in a crimson pool of blood, quickly congealing in the heat of the morning sun.

Madras wept openly, decrying, "They have murdered my cousin. See his broken body here. Surely, Yarah will punish us if we let these murderers go free."

On cue, Chu Li appeared in the midst of the gathered crowd, inwardly smiling at Madras' performance. As the golden threads of his religious robe caught the first rays of the morning sun, it looked as if on fire. He opened his arms wide to let the robe flash even more brightly.

"My children," he called. "Kena has doomed us all. He has murdered Eithan in order to resume his unholy quest for the old cities. We must find him and bring him to justice. Who will go after him?"

A dozen hands went up.

Chu Li picked seven men he thought he could trust. He chose seven because it was a holy number – the seven days of creation and the seven trials of Nuama. "Follow them," he ordered. "Find them. Bring them back to submit to the justice of Yarah and the laws of our village. Go. Gather weapons and supplies."

The seven men chosen for the pursuit sped across the bridge to their homes to retrieve weapons as Chu Li attempted to disperse the crowd. "Take Eithan's body to the Sanctuary. We must pray for his soul."

As the crowd picked up Eithan's corpse and carried it across the bridge, Chu Li spotted Kaffa standing alone, watching the proceedings with interest. He went over to Kaffa.

"See what your friend has done," he accused, pointing to the lifeless body being borne across the bridge on the shoulders of four men.

Kaffa continued to stare at Chu Li. The Elder's silence angered him.

"Your day has passed, old man," he shouted. "No one will follow you now."

Kaffa spoke quietly but with the conviction of surety. "Someday the people of Ningcha will see you as I see you, Chu Li. Eithan's life was not taken by Kena, as you well know. Beware the vengeance of Yarah on the day Kena returns." He turned and walked away, pushing his way through the crowd.

"He will never return," Chu Li shouted at the Elder's back. "They will find him, and they will slay him. He has blasphemed against Yarah, and he must pay the price. You had best watch your step, too, old man. Do not stand against me." He realized that he was shouting at the top of his lungs. He added, more quietly, "Do not go against the will of Yarah."

With the village now convinced Kena was responsible for Eithan's death, it really did not matter if they found him or not. No one would take his word if he returned claiming innocence. "Let the desert have him. Let the scavengers gnaw the flesh from his bones and those of his son."

Madras stood by the bridge waiting for him. The man was shaking from fear and guilt. Still hung-over from the *kalquat*, perspiration poured from his forehead though the full brunt of the day's heat had not yet come to the valley. Chu Li hoped the people thought he was shaking from grief and rage.

"Madras, it is done. Forget about it."

"How can I forget about it? I must look into his son's eyes each day." Madras wrung his hands.

Seeing this, Chu Li said, "There is no blood on your hands. The deed was mine. It was the will of Yarah that a sacrifice be made. Eithan's death has solidified our power. It will help bring the return of the water. Just wait and see." He added, "Eithan's son will apprentice to the metal smith as he wished, and after a suitable amount of time has passed, you will have Kena's fine house."

"If the waters fail," Madras said smugly, "our lives will mean little anyway."

"Come. Have breakfast with me," Chu Li suggested. He wanted to keep Madras from the other villagers until he had calmed down.

"No. I must go and comfort my cousin's son and wife."

"Say nothing or we will all die," Chu Li threatened in a whisper.

"I'll keep my lips sealed, as you know I must, but I fear we will all die just the same." He crossed the bridge alone and disappeared into his home.

The man is losing touch with the reality of the situation, Chu Li thought. *I must watch him carefully.*

He could not allow Kena to return to the village alive. There were those who might believe him. Kaffa was one. Madras was weak. He would surely break down if confronted by Kena. He could not leave Kena's fate entirely in the hands of his seven pursuers. No, he would have to lead them himself, to ensure a quick end to this threat to his power. He was not keen on going into the desert after Kena and Hramack, but he could trust no other to the task. Leaving the village was a risk. A flock left unattended could scatter.

Removing his robes of office, he smeared his face, arms, and pale upper body with sunscreen. The aromatic ointment, made from a mixture of cottonseed and hempseed oils added to zinc oxide found naturally in the Burning Lands, would protect his flesh from harmful Ultraviolet rays. Conditioned to the less harmful rays of the indirect sun in the village, he added a second layer for extra protection in the desert. Then he donned pants, tunic, and a cloak more suitable for the desert. In lieu of the wide-brimmed hat most favored by the High Priest, he wrapped his head in a simple white burnoose, letting the ends cover his shoulders. He brought only his knife and his staff of office. The others could bring food and water enough for him. The gathered trackers were surprised at his insistence on accompanying them but did not dare question his motives. He was the High Priest and the leader of the Council. None could prevent his joining them.

Chu Li had not wasted his many years as High Priest. On the contrary, he had read every scroll and book in the old library, many available to no other but the High Priests. He knew of the tunnel behind the springs. He suspected that Kaffa also knew and had informed Kena to allow him to escape the guard posted along the upper trail.

"Let's go," he called, and led the pursuers up the narrow stone path to the mouth of the springs. He stopped to offer a quick prayer to Yarah, and then herded the men inside the cavern. Men more used to the open air of the desert found the close, dark confines of the tunnel unnerving. The flickering torches did little to cast back the deep shadows. Chu Li admonished them often to keep them moving forward. Every little sound, every bend in the tunnel caused them to stop and discuss their pursuit.

"You will follow them," Chu Li finally shouted at them, exasperated at their constant delays. "They must be captured or killed for their crimes. Yarah demands it."

No man, regardless of his concerns or fears, could refuse such a demand from the High Priest. Thereafter, the pace of pursuit quickened steadily. When they came upon the first opening in the roof of the tunnel, casting a dim circle of light on the stone floor, several men demanded to climb out and travel in the open desert, away from the dark tunnel. They preferred the dangers of the Burning Lands to the eerie silence and the stale air of the river tunnel.

"Fools," he shouted. "It is full daylight out there. You would not last half the day before you would drop. We must use the tunnel to conserve our energy and our water."

One man, Orin, grew frightened at the prospect of continuing along the tunnel. He bolted from the group and began to scramble up the steep sides of the tunnel, frantic to reach the opening above.

"Come back, you fool," Chu Li shouted at him. "You'll never make it."

Indeed, Orin had climbed no more than five meters when the loose rock crumbled beneath his feet and brought him tumbling back to the floor of the tunnel. His left leg lay twisted at an awkward angle, a long sliver of white bone protruding through the torn and bloody skin below his left knee.

"My leg," Orin screamed in agony. "It's broken."

Chu Li quickly examined his leg. "Indeed it is. Should I now leave you here?"

"No, you cannot," Orin pleaded as he writhed in pain.

Some of the others mumbled their objections at Chu Li's suggestion.

"Very well," he said, giving in to their demands. "Tarim, see to his leg and help him back to the village. We must continue."

He chose Tarim because, of the seven men with him, Tarim was a friend of Hramack's and closest to Hramack's age. He would surely object to the boy's death. They left Tarim dutifully splinting Orin's broken leg. Tarim would drag Orin on a makeshift litter made of Orin's shirt slung between two spears. It would be a slow journey, but the two would likely reach the village before nightfall. It would be hard on both of them, but Chu Li would spare no more men. He could see in the eyes of those chosen that many considered Tarim and Orin the lucky ones.

Chu Li was growing impatient with the delays. Kena was knowledgeable about the desert and was certainly moving quickly. "We must redouble our efforts. We must catch them, soon." He knew the longer the pursuit, the more reticent the men would become at leaving their homes. All men wisely feared the Burning Lands. When each corner, each bend of the tunnel could hide an unknown predator or perhaps even Kena, a formidable fighter, the dangers became more pragmatic. Now there were five. Already their numbers dwindled, and they had traveled less than half a day. They broke into a quick trot.

Chu Li felt uncomfortable with tons of rock above his head pressing down on him, but he hid his discomfort from his men. If they sensed his fears, they would refuse to go further. The old books spoke of caves such as this as places where demons dwelt. It certainly had the feel of an evil place. Chu Li knew some of the men were probably wondering how the High Priest knew of the tunnel behind the mouth of the springs. He must push them hard until such thoughts evaporated from their minds. He muttered quiet prayers to Yarah as they marched.

By nightfall, the men were tired and hungry. He had driven them hard, but they had not yet caught up with Kena and his young whelp. He reluctantly halted their pursuit. His legs, too, were growing tired. He was unused to long marches, and his calves ached miserably. He had chosen his soft, comfortable moccasins over heavy leather boots, and now his blisters spoke to him in bloody whimpers.

"We stop and rest. Make a fire and prepare a meal. We continue the march in six hours." He could not let Kena gain too much distance on them.

Anseer, the woodcarver, slight of build and a chronic complainer, said, "Six hours. We need more rest than that." He was briskly massaging an ache in his thigh. He, too, was unused to long marches.

Chu Li stared at Anseer until the young man averted his gaze. He knew he should not have brought Anseer, but he was good with a bow. "Sleep, then. Don't waste time complaining."

The hearty aroma of soup cooking leaked from the worn water reclamation line on the pressure cooker sitting on the fire. Chu Li refrained from admonishing the men for breaking strict water rationing. The smell seemed to enliven them somewhat and alleviated a portion, but not all, of their fears. The men passed around fresh bread and dried fruit. The small fire cast an eerie glow along the uneven rock walls of the tunnel, forcing the ever-present shadows back into the corners.

Chu Li sat apart from the others, pondering his options. If they did not catch up with Kena soon, the men would press him to halt the chase and return to the comforts of the village. Could he use his power as High Priest to force them on? Perhaps, but it would not be wise to test his powers so soon. Dead or banished, Kena was no longer a threat unless he was unwise enough to return to Ningcha. On that day, Chu Li would himself end the Healer's life. He could not let Kena hold the threat of his past over him. His silence would ensure Chu Li's control of the village.

Wetting a small rag, Chu Li used some of their precious water to rinse the blood from his feet. He felt more than one pair of eyes on him as he washed his feet. These men had forgone regular bathing in order to save water for their families. To see it used in such a manner disturbed them, but they said nothing. The water stung at first as he pressed the wet cloth to the broken blisters, but soon brought a small degree of comfort to soothe the pain. He pulled a small vial of ointment Kena had given him for his dry hands and rubbed it thoroughly into his feet. The ointment dulled the ache. Why did Kena, such a talented Healer, feel the need to meddle in village politics? Chu Li respected Kena's Yarah-given knowledge of the healing arts, but still he must go. The people of Ningcha could not hope to earn Yarah's forgiveness unless they put aside the things of man's past and sought His guidance. Kena's constant digging into the past was a direct challenge to Chu Li's authority as High Priest. It would not do.

Sleep that night came slowly to him and, by the quiet whispers in the shadows, to the others as well. The unnatural silence of the tunnel was disquieting, and once the embers of the fire had gone out, the darkness pressed down on the men like a living thing. Sleep did come eventually.

✻

All too soon, one of the men awakened him from his deep slumber. "It is time, High Priest," the man said grimly.

Chu Li wiped the sleep from his eyes as he stretched his aching muscles. It had been many years since he had slept anywhere but in the comfort of his own bed. He looked up and saw Travin the hunter leaning over him. The hunter's dark eyes and emotionless face seemed to mock him.

"Tell the men to eat a cold breakfast," he said between yawns. "We must catch up to Kena."

His feet were better but still sore. To cushion the hard rock against his sore feet, he cut pieces of leather from his robe's leather sash and placed them inside his moccasins. To his delight, they provided extra protection. Walking would be much easier now.

On this day, no small talk broke the silence of the tunnel. The men marched silently, nerves taut, each man lost in his own private thoughts. Chu Li thought this was a worse sign than their constant grumbling. Silent men thought too much. By midday, they came upon another opening in the roof of the tunnel. This one, unlike the first, offered a safe passage to the surface, a gently sloping rock fall used by the desert creatures to escape the sun. To raise their spirits, he allowed the men to climb up into the daylight. In spite of the extreme heat, they reveled in the bright sunlight and open air. The confining tunnel had taken its toll on them. They exited the river tunnel opening into a shallow depression beside a massive jumble of broken red boulders. Hardy, scrub pines and dwarf mesquite grew through cracks in the rock. Ragged patches of dry sedges surrounded the depression. Even a few scrawny cacti had taken root here and there in the sandy soil. The men insisted on being allowed time to hunt for fresh game to complement their meager rations. Chu Li suspected it was mostly an excuse for them to prolong their time in the open. He divided them into two groups to explore the dell, but he remained near the tunnel entrance to prevent anyone from retreating.

"Water," one of the men shouted a few minutes later. "I found water!"

Even Chu Li's heart lifted at his shout. Water was always a welcome commodity, especially in this parched land. They hurried to see who had proclaimed his discovery. In a small natural depression formed by the slow carving of a granite slab by wind erosion, a shallow pool of water sparkled in the sun, fed by some deep artesian source. Had the shadow of the overhanging rocks not protected it from the sun throughout most of the day, it would have evaporated long ago. As it was, the pool held less than five skins of water. Still, in such times, any water was precious. Artimeer was lying with his face in the pool of water, laughing at his good luck.

"Fill our skins," Chu Li ordered him. "Fill others to leave in the tunnel for our return trip."

Such a rare find seemed a good omen to the men. Their confidence returned, and some good-natured joking started up among them. They snared a few small rock lizards and several cactus wrens with lengths of twine and a few pieces of bread as bait and quickly cleaned them. Even a scraggly hare, more bone than meat and unlucky enough to pick this particular time to seek water, soon joined their growing larder. Chu Li, no hunter himself but instilled with the lore of the desert, wondered why so few creatures inhabited such an ideal oasis. There was water, ample shade, forage, and good shelter in the tunnel below. Such a place should be teeming with life of all sorts – hares, tortoises, birds, wild goats, and even larger scavengers. Creatures should come from many leagues to such a place. Instead, there was not a bird in the sky. The water was pure and untainted. No quicksand would form in such a rocky place. They had discovered no sign of nightstalkers or other large predators. What would drive away creatures normally drawn to places of water as bees are to nectar?

"Be wary, men," he warned. "There could be danger here, unseen and unheard."

Most merely looked up and nodded at his warning, bent on watching the roasting game, but one man, Travin, the eldest of the group and a good hunter, notched an arrow and leaned warily against a boulder, his dark eyes scanning the horizon for any threat of danger.

"I must take a leak," Artimeer laughed as he stood from their feast and strode into the edge of the desert to relieve himself.

"Be sure to wash your hands before you pass the bread," Anseer chided his companion.

Artimeer made an obscene gesture at his comrade's comment. As he unbuttoned his pants, a great flurry of sand erupted around him, knocking him to the ground.

"Wha ...?" he began to yell in surprise, but his words were cut short as something grabbed his leg and pulled him toward the disturbed sand. He screamed from pain and fright. "Help! Get it off! Get it off!" He rolled onto his stomach and began clawing frantically at the ground, trying to extricate himself from the grip of his unseen attacker.

Chu Li immediately knew what had attacked Artimeer – a sand dragon. Such creatures were rare but deadly. Larger kin to the desert Gila monster, sand dragons burrowed into the sand and waited patiently until some hapless prey passed close enough to attack. Large, sharp teeth made quick work of smaller prey. For larger prey, the slow-acting venom of its bite paralyzed, and then killed, allowing the creature to drag its prey beneath the sand to consume at its leisure.

Artimeer, even in his panic, had the presence of mind to draw his knife from his belt and thrust it into the ground, slowing the lizard's progress in drawing him under the sand. Travin, prepared for danger, let loose two arrows into the beast's head, but both bounced harmlessly off the thick frilled collar around its neck. A third man attacked the creature with his staff, while Anseer grabbed Artimeer by his arms and attempted to pull him from the creature's strong grasp.

Chu Li had not spent hours in the library in pursuit of only religious knowledge. All things of the world Yarah had created interested him. "Attack the body," he shouted. He knew the sand lizard's head was as thick as armor and protected by the bony frill. One of its most vulnerable points was just behind the frill.

Travin began to hack at the creature's body with his long knife while the others delivered blows with their staffs or jabbed it with their spears. Anseer continued to pull at Artimeer's arms, drawing him as tight as a stretched hide. At first, their efforts produced no results, but soon the sand dragon, sensing it had snagged much large prey than it had intended, released its hold on Artimeer and retreated into its sandy lair, sending Anseer flying backwards. Travin began digging into the soil with his knife.

"Leave it," Chu Li shouted at him. The sand dragon would dig deep into sand below their reach.

He examined Artimeer's wounds. One leg was bleeding profusely. The sand dragon's curved, sharp teeth had ripped into his flesh like a knife. He called for Travin to apply a tourniquet to slow the loss of blood.

"I'm dying," Artimeer cried out, eyes wide with fear. He looked down at his bloody leg and sobbed uncontrollably.

"Ridiculous," Chu Li lied. "It is a mere scratch."

However, as the others watched, Artimeer slowly lost consciousness and went into convulsions. White froth dribbled from his swollen, purple lips as he shook. They held him down until the spasms subsided. By then, he was dead.

"Wha ... what killed him?" Anseer asked. "The blood loss was high but not high enough to cause death."

Chu Li shook his head slowly from side to side as if perplexed. The others might ask how he knew of the creature, or more importantly, why he had not warned them. "I don't know. Perhaps the monster's teeth were poisonous." He folded Artimeer's arms over his chest and recited the Parting Blessing. "It is the will of Yarah," he pronounced.

Travin looked down at his dead comrade and then at the others. They nodded at his unspoken thought. "We will go no further," he firmly declared. "We have lost two men already. Is Kena's death so important?"

"Yes," Chu Li shouted.

Travin took a deep breath. "Then continue alone, High Priest. This matter is between you and Yarah. We return to the village after we bury Artimeer. Our families need us."

"We must bring Kena back to answer for his crimes." Their decision angered Chu Li. Could they not see the need to satisfy Yarah's will? "You must continue," he demanded.

Travin chopped his hand downward sharply, an act of denial. "Let Yarah punish Kena if it is truly Yarah's will. Your hatred for Kena is well known, and it drives you onward beyond all reason. We will go no further into this deadly place. If such evils find us, who travel with Yarah's own High Priest, then surely it will find Kena also if he has displeased Him. Let the Burning Lands deal with Kena. We go home."

Chu Li knew they would not turn from their decision willingly. Perhaps Travin was right. How could a man and a boy endure long in such a harsh place? The desert would deal with them, as it had almost dealt with Kena on his last journey. Yet he could not chance their returning.

"So be it," he agreed. "Bury Artimeer and gather our supplies. We return to Ningcha, through the desert." He saw the relief in their faces as he made his pronouncement. They would rather face the harsh, relentless desert than endure the dark confines of the river tunnel. He added, "Bring me Artimeer's boots to replace these ill-chosen moccasins." He received several nasty looks for robbing the dead, but he did not care. His feet ached. "Cover the pool of water with flat stones. We will return later for it with empty barrels and add it to the cisterns. It is a blessing from Yarah."

The men refused to see the wisdom in waiting for nightfall. They were too eager to return to Ningcha. Seeing the futility in trying to stop them, Chu Li decided to wait until the heat exhausted them, and then called a halt until moonrise. With luck, they could be back at the village before the next sunrise. The sun beat down on their heads with the fury of a tormentor. Their pace slowed to a crawl. It seemed to Chu Li that they were standing still. The endless, flat vista before them was unchanging – sand, rock, dirt, sand, rock, dirt. No cloud painted the perfect blue sky. No hint of breeze stirred the fine dust at their feet. As the searing sun began to drop slowly to their right, into the western hills of the Burning Lands, no man doubted Chu Li's wisdom in calling a halt.

"We must rest now," he mumbled through swollen lips. "The moon will rise in four hours. We will be ready by then."

When Chu Li ordered each man to drink his fill of water, they forgot much of their earlier loathing for him. They were too tired to start a fire for a hot meal, but dried meat and fruit tasted like a feast after their day's long march through the desert. Their bellies were soon full and their thirst finally quenched. Travin passed around precious tobacco from his pouch, and smoke soon filled the night air. In spite of sore muscles and aching shoulders from carrying the water, the men began to realize they were nearing home.

"I think I can smell my wife's cooking," one man said wistfully.

"That's not your wife's cooking. That's a dead nightstalker," Anseer joked.

Everyone laughed, even the man who was the brunt of the joke. As the stars appeared in the night sky, Chu Li marked off the familiar constellations with his finger – Aspari, the Hawk; Dagon, the Dragon Lord; the Northern Ladle; the red and yellow eyes of Goliath, the giant; even the three tiny, dim stars that outlined Desert Mouse's nose, eyes, and tail. The moon would be a mere sliver tonight, but unless someone tripped on a rock or fell in a hole, it would cast sufficient light with which to see. Chu Li listened as the men joked among themselves, their past perils almost forgotten. One man injured, one man dead, and still they had not found Kena. He would have to play up the finding of water when they returned, as a sign that Yarah had not forgotten them: that their pursuit, though not fruitful, met with Yarah's blessing.

A sudden scream from among their midst split the gathering darkness. The high-pitched scream of terror did not sound as if it could come from the throat of a man. The men began to scramble for weapons thoughtlessly laid aside. Chu Li grabbed his staff.

"What is it?" he yelled over the melee as the others jumped up and down, screaming curses. Finally, one man had the presence of mind to light a torch. Chu Li saw that it was Travin.

"A scorpion," Travin replied as he smashed the large black creature beneath his boot. "It has stung Won." He held the torch over the prostrate form of Won as the man sobbed and pressed his hands tightly to his leg. In the torchlight, Chu Li could see a fine sheen of perspiration covering Won's face. "The fool failed to secure the water skin and let water drip into the sand." It was obvious from his tone that Travin had little pity for Won's plight. The waste of precious water in the desert was not a thing of small importance. "Now the smell of water will bring every creature for kilometers. We must leave."

"No," Won screamed in spite of his pain. "I can't walk." He saw Travin's cold, hard eyes and began to whimper. "Bleed my leg to drain the poison," he pleaded.

"Fool," Travin spat. "The sting of the black scorpion is always fatal. You will be dead within the hour."

Won's face turned pale, and he was silent for a moment. As in response to Travin's dire words, the haunting cry of a nightstalker drifted in from a distant hill. His lips began to quiver with fright.

"We must go now," the others pleaded with Chu Li. They understood Won's fate and feared to face a hungry nightstalker.

"Don't leave me to die," Won pleaded, trying to crawl on his already numb leg. When he reached out his hand, the others backed up, as if his touch would obligate them to help.

Travin looked at Chu Li questioningly. Understanding Travin's unspoken question, he nodded. Travin bent over Won and whispered, "I give you the blessing of Yarah."

Before the meaning of the words dawned on Won, Travin slid the blade of his knife across his throat. Won gasped and fell back onto the sand, gurgling away his life, as the others hurriedly gathered up their possessions. Soon, the area would be crawling with denizens of the desert drawn by the smell of water and blood.

"It had to be done," Chu Li said to Travin as the hunter glanced back at the body of his dead friend.

Travin's eyes bored into Chu Li's with the same intensity as a knife to the throat. "It was Yarah's will."

Chu Li said nothing more.

The call of the nightstalker grew louder. The group started across the desert at a fast trot, eager to reach the safety and familiar surroundings of Ningcha. Chu Li felt confident that not even Kena could survive long in this accursed place. For all his desert lore, every creature in the Burning Lands would be after them. When they had put what Chu Li considered a sufficient distance between them and the carnage behind them, Chu Li stopped them. A plan had been slowly forming in his mind. Perhaps he could use Won's death to his benefit.

"Yarah has blessed me with a vision," he began. The others looked at him with concern. "Yarah has spoken to me through the deaths of Artimeer and Won. He has sent water to sustain us but has punished us for our folly and lack of faith." His eyes played over the men and came to rest on Travin. "You must follow Kena into the Burning Lands, you and one other."

He remained steadfast, as Travin returned his stare with distrust before protesting, "We must all return to the village. It is useless to follow Kena. The desert demons protect his path."

"Do you think Yarah fears demons? I speak for Yarah. You will do as He bids." Chu Li spoke, as if delivering a sermon. It was a battle of wills, and as he had assumed, his will was the stronger of the two.

Travin's strong jaw quivered slightly, but finally, Travin fell to one knee and lowered his head.

"I accept Yarah's will," he muttered quietly under his breath.

Chu Li smiled. "Good. Choose one other to accompany you." He could have easily picked another man to accompany Travin, but decided the added burden of choosing would weaken Travin's resolve even further. He saw both Villas and Anseer lower their heads in shame. By rights, they should have volunteered to go with Travin, but neither offered. The deaths of Artimeer and Won and Orin's injured leg had broken their spirits. They wished only to return home.

"I'll take Anseer," Travin decided. "He, at least, has no wife to grieve over him." This last word he spat at Chu Li in defiance.

"Villas and I will return to Ningcha and bring bearers for the water Yarah has provided. Take as much water as you can carry." He handed Travin the bag of food. "This will see you for a week if you eat sparingly. Hunt when you can, but you must find Kena." His eyes drove home the intensity of his need.

Travin nodded. "I will find Kena and discover his reason for killing Eithan, who he called friend." He stared at Chu Li.

"Find him and return," Chu Li said. "Go with Yarah's blessing."

Villas gave Anseer the arrows from his quiver without meeting his friend's eyes, his shame tempered by his joy at returning to Ningcha. Anseer staggered beneath the weight of water skin, bow and arrows, spear, and extra rations.

"A beast of burden I have become," he joked, but no one laughed.

Villas clasped his arm. "Return safely." Anseer nodded absently as he tried in vain to rearrange his heavy load. Villas and Chu Li stood watching as Travin and Anseer began their long trek northwards into the Burning Lands, making a wide detour around the spot where the bones of their friend Won were being picked clean by desert scavengers. Chu Li watched until they were out of sight.

"Come," he called to Villas.

Chu Li and Villas arrived in Ningcha just before dawn tired and weary from their ordeal. He expected to find no one awake, but it seemed the entire village was waiting. Tarim had arrived only a few hours earlier with the injured Orin, and people had remained awake discussing the murder and pursuit. Chu Li brushed off Madras' silent inquiry of Kena's fate and headed straight for his home. He avoided their eyes, as the villagers noted the absence of the others of the party. He had no wish for further explanations or recriminations. His pursuit of Kena had cost him two men, perhaps four, and a great deal of his self-esteem. Kena had won this round, but even if he managed to survive the desert and return to Ningcha, one of them must surely die. Chu Li swore it would not be him.

9

MARS

C APTAIN MOORE WAS DEEPLY CONCERNED FOR HIS MISSING CREW. HE had heard nothing from them in twenty-four hours. It was not that he doubted Lieutenant Lorst's ability as a capable First Officer. Her only problem was that she did not have enough faith in her own abilities. The last message they had received from the shuttle was terse and cryptic: Taking fire from active defense satellites. The implications were ominous.

No further messages followed. Long-range scans provided no useful information. He had waited in orbit a full day, ignoring the Martians' repeated requests that he land, in hope that the shuttle would limp back to Mars. Now, he was out of options. He contacted President Anjiro of Mars.

"Mr. President," he started. He was unsure how to relate his problem. After all, the president had warned them not to visit Earth. He hated going to anyone on bended knee. "I have a problem. One of our shuttles was near Earth orbit, scanning the planet, when we lost contact with it. They reported active satellites."

"The Planetary Defense Grid," President Anjiro explained. "We warned you. We have lost many ships over the years attempting to reach Earth. I am afraid your shuttle crew is dead. There is nothing we can do."

The finality of the president's tone made Moore's blood pressure rise. He had dealt with many petty bureaucrats and local politicians in his long years of trading. They were as ubiquitous as rats. Every world had some genus of rat skulking in the alleyways and lurking in the dark underbelly of the cities. They had migrated outward with mankind, at times seemingly arriving before the colony ships. Throughout colonized space, a bureaucrat's stock response to any crisis was to wring their hands and shrug.

Putting on his best diplomatic face, he said, "We're not asking you to do anything, Mr. President. We take care of our own. What I need is all the information available on these satellite defense systems."

"I'm afraid that will not be possible. We have no such records."

With a little practice, Moore had found that could understand most of what Anjiro said. The differences between the two languages were slight even after a thousand years. The odd inflection of his words and cadence made it difficult to determine the emotion behind them, but he knew a bold-faced lie when he heard one. Bureaucrats kept records on everything. It was their only function in life. They kept records on record keeping. Enough was enough. He had no time to play silly little diplomatic games. He was no diplomat. He was a Trader's Guild merchant ship captain, and his friends were in danger.

"Mr. President," he yelled. "I refuse to believe you have no records of your encounters with the Earth defense satellites. My crew is in danger and I need your help. Our people are used to dealing with backward planets like this. Either you send over those records right now, or I shall seed your planet's atmosphere with a cloud of nano-scavengers. Within ten of your days, they will have devoured every building on this planet down to the bare metal. You'll be forced to bang two rocks together to start a fire."

Of course, he had no nano-scavengers, if such a thing existed, but President Anjiro did not know that. He hoped the president had as much difficulty analyzing his motives as he did the president. He had read something about such devices once, but couldn't remember if it was in a trade magazine or a science fiction novel. As he had hoped, his idle threat produced the desired results.

"There is no need for threats, captain. The people of Mars are concerned only for your safety. What records we have, however limited in scope, we will gladly provide. However, this might take a few days. Such records are stored in the archives. If we can help you in any way, please contact us."

Moore imagined the President was already calling a meeting of his advisors to discuss the threat of nano-scavengers. He hoped that, like most bureaucrats, he would not bother to consult any real experts in the field, but instead rely on the advice of the usual bootlicking, politically correct leeches who attached themselves to powerful people.

Alexi Secord, his engineer, interrupted Moore's pleasurable mental image of President Anjiro scrambling around his office. "Sir, I've picked up the shuttle's transponder. There is a lot of interference from solar radiation, but I'm sure it's them. It's coming from the planet."

"Good news," Moore told him "At least they made it down in one piece. Have you tried to contact them?" he asked, before realizing that Secord would have done that automatically.

"Well, yes, sir. There's no reply. I'm cutting through the interference. They're just not sending."

Moore knew that the shuttle's transponder would activate automatically in a catastrophic event. He was not enjoying the dark mental image his mind was conjuring. "They might have crashed."

"Yes, sir. I've thought of that, but I'm also picking up very faint traces of a personal transponder. Someone is alive down there. That means they could have landed safely and activated the shuttle transponder manually. Of course, I have no way of knowing what condition they may be."

Secord sounded defensive. Moore knew he was taking the blame for not being able to contact the crew of the downed shuttle. They were his friends and shipmates. He decided Secord needed a pat on the back. He was doing everything in his power to locate the crew, and he would continue to work until they had exhausted all possibilities.

"Good job, Secord. We know someone is still alive down there. Lieutenant Lorst is a good officer, and she has a good crew. The president has promised to help us rescue our shipmates, but between you and me, it will be up to us to do the job. Get with Nest and Awe. See if you can boost the transponder signal. We will need a precise location." Nest O'Conner and Awe Angina were both skilled technicians. If anyone could solve the communications problem, they could. "Also, we'll need something powerful enough to knock out a defense satellite."

Secord thought for a moment. "Our laser won't be enough, and the satellite's scanners would detect any missiles long before they reached target. If the Martians don't have anything powerful enough to do the job, we'll have to invent one, perhaps some type of Electro-Magnetic Pulse weapon. We can get close enough to launch two or three modified missiles with E-M warheads. That should confuse the scanners. Even if the defense satellite is shielded, it won't be able to handle a series of pulses radiating in different spectrums from different sources." He closed his eyes in thought for a moment or two. "We have the material here, but it will take at least five days to construct and test the devices. It's very delicate work. One mistake and I could fry the *Baldry's* electronics."

Moore knew Secord was extremely capable though perhaps a bit overly cautious. He couldn't leave his crew marooned for another week. "Don't worry about testing it, just cobble it together. We'll test it on the defense satellite. We don't have time to be cautious. Our people could be dying down there."

He knew he was taking a risk, but his crew was family to him. Most of them had been with the ship for years. He was godfather to half the children and had performed all of the weddings. He was not about to lose a single one if he could help it. Leaving Secord and his crew to work, he decided it was time to pay a personal visit to His High Uppity Lord, President Anjiro. *Time to light a fire under his bureaucratic ass*, he thought.

"Matamoras, inform the fine people of Mars that we are landing. Double check the coordinates they provided to be certain they're playing nice. We don't want any surprises."

An hour later, he was on the train running from the spaceport to Robinson City, the capital. He had learned a bit about the history of Mars from tapping into their computer network, though not as much as he would have liked. As he stared out the window, he realized Mars looked much like Earth prior to the Great Migration. The sky was a very pale blue, although even in the daylight some stars were visible overhead. The soil, where not covered by a carpet of low-growing vegetation that looked like feathers, was a rusty brown color. The atmosphere was still low in oxygen and high in carbon dioxide compared to Earth, but one could walk about unhindered by a cumbersome environmental suit or breather if they were careful not to overexert themselves.

The Great Migration had bypassed Mars and its fledging colonies in the haste to abandon Earth. The first ion-propelled multigenerational ships had been on their journey for fifty years when the first Skip Drive ship, harnessing the incredible power of artificially created miniature black holes, launched from Earth's orbit. Many of the lumbering multigenerational ships arrived at their destinations only to find thriving colonies already planted by the faster Skip

Drive ships. Some, learning of the likelihood of finding their chosen planet already colonized, chose new destinations. However, a few, dismayed by the poor likelihood of success, returned to Earth.

They arrived during the height of the solar flares engulfing Earth and chose to settle on Mars. The fourth planet's distance from the sun offered some protection from the massive solar bombardment. They expanded the struggling existing colonies underground for protection. Then, they pumped water from vast subterranean caverns, cracked it into oxygen and hyrdrogen, used the hydrogen as fuel, and released the oxygen into the atmosphere, slowly creating a protective ozone layer. The thin atmosphere trapped the additional solar output, raising the planet's mean average temperature by eight degrees Celsius, making seeding the planet's surface with ground cover to provide more oxygen and as a source for carbon more viable. In a way, his ancestors, the Scattered Ones, had settled Mars. It even looked much like his childhood home on Sanchez. There were no oceans, but a chain of shallow interconnected seas dotted the planet's surface.

The Presidential Palace was an imposing hexagonal building constructed of Martian red limestone topped by a mirrored glass dome. It offered a magnificent view of the Thesis Bulge and a small forest of cedars marching majestically along a waterway. President Anjiro was nervous, wringing his hands as he met Moore. Surrounding him was the usual perfunctory group of lackeys carrying computer slates. A tall man, the President appeared short surrounded by his even taller, lanky staff members. Almost all the Martians Moore had met so far were tall and thin. The slightly lower gravity explained the increased height. Their habit of consuming numerous small but elaborate meals and years of genetic modification had eliminated obesity and encouraged a svelte physique.

Carrying a slightly larger stomach than he wished and standing barely one-hundred-sixty-seven centimeters tall, Moore felt somewhat uncomfortable among such gaunt company. Then he remembered his threat to the President. He would bluster his way through as he had done so often before. He sucked in his gut and stood as tall and as proud as he could manage. To these people, he was the representative of a foreign and possibly extremely advanced culture.

"Ah, Captain Moore," Anjiro called as he spotted the captain. "We have all the information on Earth's defenses we could find on such short notice." He indicated a slate one of his attendants held out in the open palms of his hands, as if an offering of gold or jewels.

Moore accepted the slate graciously and bowed slightly. "I regret my earlier incivility, Mr. President. It's just that my crew is my only family, and I was driven by my deep concern for their safety." He swallowed hard to force down the taste of bile his apology was creating in his mouth. He hoped the Martians had something suitable with which to wash out his mouth. "I withdraw any threats I have made and gladly accept any and all assistance you can offer." He felt that apologizing now that the president had already acceded to his wishes was perhaps a bit magnanimous, but it indicated a willingness to allow the president to appear to be in charge, saving face.

As he expected, President Anjiro seized on his conciliatory gesture with all the tact of a true diplomat. He puffed out his chest and smiled broadly. "No apology is necessary, my dear captain. I fully understand your, er, ah, somewhat emotional outburst. I show the same concern for my people. Rest assured my people are even now at work on several methods of rescuing your downed ship."

He smiled at the president. "We may have come up with a solution, but I will require the assistance of some of your asteroid miners."

Moore had already made the acquaintance of several miners when he had sold his mining equipment to them for a tidy profit and had found them to be a down to earth people, more like Traders than Martians. With no common currency, he had accepted items he hoped would be in high demand back on the settled worlds. With such deals came the risk of failure, but his innate sense of what would sell hadn't failed him yet. The Altruscon nuclear drilling rigs he carried were far superior to any the Martians had in operation.

Manned by crews of two instead of the usual ten men, they proved a valuable trade item. In gratitude, the Miner's Alliance had promised to assist him in his endeavors. The approval of the president was merely a political maneuver designed to garner more votes in the ruling council for the miners. Moore figured having political influence could not hurt in future dealings with Earth or Mars. The Traders Guild had operated in this manner for centuries. "If it works, use it" was his motto.

The president looked shocked and somewhat annoyed that Moore had arrived at a solution before his people could, but he recovered quickly. "That is wonderful!" he gushed. "I assure you anything I can do to, er, facilitate the assistance of the miners will be done. Can you tell me what your plan is?"

"I had rather wait until my engineers report their findings, Mr. President. Things may change several times before plans are finalized." Actually, he did not want Martian engineers bothering him with their contributions. They had never recovered a ship from Earth space. It was unlikely that any plan they contrived would be viable. *Besides,* he thought with amusement, *they might not like my solution.*

"Ah, yes. It is the same in politics also: so many variables to be considered, so many egos to be salved."

Moore barely covered a chuckle with a strategic cough.

"Well, dear captain, I know you are a busy man, but would you honor me by having lunch with me? It has been a trying day. A delicious meal and a glass of local brandy would do much to ease the burden of command."

Moore sighed. He hardly had the time to spare, but brandy – that was another matter entirely. He could put up with the pompous twit at least long enough for a bite to eat and a glass, or perhaps two, of brandy. He had been fortunate enough to sample Martian brandy during his meeting with the miners. So far, the local liquor was the only thing about Mars he liked. In fact, part of his deal with the miners had included several cases of Martian brandy. He hoped it would prove as profitable a trade item as the drilling equipment.

"I would like nothing better, Mr. President," he answered with a broad smile.

"Please, call me Alfons."

"Certainly, Alfons. Call me Captain. It's the only name I answer to. I've forgotten the others."

The humor was lost on the president. "Come then, Captain. Let us dine."

He walked beside the president while the entourage followed dutifully a few steps behind. He could not help feeling that next to the Martians, he looked like a barbarian invader from some nether region of space. Perhaps when he returned to the ship he would trim his beard and hair. He ignored the slight tittering of onlookers as the bells in his braided beard tinkled as he walked. He quietly reached up and removed them, then surreptitiously placed them in his pocket.

10

THE JOURNALS OF ARUN KANE

"I HAVE SET THESE WORDS TO TABLET IN ORDER TO HELP OTHERS UNDER-stand the reasoning behind my actions," Hramack read from the journal Kaffa had given him. In the back of his mind, he wondered what process the ancients had used to etch the words into the metal pages, but the enormity of hearing a voice from the past overcame his curiosity. "History will judge me as it will, for I have done what I thought necessary in order to save mankind and to end the bitter enslavement of our people.

"When it was first discovered that the Earth's sun was slowly increasing its radiation output to a lethal level, the nations of the world reluctantly set aside old wounds and differences to unite in a noble effort to reach the stars. The newly formed Alliance of Nations oversaw the construction of a fleet of two-kilometer-long multi-generation ships in Earth's orbit to transport carefully selected crews and passengers to new homes beyond the stars. Recently developed antigravity drive engines lifted great tankers of water to provide fuel for the fusion reactors and radiation shielding for the ships. The undertaking was monumental. Tankers of water, freighters filled with supplies, and shuttles filled with lucky passengers left the surface at the rate of five hundred a day, forming a cloud in the sky. This continued for forty years. Even so, only a small fraction of Earth's population went aboard the ships, less than eight million people. Many people chose sterilization to reduce the population. Some governments enforced mandatory sterilization on all but a carefully selected few destined for the ships.

"Sadly, the initial cooperation of nations fell apart under the financial and political burdens of such a mammoth undertaking. Petty jealousies, the hoarding of dwindling resources, the reluctance to allocate food and medicines to the most impoverished nations, and waves of religious fervor simmered and festered until wars broke out. Most were small border wars, but ensuing famine and disease killed tens of millions in the most affected nations.

"Skip Drive technology developed in the late Twenty-Third Century reduced the stellar journeys to mere weeks instead of decades or centuries, allowing cheaper and smaller ships to make multiple journeys to distant worlds. Over a hundred-year period, half of Earth's remaining population abandoned their birth world for new homes beyond the stars, leaving only a dozen domed cities as refuges against an environment steadily growing more hostile to life. Those not selected for the domes or those who refused to enter the domes for whatever reason established what shelters they could, but most perished.

"For hundreds of years since that great migration of our ancestors to the stars, the Abandonment, as it has since become known to those who remained on Earth, humanity huddled in enclosed cities as the outside world became too hot, too dry, and too flooded with solar radiation from our angry sun. The planet became enshrouded in clouds, holding in the heat and creating massive storms that lasted for weeks and months. Crops failed. Starvation became routine. Resources dwindled. Then, the wars came between those outside the domes and those inside, and often between rival domes. They ended with the destruction of many domes and the deaths of hundreds of millions. The great Upheaval that followed as the Earth tried to restore balance after the destructive conflict killed many tens of millions more. In the end, only Denver Dome and Kolkata Dome in the subcontinent of India remained. Kolkata Dome has completely shut itself away from the world, and we do not know if it still exists.

"Seven hundred years into the life of Denver Dome, a new socialist regime gained control. People became mere slaves to serve the needs of the city and its Elite controllers. Religion had been on a decline for centuries. Some had faded away completely. Now, faced with nowhere else to turn, people began to worship a greater deity once again. Old religions melded and old schisms were forgotten. A new religion was reborn: Deism. Yarah became the new name for the One Powerful Force in the Universe, the One True God. With the discovery that our sun had passed through its unstable phase and radiation levels were dropping substantially, the innate desire for freedom and the need to set straight the plight of the Earth united under a religious banner. A great cry went out to open the doors of the dome and let man once again move into the wilderness to make of it a garden. The call went unheeded by the Elite rulers, who feared to lose control. They took harsh measures to maintain their authority.

"People became desperate to leave and civil order broke down. The authorities arrested thousands and killed hundreds more. I was a computer controller in the communications center, a Tech II, mate to one of the Elite. Though I loved her desperately, I could not sit by and watch citizens killed simply for their desire once again to breathe fresh air. I stole secret codes and reprogrammed one of the satellites of the Global Defense Network. I unleashed the awesome power of its laser upon Denver Dome's massive outer doors.

"The destruction was horrific. Hundreds died as a whole section of the dome collapsed where the great doors had once stood. I had greatly underestimated the power of the satellite's laser. Chaos erupted. Fires raged and people turned on one another in fear and in anger. Sensing defeat, most members of the Elite fled, including my mate. Some say they sought asylum in Kolkata Dome. I do not know. I thought my actions would free our people, but I underestimated their ability for self-destruction. Factions went to war with each other. A radical group captured the water aqueduct that supplied the dome from the Mount Lincoln collection system and destroyed it when driven back, thereby depleting our water supplies.

"Within weeks, people began dying of thirst. A sense of finality settled upon the people. Then the looting and wholesale slaughter began. It was one of Man's darkest days: one I wish I had never witnessed. I precipitated it all, I who had underestimated the satellite's awesome power of destruction and man's unholy appetite for self-annihilation.

"I gathered as many people together as I could find: people appalled at the destruction, people who had expressed a deep belief in Yarah and a desire to leave the dome to establish a colony. I knew of a place to the south along the old Rio Grande River system, where underground tunnels had once channeled the overflow from the mountain collectors to the city of Albuquerque. The river is long dry, but the water from the facility still flows periodically through the underground aqueduct. It offers a chance at survival.

"On Easter morning by the ancient reckoning, we set out on foot for our new home, deciding to leave those bent on destruction to their own fate. It was a hard journey. Within a week, we had lost twenty to thirst, roving gangs from the city, and the hidden dangers of the desert wastes that we had made of our country, our planet. It took two months to make the trip. Of the 325 people who accompanied me, only 205 arrived. The dead marked our trail as surely as a road sign.

"To our horror, scouts sent ahead reported Albuquerque was long dead. The water no longer flowed. Faced with a lingering death, we changed our line of march to intersect the aqueduct. We found the cause of lack of water. A great earthquake had split the earth, severing the underground channel, but there was no water. We searched but could not find the outlet of the overflow. A landslide had blocked it. A small explosive charge loosened the slide. As I pushed aside one boulder, sweet, clear water burst forth from the crevice in the canyon wall and filled a natural stone basin. We built our homes along the sheltered steps of the canyon, protected from the occasional ravages of the sun and the western winds that scoured the sandy plains.

"Our technology was limited, but we survived. Over a year after we had established our village, named Ning Cha for Lei Ning Cha, a holy man who gave his life to protect others, I led an expedition back to Denver Dome to try to salvage parts for our electronic devices and see what had become of the other survivors. I should not have gone. The memory of what I witnessed will haunt me forever.

"The once-proud monument to mankind's technology was now nothing but a crumbling glass shell surrounding a burned-out city. The desert sands had already claimed large parts of the city for their own. We lost five men to roving bands of cannibals. The rabble groups staking claims to small parcels of city for looting were no better. We had to fight our way through them to exit the city. What had once been a proud and beautiful city was now just another of Earth's multitude of ruins. Of its two million inhabitants, scarcely a thousand remained in the city and they had fallen to savagery, or worse. If any more survived, I do not know. If they did, they wisely left no signs for us to follow.

"I alone bear responsibility for what has occurred. I sought to free us from an oppressive government. Instead, I condemned us to death or savagery. I do not take comfort in our religious leader's claims that Yarah guided my hand and chose us to rebuild Earth. I will pay for my crimes, of this I am sure. I can only hope that the seeds of the future I have planted at Ning Cha will grow to spread over the empty lands we once owned.

"With the instruments and equipment we recovered at Denver Dome, we can make our life here much easier. We will start afresh and begin to rebuild. Perhaps our brethren will return from the stars one day to find a thriving civilization where they expect to find a burned-out husk. I can only hope.

"I fear what I have seen has taken its toll on my soul and my body. I am sick of heart and weak of limb. I offer these words not as an excuse but as a history. I did what I did for good, but as often happens, evil came of it. The future should know the truth. Already, the people of Ning Cha are trying to deify me in spite of my protestations. Luckily, I will not live to see it happen. I know I am not long for this world. I pray Yarah will give me the balm my soul yearns for. For you, my descendants, I give the truth. I have asked Nuama Lon Makimbo to see to it that this record remains in our library for all to see. He has become our official chronicler and spiritual leader. Yarah forgive me my sins."

Arun Nevil Kane   2-19-3257 AD

11

INTO THE LIGHT

A S HE READ ALOUD THE FINAL REVEALING WORDS OF ARUN KANE, TEARS filled Hramack's eyes – tears of sorrow and tears of anger. All he had learned since childhood was a lie. Kane was no Prophet of God. He was a man, fallible and all too human. Hramack could not understand all of the narrative, the technological terms were a mystery, but he knew Kane had tried to do what he thought to be right. He had simply underestimated man's ability to sink to its lowest level.

He had gleaned one bit of good news. Kane had described a water collector in the mountains northwest of Denver Dome that overflowed into the canyon system through the very tunnels they were traveling. If so, they could easily find the site and set about to once again free the flow of water for the village, though he had to admit to himself, he had no idea how they would accomplish this feat.

Hramack shrugged off this negative line of thought. There could be no room for doubt or they might as well turn around now. Their fate in Ningcha was sealed. They could not go home. They were wanted men under penalty of death. Ahead lay the unknown. The unknown was far better than certain death.

Kena had said nothing as Hramack read Kane's words, but Hramack had seen the anger building in him. "Our village founders used religion as a means of controlling the people," he burst out, "to keep them together, even if it was for their own good, in much the same way as the Elite used their authority over the populace of Denver Dome. Nuama controlled the records. Eventually, the truth was forgotten or purposely hidden. That is why we are such a threat to the Council and Chu Li. Kaffa knew the truth but could not reveal it. As High Priest, Chu Li knew as well. I wonder if all the Council is implicit in the charade. They cannot allow us to tear down what they have worked so diligently to build. They are afraid, Chu Li most of all. Not of us, but of what we may find. It's understandable."

Hramack listened to his father's words, but was not comforted. "How could they lie to us to keep us hidden away in Ningcha?" he shouted. "We are fewer in number than those that founded the village. Kaffa knew, or surely suspected, that the village was slowly dying, and yet, they did nothing. Now, it may be too late."

"We will try though," his father said as he stretched out on his blanket to sleep.

Hramack tried to stay awake to brood, to give vent to his anger, but exhaustion soon closed his eyes, too.

He awoke with his father standing over him, shaking him gently. "What is it?" he asked.

His father placed a finger over his lips to silence him. "Come. I smell cooking behind us."

Silently, he and Kena crept back down the tunnel until they could see the dim glow of a campfire. The aroma of roasting meat filled the tunnel. They heard voices speaking softly. On their bellies, they crawled closer. Chu Li and five others sat around the fire. Kena and Hramack hid behind an outcropping of rock and listened to snatches of conversation among the men. In that way, they learned of the murder of Eithan and that they stood accused of his death. Kena pointed one man out to Hramack.

"Travin is a skilled hunter. He could track us even in the desert above. We must be very careful."

When the men had settled in for the night, Kena and Hramack returned to their own camp.

"They think we killed Eithan, father," Hramack gasped. His mind whirled with emotions. Anger, surprise, and fear fought for dominance. "But it was he who freed us."

Kena shook his head in dismay. "I see Chu Li's hand in Eithan's death. He means to give us no out. If we return to clear our names, he will have us killed for Eithan's death."

"Can't we talk to them? You know Travin. He's a good man."

To Hramack, it seemed only reasonable that men who truly knew Kena would know him incapable of murder. He worried that Teela would believe the lies about them. Could she think him capable of such a thing? No, Kaffa would know the truth and would reassure her. He felt better knowing that she, at least, would not believe the lies.

"Chu Li would not give us the opportunity to speak to him. We must outdistance them. Gather your possessions, quickly."

They breakfasted only on dried fruit and water. By midday, they had covered many kilometers. The tunnel widened and the going became easier. Both felt relief as the tunnel became less confining. Periodically, they caught brief glimpses of the sky through cracks in the tunnel's ceiling high above them. Throughout the day, they trudged steadily northwards. Protected from the full wrath of the sun above, they were able to make good time.

Because of the threat of pursuit, they did not tarry long to eat or sleep. Quick meals on the run and short rest periods wore on Hramack, but they covered many kilometers. As dawn arrived on the morning of their third day out, they came upon a section of the tunnel that had collapsed, leaving a steep pile of rock and dirt along one wall. They had not seen nor heard any sign of their pursuers all day. Hramack hoped they had abandoned the chase and returned to the safety of the village. Few people, aside from Kena, had gone as far into the Burning Lands. Hramack looked up at the sunshine and open space with longing.

"Can we not take a look around?" he asked.

Kena stared at Hramack for several moments before nodding. "By my account, we should be almost to the wall of mountains north of the Burning Lands and well into the Empty Lands beyond," he said. "This journey would have taken us twice as long if we had been forced to walk above. Perhaps a short rest above will relieve your claustrophobia."

Hramack started to protest, but his father's smile told him he was not mocking him. They scrambled up the slope over the rocks and debris, careful that each step could send them plummeting to the bottom of the slide. Already the heat was becoming almost unbearable after their three-day respite underground.

Hramack struggled with his heavy pack and missed his footing on the loose rocks. If not for Kena's quick reaction in catching his shoulder, he would have fallen the ten meters to the floor of the tunnel.

"Careful, son," Kena admonished. "If you are injured, we would be forced to return to Ningcha."

Hramack understood the unspoken implications. "Yes, father," he answered.

He tested his footing at each step before placing his full weight on it. As he emerged from the tunnel, the full intensity of the sun hit him like a physical blow. He donned his sunshades to shield his eyes from the sun's harsh glare. As he looked around, he noticed a grove of trees ahead of them, between them and the mountains.

"Look, father! A forest," he shouted.

Kena, too, wore his shades made from smoked glass. He turned to peer in the direction Hramack was pointing. After a few moments, he answered, "No, not a forest, I think. It is a large grove of cacti, giant saguaro. I have seen smaller ones in my travels."

Hramack was disappointed. He had seen pictures of forests and would like to see one. He satisfied himself with the knowledge that he had never seen a cactus grove either. Scattered cacti grew in the Burning Lands near their valley, but mostly smaller species such as cholla, hedgehog, and fishhook barrel cactus. Sedges, bitter grass, mesquite, and creosote were more prevalent.

"Why don't we take a look?" he suggested. "Maybe we can find food there."

Surprisingly, Kena agreed. "We can get water from some of the cacti. That will make our meager supply last longer." He looked at the grove, and then back at the tunnel. "The grove seems to be growing in a line directly along the tunnel. Perhaps we can find another entrance further ahead and we won't have to backtrack."

Hramack was overjoyed at the prospect of leaving the dark tunnel if only for a few hours. As harsh as the heat was, he could endure it better than the pressing darkness. It was less than ten kilometers to the cactus grove, but compared to their rapid progress underground, the journey seemed to take forever. After an hour and a half of walking up one hill and down the next under the grueling morning sun, they finally reached the edge of a wide depression in the desert floor. As he neared the edge, Hramack began to realize just how tall the saguaros were. The lip of the depression had hidden their true height from view. They seemed suddenly to leap upwards at him, thrusting straight into the sky. The smallest were at least five times the height of a man. Many were ten times a man's height. They towered over Hramack and Kena, marching left, right, and onwards as far as they could see.

In the shelter of the giant saguaros, a mini-ecology thrived. Dwarf creosote plants fought for space with bitterroot and sage. Many of the plants Kena sought for his medicines grew here in great abundance. Almost without thought, Kena began to gather specimens and catalog their location in his mind. Hramack wandered around the grove marveling at the many-armed giants surrounding him. He caught glimpses of desert hare and lizards scurrying through the brush. He even saw a pair of roadrunners nesting beneath a cholla.

"I think I'll set out a snare or two," he said, but Kena was intent on his specimens and did not acknowledge him.

Two hours later, Hramack found Kena sitting in the shade of a gnarled old saguaro tasting bits of cactus fruit. He quickly spat them out saying, "They aren't ripe yet."

Hramack held up two lizards and a small hare and smiled at his father's approval.

"You caught them; I'll cook them. I found some sage and wild garlic that should improve their taste." As Kena spoke, he gathered a small pile of dry cactus skeletons and placed them inside a circle of stones. Across the stones, he laid a long, thin, flat stone. He set fire to the wood and waited until the flat stone became very hot, like a griddle. Cutting thin strips of meat from Hramack's kill, he laid them on the stone to cook. As they began to sizzle, he crumbled the herbs onto the cooking meat and added small pinches of salt and pepper that he carefully rewrapped and placed in his pack. "We'll feast today," he said as he pulled out pieces of bread and cheese from his pack.

Hramack and his father sat quietly in the shade of a saguaro and watched the meat cook. The aroma made Hramack's mouth water. So intent was he on the meal, he failed to hear the snapping of a twig nearby. However, his father was more vigilant and slowly reached for his bow. The thud of an arrow sinking into the cactus above his head stopped him. Hramack watched in surprise as his father stood slowly with his arms spread wide. Hramack rolled across the ground and grabbed for the bow. A heavy blow to the side of the head sent him reeling. Blackness rushed in.

✳

Hramack slowly regained consciousness with the tall figure of Travin standing over him, a look of disgust on his face. Nearby, Anseer stood aiming an arrow at Kena's chest.

"So, young one, you finally join us." Travin's words were bitter. He seemed unlike the man Hramack remembered. The blue eyes that once sparkled with laughter now flashed anger.

"You are wrong about us, Travin," Kena said. "We did not kill Eithan."

"How did you then know of his death?" shot Anseer. He stood a few steps from Kena and kept his bow pointed at Kena's heart.

"We crept within a stone's throw of you in the tunnel and over-heard," Kena explained.

Anseer sneered. "I kept watch. You could not have gotten within a bow shot of our fire." His words spoke of his certainty of Kena's lies. It was a challenge to his manhood. Hramack saw doubt in Travin's eyes.

"We must take you to Ningcha to stand for your crimes," Travin said slowly but without his earlier anger.

"Chu Li will never allow me to speak at a trial," Kena said. "He will see to my death as he saw to Eithan's and Herat's."

"You accuse the High Priest of not one, but two murders," Anseer challenged. He drew back the arrow. "Better I kill you here and now for the desert creatures to feast on your treacherous bones."

Hramack started to cry out.

Travin held up his hand. "Stop! Our job is to return them, not punish them."

After a few tense seconds, Anseer lowered his bow. Hramack breathed once more.

Travin turned to Kena. "Your word has always been true to me, yet you defy the Council's wishes. Tell me truly, did you kill Eithan?"

Keenly aware of Anseer's anger, Kena rose slowly to stand before Travin and look him in the eye. "In the name of my dead wife, Allana, I speak the truth. Eithan gave Kaffa the key to our cell. Kaffa released us. We had no wish or reason to harm him."

Travin nodded. "Your words ring true, Kena. There is more here than Chu Li has said. Chu Li's ire at your escape seemed too personal, else why would he insist on accompanying us. I pledge that you will be given the opportunity to speak."

Anseer burst out, "They are murderers. We cannot watch them the entire journey. I say, kill them now."

"Silence," Travin demanded. Anseer obeyed. "Kena has been my friend for many years. His Healing talents saved the lives of my wife and my son during his birthing. I owe him. His words carry the weight of truth. We will bring them back with us to Ningcha."

"No," Kena called out. "We must continue our journey."

Kena's outburst stunned Travin. "That is impossible. I have said I will stand with you. Is this not enough?"

"Your belief in my innocence honors me, but there is much more to be considered. Ningcha is dying. Without water, we are doomed."

Anseer spoke up. "Your blasphemies have dried the Pools of Yarah. Now that we have you, the waters will return. Perhaps they flow even now," he challenged.

Kena shook his head. "No. If the waters were again flowing, we would hear them rushing through the river tunnel. They will not flow again until we find the source of the water and free it, if we can."

Anseer was livid. "He seeks to trick us," he pleaded with Travin. "Let us at least bind his mouth so he cannot cast a spell on us."

"Fool," Travin shot at him. "You chatter of demons and spells as if you were a child sucking at your mother's teats. My belief is in Yarah, not Chu Li. His cold eyes harbor dark secrets." He looked at Kena. "How can we few seek out the source of the Pools of Yarah? I have heard that you claim the source is near the old ruins of Denver Dome."

"Denver Do ..." Anseer started to protest, but Travin silenced him with a sharp wave of his hand. Anseer grumbled quietly under his breath.

"The water supply was probably automated, or it would have stopped many years ago," Kena suggested. "Unless the path is blocked by collapse or landslide, we should be able to bring about its return."

"It would be the will of Yarah," Travin whispered, more to himself than the others. He cocked one eye at Kena. "Will you return to Ningcha once this thing has been accomplished or proven to be beyond our ability to accomplish?"

Hramack stared at Travin. Hope surged in his chest. Was he offering to go with them?

"Absolutely," Kena swore.

"You can't mean this," Anseer cried. "We will die if we venture into the Empty Lands. None can survive there."

"Then return to Ningcha if you will," Travin replied. He looked at Kena. "I will accompany Kena and Hramack on their quest. It would seem far nobler to die doing such a thing than to hasten back to Ningcha and bow before Chu Li."

Hramack could not believe it. One moment he and Kena were prisoners; the next, they had help on their journey.

"It is surely the will of Yarah," Kena claimed.

Travin turned to Anseer. "Do you go back or come with us?"

Anseer was almost in tears with indecision. Hramack knew the woodcarver could never survive the journey back alone. He almost felt sorry for him.

"But what of your family?" Anseer whimpered. "Your son?"

"I serve my family best by helping to save the village."

Anseer's shoulders slumped in defeat. Finally, barely above a whisper, he said, "I will come. I knew I was doomed the moment you chose me to accompany you." He lowered his bow and picked up his pack. He walked over to the fire and looked at the lizards and hare searing on the hot rock. "If we must die, at least let us go with stomachs filled."

Travin laughed and helped Hramack to his feet. "Well, boy, do not look so pleased," he said as he saw Hramack's wide grin. "There will be many opportunities to die between here and our destination, wherever that may lie."

"Perhaps," Hramack replied, "but it will be a more pleasant journey with friends."

"Friends," Anseer sneered. "You take your friends to die."

Hramack hoped Anseer's words were merely the whining of a frightened man and not a prophecy. More problems erupted when Kena proposed to continue their journey north by using the river tunnel.

"Into the bowels of the earth again?" Anseer questioned. "I will not!"

Travin, too, appeared reluctant to return into the dark, winding passages far away from the sun he knew so well. "Is there no other way?" he asked quietly.

Kena shook his head. "If we travel above ground, we will exhaust our water supply twice as quickly, and we both know the dangers that patrol the deserts." Travin had related the story of Artimeer and Won's deaths.

"Very well," Travin decided. "We travel underground."

Anseer kicked at the sand with the toe of his boot and howled, "You will kill us all!"

Travin shot the woodcarver a withering look that made him back up a pace. Anseer shut his mouth and gathered his gear, but he did it with much slamming and grumbling to show his anger. With Kena leading the way and Travin bringing up the rear, they marched back to the opening and plunged into the earth. The descent was perilous, filled with loose rock and crumbly clay, but they safely reached the bottom. Kena lit a torch and set the pace for their march.

Hramack felt much safer in the knowledge that Travin was with them. Travin was a good hunter and knowledgeable in the ways of the desert. He and his father had often hunted together and enjoyed each other's company. He made a welcome addition to the group. Anseer was slightly older than Hramack but still unmarried. He had apprenticed as a woodcarver and carpenter and had little practical knowledge of the desert. Hramack had overheard Travin's explanation to Kena of his reason for choosing Anseer: his bachelorhood. Hramack knew it must have been a hard decision for Travin to make. Travin had assumed they were going to their deaths but feared for his family if he opposed Chu Li's authority. They must wrest the High Priest from power.

The tunnel made fewer twists and turns and widened considerably. The torches cast their light farther ahead, quickening the pace. The polished stone of the walls shone like milky glass. Indeed, when Hramack observed the walls closely, he found them to be comprised of white quartzite. No amount of water pressure or stretch of time could account for this. True, given sufficient time, water could grind stone in ways difficult to imagine. He had seen such examples before, but given the hardness of quartzite, it would have taken millennia for water to work its magic here. These tunnels had not been there for nearly as long.

The section of tunnel they were in had been made by the hand of man. He showed Kena his discovery.

"See this wall. Our ancestors must have carved it for the passage of water." Hramack ran his hand over the almost perfect smoothness of it. "We could not do such fine work today," he said with awe.

"It is the work of Yarah," Anseer claimed. "His hand carved the way for His water."

Travin snickered. "Better Yarah had created the water closer to His Pools than dig this dark hole."

"Blasphemer," Anseer cried.

"Enough," Kena erupted. "There are no blasphemers here. We all do the work of Yarah."

"If Yarah used Kane to bring forth the water of the springs, could he not also have used others' hands to provide the means?" Hramack postulated to them.

"Yarah needs no man's hand," Anseer insisted.

"Then Yarah indeed has a sense of humor." Travin pointed his torch to a spot high on the wall. There, carved long ago by one of the tunnel's builders, was a sign, the kind left for millennia by such men intent upon leaving some sign for posterity.

Hramack read the words aloud. "Crew # 3, 6-2-2879, Denver Dome."

Denver Dome!

"This was made over six centuries ago by men like us," Kena told them. His face was glowing with excitement.

Travin shook his head. "We have fallen far."

Kena clasped his friend's shoulder. "We will reach such levels again," he promised.

"Not as long as Chu Li holds power."

Hramack spoke up. "When we return the waters, he will be finished."

Kena shook his head. "Chu Li will not easily relinquish power." He glanced at Anseer, who had grown uncommonly quiet. He was running his hand over the smooth surface of the walls and mumbling to himself.

"We must continue," Kena told them. "We must cover many more kilometers before we camp."

Reluctantly, Anseer turned away from the wall and followed.

They stopped twice for rest and water but made good time. Hramack estimated they had covered nearly twenty-five kilometers since leaving the cactus grove. They were all exhausted, Anseer especially so. His face was drawn and pale, and the sound of his labored breathing filled the tunnel. He fell to the floor without removing his pack.

"Rest," Kena told him. "We will make camp."

He nodded weakly and fell asleep face down on the ground. Hramack doubted Anseer had ever walked farther than to the bottom of the canyon in his life. One more day of this and he would be too weak to continue. They would have to slow their pace or risk pushing him beyond his limits. Travin started a fire while Hramack peeled a handful of wild root vegetables he had gathered. A hot, hearty meal would revive all of them, especially Anseer. In spite of the oppressive heat, Hramack knew cooked food took fewer calories to digest, leaving more calories for the hard journey.

As the food cooked, Travin sat and carefully put a fine edge on his spear and his knife with a whetstone he carried in his pack. He appeared to focus his entire attention to the honing, but Hramack suspected his thoughts were of home. Kena, too, sat alone in thought. Hramack knew what was on his father's mind. His father wondered if he had made the right decision about traveling underground. While it was true they could make better time away from the heat of the sun, they were pushing themselves far harder than they would have above. In the open, moving only at night, the terrain and the need to seek shelter before sunrise set the pace. In the cooler, time-less dark of the tunnel, they traveled until exhausted.

Hramack glanced at Anseer. Perhaps he should suggest they travel at a slower pace tomorrow. It would cost even more time if they were to wait on Anseer to recover or carry him. No matter what, he would not leave him behind.

The vegetable stew's aroma roused Anseer from his sleep, but he was too exhausted to move. Hramack spoon-feed him and forced water down his throat before allowing him to succumb to sleep's pull once again.

"He will not last long, I fear," Travin spoke.

Hramack, overhearing, warned, "I will not leave him."

Travin cocked his eyebrow at Hramack. "Nor I."

"Maybe we should travel slower tomorrow to allow him to get his legs," Hramack suggested.

Travin nodded. Kena agreed. "Perhaps you are right." He looked at Hramack. "Perhaps Travin should understand what we are trying to accomplish. He should know the truth."

Hramack raised his eyebrows and returned his father's look. "You are sure?"

"Yes. Give Travin the book Kaffa gave you."

Hramack pulled the book from his pack and handed it to Travin.

"Read this," Kena said. "It contains the words of Arun Kane concerning the fall of Denver Dome. You should know why I am doing this."

Travin took the book and held it in his hands for several seconds, as if afraid to open it. Finally, he moved closer to the fire and began to read. Later, after the others had gone to sleep, Hramack watched Travin. Tears glistened in the hunter's eyes, reflecting the flickering light of the fire. *Good*, he thought. Travin was still reading when Hramack pulled up his covers and went to sleep.

✳

The fire had died during the night. Hramack awoke to total darkness. He could feel the walls of his stone coffin closing in on him, pressing him down into the dirt. The echo of his rapid breathing drowned out all other sounds. It was as if the darkness had swallowed the others.

"Father," he cried into the silence. Light flared as Kena switched on one of the lanterns.

"Are you okay?" Kena asked. His face showed concern over his son's sudden outcry.

Hramack's heart slowed to a more normal beat. "Yes, I'm all right," he gasped. "Just alarmed by the dark."

"Here, I'll light a torch." Kena struck a match and lit two torches. He stuck one in the ground on each side of Hramack, and then extinguished the lantern to save batteries. By now, the others were awake.

"Wha...?" Anseer mumbled, still half asleep.

"Nothing," Kena reassured them. "Just starting breakfast."

Hramack was ashamed by his outburst. He rushed to rekindle the fire for breakfast using twigs he had gathered at the cactus forest. When the flame was high enough, he placed the coffee pot over it. They would eat cold biscuits and fruit to save time, but the hot coffee would warm their bellies.

Travin was very quiet. He had been up most of the night reading the Journals of Arun Kane. Hramack noticed the tightness around the hunter's eyes and wondered if what he had learned had shaken the taciturn hunter's faith as much as it had his. He knew having faith in nothing meant not having faith in oneself. He hoped that somewhere along the way, he would find reason to believe once again.

Anseer awoke surly and unapologetic, complaining about everything from the coffee to the cold breakfast.

"The least we could do is have a decent breakfast," he whined. "My muscles ache as though I had been stomped in my sleep. I need nourishment."

Finally, Travin broke his silence. "Stop your whining and get ready. We must cover a lot of ground today."

He handed the book back to Hramack without comment and chewed his cold fruit in silent thought. As they were packing up, he asked Kena, "Chu Li knows of these things also?"

Hramack nodded. "He must. He knew of the tunnel behind the mouth of the falls didn't he?"

Travin hung his head and slowly shook it side to side. "He has much to answer for."

"He won't unless we reach our goal," Kena commented, slinging his pack over his shoulder. "Let's go."

12

HELL ON EARTH

THEY WERE ONLY THREE DAYS INTO THEIR JOURNEY, AND WHITEHALL DID not look at all well. Cathi watched him closely as they walked. His ragged breathing produced small droplets of blood that speckled his chin. She suspected that a broken rib had punctured his lung. She had done all she could. Without proper care, he could soon die. The long trek had burned up all his reserve energy, and his health deteriorated rapidly. He was feverish, and she suspected an infection by some native bacteria to which they had no immunity. Almost all the heavier pain medication was gone from the first aid kit, as were the antibiotics. All that remained were mild sedatives for minor aches and pains. If Whitehall's fever did not abate soon, they would not be able to continue their journey, which could mean all their deaths.

She studied Anderson as he trudged along almost in a trance. He was pretty well done in as well. She couldn't see his eyes beneath the brim of the cap pulled low over his forehead, but she felt certain they noticed little of the bleak terrain through which he marched. Life aboard the *Baldry* was not conducive to physical endurance. They spent much of the time at less than .8 G's. Most Traders exercised periodically, but it was a personal choice. She forced herself to endure a strong regime of exercise each morning while aboard ship to keep in shape, and she ran for several kilometers each time they were in port, but even she now felt the need to rest more and more often. The insipid heat was sapping their energy, and at half rations, they would only grow weaker.

She envied Anderson his swarthy complexion. The extra melanin in his skin cells provided an added degree of protection against the sun's harsh UV rays. In stark contrast, her pale skin was already beginning to show the debilitating effects of the intense sunlight. She felt flush, and the exposed areas of her body were red and tender to the touch. The one thing she needed most, a heavy UV sunscreen, was not included in the first aid kit. They had used up the small tube aboard the shuttle.

She was determined not to lose any more of her crew. Pegari was dead. They had buried her body and left the grave behind as a testament to her failure to keep Pegari safe. Whitehall's condition was deteriorating and he was in danger of dying as well. She was a ship's officer, and her crew needed her guidance, her leadership, and her strength. Was she marching them to their deaths? Denver Dome seemed as far away as ever, yet if they were to find help, it would most likely be there.

They staggered in a ragged line through a barren land, seeing nothing alive – neither plant nor animal, nor bird in the sky. The devastation of the old war had sterilized the soil and ripped the land into an unreadable mosaic of broken tiles. Fractures too wide to cross, they went around. At times, they climbed up and down vertically farther than they progressed horizontally.

"This hell hole goes on forever," she grumbled to Anderson, looking out ahead of them through her field glasses. She saw nothing but broken rock and heat swirls. "Whitehall needs shelter from this heat. We'll look for some shade and wait until dark to continue."

They had gone through the same routine for three days. She did not need to tell Anderson anything, but it made her feel in command. He did not complain as he trudged off wearily in search of an overhang or a crevice in the rocks – anything that would get them out of reach of the sun's fury.

Cathi's limited knowledge of Earth's history did not include the reason for Sol's flaring. It was not bad enough that the flares had forced humankind from its birthplace. Those who had chosen to remain had let loose the Hounds of War and finished the job nature had started. It seemed increasingly likely that only those who had re-settled Mars had survived. The age of flares had long passed, and the sun had again stabilized, yet it beat down upon her like an angry god. She could not imagine anyone thriving in such a barren waste.

Anderson located a small overhang nearby and directed the others to it. Whitehall collapsed in a fit of coughing as soon as they stopped walking. She checked the transponder unit, as she had every few hours since they began their journey. It was still sending. At least Captain Moore could find them. If – and it was a big if – he could knock out the defense satellites and bring the *Baldry* in. She hoped Anderson's last message had gotten through. Maybe the people on Mars had not been hiding anything after all. Maybe they had simply tried to warn the *Baldry* away from Earth because of the dangers they had faced.

Too late for regrets, she mused.

As the sun began to set in the blood-red western sky, she stood at the edge of the overhang, shaded her eyes, and stared out at the bleak vista before her. She caught a glimpse of the ragged peaks that still lay many days' journey ahead. The ruins of Denver Dome were there somewhere, in the foothills, out of sight behind the intervening mountains. She feared they would never make it.

Just as the blazing sun slipped over the edge of the horizon, she noticed a small flickering light just southwest of them. It looked like a fire, and a fire meant people. She rejoined the others and checked Whitehall's pulse and temperature with the scanner. His pulse was weaker, and his breathing was rapid and shallow. His rising temperature concerned her. It was placing a strain on his already over-taxed system.

He looked up at her with his sunken hazel eyes and smiled. "Don't worry about me," he said with a raspy voice. "I've suffered worse."

His attempt to reassure her touched her, but she knew he would not last long without help. She refused to let him die.

"Anderson, watch Whitehall," she said. "I'm going to scout ahead. I saw a bit of light. It may be nothing, but I have to check it out. I'll be back in four hours tops."

Anderson looked at her questioningly, but merely nodded. He settled down on the ground and fell into a heavy slumber. She wondered if Anderson thought she was abandoning him and Whitehall, trying to save herself. If so, he did not have the energy to fight, and she certainly did not have the heart to argue. It would take every bit of willpower she had to force her weary legs to push on. She checked her chronometer again. Four hours should be plenty of time. She estimated an hour and a half there and the same back. That left an hour for reconnoitering and, if possible, to find help.

She left the flashlight with Anderson. Without the illumination of the moon to light her way, she fell often over loose stones and twisted spires of molten rock. It took longer than she had calculated to reach the small rise upon which she had earlier spotted the flickering light. Once there, she found a small circle of stones and the still-warm ashes of a fire, but no people. There were no other signs that a living soul had been here. Still, fire meant people nearby. The idea of rescue lifted her flagging spirits. She searched for another hour. Just as she was beginning to give up hope and return to her friends, a small scraping sound behind her attracted her attention. She started to turn around but never completed the move.

She awoke with a throbbing pain in the back of her head and the sound of laughter ringing in her ears. She attempted to sit up and found her hands and legs tightly bound. She was also naked. The stones beneath her were uncomfortably hot. Looking around, she saw a band of seven men in ragged clothing rummaging through her clothing. One removed the laser from her belt, examined it for a moment, and then tossed it aside. It clattered against the rocks as it bounced down the slope. *That can't be good for it*, she thought wryly. One man with a toothless grin was fighting a smaller comrade for her jumpsuit. In their rage, they had failed to notice that she had regained consciousness. She worked frantically at the knots of her bindings, which they had not tied very securely. Given time, she was certain she would be able to work them loose, but depending on the intentions of her captors; she doubted she would have any time.

The men, all painfully thin, wore a loose collection of various colored bands of cloth draped over their bodies bound together with leather cords and other strips of cloth. Over this, several wore a kind of poncho or serape and either a leather hat or burnoose to protect their heads from the sun. One wore her cap. The prevalent footwear was leather sandals, decidedly unsuitable for the sandy terrain. They were particularly interested in her boots. Their exposed flesh was smeared with a foul-smelling white cream that had caked and cracked as it dried, lending them the impression of old age, but she doubted the oldest was more than thirty. By the coughs and wheezes they emitted as they laughed and argued over her belongings, she doubted most of them would live beyond thirty-five, their lives shortened by constantly breathing in the prevalent dust.

Toothless won the argument over her clothing by the expedient act of kicking his opponent in the shin. Bearing her jumpsuit draped over his arm, he sauntered over to her triumphantly and stood at her feet. She feigned unconsciousness.

"No fool," he snapped. "Hear your heart. Looky me." He followed this command with a swift kick to her leg.

She had barely understood what he had said. His words were slurred by his lack of teeth, and his double O's sounded like short U's. His kick had been easy to interpret. Realizing her unconscious act had not worked, she sat up, wincing at the pain. Toothless leered down at her. She stared back at him.

"Hey, Toothless, what do you want with me?" He took no notice of her nickname for him.

"Big tits, bitch. Hardy will like." He chuckled. "Much to play with. Give me much riches." He shook his head. "No. We don't touch you, bitch. But we look."

"It's nice to know the word bitch hasn't changed meaning in a thousand years," she replied.

His comrades, including the small one now limping, joined him and stood in a semicircle leering down at her. She did not like the idea of being on display. Normally, nudity did not bother her. Aboard the *Baldry*, they had no inhibitions about the human body, especially while sharing baths or massages. Seeing a comrade parading naked from the bath to their cabin was commonplace. In this instance, as a recipient of their vulgar lecherous stares, she felt dirty, dirtier even than the layers of filth accumulated by her long journey could account for.

When Toothless drew a long, double-edged knife from the band around his waist, she thought for a terrible moment he had changed his mind. In a display of domination, he shredded her jumpsuit, smiling his toothless grin the entire time. He dropped the pieces at her feet one at a time. Her undergarments quickly joined the pile of scrap. Judging by the group's bedraggled attire, her jumpsuit would have been a valuable trophy. His costly display of destruction was a warning to her.

"Eat," Toothless said and nodded to one of the men, who tossed her a scrap of meat. She felt her stomach began to heave when she saw that the piece of meat was a human finger, roasted earlier over the fire that had drawn her here. Intellectually, she understood their fall into cannibalism. High protein foods, especially meat, had to be scarce in such a desolate place, but the thought of actually killing and eating a fellow human being was repulsive. She was not a Vegan as were many of her comrades, but she certainly drew the line at eating people.

Luckily, they valued her more as a female than as a food source. *Of course*, she reminded herself, *they could always eat me later, after satisfying their more basic carnal urges.* Looking at them, she wasn't sure which would be worse. They were little more than savages. Her only hope lay in the fact that the one they called Hardy wanted her brought to him. If he was their leader, perhaps she could work out a deal with him that would save her two companions. She despised the idea of using sex as a bargaining tool, but if it kept her and her companions alive, she would subject herself to whatever debasement he required of her.

Looking at the sky, she judged that dawn was only an hour away. She had been unconscious for hours. If she did not return to her companions soon, she hoped Anderson wouldn't think she had abandoned them. Not that she would blame him. So far, she had accomplished nothing but crashing the shuttle and stranding them in the middle of a desert. She had sought rescue for them. Now, she was the one in need of rescue. She couldn't use her hands. Bending over as far as she could, she jammed her knee into her sternum to activate her sub-dermal communicator. She didn't have to speak aloud. The induction mic embedded in her mastoid bone would pick up her sub-vocalizations.

"Anderson, this is Lorst. A band of savages has taken me captive. They don't look very friendly. I think I'm about two kilometers southwest of you. I could use some help."

To her dismay, she received no answer. *Too far away*, she thought, *or maybe Anderson thinks he and Whitehall are better off without me. I don't blame him.*

Before she could make a second attempt at contacting him, Toothless dragged her to her feet, being none too gentle about it, loosened the bindings around her ankles, and tied a length of braided leather rope to her left ankle. He wrapped the other end around his wrist. He did not remove the thong securing her wrists.

"Walk," he told her, shoving her forward.

Walking hobbled proved awkward, and Toothless enjoyed jerking her down to the ground just to stand over her and laugh while she struggled to her feet. Many hours passed in this manner. Her naked feet began to bleed from sharp rocks, and her knees and forearms bore numerous cuts from breaking her frequent falls. The sun rose in all its fury. Within two hours, the heat had become unbearable, searing her naked flesh, sucking the moisture from her body. The rocks and sand roasted the soles of her bare and abused feet.

To her immense relief, Toothless halted their march and sought shelter beneath the meager shade of a great spire of rock. She collapsed on the scorching rock while the others spread blankets to lie on. Toothless untied the cord from his wrist, looped it over a knob of rock, and walked the perimeter of their camp. Finally, satisfied they were safe, he, too, lay down, after first looping the cord around his wrist. An experimental tug on the rope showed her that he awakened easily and that escape would be difficult if not impossible. Besides, where could she go naked, barefoot, and lost in a desert? She sat quietly and tried to think of a way to free herself and find the others. Her dismay mounted. There appeared to be no solution to her dilemma.

The slight sound of falling rock instantly brought Toothless to his feet. He hissed a warning, and the others scrambled for their weapons. She searched for the source of their concern. Suddenly, one of her captors screamed out and collapsed with a neat hole burned through his chest. A wisp of smoke rose from his leather shirt, still smoldering from the intense heat of a laser. *Whitehall!* He had come for her. When one of her captors raced toward her with a spear intent on skewering her, she tried to roll away, but Toothless still held firmly to the rope attached to her ankle. A second blast from the laser vaporized the side of the spear bearer's head. He fell dead across her legs. The spear landed inches from her head. Unable to locate their silent attacker, her captors began firing arrows blindly in all directions.

Using the confusion as her chance to escape, she rolled the dead weight of the body from her legs and scooted closer to the spear. Grasping it behind her back with her hands, she worked the bindings on her wrists against the sharp metal point. They parted quickly. She slipped the rope from her ankle and made a dash for freedom. Toothless noticed her movement out of the corner of his eye and dove for her. A laser bolt shattered the stone between them. He fell back brushing chips of hot stone from his skin and clothing. Running as quickly as she could on cramped muscles and bleeding bare feet, she rounded the rock spire and almost tripped over Anderson.

"This way!" he yelled, firing twice more to cover their retreat. A third man fell as he pursued them. The others fell back in confusion. He looked at her. "You'll burn to a crisp in that outfit," he commented as he handed her a jumpsuit.

His demeanor was matter-of-fact, his eyes never straying from the retreating savages to her naked body. They had seen each other nude many times, and even though he had never been one of her lovers, she admired his sense of decorum. She was his superior officer. Casual nudity was far different from being stripped naked by force. She noticed the jumpsuit he produced was Whitehall's. She glanced at Anderson. He nodded.

"He died an hour after you left. He passed quietly in his sleep. When you didn't return, I became concerned and searched for you. When I discovered your tattered jumpsuit but no blood or body, I figured you had run into trouble. I went back for our packs and took

Whitehall's jumpsuit. Sorry for the delay. Looks like I was just in time." He jerked his thumb back over his shoulder. "Who were your friends?"

"Thanks, Anderson," she said as she slipped on the jumpsuit. She winced as it touched her tender flesh. Heavy perspiration had washed away the last of the sunscreen she had applied before they began the trek. She didn't worry about carcinomas. Her annual gene-booster therapy prevented most cancers, but they didn't prevent serious sunburn. Large blisters pocked her arms, face, and neck.

Anderson kept watch while she dressed. She had been wrong to think he would abandon her. He hadn't received her com call, and yet he had searched for her. "Too bad about Whitehall," she said. "His death is my fault. I guess I haven't been a very good officer."

Anderson looked at her. She had never been good at reading his face when playing cards. Some thought him stoic and cold, but she knew he simply kept his emotions in check. She thought it was part of his religious upbringing on Brosnia, a decidedly theocratic planet. His religion had placed him at odds with most of colonized space, which was agnostic, atheistic, or apathetic. Centuries of wars between religious empires had left a bad taste in people's mouths. He spoke little about his past and revealed even less about himself. She herself believed in the possibility of a Creator, but was certain he or she did not care much for his or her creations.

"You brought us down in one piece, lieutenant. No one else could have done that. Pegari and Whitehall aren't your fault. Chalk them up to this damned planet. We're still alive. Now let's try to stay that way. You're still in command, lieutenant," he continued.

"You can call me Cathi, Kal. We're not on duty and I'm not in command of anything."

A brief flicker of something she could not identify crossed his face. *Was it fear?* she wondered. "I would prefer to continue to call you lieutenant. It . . . helps me keep myself oriented. Who were those guys?"

"A local welcoming committee, I suppose," she replied as she slipped on Whitehall's boots. She winced as she worked the boots over her damaged feet. His jumpsuit was a too large for her, but it covered her body. His boots were too large as well, but they were better than walking barefooted on the treacherous, searing rocks.

He handed her the transponder and her laser. "Sorry, that's all I could salvage. They took or destroyed the rest. The laser is badly damaged. I'll try to repair it later." He looked around. "Which direction?"

"We head west. We follow them." She nodded towards her recent captors. She transferred everything from Whitehall's backpack into hers and slung it over her shoulder. It was a heavy load but she wanted to leave nothing. Fully dressed, she regained some of her lost composure. "Let's go."

Toothless's band moved swiftly. Following them was not easy. They knew they were being pursued and attempted several times to throw Cathi and Anderson off their trail. Luckily, the medical thermal scanner they carried was powerful enough to pick up traces of their trail, even in the heat of the day. Anderson had used it to follow her after Whitehall's death.

Eventually, Toothless's band gave up trying to throw off pursuit and headed due west at a rapid clip. Her biggest concern was that Toothless could pick up more men and return to recapture her and Anderson. To continue following them was risky, but they needed supplies soon. Moreover, the group lay between them and Denver Dome. Denver Dome, she was sure, was their only chance for rescue.

"Did Whitehall say anything before he died?" She had been silent for hours as they marched in the relentless heat. She was angry at herself for being captured and even angrier at not present when Whitehall needed her most.

Anderson stopped walking and looked at her questioningly. "Like what?" he asked.

She sighed. "Like maybe he blamed me for his death."

Anderson shrugged noncommittally. "He was raving a bit from fever, but no, he didn't really say anything."

She felt no reprieve at his answer. "Do you think it's my fault?"

"Look, lieutenant, you got us down. Pegari died in the crash. She saved our asses. Whitehall died of his wounds. It's no use dwelling on the past. We're alive. Just try to keep us alive." He pushed ahead.

She could tell by the set of his shoulders that Anderson was struggling to keep going, but he did not complain. By mid afternoon, the heat was too much for them. They found respite from the heat beneath an overhang of rock. She felt a little guilty as she took a long sip of water. Whitehall's death had increased their daily water ration.

She abandoned pursuit during the day, but for two nights, they trudged through the twisted and burned-out landscape, playing hound to Toothless's hare. By then, she had guessed that Toothless was making for the dome, too. Rescue seemed remote now. If Toothless' people lived in the ruins of Denver Dome, she doubted they would find help. If they were lucky, perhaps they could steal supplies and hide out until Captain Moore located them, if he managed to overcome the killer satellites. The batteries on the transponder that relayed their location would last for months, but she was certain that she and Anderson could not. The crew of the *Baldry* would find only their bleached bones.

She was willing to bet her life that the controls for the orbiting defense satellites were located in one of the domes, but which one. The odds of it having been Denver Dome were one in ten, but it was the only one within reach. If anything had survived the dome's destruction, the satellite control system would have. It would have been the most protected area of the dome. The problem was that she was betting Anderson's life as well as hers.

The sun broke free of the intervening hills and scoured the blasted landscape. By following a deep ravine that led south, they were able to take advantage of the shade for a short while longer. All too soon, the overpowering heat forced them to seek shelter. They crammed themselves into the shade provided by a very narrow cleft in the rocks. It was a snug fit, but both of them fell asleep almost immediately.

They resumed their journey after dusk, trying to follow the rills and valleys to avoid discovery by Toothless's men. It took longer, but they could not afford another encounter with her former captors. This was Toothless's territory, and he probably knew every rock and ridge. An ambush could cost her and Anderson their lives, in spite of their superior firepower.

Near dawn, they reached the rim of a high ridge. Her hopes sank as she topped the rise. Ahead lay kilometers of flat, empty land. She eagerly scanned the horizon for any sign of civilization but saw nothing – no buildings, and no ruins, not even an old road. The area was an ancient battleground, the target for massive laser blasts with heat so intense it had fused the soil and rock into glass. Over the centuries, the plain had cracked like a giant mirror and weathered. She glanced at Anderson. His glare told her all she feared. She had already lost two of her crew. Now, she was in danger of losing another, this time to mistrust and a perceived lack of leadership.

Maybe Anderson was right in his unspoken assessment of her abilities. She had gotten them down alive, at least most of them. Even Anderson would not dispute her piloting abilities, but since then, her every move had been thwarted. They were wandering aimlessly. She turned to Anderson.

"I'm sorry. You take command. I may kill us both." At this, her will to continue fled. She collapsed on the ground, spent.

After a minute or two, the hard look on Anderson's face softened. He gently rested his hand on her shoulder.

"You're in command, lieutenant," he assured her. "I'm not one to make decisions. I follow, but I can't lead. I'm sure it's logged somewhere on my fitness report. We're still alive, and in spite of my doubts, I believe your decisions are sound. I couldn't have done as well. Left to me, we would still be back at the shuttle, probably dead by now. Now, straighten up and get us the hell out of here."

She stifled a last sob and stared at her companion, heartened by his words. He was made of sterner stuff than she had believed. Beneath his cold, impertinent façade, he was a true Guild Trader. "You're sure?" she asked.

"Hell, yes. Now, let's go before I change my mind."

Buoyed by Anderson's vote of confidence, she checked her compass to get her bearings, shouldered her pack, and took the next step toward Denver Dome.

13

OBSERVED

ANSEER HAD DIFFICULTY KEEPING UP, EVEN THOUGH KENA HAD DELIBER-
ately set a slower pace for him. They stopped and waited for
him many times that morning. By noon, Anseer's slow plod-
ding dismayed even Hramack, who was rapidly losing patience with
the woodcarver. After they had eaten bread and fruit and rested for
half an hour, Hramack relieved Anseer of part of his load. Combined
with his own pack, he was now carrying over thirty kilos, but Anseer
seemed to manage better, and they made better time.

By late afternoon, Hramack was the one struggling to keep up.
His shoulders ached from his heavy burden, and his legs tried to
rebel with each step, yet he refused to complain. Throughout the
long afternoon, he stumbled along, oblivious to his surroundings,
following his father's back. That evening, they came to a series of
shallow natural steps carved in the differing layers of sandstone.
Above, through a small crack in the ceiling, stars twinkled in the

night sky. To his weary eyes, the steps looked like a stairway to the stars.

"I'm sorry father," he moaned and collapsed on the floor of the tunnel. "I must rest."

Kena helped him with his pack and, when he saw the raw wounds on his son's shoulders, he rummaged in his pack and removed a carved stone jar. "You carry too heavy a burden," he said as he rubbed a strong-smelling ointment on the wounds.

"Yours is the heaviest," Hramack answered brusquely. He immediately regretted his tone. "I'm sorry. I'm tired."

Kena nodded and continued to rub in the soothing cream. "We have covered less than ten kilometers. At this pace, the northern mountains are still a week away. We will remain here a while. You and Anseer need rest." He looked at Travin. "I will leave a torch. Travin and I will scout ahead a short ways."

He set a torch in a crevice in the wall and walked ahead with Travin. When the two were out of sight, Anseer rolled over and looked at Hramack. His face bore the look of a chastised child. "Thank you for carrying part of my pack today. I didn't know it was hurting you."

Hramack shrugged, and then winced as the action sent pain running down his arms. "You are unused to long marches. I only sought to help you."

Anseer laughed.

"What's so funny?"

"I was just thinking. I started out to capture, perhaps kill you and your father. Now, here I am beneath the earth helping you reach some unknown destination, and you injure yourself trying to lighten my burden. Strange, is it not?"

Hramack chuckled. "Perhaps you are learning to think for yourself. I don't think you regret your decision to accompany us as much as you let on."

Anseer sneered. "Don't kid yourself." However, Hramack noticed a slight smile curling around the corners of his mouth.

"Rest now. Father will be back soon and we must leave."

Hramack closed his eyes but could feel Anseer's dark eyes staring at him from across the tunnel. Hramack assumed Anseer could not understand anyone wanting to help him. His father had told him Anseer had been headstrong and a loner even as a child. Hramack knew him as a quiet young man, not very well liked by the others in the village, but he did not know him very well. One reason was that Anseer was not easy to like.

Kena had also explained about Anseer's problems with his father. Anseer's father had wanted Anseer to become a stone craftsman or mason but Anseer, instead, had chosen woodworking. The entire village acknowledged his carving abilities, but his hidden anger often bled through into his carvings, revealing delicate twists and whorls that, when followed by the viewer's eye, left a queasy feeling in the pit of the stomach. Hramack was beginning to wonder if Anseer craved friendship.

All too soon, Kena and Travin returned, and the four continued their trek northward. Travin insisted on dividing the packs more evenly to give Hramack's shoulders a chance to heal. Hramack did not object. They made much better time in this manner. Just after moonrise, they came upon a crumbled section of ceiling through which they could safely ascend to the surface, if only long enough for Kena to check his bearings and for them all to catch a breath of fresh air. Anseer needed assistance up the steep path but was visibly delighted to be free of the dark confines of the tunnel. Exhausted, the trekkers fell onto the sand and removed their heavy packs.

The planet Venus shone brightly just to the right of and slightly below the rising moon. The light cast by the moon was sufficient to see that they were in a long, narrow valley enclosed by steep cliffs. No easy path out of the valley presented itself.

"It would be too dangerous to try and climb out tonight," Kena suggested. "We should rest and wait for sunrise to show us a path upwards."

Travin agreed. Hramack began to hunt for dead wood for a fire. Kena stopped him.

"We should not build a fire out in the open. The smell and the smoke might draw predators."

Hramack dropped his load of twigs. "I had hoped for a warm meal," he complained.

Kena shook his head. "We are in unfamiliar country with no escape except back down the tunnel. A cold meal will suffice. Tomorrow, if things look good, we may chance a fire for breakfast."

Hramack noticed the way his father's eyes scanned the valley ridge.

"It's not predators that worry you, is it?" he asked.

"I'm not sure," Kena admitted. "It's strange, but I feel as if we're being watched."

Hramack followed his father's gaze but could see nothing out of the ordinary. He reluctantly brought out a piece of hard bread and dried fruit. Tearing off a piece of the chewy bread with his hands, he said, "Unless we hunt soon, we will have to continue our journey on only traveler's bread and dried fruit."

"When the sun rises we will know more about our location. Perhaps we can hunt then," Kena promised.

Travin nodded his approval. He pointed to a haze surrounding the moon. "Dust storm. I'll keep watch. If it veers toward us, I'll warn you, and we can seek shelter in the tunnel."

Travin tore off a chunk of bread, picked up a handful of dried dates, and walked to the far end of the valley to stand guard. When he was out of earshot, Hramack whispered, "Travin is a quiet man, isn't he?"

Kena smiled. "When we hunt together, he sometimes says nothing all day. At other times, he talks your ear off. I think he is nervous about being in unknown territory."

"Who isn't," Anseer snapped. "We don't know what's out there." He waved his finger vaguely in the direction Travin had gone.

"We're well armed. We should be able to handle most threats," Kena assured him.

"Can your arrows stop a scorpion? I don't want Travin to slit my throat like Won's." Anseer was speaking loudly. Hramack tried to get him to keep his voice down, but Anseer ignored him. Suddenly, Travin was standing over Anseer, his face twisted into a mask of agony. He gripped his knife in one hand. The blade trembled with his rage. When Anseer saw him, he began to scoot backwards across the dirt. Travin smirked at him and tossed a handful of water roots at his feet. He had dug them out of the soil with his knife.

"Use your big mouth on these and save our water supply." He looked at Kena. "Won was dying. A nightstalker was coming, drawn by his screams of agony as the scorpion's venom found his heart. I ... released his spirit."

Kena nodded his understanding, and Travin turned and walked silently into the darkness.

Hramack could not believe what he had just heard. "Travin killed Won?" he whispered.

Kena's glance was enough to stop Hramack's speaking further. It contained an odd mixture of sadness and pity.

"There is no cure for the black scorpion's sting," Kena explained. "It is a slow and agonizing way to die. Travin could do no less. Other lives were at stake."

Hramack nodded his head slowly. Maybe he understood, but he did not know if he, when faced with a similar situation, could take a life.

"Get some rest," Kena suggested. We must move before sunrise."

The wind picked up throughout the night, but the steep cliffs protected them from the brunt of the storm's fury. The sandstorm blew past them but caused no damage except to keep them awake. The wind's howl sounded like a pack of nightstalkers on a fresh blood trail. The eerie undulations sent shivers up Hramack's spine as he remembered his own almost fatal encounter with a night-stalker. Before dawn, the wind died to a whisper. They arose and made their way up the steep slope using a path Travin had located during the night. They exited in a shallow defile filled with cactus and stubby plants. A slender finger of red rock towering over their heads pointed skyward. Hramack was afraid it would fall and crush them. As he stared up at it, it seemed to sway in the breeze.

Around them as far as they could see stretched the Empty Lands, a land totally devoid of tree or shrub, a vast rocky plain whose endless expanse was broken only by the occasional sand dune or large boulder. Nothing moved either in the sky or on the sand.

It was a dead land.

"We can't cross that," Anseer cried.

For once, Hramack agreed.

"No, it is too desolate," Kena concurred. "We'll have to return to the tunnel."

Kena sounded as disappointed as Hramack felt. Hramack felt as if he had been born in the narrow river tunnel through which they traveled. He yearned for the sky over his head, but not this sky. He shaded his eyes and glanced upward. There was no cloud, no feathered creature, not even an insect visible. The bright sun blazed down on the sand and rock like the fiery hand of Yarah smothering all life from the blighted land. A heat shimmer danced on the horizon. They would not last out the day beneath its fury.

As he scanned the horizon, he thought he saw a brief flash near a group of boulders to the northeast. He strained to see more clearly, but the flash did not repeat itself. He turned to inform Kena and saw his father staring in the same direction.

"Did you see it?" Hramack asked quietly.

Kena continued to stare a moment longer, then glanced at his son. "Perhaps," he murmured. He looked back at the others. "We had better get started now."

"Don't you want to ..." Hramack started to ask about searching for the flash. Kena stopped his question with a withering look. Kena did not mention it to the others.

Back in the river tunnel, they traveled less than two hours before encountering their first major obstacle. Kena was leading the group. As he rounded a turn in the tunnel, he almost fell into a deep pit. The light of the torch could not reach the bottom.

"Stay back," he warned the others.

Hramack crept up slowly to his father's side and whistled softly as he saw the yawning chasm before them.

"The water must have broken through into a cavern below the tunnel," Kena explained.

"Is this the reason the water stopped flowing?" *If so*, thought Hramack, *there is no way we could correct the problem.*

After a moment or two, Kena answered. "No, there is no water pouring into the chasm from the other side. The water stopped before reaching this point." He took out an extra torch and dropped the first into the pit. It rapidly dwindled in size, almost disappearing, before Hramack saw a splash of light as it splattered against the bottom six seconds later.

"About forty meters deep," Kena exclaimed.

"How do we cross?" Travin asked. He had walked up quietly and looked across the pit to the other side.

Kena played the light around the edge of the pit. A narrow, meter-wide ledge jutted into the empty space from the right-hand wall of the tunnel. "There's a ledge wide enough to use." He looked at Travin. "We could string a rope to an outcropping and use it for a safety line."

Travin shrugged. "It would seem our choices are limited," he admitted. He pulled a coil of rope from his pack.

Kena looked across the gap, and then down into the pit. "I'll go first." He carefully stepped out onto the slender lip of rock, pulling himself as close to the wall as possible. Halfway across, he secured the rope to an outcropping and continued to the other side. After tying off the other end of the rope, he called out heartily, "Who is next?"

Hramack swallowed heavily and volunteered. He tried not to stare down into the dark void at his feet, concentrating on placing his feet carefully with each step. He kept one hand on the rope at all times. He reached the outcropping without mishap, took a deep breath, and began the second leg of his journey. Stepping on a loose stone, he skidded, and one foot slid off the ledge. He fell to one knee and gripped the rope tightly with both hands, but the linen rope stretched under his weight. Slowly, unable to halt the inevitable, his knee slipped off the ledge. He dangled precariously over the chasm, swinging like a pendulum. Now, panic rose in his chest as the rope began to slip from the rock to which Kena had secured it. He struggled to find purchase on the slippery rock wall with either foot. Finally, he managed to throw one leg onto the ledge, but the rope and his body were below the ledge. He used the rope as he would the twine of a bow, pushing down and out against the rope with his other foot. When he removed his foot, the line snapped taut, bringing his hands above the level of the ledge. He used the momentum to grab the ledge with one hand and slowly lever his body over the edge.

He lay there panting for a few moments, trying to catch his breath while his father continued to bombard him with queries about his health. He waved his hand at Kena to show he was okay. Kena took the slack out of the rope and re-secured it to the rock. Hramack stood and completed the remainder of the trip. Kena shot him a broad smile and reached out to grab his hand, but Hramack could barely manage a weak grin. His heart still pounded in his chest.

Anseer had watched Hramack's near fall with horror. "No way," he protested when Travin waved him forward. "I'm no acrobat."

Travin ignored Anseer. He removed a second coil of rope and tossed one end to Kena. He then made a loop in the middle and slipped the loop over Anseer's head, tightening it beneath his arms. "You won't fall," he said.

Anseer moaned and complained loudly as he stepped out onto the ledge, but he quickly scurried across, buoyed by the rope held securely in Travin and Kena's hands. Travin crossed last, but first he secured all their packs to one end of the rope. Once across, they hauled them across the chasm.

"Even if we return the water, it will spill into the pit," Hramack said. He had been studying the pit as he rested from his ordeal. In his mind, the pit presented as great an obstacle to the water as it had to them.

"No, I don't think so," Kena mused. "The pit will eventually fill and the water will continue to flow."

His father spoke with confidence, but Hramack still had doubts. "How do you know?"

"The pit is old, far older than you or I, yet the waters flowed last season. It failed to stop the water."

Hramack could find no flaw in his father's logic. "I guess you're right," he conceded.

Travin stood up and brushed himself off, unperturbed by the hairy crossing. "We should continue," he said stonily and picked up a torch. Without waiting for the others, he began striding down the tunnel.

Hramack heard Anseer muttering under his breath.

"What?" he asked.

"I said Travin acts as if he has a bug up his rear," he repeated loudly.

Hramack started to respond acidly to Anseer's unkind remark, but Kena stopped him with a glance.

"Perhaps Travin likes this tunnel even less than you do," Kena suggested.

Hramack smiled as Anseer glared at Kena but said nothing as he picked up his pack and followed Travin. Here, the tunnel was less smooth. The rock surrounding them was mostly loose shale and gravel, deposited many eons earlier when the area had been the bottom of a great inland sea. The walls and floors were pitted and irregular, making walking difficult. There were many false tunnels and small caverns, but Travin continued unerringly down the main tunnel, his hunter's sense as accurate below the earth as above it. They marched without rest until early evening.

"Look at this," Kena called out eagerly as he pointed to one small niche in the wall. A pile of dried straw and feathers indicated an abandoned bird's nest. Hramack soon spotted several more, many looking less abandoned.

"We must be near another opening. Feel the air moving?"

Hramack nodded. He had spotted a dim glow coming from around the next bend in the tunnel. As he turned the corner, he saw an almost circular opening in the ceiling. Just below it ran a ledge with a series of irregular steps that descended to the bottom of the tunnel. He pointed it out to Kena.

"It looks manmade," Hramack observed excitedly.

"It looks like an ancient well," Kena exclaimed. "Someone used it to draw water from the river when the water was flowing. Look," he said. Kena's face betrayed his excitement. "There is a piece of broken pottery."

Hramack picked up a shard. It bore a depiction of a colorful stylized wading bird, long-legged and graceful. He recognized the bird from an old text of his father's.

"It's a crane. It must be ancient."

"No," Travin replied. "It would be buried by debris falling in from above. It was lying on the ground exposed and barely dusty."

"Who left it there?" Hramack asked. Travin's observation perplexed him, but had too much respect for the experienced hunter to doubt his word.

Kena shook his head absently as he stared at the opening. "I don't know."

"Perhaps we should investigate," Travin suggested. He pulled his knife from its scabbard and began to climb the stone steps. Curious to see what lay above them, Hramack followed.

They emerged in a bowl-like depression similar to the cactus garden that he and Kena had found earlier. This one was smaller, less than fifty yards in width, but the ruins of a rough stone building nested into a rocky shelf along the edge of the depression. A few saguaros grew in the center of the bowl, along with several stunted mesquite and pinion pine trees.

"People once lived here," Kena marveled as he examined the depression.

Travin had been studying a pile of ashes in a small rock-lined pit as Kena had walked the circumference of the bowl. "They have been here recently," he commented warily, keeping one eye on the horizon.

Hramack joined him. "How can you tell?" he asked, stirring the ashes with the tip of his boot.

"The ashes are still black." He picked up ashes from a second pile. "These are older. They are bleached by the sun."

Hramack noted the difference, intrigued. "How old are they?"

Travin thought a moment before answering. "Three days, perhaps four."

Four days. "There were people here four days ago?" he stammered. He turned to his father. "If there are others out here," he almost shouted, "we must find them."

"They could be some of the people Kane mentioned in his journal, the cannibals," Kena cautioned.

Hramack's smile quickly vanished at the thought of being eaten. He helped Travin scan the horizon. "Should we leave?"

"I think we can risk a small fire and hunt for game," Kena conceded.

They set out several snares and Kena discovered some edible fruit growing on the saguaros. With much effort, he managed to knock down several of the sticky, sweet fruits with his spear. Hramack got down on his hands and knees to follow the trail of a quail through the brush and down a small arroyo. Suddenly, a shadow fell over him. Before he could look up, a blow to his head sent him reeling into darkness.

14

TEMPERS FLARE

TEELA ROSE EARLY EACH MORNING AND WALKED TO THE RIM OF THE CANYON hoping to see some sign of Hramack, even though she knew his return could mean his death. Her heart conflicted with her mind, trying to dismiss any thoughts that she might never see her love again. If he and Kena failed in their task in returning the springs, the village was doomed. Since Chu Li's return to the village, it felt as if all hope had died. A morbid air of despondency had settled over the village like dust from a storm. No one sang anymore. The children no longer played. They sat at the doors of their homes as if afraid to venture outside.

When the three men sent out to fetch the water Chu Li's party had discovered returned, a score of women demanding water for their families mobbed them. Their frustration quickly turned to anger, and then blind rage. They fought among themselves; then, when others came to break up the scuffle, they quickly became embroiled in the melee. Chu Li stopped the fight by wading into the middle of it wearing his full robes of office as High Priest complete with staff and miter. Reminded of their faith by his presence, the fight ended with only a few bruises and scratches. The biggest wound was their pride. As penance, he urged everyone to meet near the Pools of Yarah each morning and each evening for prayers, but his manner left little doubt that attendance was compulsory. Since Kaffa's resignation from the Council and Kena's absence, it might as well have been a crown. Chu Li now controlled all aspects of village life. No one openly opposed him.

She left her vigil and joined the others as they gathered for prayers. Teela noticed the High Priest wore the white conical gold-trimmed miter atop his head like the crown he sought. Each day, his prayers became more ardent, often returning to Kena's blasphemy and his murder of Eithan as the root of their suffering. The fact that the pools had been dry for months had no bearing on his rants. Surely, no one believed Kena, a Healer, capable of murder. To her horror, many of the villagers mirrored his sentiments, even blaming him for the deaths of Artimeer and Won, instead of Chu Li where the true blame lay. She was appalled that people, her friends, could blame their ills on the man who had so selflessly strived to save them when they were ill or injured. It was as if all reason had fled, replaced by a kind of religious fervor that ignored the *Teachings* and focused on the High Priest.

Today, he had added a new spectacle. As he stood before them, two men brought a goat, its legs bound together, to the edge of the canyon. Its pitiful bleating seemed to delight the High Priest.

"Yarah demands blood," he said. "Kena shed innocent blood. Until he is apprehended and punished as Yarah wills, we must offer a substitute."

She waited for someone to rush up and free the hapless goat, but no one did. "Have we come to this?" she cried.

Faces turned toward her, faces she no longer recognized, subtlety changed by fear, frustration, and doubt.

"Your betrothed placed us in this position," Chu Li replied.

"Hramack? How?"

"Kean is a Healer. It has been suggested that perhaps he is incapable of murder, that blasphemy is his only crime."

Teela was confused. "Then, what . . . " Chu Li's meaning suddenly became clear. Her heart caught in her throat. "You cannot believe that Hramack would . . ."

"One is a murderer: father or son."

"No, you are wrong. Neither would kill anyone."

Chu Li opened his hands wide. "And yet Eithan is dead."

She realized he was playing her, using her as a foil to manipulate the crowd. "You are wrong." She waved her hand at the bound goat. "This is wrong. We are better than this."

His voice became cold. "Do you dispute the word of Yarah?"

"I dispute the word of Chu Li," she returned. She heard mutterings in the crowd and realized she was attacking their faith, the same faith that she once followed.

Chu Li smiled. "I will forgive your transgression. You are young and distraught, concerned for your betrothed. Your loyalty is admirable but sadly misplaced. Who but Kena or his son would murder Eithan and release them from their confinement?"

She held her tongue. The High Priest was making veiled accusations toward her. *Or Grandfather*, she realized in horror. As she stood there, afraid to speak up for fear of making matters worse, Chu Li removed a dagger from his sash, raised it, and plunged it into the goat's heart. It shrieked and kicked madly for a few moments, and then he sliced its throat. Finally, it was still. Blood ran from the wounds and pooled around the goat's body like a crimson robe.

She was in shock. She had watched goats and sheep being slaughtered and understood the necessity for the life of the village. Their meat sustained them and the cured hides provided material for boots, belts, and other items. The wool provided clothing. Their slaughter was accomplished with reverence and as little pain as possible, not the brutal butchery the High Priest had just performed.

What troubled her most was the reaction of the crowd. They stood silent, expectant, watching the High Priest.

Chu Li dipped a silver goblet into the blood and lifted it above his head. "This blood we offer to Yarah." He then spilled the blood into the canyon below.

She had seen enough. Almost in tears, she raced across the bridge to the home of Kena and Hramack, now empty. She wandered through the house, touching objects she knew Hramack had touched, hoping to feel some connection with him as strong as the one he had confided lay between father and son. She felt only a deep sense of loss.

"Don't despair child."

She whirled. Kaffa stood in the doorway. "Oh, grandfather, we are lost!" she cried.

He nodded sadly. "I watched the spectacle. It was Chu Li at his best.'

"He accused you or me of murdering Eithan."

"Yes, he knows that I know the truth, yet he cannot move openly against me. I am no longer Precept, but people still trust me."

"Then he accused me."

"He wishes to draw attention from himself by providing other probable suspects. All know of your love for Hramack and believe youth is impetuous. Many think me too old and weary to best a man like Eithan."

"Why not simply tell them that you spoke with Eithan, and he gave you the key?"

"It would be my word against that of a dead man. Chu Li will speak for him. It would sound too much like an old man trying to protect his granddaughter. Such an admission would give Chu Li all he needs to confine me and take away my ability to sway others."

"You are indeed wise, grandfather. It is better that I be suspect than you. People will forgive a heartbroken youth, especially a girl."

"You must not confront Chu Li again," he warned. "He has grown too powerful."

She knew her grandfather was right. "What of Travin and Anseer? What if they find them? Will Kena …"

"You wonder if Kena will kill to remain free. I do not know. Travin is an honorable man. He is also Kena's friend. I have faith in his judgment."

"Faith?" she questioned. It was an odd word to use for a hunter sent to track down and capture Kena and Hramack.

"Travin chose Anseer because he has no wife. He fears that he will not return, or he believes in Kena's cause. He knows that if Kena is right, his family is at risk, as is the whole village. He is no friend of Chu Li."

"I pray they are safe."

"Yes, pray for their safe return, but they are safe for now."

She looked at her grandfather. His eyes were closed, and he looked lost in thought. "How do you know?"

He smiled and touched his heart. "Because there is no emptiness here."

His words and his certainty gave her renewed hope.

"Now, Teela, fetch some of our water. Kena's herbs need tending."

Her heart was much lighter as she walked back across the canyon, that is, until she saw Chu Li standing outside the temple staring at her with a smile on his face. Then, her heart went suddenly cold and her steps faltered. Putting on her best façade of indifference, she went home for the water for Kena's herbs. He would need them when he and Hramack returned.

15

GREY EAGLE'S BAND

WHEN HRAMACK CAME TO HIS SENSES, HIS VISION WAS BLURRY, BUT he saw the images of three men standing over him. One held a bow on his father, Travin, and Anseer, a razor-sharp, metal arrow point glinting in the sun. As his vision cleared, he saw the men all wore leather britches with cloth shirts sewn with intricately crafted beaded designs over their hearts and along the sleeves. Over this, they wore heavy leather vests with armadillo shell pieces connected by wire over shoulders, chest, and forearms. Even this protective garb bore remarkable painted likenesses of animals and plants. The care given to their garments made him ashamed of his plain, woven outfit and loose outer robe. All three men wore their long, black hair in tightly woven braids that fell loose around their shoulders.

"*Taadoo Nahi nani,*" one of the men said, giving Hramack a kick to the ribs. The words meant nothing to Hramack. When he ignore the man, he drew back his foot to deliver another blow. The oldest of the three stopped him. Hramack vaguely heard his father's voice through the pounding in his head and the ache in his ribs. "We didn't know we were in your territory. Take your food and let us return south."

"*Bilaganna she' enaii,*" the bow holder said to the older man.

"I don't understand your language," Kena said.

The elder man said, "He told the young one not to move. He thinks you are the enemy, pale Marauders from the south."

Hramack was glad the man spoke English even if the enunciation was strange. "We come in peace."

"We shall see. We will take you to our *nihinahdodekaad,* our leader. He will decide your fate." He carefully looked Hramack over, noting his clothing. "You do not dress like Marauders, but I have not seen your kind before. Where are you from?"

"South," Kena replied, "Six days' journey from here. We are bound for the ruins of Denver Dome."

The three made a quick sign above their heads with one hand. "Never mention that place," the oldest said. He seemed to be the group's leader. "The Marauders come from there. It is a most evil place." Again, the three made the sign, thumb and pinky fingers extended from a closed fist held above the head.

"What is your name?" Kena asked.

The eldest stared at him a moment before replying. "I am Grey Eagle, the leader of this band. The others will remain nameless for now. You now know my name. What are you called?"

"I am Kena, a Healer in my village." He indicated Hramack. "This is my son, Hramack. The other young one is Anseer, a woodcarver. Travin is a hunter."

Grey Eagle looked Travin up and down. His survey appeared casual, but Hramack was certain the group's leader was making careful note of Travin's bulging muscles and great size. He came to a decision.

"I think you are not Marauders, but you are strangers. We will take your weapons, but will not bind you if you give your word not to escape. We travel to Pueblo Nuevo, our home three days north of here. There, our Chief will judge you. I do not wish to bind you for that length of time should you prove a friend." Seeing the angry look on Hramack's face, he added. "These are dangerous times, and I will take no chance with the safety of my people. Our Chief will hear your words. At any rate, you will be safer traveling with us than alone. We have seen signs of a small party of Marauders nearby. Come, we must hurry. The day grows hotter, and we must reach the Wall soon and find shelter." He pointed towards the mountains north of the grove.

Kena spoke, "We can find shelter there." He pointed towards the tunnel entrance. "There is a cavern, an old river channel."

One of the three exclaimed, "What! Into the *o'ann*. You expect us to walk with the *chindi*. Better to face the Marauders or to burn in the desert."

The leader of the group explained. "We know of the tunnels below ground, the *o'ann*. Usually they run with water in the spring. This place is an oasis, a way stop for our southern patrols. The tunnels are near our village also, but we do not venture into them. They are dangerous, and some of our people have died in them. When the water flows, this well is the only source of water for many days' march. Many of the foolish think them haunted by *chindi*, the spirits of the dead." He looked towards the one who had first spoken with a look of disdain. "I went down into one once. It was ... disconcerting." He turned his back and began to walk away, deflecting further conversation.

Shouldering their packs, the four set off with their captors watching their every move, one in front and two in back. Their captors did not bind them, but there was no mistaking who was prisoner and who was guard. Their leader's pace was rapid and punishing. By the time they had reached the meager shade cast by the mountain peaks ahead of them, Hramack was breathing rapidly and stumbling over the uneven ground. Anseer was too tired to complain. He fell onto the ground exhausted, unable to get up. Travin stopped, ignoring the not too gentle prods of his captors.

"Our companion can go no farther," he said. "Nor will I."

Hearing this, Grey Eagle grunted and called a halt. Kena and Hramack collapsed gratefully on the ground. Their captors sat down around them, trying to mask their own exhaustion. Travin stubbornly remained standing, refusing to betray his fatigue to the others. Though they would not admit it, Hramack could see their new companions were clearly afraid of Marauders. Perhaps it was a wise move to remain with them, since north was both their goals.

They rested for half an hour, then Grey Eagle stood. "We must continue."

Hramack groaned from aching muscles as he stood. The long journey was wearing him down. They pushed on at a brisk pace toward the peaks thrusting skyward before them. Hramack thought the mountains were beautiful, the tallest one with an almost sheer vertical rise of over 700 meters. Hardly a blemish marred its reddish surface. Flanking it were two smaller, but daunting, massifs. Unlike the former, eons of wind and rain had scored their grey faces into a series of channels and cracks. Piles of debris marched up their flanks, and great boulders lay strewn about like marbles scattered by a giant. Dark scars in its sides marked the location of caverns and deep clefts in the rock. It was towards one of these openings that Grey Eagle led them.

"The Wall," Grey Eagle said, as he pointed at the sheer wall of red rock. "But we go there," he pointed to the grey mountain to the right, "the Cavern of the Dead. The Marauders fear this place. We will be safe. There we will find *kuuyi*, water. Come."

The cave was larger than Hramack imagined, as they emerged from the five-meter deep slit that was the entrance. He noted that the narrow entrance was easily defendable. Inside, the cave was cool and dark. Grey Eagle lit several torches he picked up from a pile beside the entrance and set them around the cavern. Their flickering light dappled the cavern's ceiling a dozen meters above their heads. The rear wall stretched beyond the pool of light.

One of Grey Eagle's men removed a large urn of water from a cleft in the rock and passed it around. Hramack had difficulty refraining from draining it in his thirst. As a gesture of good will, he took out a package containing dried fruit and travel bread and laid it on a rock in front of him. Seeing this, Kena added a handful of vegetables from his pack. Grey Eagle nodded at the offering and produced a pot into which he poured water, their contributions, and added meat from a hare from his pack.

Hramack noted that the men of Pueblo Nuevo did not use any type of water recovery system. He watched the steam rise from the open pot with dismay, but soon the tantalizing aroma of stew filled the cavern, making Hramack's mouth water.

As they rested in the safety of the Cavern of the Dead, refreshed by cool water, eagerly waiting for the stew to cook, Grey Eagle and one of the men came to sit and talk with them. They passed around tobacco to show that they did not consider Hramack and his companions as enemies. Grey Eagle's younger companion offered his name.

"I am called White Elk," he said in halting English. A slight smile quivered on his lips before disappearing.

"Why is this place called the Cavern of the Dead?" Kena directed this question at Grey Eagle.

Grey Eagle knocked the ashes from a small soapstone pipe and filled it with tobacco before answering. "About thirty years ago, a large band of Marauders trapped a small group of our people here – twenty men, women, and children. My father was one of those twenty. They fought bravely, the wounded binding their wounds and returning to the fight. The Marauders were convinced the dead were coming back to life and fighting alongside the living. Eventually, all our people died, but Marauders are a superstitious lot. They now fear this place and avoid it at all times. We will be safe here."

He lit the pipe with a burning sliver of wood from the fire, inhaled deeply, and then slowly exhaled a stream of smoke. Hramack noticed that his teeth were yellow with tar.

"Do your people know much of the tunnels under the ground?" Hramack asked.

"Yes, we know of them, but we avoid them. They are dangerous. Each spring they run with swiftly moving water. They are dry now though."

Kena spoke up. "Yes. Our people suffer from lack of water as well. We seek the reason for the water's failure to return. Will you help us?"

Grey Eagle glanced at White Elk before replying. "We must bring you to our Chief, but if you speak *aaniigoo*, the truth, we will help you. It would serve our needs also." He looked over at Anseer lying alone away from the group. The woodcarver had fallen asleep almost immediately after collapsing. "What of this one? He is almost beyond his limits now."

Kena eyed Anseer. "He is unused to hard travel. Perhaps he can remain in your village while we continue our journey."

"Perhaps so," Grey Eagle agreed. "If Chief Kosono agrees."

Hramack smiled. *At last, a bit of luck.* They would need all the help they could find in this inhospitable country. "We did not know of other people still alive until we met you. Are there many others?"

Grey Eagle took another long draw from his pipe. This time he let the smoke trickle from his nostrils. Hramack thought he was stalling before answering. "Our village is the only I know of. The Marauders are nomads scavenging the ruins and stealing from us when they can. They are like wild animals nipping at our heels." He spat on the ground to show his contempt. "Are there many men in your village?"

Hramack started to answer, but Kena shot him a fierce look. "Too many for the water we have left," Kena answered.

Grey Eagle raised his heavy eyebrows. "You think we might attack you?" he asked harshly; then he softened his voice and nodded.

"*Ya'ateeh*. It is good. It was a wise answer between strangers. Later, perhaps, we can speak to each other as friends."

He tossed a stick on the fire and watched it catch. Then he settled back against a rock. "Rest now. We leave at sunset. It is still two days' march to our village."

With renewed hope, Hramack lay down to sleep, the most restful sleep he had managed in weeks.

For two days, they traveled only by night, keeping to the shelter of the mountains as protection against any Marauders that might be lurking. Little by little, Hramack learned of their new friends' ways and of their village. He also picked up a few of their words. They were Pueblo Indians, a mixture of Diné, Hopi, and Zuni whose ancestors had refused to enter Denver Dome. Diné was the most prominent language among themselves, but most spoke at least some English or Spanish, passed down the generations by their ancestors as had their own language. It astounded him to learn that people had lived for hundreds of years less than two weeks' journey north of Ningcha.

The people of Ningcha, including himself, had arrogantly believed themselves the last bastion of civilization on Earth. Once they returned, their discovery to the contrary would irk Chu Li. *If we return*, Hramack corrected himself. He especially liked the group's leader, Grey Eagle. Though almost as old as Kaffa, he retained the stamina and vigor of one used to surviving in harsh conditions. A union of their two peoples would benefit both cultures. It would take new blood to repopulate Earth.

Near dawn of the third day since encountering Grey Eagle's small band, the sky became red and hazy, obscuring the distant mountains that had been prominent the day before.

"The Devil Wind comes soon," Grey Eagle warned. "We cannot remain here. We must seek better shelter."

Hramack looked at the sky. "How can you tell?" he asked.

Grey Eagle pointed to the red dawn and line of haze that seemed to be getting darker as he watched. "Dust colors the dawn. The winds can be strong and the dust can kill. We must hurry."

They picked up their pace and jogged for almost an hour. The heat was unbearable, their pace relentless. Travin supported Anseer with one arm as he stumbled more often. The wind steadily increased in intensity and dust swirled around them, stinging Hramack's skin even through his shirt. The flinty smell reminded him of the mine tailings of the Red Valley. Visibility was now less than half a kilometer. A wall of rocks loomed out of the dust cloud, the shelter Grey Eagle had promised, but it looked impossibly far away. The wind tore at Hramack's feet, threatening to trip him. He feared that if he fell, he could not rise again.

"Take this," Grey Eagle shouted as he handed Hramack the end of a rope. Hramack wrapped a loop around his body and passed the rope on to Kena. With all seven bound securely by the rope, Grey Eagle planted his feet firmly and, with the aid of his spear, began to pull the others through the screaming wind to the safety of the rocks.

Sand filled Hramack's mouth as they struggled forward. Twice, he fell and felt someone's arms pick him up. They reached the wall of rock and collapsed on its leeward side. Out of the cutting wind, breathing was easier. The roar of wind around them sounded like the thunder of long-vanished herds of bison as they roamed across the plains in search of food. Hramack had often thought of these great beasts. He had seen pictures of them in books and even had an ancient coin with an image of one of the shaggy beasts stamped onto it.

The group huddled together out of the wind for hours. At times, the shriek of the wind increased until it hurt Hramack's ears. Dust swirled until it was impossible to see. Hramack placed a scarf over his face, and still the fine dust penetrated the cloth and worked its way into his eyes and throat. He wanted badly to take a drink of water, but knew if he opened the water skin, it would almost assuredly become contaminated with the all-pervasive dust. Then, the wind subsided as quickly as it came, leaving them in silence.

"Does the wind often do that?" he asked Grey Eagle as he shook the dust from his clothing.

"Many times each year," Grey Eagle replied. "This was but a breeze. I have seen winds strong enough to flay the skin from a man unlucky or unwise enough to be caught in it. Such winds are called The Hammer of God."

"Will we encounter more?"

Grey Eagle pointed to the mountains. "We travel there. As we go higher, the winds will be lighter, but breathing will be more difficult." He looked up at the sun. With no dust cloud to temper its fury, the heat had returned like a blast furnace. "We must hurry before the sun passes its zenith or we will perish."

By noon, they had reached the foot of the mountains. The mountains rose slowly at first, like folded blankets, and then shot abruptly into the air sheer-sided until they almost touched the sky. Hramack stared at them, hoping they would not have to climb to the top. The day's heat was sapping his strength. To his relief, Grey Eagle called a halt in a narrow defile shaded from the sun.

"Climbing will be more difficult at night," he said, "but the moon will help. We would never make it in the heat of the day."

Hramack was glad for any chance to rest. The company was too tired to cook. Chewing on a piece of dried meat as he rested, he surveyed his companions. Grey eagle, White Elk, and his companion were economical in their movements, using as little energy as possible as they removed their packs and chose spots to sleep. Kena, though exhausted, was examining the walls of the ravine. Travin brooded as he stared at their captors. Of them all, only Anseer's condition disturbed him.

The young woodcarver had stopped his usual complaining. In fact, he had not spoken all day. He slept fitfully, moaning and his legs thrashing. His breathing was ragged. Hramack was concerned about his poor health and the climb they faced, but he could do little about it.

Hramack managed to doze a few times but did not sleep soundly. He awoke once to see his father bending over Anseer.

"Is he all right?"

His father shook his head. "He is very weak."

"Will he live?"

"I don't know. If we can reach Grey Eagle's village, perhaps."

Sometime before sunset, he fell asleep. He dreamed of Teela. She stood beside the wooden bridge in the village with the moonlight shining through her golden hair, but she did not smile. Her tear-filled eyes pleaded with him. He ran toward her, but she seemed to retreat farther with each step. Exhausted he fell to his knees and called out to her. "Teela!"

Her voice, faint and trembling, answered, "Come to me, Hramack. I need you."

He awoke with a start, troubled by his dream. Around him, the others were stirring. He picked up his pack and joined them.

Grey Eagle led them up a well-worn game trail, climbing higher hour by hour, often scrambling upwards on hands and knees up loose slopes of scree. Hramack felt the change in altitude in his chest, laboring for each breath. The thin air forced the group to halt more often than Grey Eagle obviously liked, but he did not complain.

"Once, a man could once climb Mt. Everest in Asia without oxygen," Kena said, "albeit at great risk, and it is many times the height of this mountain, over 8800 meters. Today, he could climb less than 3500 meters without suffering from oxygen deprivation. The atmosphere is much thinner now. With the forests gone and the ocean's plankton vanished, there is less oxygen."

"My ears," Hramack complained. "They popped." He rubbed his ears with his hands.

Kena smiled. "Mine also. It is the change in air pressure as our bodies adjust to the height."

As the ache in his ears slowly subsided, Hramack looked at Travin. The hunter had grown even more taciturn than usual since their capture. Hramack hoped Travin would not try to escape. They would need his strength later. Anseer was too weary to attempt an escape. The lower oxygen did not help the woodcarver's breathing. Travin fussed over him as if he were his own son. Hramack thought the hunter's concern for the woodcarver was the only thing preventing him from escaping. His guilt at bringing Anseer with him weighed heavily on his conscience.

Finally, they were able to look out over the valley floor from a ledge some 700 meters above it. Hramack felt dizzy as he looked over the edge back down the way they had come. Though it was no cooler even at that altitude, a slight breeze helped ease their heat burden somewhat. The view was spectacular.

The land was awash with moonlight, softening the harsh terrain. Somewhere below them far to the south lay the valley in which Ningcha safely nestled in its canyon rim. Hramack could see for scores of kilometers. The cactus grove of their capture was clearly visible, as were other small copses of cactus or trees dotting the horizon running in a straight line above the underground river. The flow of water that allowed Ningcha to survive also provided life for many others, including Pueblo Nuevo. They must see their mission to its end. Ningcha, Pueblo Nuevo, and the land itself depended on them.

Reluctantly, he turned away from the riveting view and followed Grey Eagle towards a small flat mesa some ten kilometers across the plains on the other side of the plateau upon which they now stood. Grey Eagle pointed towards a small speck at the mesa's base, barely visible in the distance.

"Pueblo Nuevo." He beamed proudly as he spoke. "We will be there *abinigo*, before sunrise."

From the edge of the plateau, Hramack could see several points of light flickering around the base of the distant mountain. "What are those?" he asked Grey Eagle.

"Some choose to live away from the village in their own *hogans*. They grow their own crops but help the village as needed. They are protected from danger by the steep cliffs surrounding the village." He lit a torch and waved it a few times before extinguishing it. "They will know we are coming."

Their path wound down the side of the mountain, curving westward until their destination vanished from view. Large slabs of rock had cracked and slid down the mountain, leaning against its flanks like stone buttresses. Their path led them beneath several of these splinters of stone. One such passage contained carvings of long-vanished animals men had scratched onto its surface. A large spiral dominated one wall. Hramack stopped to rub his hands appreciatively across the spiral, knowing that those who first settled the land centuries ago had carved them.

"These were carved by the *adaadin*, our ancestors," Grey Eagle said proudly. "Long before white men came to this land my people lived here among these mountains." He touched the spiral almost reverently. "At certain times of the year, a sliver of light entering through cracks overhead bisects the spiral markings or touches its outer edges. My ancestors knew in this way when to plant crops or when the snows would come."

Hramack noted the pride with which Grey Eagle spoke of his ancestors. Such a calendar was a great accomplishment for a civilization that had neither wheel nor machines and saw the stars above solely with the naked eye.

"There are many such places throughout the lands," Grey Eagle continued. "Some have hundreds of animals carved or painted on the rocks. They were an artistic people."

"I see your people decorate your clothing. You are the inheritors of your ancestors' artistry."

Grey Eagle smiled at Hramack's words of praise. "Some things should not be forgotten," he said as he walked away.

The terrain at the base of the plateau was uneven, and small clumps of cacti thrust upwards between cracks in the rock, reaching out to prick him as he passed almost as if on purpose. Hramack envied the men of Pueblo Nuevo their leather britches. Dozens of small quills stuck him through his thin trousers. He plucked them out, but the small punctures still burned. As they descended one steep arroyo to a well-worn path below, Grey Eagle observed the shadows apprehensively. His companions also seemed uneasy.

Kena questioned Grey Eagle's behavior. "You look worried. Are we in danger?"

Grey Eagle replied without taking his gaze from the horizon. "We should have been met by scouts from our village. There is no sign that they have been here, but there are signs that others have passed through and tried to cover their tracks."

Even as he spoke, the first arrow struck the ground at his feet.

"Take cover!" he yelled. "Over there." Grey Eagle pointed at a pile of nearby boulders.

As Hramack ran, he saw one of Grey Eagle's men lying on the ground with an arrow protruding from his back. The man had not screamed. It was the first time he had seen someone killed other than by accident. He did not even know the man's name. Then he noticed the dead man had carried all their weapons. They lay scattered across the ground where he dropped them. Without weapons, they were defenseless. Ignoring the danger, he took a deep breath, leaped from the protection of a small shrub, and ran to retrieve the fallen weapons. Another arrow sang, passing within inches of his ear as he sprinted for the cover of the rocks. He smiled as he handed his father his bow. Kena's stern look wiped the smile from his face.

"That was dangerous," he snapped.

"*Tsosts'id,*" White Elk broke in. He held out his hand with fingers spread widen and raised two fingers on his other hand. "Seven of them." He looked at his companion lying on the ground and frowned. "Little Otter is dead."

Grey Eagle at Kena grimly, then at Anseer cowering behind a boulder. "If you three can fight, we may have a chance. I see you have your weapons." He glanced at Hramack with admiration in his face for his Hramack's quick actions.

Kena strung his bow and, after taking careful aim, let fly an arrow. A sharp yell erupted from the tangle of shrubs. He looked smugly at Grey Eagle.

"You'll do," Grey Eagle replied.

"Little Otter carried most of the water," White Elk said. "We cannot wait them out until help arrives. It will be sunrise soon. We must make our move soon while it is still dark enough for cover."

The others nodded their agreement.

"Travin and I will work our way down that arroyo and try to get behind them. You two can cover us." Kena looked at Hramack. "Watch our flank, son."

Hramack gripped his Little Otter's bow and took a deep breath before signaling his readiness. He lacked his father's skill with a bow, but his knife was of little use to him in this situation. He felt an uneasy queasiness in the pit of his stomach much like when he had faced the nightstalker, but knew he had to summon his courage. This was no time to let his fear endanger the others.

"Try to stay low," Grey Eagle advised. "If things go bad for us, go to Pueblo Nuevo. Tell them Grey Eagle vouches for you." He clasped Kena's hand firmly. "*Et eh*, together." When Kena opened his hand, a small, carved wooden amulet lay in his palm in the likeness of an eagle. Kena thrust it into his pocket.

Grey Eagle and White Elk let loose a flurry of arrows as Kena and Travin crawled down the length of the small arroyo. Hramack slipped into the brush on his hands and knees, paralleling his father. Cover was sparse, but he used the deep shadows cast by the moon. The soft whisper of the bowstring came from just ahead of him as one of the hidden Marauders fired an arrow. He watched with apprehension as his father worked his way out of the arroyo and into a mesquite thicket. Kena drew himself to his knees, sighted along an arrow, pulled tight the string, and released it – all in a split-second.

A yelp of pain and the thud of a body falling signaled his arrow had found its mark. As Kena turned to motion for Travin to join him, two men suddenly jumped him. They wore rags for clothing and had rags wound around their heads and faces like a burnoose. Their hands held long knives whose blades gleamed wickedly in the moonlight. Kena parried their blows with his bow, trying to pull his own knife with his free hand. Before Travin could assist Kena, a third Marauder attacked him as well.

Without thinking, Hramack dropped Little Otter's bow, rushed across the open ground, and leaped into the fray, quickly knocking one man from his father's back. This gave Kena the time to draw his knife from its scabbard and plunge it deep into the second man's chest. Hramack's foe picked himself up and turned to flee. He had gone less than three paces when he staggered, an arrow suddenly protruding from his neck. Grey Eagle stepped from behind a boulder.

"I thought you might need some help. I saw them headed towards you and decided to join in." He used his foot to turn over the Marauder lying on the ground with a deep wound in his chest. Barely visible through the folds of cloth encircling his face, the man's skin was alabaster white. Dark bands circled his eyes, giving him a skeletal appearance. "Dead."

"This one still breathes," Travin said. He stood over a third Marauder. His knife protruded from the man's shoulder. The Marauder moaned in pain. Travin ground his foot into the wound and yanked his blade free. His moans turned to screams of pain.

"Good. We'll take him to the village for questioning."

Hramack examined the dead Marauder more closely. The Marauder had filed his teeth to sharp points. Grey Eagle's tales of cannibalism seemed less a fantasy now. The idea of eating human flesh sickened Hramack. He rubbed his finger along the man's cheek. It came away white, revealing heavily tanned flesh beneath it. He sniffed the greasy smudge on his finger and snorted.

"It smells like rancid meat."

"They cover their flesh with a mixture of rendered fat, talc, and creosote to protect them from the sun," Grey Eagle said. "It smells slightly less offensive than their bodies."

A scream in the distance made Hramack to jump. Grey Eagle shrugged. "The remaining three tried to flee, but one carries your father's arrow. White Elk sees that they do return to carry word to his friends. He will also make certain no more marauders are near. He will catch up later. Come. Let's carry this devil spawn with us." He looked at Kena, Travin, and Hramack and grinned broadly. "You did well. I will speak for you before our Chief."

Travin stared toward the scream and growled, "I will help White Elk."

Before Kena could stop him, he loped away. Grey Eagle watched Travin's departure with a frown.

"Your companion is fearless, but he carries a heavy burden on his shoulders. Darkness surrounds him like a cloud. I fear for him."

Hramack wanted to go after the taciturn hunter, but Grey Eagle was eager to leave. Binding the wounded Marauder securely, they half-dragged, half-carried him back to where they had left Anseer. The young woodcarver leaned against a boulder with his knife in his hand, trembling in fear. He lowered it when he saw them.

"I thought you were dead," he gasped.

No," Grey Eagle said. "Your friends fought bravely."

"What of Little Otter?" Hramack asked, glancing at the fallen man.

"White Elk will bury him when he returns this way." Grey Eagle walked over to Little Otter and removed a colorful beaded necklace, carefully worked with silver threads, from around his neck. "We will return this Betrothal Locket to his wife. It will serve for the Parting Ceremony."

The Marauder moaned. Grey Eagle hit him with his bow. "Walk, carrion," he yelled. "I will not carry you. I will stake you to the ground for the vultures to enjoy."

Hramack was not certain if Grey Eagle would do such a barbarous thing, but the Marauder seemed to have no doubts. He walked. Hramack studied the Marauder carefully.

The Marauder wore a mix-matched set of ragged, filthy clothing made from roughly woven cloth and poorly cured leather and a pair of worn leather boots. Angry black and brown patches, like a rash, covered his skin visible through the foul-smelling grease covering his flesh. He was filthy and stank like carrion. His body was emaciated and most of his teeth had fallen out, leaving only the sharply filed canines.

"Scurvy," Kena said, noticing Hramack's interest in the man's missing teeth. "A lack of fruit causes it. I imagine his bones are brittle also."

"I will break them for him if he dawdles," Grey Eagle threatened.

"What is the rash?" Hramack asked.

"Probably skin cancers caused by prolonged exposure to the sun," Kena replied. "The animal fat they rub over their bodies might reduce sunburns, but it won't keep out Ultraviolet radiation as well as our sunscreen."

"Is he dying?"

Kena nodded, his face expressing deep sorrow in spite of the fact the marauder tried to kill him. "He will never see thirty years."

It was more than Hramack could imagine – dying so young because of your lifestyle. Most villagers in Ningcha lived until their eighties, some longer. They would have to do something for these people if they were to rebuild the world. With their prisoner in tow, Grey Eagle, Kena, Travin, Anseer, and Hramack soon came within sight of Pueblo Nuevo. White Elk and Travin caught up to them a short time later, but said nothing about the other Marauders, though the blood smears on their clothing spoke volumes. Grey Eagle merely nodded at their arrival. Hramack noticed a look of satisfaction in Travin's eyes, as though he had finally found an outlet for his suppressed anger. The village hunter had become warrior.

Though he could not see the dark cloud Grey Eagle had described, Hramack worried for him.

16

PUEBLO NUEVO

A S THEY CAME TO THE FIRST BUILDING AT THE OUTSKIRTS OF THE VILLAGE, Kena stopped and retrieved the amulet from his pocket.

"You might need this," he said as he returned it to Grey Eagle.

Grey Eagle took the amulet and placed it around his neck. "I thank you. It was given to me long ago by my wife the night before our Betrothal."

"I noticed the word Nada inscribed inside. Isn't that Spanish for nothing?"

Grey Eagle chuckled. "Nada is my name, Nada Puhuyesva. I am Hopi of the *Mishungovi* clan of the Third Mesa. Grey Eagle is my warrior name."

"We have no other name. I am simply Kena."

"Then I will give you one for your bravery. You are *Toho*, the cougar, for your bravery."

"Toho, I like it."

Grey Eagle nodded. "*Ya'ateeh*, it is good."

"What about me?" Hramack asked, feeling left out. The idea of having a second name that described your attributes delighted him. Others often called his father, Healer; Kaffa was Precept. Even Chu Li was High Priest.

Grey Eagle smiled. "You will be *Ta'avo*, the rabbit, for your speed."

"Ta'avo," Hramack repeated to get the pronunciation right. "I suppose rabbit is better than mouse."

Shouts of joy greeted them as they entered the village. The chorused ululations of the women startled Hramack, but he soon realized they were vocal displays of happiness. Hramack counted over five hundred people who had turned out for their arrival, more people than he had ever seen in his life. Grey Eagle, it seemed, was a well-respected member of the pueblo.

White Elk quickly disappeared into the crowd with a beautiful young girl, who Grey Eagle explained was White Elk's fiancée. Hramack felt a pain of longing for Teela, but his curiosity drew his attention back to the village. He was amazed at the pueblo's strategic location. Built into a massive hollow carved by the wind into the native rock much like Ningcha, it was high enough above the valley floor to provide protection, yet was easily accessible by a broad, winding path. Two stone towers, one on each side of the path, guarded it from attack. The overhang of the cliff protected them from dangers above as well as from the worst of the sun's fury and the elements, yet it had none of the rough, unfinished feeling of Ningcha.

Groves of trees, most of them bearing fruit, lined the path and were scattered in small copses across the valley's broad floor. Carefully constructed stone aqueducts carried precious water from large, rock-lined pools and cisterns higher up the mountain to each small grove and garden. The roof of each pueblo contained a small garden, many with vines cascading over the edge of the roof and down the sides of the walls. The people of Pueblo Nuevo utilized every square meter of their small domain to provide sustenance both for the body and for the soul. The village was hauntingly beautiful. Hramack thought Pueblo Nuevo made Ningcha look like a ground squirrel's burrow hastily scratched in the earth. Grey Eagle was right to be proud of his village.

"How do you maintain the plants without the water from the springs?" Hramack asked of Grey Eagle. He hoped he could learn how to save Ningcha's slowly dying crops.

"There is a small artesian spring bubbling from the back of the overhang," Grey Eagle explained. "It provides enough water for now, along with that which we have stored in our pools, but without the underground wells, our cattle and sheep will soon die. We cannot provide enough water for the grasses they eat, and we cannot move them elsewhere with the threat of Marauders looming."

"Then it is to both our village's mutual benefit to seek out the source of the springs and try to aid their return," Kena added.

As they spoke, a small entourage of men made their way through the gathered crowd toward them. The woman leading them wore a long tunic of brightly colored woven wool. She carried a long shepherd's crook with bands of around the crook glinting like fire in the bright sunlight. Though her long, white hair showed her to be older than Grey Eagle, she retained a look of vitality and strength that marked her as a vibrant leader. She walked proudly, her sandaled feet almost gliding along the path.

"Our Chief, Kosono the Seer," Grey Eagle presented his leader to them.

Hramack noticed the sudden tenseness in Travin's stance as the leader approached the group, though he did not know if from fear or respect. The hunter's hand tightened on the hilt of his knife, whose blade still bore traces of blood, and then slowly relaxed, as she smiled.

Chief Kosono halted her small train of attendants a few steps from the group and raised her hand palm outward. Her languid but intense eyes scanned each of them for a long moment. Hramack felt certain the Chief could read his mind and tried to quiet his thoughts.

His anxiety vanished as the Chief extended both her hands to Grey Eagle, who clasped them and touched them with his forehead. She repeated the gesture for Kena and Hramack, who followed Grey Eagle's example. Hramack noted the leader's hands were wrinkled and calloused, but her grip remained strong.

"So, Grey Eagle, I see you have returned with friends," Chief Kosono said with a glimmer of laughter in her eyes. "It is good. This I saw in a vision. I have arranged for their comfort. It may be that they are our only salvation. The stars themselves move for them." She turned to Kena. "I bid you welcome to our pueblo and extend to you all that we have to offer." As she waved her arm to encompass the village, two women came forward, took Kena and Hramack by their arms, and began to lead them towards the pueblo through the throng. Kena glanced at Grey Eagle questioningly.

He smiled broadly. "Please go with them. You will be able to bathe after your long journey and to eat. I will inform Chief Kosono of all that has occurred and of what you seek. She will seek council with the Elders and call for you soon. Go. Rest."

"What about Anseer and Travin?" Hramack called out.

"Your weary friend will be sent to our *hataalii*, our medicine singer, to tend to his needs."

Kena protested. "He needs more than songs sung over him."

Grey Eagle smiled. "Our *hataalii* is wise in our traditional ways and natural remedies, but she also employs knowledge and tools gleaned from the *biligana*. He will heal." He pointed to Travin. "This one will accompany me to my home."

Travin turned to Grey Eagle and nodded his acceptance to the invitation. Hramack glanced at his father. "They will be safe, as will we," Kena said.

Worn out from the long journey, the idea of a bath and rest sounded too good to be true. Hramack allowed the young woman who held his hand to lead him away from the crowd. He caught a glimpse of Kena ahead of him. He turned to his sponsor. Her dark eyes looked him up and down appreciatively.

"What is your name?" he asked.

"Aseara," she answered smiling. Her voice was a song spoken. Her lips were full and colored with a red substance that made them luscious and inviting. "What is yours?"

"Hramack," he answered, trying not to stare at her.

"Come, Hramack."

Aseara took Hramack to a small but comfortable pueblo near the edge of the canyon. Her home was on the lower floor. It consisted of a large open great room with comfortable couches and chairs, a kitchen that opened onto a covered veranda, and a bedroom. A fireplace dominated the great room. A large black kettle hung suspended over a low flame from a metal rod. The people of Pueblo Nuevo cooked with fire, as did his father. A neat stack of twigs and small sticks gleaned from the grove of trees for fuel rested beside the hearth. The fireplace, like the walls, was made of stone covered with a smooth, plaster-like substance. Hramack ran his hand over it.

"It is adobe," Aseara told him. "We make it from clay."

Many colorful tapestries depicting stylized figures of people and animals hung from the walls. Similar rugs covered the mosaic tile floor. Small, delicately carved animals sat in niches in the walls. The villagers of Pueblo Nuevo surrounded themselves with art.

Trying not to be too obvious, Hramack examined his hostess. Aseara was older than he by a handful of years, but her dark eyes were bright and full of mischief. Her long, silken hair reminded him of Teela, though Aseara's hair was as black as a moonless night and as straight as the fall of water plunging into the Pools of Yarah. When she stood near him, Hramack caught the faint scent of apple blossoms. In spite of his thoughts of Teela, Hramack felt himself drawn to this exotic woman.

"You must remove your clothing now," she said.

"What ... I don't ..." he stammered in embarrassment.

Aseara smiled and pointed to the veranda. Hramack noticed a paper screen at its edge. "You may bathe there. I will take your dirty clothes."

Hramack's face reddened. "Oh."

He stood behind the screen painted with a waterfall scene, removed his filthy clothing, and handed them to Aseara. He felt slightly uncomfortable standing naked near her in spite of the screen between them, but she showed no sign of embarrassment.

"I will bring clean clothing for you," she offered, wrinkling her nose in disgust. "These garments have lost their usefulness." She tossed them in a pile on the floor.

The shower was open to the sky, but the screen and a row of young trees provided ample privacy from passersby. Wastewater ran down a gutter to a stone tank downslope. Pipes ran from a wooden tank on the roof to the showerhead above him. Unsure of the proper etiquette of bathing with a water shortage, Hramack asked Aseara. Her voice was as soft as her skin and as gentle as her eyes.

"First, wet your skin with a small amount of water. Then use this gel," she offered him a small bowl of pale green paste. "We gather it from a cactus flower. Rub it over your body." She gently rubbed the cool paste onto his arms. Its white lather produced a mild tingling sensation on his skin. Aseara's ministrations were soothing, but Hramack's embarrassment got the better of him.

He gently removed her soft hands from his body and said, "Perhaps it would be best if I do this."

Aseara giggled. "As you wish." She wiped her hands on a towel, and then continued with her instructions. "Lastly, rinse it off. The gel will remove all dirt and leave your skin soft and clean. It takes very little water to remove it. The wastewater will feed the trees. The cleanser will not harm them."

Hramack followed her instructions, surprised that the shower provided both hot and cold water. He had seen no evidence of electricity in the village.

"The water is hot. How do you heat it.?"

From deeper in the house, she answered, "One line runs directly from the water tank on the roof, but a second snakes around the roof, allowing the sun to heat it."

Passive solar heating, he thought. The people of Pueblo Nuevo were not primitive in spite of their clinging to their ancient roots. In fact, in many ways they were more advanced and in tune with their environment than the people of Ningcha.

After he finished his relaxing shower, he dried off with a large, soft towel and felt remarkably clean and refreshed. It had been many months since he had felt as clean. He would try to take some of the gel back to Ningcha. It saved a remarkable amount of water, and from the fact that the cactus quill punctures in his leg were no longer burning, he suspected the gel could be useful as a medicinal balm for burns and cuts.

Thoughts of Ningcha quickly reminded him of the reason for his journey. Things could be bad there for his people already. It was imperative that his father be able to convince Chief Kosono to help them in their quest. A yawn cut his thoughts short. First, he would rest. Aseara had left a thin robe in hanging beside the shower. He donned the knee-length robe and eyed the comfortable looking bed but instead chose a rope hammock strung between two poles used to support the roof of the veranda. Several wool blankets with intricate designs lay folded on the hammock. He sat down on the hammock experimentally. Its swinging motion startled him at first, but as he lay down, he was pleased to find it surprisingly comfortable.

In spite of his fatigue, Hramack found sleep too elusive. His mind overflowed with thoughts and questions. He was eager to find out about these strange, new people. Until their encounter with Grey Eagle and his men, he had thought the villagers of Ningcha the only survivors in the world. There were also the savage Marauders to consider. If these two groups survived and flourished in spite of the wars, the Upheaval, and the centuries of solar radiation, it was possible that many more had survived. How did so many people manage to eke out a living in such inhospitable surroundings? Were there places on Earth less ravaged by the Upheaval and by the sun's deadly flares than the lands of the Southwest? Perhaps it was time to seek them out. Only by acting as a united force could they hope to overcome the inhospitable climate and lack of resources. Perhaps they had already made a small start with this meeting.

Aseara returned with clothing similar to that worn by Grey Eagle and White Elk: leather pants and jacket with a shirt and under-clothes made of a soft material.

"Cotton," she told him as he gently rubbed the cloth. "It comes from fibers of a plant we weave. We also weave wool and work the leather of our cattle."

Hramack donned his new clothing and walked around the room. The leather britches were surprisingly light and comfortable, and the cotton underclothing much more supple than the linen he had been wearing.

"Thank you," he said.

She bowed her head. "They belonged to my husband."

Hramack glanced at her. "I ... I didn't know," he stammered. His sexual thoughts about her embarrassed him, causing his cheeks to redden.

She smiled and touched his hand gently. "Do not be embarrassed. It has been a year since his death."

Under Aseara's guidance, he began to explore the village. Like Aseara's home, the other apartments of the pueblos were large and open, blending seamlessly into the environment. Each home possessed many doors and were open to covered verandas, which the villagers seemed to prefer. Those homes on the top floors of the pueblos contained frosted glass skylights to allow in light but shaded to reduce the intensity. Though most people lived in the main build-ings of the pueblo itself, many smaller, single-family dwellings Grey eagle had called hogans lay scattered about the area. Even here, it seemed some preferred their privacy. One building bore many floor-to-ceiling glass panels etched with scenes of forest and lakes.

"A reminder of what we have lost," Aseara replied to his unspo-ken question.

Although now empty, the building once held a pool for swim-ming. The thought of swimming in a pool of water prompted visions of the empty Pools of Yarah. He sadly turned away. The walkways were works of art: colored stones intricately fitted together in mosaic patterns and cemented in place. The walkways curved whenever possible with wide, flowing steps to negotiate slopes. A stream cascaded alongside one walkway, providing music as it poured from between thin, flat stones into catch basins filled with hollow metal balls. Even the trees bore decorations. Ribbons and carved wooden ornaments hung from the lower branches and whirled in the wind. Black and gray squirrels leaped from branch to branch, chattering at Hramack as he walked past. A myriad of birds, most of which he did not recognize, flitted through the branches. Compared to Ningcha, Pueblo Nuevo was an Eden.

From a rise, he spotted many pueblos and small hexagon-shaped buildings Aseara called hogans dotting the valley. Many appeared empty and abandoned. Noticing the direction of his gaze, Aseara said, "Today we number less than a thousand. Once we were five times that number. Our numbers grow fewer, while our enemies increase."

Hramack nodded. "Our village suffers the same problem."

A deep, circular pit in a clearing away from other structures intrigued him. Unlike other roofs he had seen, roughly split cedar logs covered this one. The only entrance was a square hole in the roof's center. The end of a wooden ladder protruded through the opening.

"Is this a cistern?" he asked.

Her smile was slightly chiding but kind. "No this is the village *kiva*, a holy place. It is for our religious ceremonies. Our legends say our ancestors came to this world through a *sippapu*, or hollow reed. The *kiva* is round for this reason. It represents our beginnings."

"At least your people remember and honor your past," Hramack said bitterly. "Mine seek to forget it."

"Even our past has dark moments, but these, too, are a part of it and must be remembered."

Hramack smiled. "Show me more."

Many walls and the sides of homes displayed intricately designed, multi-hued mosaics and vibrant paintings. Each home seemed in competition with its neighbor for attention. Hramack remembered the dull, white-on-white homes of Ningcha and felt shame. It was as if his people had built their homes with only refuge from the weather in mind. In Ningcha, each person strived to become one with the village, a part of the whole. Here, each took pleasure in their individuality, yet the whole became more than the sum of those individuals. The pueblo took on a life of its own.

He discovered a forest of windmills sprouting near the desert's edge, providing electricity for the village's buildings, yet they chose to cook with fire and light their homes with candles. Unlike the looping metal bands of Ningcha's windmills, these were circles of woven thin wooden strips atop stone towers, a low-tech approach but just as efficient. Aseara showed him a fountain in a small alcove near a vine-covered walkway spraying water into the air. The water fell onto a series of metal dishes before cascading back into the fountain. Netting above the fountain prevented evaporation from the sun.

Hramack reached down and splashed a handful of the cool water on his face. On an impulse, he splashed Aseara. She laughed and pushed him to the ground. She was surprisingly strong for her slender frame. As she reached to help him up, he tripped her. She fell on him laughing and throwing handfuls of a creeping groundcover into his face. He rolled away spluttering, picking tufts of pungent leaves from his mouth.

"You have little water," he commented, holding out one flowered stem, "Yet you use it wisely." He sniffed the plant, pleased with the scent. "What is this?"

She wiped dirt from his brow and laughed. "It is called wild lilac. This, cotoneaster, creeping juniper, and coyote brush are hardy xeric groundcovers to keep the soil from blowing away. Water is scarce, but they use very little water." She pointed to the fountain. "This water is for all to use. We could not bear to forego its soothing music at night. Treated wastewater irrigates the plants. It would better serve to water trees or food, but it is a small price to pay for the comfort it gives in return."

Hramack nodded. His own people took the same care with potted flowers. At least they had until the Pools of Yarah had dried up. Most were now leafless stems. He listened to the soothing metallic tinkling of the fountain with his eyes closed and smiled. He roused only when Aseara nudged him.

"Come," she said.

They walked down the sidewalks between homes as both men and women prepared vegetables for their midday meals, but there seemed to be more women than men in the village. He asked Aseara the reason.

"Many of our men have died fighting Marauders. Others are away guarding the passes." She stopped talking and glanced away. She looked back with tears forming in her eyes. "My own man died last year while protecting one of our distant cactus groves from Marauders."

Hramack tried to offer words of sympathy, but they sounded weak in his own ears. Aseara, though, accepted them for what they were and thanked him. "What of your village?" she asked. "Are there many women there?"

They had come to a small grove of citrus trees, dozens of them: lemon, orange, and grapefruit. There were only two such trees in Ningcha, and it was one of Teela's favorite spots, especially when the trees were blooming, filling the air with their fragrance. Hramack thought of his beautiful Teela. "Only one I care about," he answered.

Aseara saw the look on his face and replied softly, "She is a lucky woman, I think."

Hramack blushed. "We have many young men without wives or hopes of one. Perhaps our two villages could arrange an exchange of people and of cultures."

"That would be a blessing to our women," she agreed. "Many sleep alone at night. That is not good." She looked into Hramack's eyes and squeezed his hand. "It has been many months since my Long Walker's death. Will you sleep with me tonight?" she asked.

Her unexpected request dumfounded him. He was also flattered. She was very beautiful, but he loved Teela very much.

Aseara noticed his reluctance and perhaps understood the reason. "In my culture, women choose the men. Sex is a way of giving to each other and a means of strengthening bonds. Between husband and wife, it is more. Between you and me, it will be a release. Nothing more if you wish it so, just a way to explore each other's sexual urges and to fulfill them."

To show Hramack her desire, she took his trembling hand and gently placed it on her left breast. Her nipples were large and hard and twitched slightly as his eager hand seemed to explore her breast with a mind of its own. She slowly pushed the top of her tunic down and exposed her breasts for Hramack's view. They were magnificently large and shaped somewhat like the pori fruit. The skin between them blushed red with excitement.

His breath came faster as Aseara's hand guided his over her warm breasts, exploring their softness and warmth. "I've never... I don't..." he stuttered.

"We do not have to wait until tonight," she moaned softly. "I will teach you all you need to know. Your woman will be grateful."

She took him to a stone bench behind a grove of trees. She lowered his head to her breasts and he kissed them softly, hesitantly, exploring her nipples with his tongue. Her soft moans excited him as she first pulled his hair, and then pushed his head into her bosom.

Her hands were not idle and explored Hramack's eager body beneath his tunic. All thoughts of Teela disappeared from his mind by the rising heat of passion. Lost in each other's desire, they fell to the ground sheltered from view by the trees. Aseara patiently helped Hramack through the awkward phase of becoming a man while fulfilling her own needs. Any person passing by would have heard and recognized the sounds of passion, but they were alone. Hramack's cries of release caused a flock of birds to take flight.

Aseara pulled Hramack to her and cradled his head on her heaving belly.

"I have failed Teela," he moaned. "She will never forgive me."

"No, you have not failed her. She need never know. Admitting what we have done to her will only confuse her. She cannot understand my peoples' ways. It will be a secret between us. I shall cherish it dearly."

Though he believed her words, his heart told him different. However, she was right. He would never tell her. It was his burden to bear alone. *Why then, do I not feel guilty?*

Kena awakened from a refreshing sleep and changed into his clean, new clothes. Chief Kosono and Grey Eagle entered the room.

"I hope you have rested well," Chief Kosono ventured.

"Yes, indeed," Kena replied. "And I am cleaner than I have been in weeks. Your cleansing gel is marvelous, and your hospitality has been excellent," he said, showing them his new leather pants and jacket. "Is Hramack enjoying his visit?"

Grey Eagle chuckled. "I am told he is enjoying himself very much under the tender care of Aseara, my cousin." He motioned all to seat themselves on the large pillows strewn about the room.

"And the others?"

"Travin is eager to learn our fighting ways. White Elk says he will make a fine warrior." He rolled his eyes. "The small one is being attended to. Though his mouth belies it, he will recover." He turned to Chief Kosovo. She nodded. "I have spoken with Chief Kosono concerning all we have seen and all that you have told me. She agrees with me that it is in both our best interests to seek out the source of the underground river and try to bring about its return."

Kena released his pent-up breath and sighed with appreciative relief. "I hoped that that would be your answer. I have come a long way and there is farther to go still. It will be good to make that long journey with friends."

The chief spoke, "I will send ten of my men with you and your son. You will guide them, but Grey Eagle will be in charge of all things concerning security. He knows the area well and there are Marauders about. The desert north of here is in the heart of their territory."

"Perhaps there is a safer way," Kena ventured.

"How is that possible?" she asked. "There is only one way north, through the pass."

"We can follow the river underground."

"Impossible," Grey Eagle exclaimed, jumping up and staring at Kena as if he had suggested trying to fly.

"No, wait!" he interjected. "Hramack and I followed the river's course from our village to where Grey Eagle found us. The only danger is that of the river itself, but since there is no water flowing, there will be no danger. We can save many days' water rations by avoiding the searing heat of the sun and travel by day or by night. More importantly, we can travel undetected." He paused to allow the significance of that fact to sink in. "Once there, we can return overland from the north, if we wish. The Marauders will not expect us to enter their territory beneath their feet."

Grey Eagle stood quietly in thought. He became calmer as he pondered Kena's reasoning. Finally, he spoke. "There is wisdom in your idea, Kena. Our greatest danger is that of discovery by the Marauders. If we can slip through their border undetected, it will greatly improve our chances of completing our mission." His vision narrowed as he looked at Kena and admitted, "I tell you this: I do not like this traveling underground. It is ... unnatural. I will agree only because it is necessary."

Chief Kosono nodded. "Grey Eagle agrees with you then, friend Kena," she said. "I trust his judgment. He will choose the men to accompany you. It will be best if you leave soon, before the Marauders learn of their scouting party's demise."

"We can leave tonight," Kena replied.

Grey Eagle raised an eyebrow at this, but said nothing except, "Then I will start gathering supplies and choosing our men."

Chief Kosono stopped him. "No, it is best you wait one more day. You all need rest. Little Otter's spirit must be set free. Even so, the young woodcarver will not be ready to travel."

Kena turned to Chief Kosono. "Can Anseer remain here? He would be of no use to us on this journey."

"Your friend is a talented woodcarver. Our people respect craftsmen. Of course, he may remain here if he wishes. He seems intrigued by the fact we have more women than men."

Kena chuckled. "He would be. What of Travin?"

Grey Eagle spoke up. "He will accompany us. He has said so."

To Chief Kosono, Kena said, "When we met, you said the stars move for us. What did you mean by that?"

The chief closed her eyes as if deep in thought before replying. "I am not sure. Many things I see on my dream walks are unclear. You and your son are our village's best hope. This I see clearly. Without your help, both our villages will die. I see the stars falling to the earth to aid you. This I do not understand. A woman with a head of fire will come to your aid." She sagged as if exhausted by this interpretation of her dreams. "I am old and weary," she apologized. "I must rest."

Chief Kosono and Grey Eagle exited the room, leaving Kena alone with his thoughts. "I hope I know what I'm doing," he said to himself.

17

NIGHTMARE

TEELA AWOKE CRYING AND STRUGGLED WITH THE COVERS OF HER BED. A fine sheen of perspiration covered her trembling body. A nightmare, one so vivid and clear that Teela had watched as if there by Hramack's side, had roused her from her slumber.

Hramack was crawling along a shallow arroyo. She could hear the sounds his body made on the sand. She could even taste the flinty dust he kicked up at the back of her throat. Suddenly, a wild-eyed man leaped from the brush and attacked him. It was at this point that she cried out her useless warning and awoke screaming.

Kaffa entered her room. "Are you all right, granddaughter?" he asked with deep concern, breathless from his hurrying.

As realization came to her of where she was, she fought to control her racing heart. "Yes, Grandfather," she moaned. "I had a terrible dream, a nightmare about Hramack." She sat up on the edge of her bed. "I fear for him. He is in terrible danger; I feel it."

Kaffa brushed her hair with his hand. "There will be danger, yes, but I feel he is equal to the challenge. He is under the protection of Yarah. Help will come from an unlikely source." He smiled. "I too have dreams."

Teela looked at her grandfather, studying his face. He seemed so certain of the truth of his words. His visions had often guided the village through difficult times. *Is he just trying to comfort me, or does he speak the truth?*

"Go back to sleep, Teela. Hramack will return to you soon. His love will see him through."

Kaffa pulled the door closed behind him as he left, but left it open just a crack, as he often did when she was a child awakening from a nightmare. She listened to his footsteps recede as he returned to his room. Sleep did not come for her. She lay there thinking about Hramack until the first light of morning.

✳

Kaffa did not sleep. He pondered his conversation with Chu Li when the High Priest had returned from his unsuccessful attempt to bring back Kena and Hramack.

"It was you who freed Kena and showed him the tunnel, was it not?" Chu Li accused.

"I have heard Kena murdered Eithan in order to escape. Is this not so?" Kaffa answered.

Chu Li seethed. "You meddle too much, old man. It could bring harm to you or your granddaughter."

The threat to Teela energized him. He strode quickly to stand directly in front of the High Priest, towering over him. "If harm comes to Teela, I will see you dead." His voice was firm and filled with conviction. Chu Li backed up, startled by the old man's words. "Perhaps Madras would be willing to speak of his cousin's death. He seems to be in a most somber mood. Perhaps he knows something of Herat's death as well."

Chu Li exploded. By his reaction, Kaffa knew Kena's suspicions concerning the old High Priest's death were true.

"Watch your words, Kaffa. Do not threaten me with your baseless accusations."

"True, only Kena knows the truth about Herat, your High Priest predecessor, and he is not here, but someone other than I saw Eithan summoned to your quarters after Kena and Hramack had fled."

"Who else?" Chu Li demanded; then his eyes lit up. "Teela? It would be wise to watch your tongue, old man."

"I say nothing for now. When Kena returns, then will I speak. Your days are numbered, Chu Li. Mark them well."

Chu Li glared at Kaffa before turning and racing to his home. Kaffa hoped Kena would return soon. Life in the village would be harsh with Chu Li controlling the Council. There was some grumbling already. Many found it difficult to believe Kena capable of murder in spite of Chu Li's assertion to the contrary. Chu Li's disappointing return with two men dead and one injured did nothing to lift people's fallen spirits. Sending Travin and Anseer in pursuit of Kena seemed to many petty and a misuse of good men.

As he had on many sleepless nights of late, Kaffa sat in his comfortable chair staring out the window at the sleeping village. Thoughts of the dying village plagued him. If the waters did not flow soon, it mattered little if Kena returned or not. He was an old man. Teela needed someone more able to protect her from Chu Li. She needed Hramack. He hoped his dreams did not mislead him.

18

INTO THE BOWELS OF THE EARTH

A T THE RISING OF THE MOON, A PARTY OF FOURTEEN MEN SET OUT FROM Pueblo Nuevo for the nearest entrance to the dry river tunnel, ten men from Pueblo Nuevo and Grey Eagle at their head, and three representing Ningcha – Kena, Hramack, and Travin. Fewer men would have left them vulnerable to attack. More would have been logistically impossible to feed in the sparse country through which they would pass and would have seriously diminished the village's capacity to defend itself. Hramack wondered what Grey Eagle would think if he learned that he and his father were outlaws accused of murder, and that Travin and Anseer had been dispatched by the High Priest to apprehend them.

Anseer had followed Kena's advice and accepted Chief Kosono's invitation to remain in Pueblo Nuevo. He made no pretense of his doubt about the wisdom of their journey. To Hramack's amazement, several single females had shown a romantic interest in him, and the villagers found his woodcarving skills intriguing. Travin, more taciturn than ever but changed in some sublime way by his fight with the Marauders, had shown some amusement at Anseer's decision.

"His injuries are too severe for our journey but too insignificant to interfere with his attempts to woo the women," he said.

The most accessible entrance to the river tunnel was located at the edge of the desert nearly five kilometers from the village. The journey there was uneventful. The songs of night birds and the chirruping of crickets set the pace of their march. Though the aqueducts did not extend that far from the village, groves of trees and small patches of melons and other vegetables lined the road. Carefully maintained by the villagers in plots of rich soil and compost, the gardens provided both vegetables and a diverse habitat for wildlife that somehow managed to dig under or crawl over the fine mesh fences surrounding them.

Just outside the village, Hramack saw his first cow. The skinny, buff-colored creature had long horns and a sad face. It stood staring longingly over the fence at a patch of squash as it chewed on a clump of ground cover. The tantalizingly delicious aroma of squash blossoms and ripe tomatoes filling the air made Hramack's mouth water in spite of their large send-off banquet. He recalled the banquet as he walked.

Aseara had sat next to him on the ground around a large bonfire playing, stroking his thigh when no one was looking. He had been embarrassed when she had presented him a beautiful silver wristband inset with polished pieces of turquoise.

"It is for your Teela," she explained. "My heart goes with you on your journey to the north. Guard yourself well and return to her."

Kena looked at him questioningly. Hramack merely shrugged his shoulders.

"You are very brave to undertake this journey," she added. "You must love your people very much."

The thunder of a dozen drums drowned out further conversation, as twenty young women dressed in long, flowing blue and red skirts and colorful blouses entered the circle and began to dance clockwise slowly around the fire. The tiny bells they wore around their ankles and wrists tinkled a counterpoint to the pounding of the drums. Their feet stamping the hard earth mimicked the rhythm of the drumbeat. Young boys stood at the edge of the circle shaking rattles made from gourds.

"What is this?" Hramack asked Aseara. He had to lean close to her for her to hear, and the scent of her perfume forced his mind back to their lovemaking. He fought the urge to kiss her.

"It is the *Hozhoo ji*, the Blessingway ceremony. We perform if for our young men who are leaving, to protect them. It is for you as well," she added with a wink. She pointed to a man sitting across the fire from them making a sand painting by carefully sifting colored sand through his fingers. "Masali is our hataalii, our Healer and spiritual leader. The sand painting will guard you against evil spirits."

"Do you believe in evil spirits?" he asked, surprised.

"No, but there is evil out there."

The women began to chant in their native language. He could not understand the words, but felt the energy of their message. Eventually, more of the villagers got up to dance. Aseara tried to get him to dance, but he was too uncomfortable with his lack of rhythm to try.

He had not answered question her then, but her words had set his mind to the task of discerning the real reason for his going. It was not bravery. The prospect of death frightened him. The needs of the village were great, and his father had taught him that often one man willing to risk his life for the welfare of others could make a difference. His father was determined to be that one man. He was the brave one. Kena would have gone alone if necessary, but he could not allow that. Devotion, not bravery, compelled him. His place was by his father's side. Even as he thought it, he knew that was not the entire truth. The real reason was less altruistic – Teela. She would never leave the village. If the village died, she died with it. It was for her that he was willing to risk everything. He could not contemplate a future without her. That thought quickened his steps.

When they came upon the hole leading to the river tunnel, he cast one last look at the familiar stars above. Reluctantly and with great trepidation, he began the descent of the steeply sloping path down into the bowels of the earth.

"It is called the Demon's Mouth," he heard one of Grey Eagle's men say, sounding as reluctant to enter as he was. "It is in such places Skeleton Man dwells."

"Skeleton Man?" Hramack asked. "Who is he?"

"*Masau*," Grey Eagle answered his voice barely above a reverent whisper, "the Spirit of Death."

In silence, they threaded the winding dry river course, only the soft scuffling of their leather boots and moccasins echoing from the cold, rocky walls. Hramack noticed that the strained look of concentration on Grey Eagle's face pulled great valleys into the parched skin around his eyes as he glanced around furtively, searching the walls for some sign of hidden danger. He paused at every turn of the tunnel, listening and peering into the darkness. Grey Eagle appeared more afraid of the tunnel than of any dangers they might have faced above ground.

Hramack agreed with the old man's assessment. His earlier underground journey had been disconcerting. Now, as then, the air seemed much too stuffy and tasteless, and the walls had an unnatural way of advancing and receding in the flickering torchlight. Shadows danced and leaped along the walls, as if in some parody of the ancient ritual dance the villagers at Ningcha performed each year for the return of the life-giving waters.

They marched single file for long hours. When the need for words arose, they whispered. Grey Eagle's nervousness spread among the men like a virus. Men continuously looked over their shoulders to reassure themselves that the others had not abandoned them. Tensions ran high.

Hramack stopped at a sudden movement to his right. Grey Eagle turned quickly at Hramack's sudden pause. A shadow, twice as high as a man, advanced on them. Grey Eagle dropped his torch to the ground and quickly drew his knife. Hramack held his staff before him. The others silently began to reach for weapons. Then, Grey Eagle let out a mighty yell and leapt forward at the shadow. Hramack braced himself for an attack.

The intense light almost blinded Hramack as Kena brought the electric lantern up to full intensity, throwing the entire tunnel into view. Grey Eagle's yell turned into a howl of laughter at the sight of the frightened hare frozen in the lantern's bright light. Everyone began laughing at the top of his lungs, dissolving the long march's tension. Hramack's eyes filled with tears of laughter at the sudden release. When the laughter subsided, they resumed their march a little more lighthearted, leaving the bewildered and confused hare behind them. Their bellies were full and they had no need for meat. It was the hare's lucky night.

"Aye, Grey Eagle, good thing there was only one," yelled out one man in jest. The withering look he received for his comment shut him up quickly. Though the tension had lessened, it was obvious Grey Eagle still did not like the tunnel.

For two days and nights, they carried on, stopping only briefly to sleep and eat with Grey Eagle always taking the first watch, and then pushing them hard to continue. Everyone was eager to leave the tunnel behind him. The endless burrow wore on them, sapping their humor and setting them on edge. Hramack began to doubt the wisdom of his father's plan. He longed for the sky overhead instead of the pressing weight of stone above him. He was relieved when they came upon another space open to the sky. The stars twinkled overhead like familiar friends.

The collapse of the roof was massive. A huge bowl had formed around the hole, teeming with stunted cottonwoods, scraggly pines, mesquite, and dozens of species of cacti.

"This would be an excellent spot to make camp," Kena suggested. "The men need rest and a proper meal."

Hramack watched in amazement as Grey Eagle, who had to be as exhausted as the rest of them, went about the men, talking and joking with them, assigning duties and questioning them about any aches and pains or blisters, a serious problem with such a long distance yet to travel. All the men professed to be in fine spirits and free of any serious injuries.

Travin, however, sat by himself, looking forlorn. Hramack had not spoken to him since they had entered the village of Pueblo Nuevo. He walked over to him and sat down beside him. Travin glanced at Hramack but said nothing.

"Grey Eagle says you are a good warrior," he started.

Travin shook his head. "A good warrior does not fear death," he said sadly.

"Everyone fears death," Hramack replied, relieved that he was not the only one with death on his mind.

"No, a warrior will give his life without thought to save others when the need arises. This I can do."

"Then why the long face?"

He looked at Hramack, and for the first time Hramack saw the haunting fear in his eyes. "I have seen my death," he said through clenched lips, as if trying to prevent the words from leaving his mouth. "I saw my death in the eyes of one I killed, and I know I cannot run from it."

Hramack was silent for a moment. He could see Travin was upset but could not understand why. "Every man dies," he ventured.

Travin nodded. "True, death comes to all whether they wish it or not, but my death will not be an easy one."

Hramack was almost afraid to mention it, but the thought occurred to him. "Is it because of Won?"

Travin shot him such a withering look of despair that it seemed to rush from the man's pores and surround him. His eyes filled with tears as he spoke. "I did what had to be done, but that does not free me from the consequences of my actions. I should have remained by his side until he had Passed."

"Father said nightstalkers were coming."

Travin gripped his spear so tightly the leather bindings squeaked. "Even you have conquered a nightstalker," he said sadly. "I let my fears and Chu Li's words sway me, and now I must redeem my soul."

"Was coming with us an act of absolution?"

Travin shook his head slowly side to side. "No, it was an act of desperation."

He stood and walked away, leaving Hramack disturbed by his words. If Travin sought absolution from his supposed sins, would it affect his judgment? Perhaps he should warn his father. Having Travin in a morose state of mind was not good for the company. He glanced at his father and decided he had heard enough bad news for one day.

Grey Eagle deployed two hunting parties to leave the dell and scour the land for food. Hramack volunteered to accompany one. He needed to be out in the open for a while to think. He and two others headed eastward. Two Clouds was his age but already a seasoned warrior. His arms bore the scars of his battles. Stone Thrower was a year younger, not yet a warrior, but a good hunter. He smiled constantly, cracking jokes to which Hramack seldom got the punch line, but he continued a running barrage as they walked.

The land spread out flat and desolate before the wan light of a crescent moon. The high flat ridges of mesas and sharp peaks of taller mountains surrounded them. With only six hours of moonlight remaining before sunrise, speed was of the essence. He and his companions broke into a trot across the Empty Lands. The trio split up to make their search more effective, but remained within earshot of each other.

Just before dawn, when the eastern sky was beginning to show a reddish glow, he and Two Clouds met to take stock of their finds: two large lizards, several edible fruits, and even a pair of fat rock wrens. Stone Thrower had wandered farther afield. If he had anything to contribute, they could begin the return journey. They had traveled far, and the heat would be intense before they reached the others.

A long, low whistle erupted from a distance ahead of them. "Stone Thrower," Two Clouds said. "Come." He began to run ahead. Hramack followed.

They soon saw Stone Thrower standing in the fading moonlight by a twisted spire of metal. His stance betrayed no danger. He was staring down at his feet. As they came closer, they saw what had caught his attention.

At his feet, a great gash in the earth ran as far as they could see to their right and to their left. The far side was barely visible in the pale moonlight. The bottom was lost in the depths of the darkness, but they knew it was very deep. No stranger to canyons, mountains, and valleys, the beauty and grandeur of the cleft struck the trio with awe.

"*Tsehaaji*," he said.

"A rock canyon," Two Clouds translated. "Surely this was a place of power of the Ancients," he whispered.

Hramack could only agree. He surveyed the area. One of the standing stones near them bore carvings. Hramack traced the words with his finger, wiping the dirt from the grooves. Well-weathered and chipped in places, he could still read them.

"Royal Gorge Bridge. Built 1929," he read. "Yes, Gorge. That is a fitting name for this place." The bridge, of course, had long ago fallen into the gorge, leaving only stone and twisted pieces of metal as reminders that man had ever been there. They walked along the edge of the gorge. As the sun began to creep over the horizon, casting an orange pall around them, they could see the steep granite walls plunging to a dry riverbed below.

"It must be well over three hundred meters to the bottom," Hramack exclaimed. "I can see two lines of metal running beside the river. They look like the rails for a train." He was as excited as a child. He had seen such things in books, but to think that man had once been able to build rails in such difficult places was almost like magic. And the bridge. It put the small bridge over their canyon to shame. Two Clouds called out to him. He was standing beside another twisted piece of metal.

"Look," he said, pointing to a few words visible through the rust. It was a sign. It read, "Denver ... 115 kilometers"

Denver. He knew from history that Denver Dome was located south and east of the old site of the ancient city of Denver. It lay only a tantalizing 4-5 days distant, but the ruins were not their destination. He looked around. According to the old map his father had found, Pueblo had been located nearby. He saw the ruins of a building perched on the cliff opposite them, and twin rails of steel were still visible along the cliff on which they stood. Perhaps one of these railways led to Pueblo. He could simply follow the rails to see the ruins of an ancient city.

A rustle in the brush behind them jolted him out of his daydream. Two Clouds pulled his bow and crept closer. Suddenly, a large deer leapt from the brush and almost landed on top of him. His arrow flew wild. Hramack just stood and stared at the magnificent, startled beast. Two long, spiraling horns rose from its skull and ended in sharp points. The deer stood and stared back at Hramack before resuming its journey. Stone Thrower had better presence of mind and let fly a large rock from his leather sling. True to his name, his throw hit the mark, and the deer fell dead at Hramack's feet.

"Aai! Aai! Aai! Aai! Aai!" Stone Thrower yelled as he danced with glee around the fallen animal. "One throw, and look, more meat than we can carry."

Hramack realized Stone Thrower was right. The sun was now well above the horizon. Loaded down by the weight of the deer, they would be hours on the return journey, and the smell would attract predators and scavengers from kilometers away.

"We must butcher the beast here and take only the best meat and the hide. It is too large a burden to bear in the heat of the day."

"But the horns . . ." Stone Thrower protested.

Two Clouds quieted him. "Hramack is right. The sun is climbing high in the morning sky. We must hurry." He pointed to a carrion bird already beginning to circle above them. "See! Any Marauders about will know exactly where to find us. We must hurry."

They set about quickly removing the deer's hide to repair boots or britches and taking the choice of meat, the heart, and the liver. Reluctantly, they left the remains for the scavengers, first dismembering the carcass to look like scavengers had done it in case Marauders should stumble upon it.

"Look." Stone Thrower pointed to a sign twenty meters below them on a ledge of the gorge. "What does it say?"

Hramack stared down at it, but could not read the faded writing. "I don't know."

"I bet it is important," Stone Thrower said as he unrolled a thin rope he wore coiled around his waist.

"We don't have time to waste," Two Clouds protested. "Besides, it is too dangerous."

"For you, perhaps," Stone Thrower chided. He securely attached the rope around an outcropping of rock and dropped nimbly over the side of the cliff.

Hramack watched in awe as he slid down the rope using hands and feet to slow his descent. He reached the ledge and tried to pull the sign from the tumble of rocks that held it in place, but it was wedged too tightly.

"Come back up," Hramack warned him. "You can't move it."

Stone Thrower dismissed Hramack with a wave and let out a loud 'whoop'. It echoed off the walls – 'whoop-ooop-oop'. Pleased with his new discovery, Stone Thrower called out several times and laughed at the echo.

Two Clouds looked at Hramack in mock disgust. "He is like a child with a new toy. We'll never get him back up."

Hramack listened to Two Clouds with one ear. His other heard a strange, new sound coming from farther down the gorge – like the whistling of the wind. It sent shivers up his spine.

"Stone Thrower," he called again. "Come up. Now!"

Stone Thrower, too, had heard the strange sound. He looked up the canyon, toward the sunrise. "I see something," he yelled up at them.

Dust. Hramack knew then that it was an approaching dust storm causing the whistling sound. The haboob roared down the gorge like a flash flood. There was no time for Stone Thrower to ascend the rope.

"Hold on tightly," he called down, and saw Stone Thrower wrap his arms and legs around the sign's metal support. He turned to Two Clouds. "We must find shelter, too."

Already, the steady roar filled the gorge. He looked around and saw a metal ring embedded in the stone pillar. He pulled on it experimentally and judged it sound. He grabbed Two Clouds by the shoulder and pulled him to the ring. Grabbing the metal ring tightly with both hands, he yelled in Two Clouds' ear.

"Grab me around the waist."

The wind now swept down the gorge like a hurricane. Luckily, only the fringes reached above the lip of the gorge. Even so, Hramack fought to retain his fragile grasp on the ring and that of Two Clouds on him. Almost as quickly as it appeared, the wind was gone. Hramack wondered if it repeated this ritual each day as the rising sun heated the cooler air of the gorge. They hurried to the gorge's edge and looked to see how Stone Thrower had fared. He was not there. The wind had scoured the ledge clean but for the boulders and the metal sign still wedged within them.

"Stone Thrower," Two Clouds yelled uselessly into the depths, but Hramack touched his shoulder to silence him. Stone Thrower was gone, taken by the wind.

They stood for a few minutes as Two Clouds offered prayers for his friend. He withdrew a pinch of white cornmeal from a leather pouch around his waist and sprinkled it into the gorge. A moment later, the gorge sighed. Hramack thought it was just a gust of wind blowing through the gorge, but Two Clouds smiled and said, "Masau accepts Stone Thrower's spirit to the underworld."

Hramack silently asked Yarah to accept his new companion's soul as well. Then, in silence, they gathered their supplies, Stone Thrower's deer, and left.

Upon their return to camp, a great feast was in progress. The other hunting party had also been successful. They had come upon a Bighorn sheep on a small hillock of boulders. It was now roasting over the fire. Kena had seasoned it with herbs he had gathered. Two Clouds and Hramack delivered their meat.

Grey Eagle looked at them, and then searched in the direction from which they had come, instantly alert that something was amiss. "Where is Stone Thrower?"

"Dead," Two Clouds replied, "taken by a foul wind." In silence, he sat down and began to slice their meat into thin strips to dry over the fire.

Hramack described Stone Thrower's death in the gorge to the others. The lively feast quickly became a wake as others joined in with tales of Stone Thrower's deeds. His death was a great loss to the tiny band of explorers. In a harsh life fraught with dangers, death was never welcome, but they understood it. Hramack wondered how the people of Ningcha would handle death. Few of their number died except from old age and more rarely from disease. Death was a relative stranger to them. That might soon change if their journey were not successful.

Hramack had never witnessed death until this journey. His mother, Allana had been the last death in the village, until Ethan's murder. Now, he had seen more deaths than he had his entire village in the last twenty years. It was a harsh world the Scattered Ones had left them.

Satiated by their meal and fortified by swigs of beer from a flask one companion had brought along, they sat back to rest before their return to the inky darkness of the underground river. Hramack told Kena of the gorge and the sign pointing towards Denver.

"115 Kilometers," Kena mused. "If we push ourselves, we could be near Denver Dome in four days." He listened as Hramack described in detail the gorge and the wonders he had seen there. "Perhaps we should explore. You saw a lot of steel, you say. That could be very useful."

Two Clouds walked by and overheard. "We do not have the time, my friend. Every day is precious to us and to our villages. Perhaps later we can visit this place and salvage the steel. I would like to catch a few of those whitetail deer to bring to my people. If we could breed them, they would provide much meat. They seem to be able to graze in much wilder country than our cattle or sheep." He lowered his gaze. "And too, I would like to look for Stone Thrower's bones to return to Pueblo Nuevo for the death rites."

Reluctantly, Kena agreed with Two Cloud's assessment. The sun was already past its zenith. Though not wasted, this day had brought them no closer to their journey's end. The party gathered their supplies and re-entered the daunting darkness of the cavern.

This time, though, Kena produced two lanterns from his pack and their brilliant, white light held the darkness further at bay than the torches. He confessed to Hramack that he did not know how much longer the batteries would last, but weighed the psychological benefits against saving them for later use.

This time the men spoke, joked, and laughed with one another. Even Grey Eagle seemed more at ease. Their bellies were full, and the soothing effects of the beer had not yet worn off.

"They act as if Stone Thrower's death means nothing," Hramack complained.

"Do not be bitter. They see more death than we do in their fight with the Marauders. Because they do not mourn and wear black or sing of his death does not mean they have forgotten. This journey is dangerous and it is not good to dwell too much on death. It could come to any of us at any moment. When they have returned, I'm sure Stone Thrower will be remembered, as they did Little Otter."

His father was right, of course. Dwelling on death only darkened the heart. They would certainly face many dangers in the days to come. Little Otter had been the first man Hramack had seen die.

He imagined there would be many 'firsts' for him on this journey. Attaining adulthood, he was learning, was more than learning the proper way of repairing the windmill or cleaning a solar panel or even healing a fever. Things happened that could change or harden a man's heart if he allowed it. Perhaps this was what had happened to Chu Li. He did not think he could ever be sorry for the High Priest, but now he at least understood the penalty a man pays for losing heart.

A week earlier, he had been concerned only for his father. Now, he and his father were betting their lives and the lives of these new-found friends that they could find the source of the water and return it to Ningcha. It sounded like an impossible task, like reaching for the moon. If they found the water, what could they do? What if a mountain had fallen in its path? Could they dig it out?

Like many other things his father said, Hramack was learning one moved forward with the willingness and trust in Yarah to provide the means. He looked at the men in the line. They had placed their trust in him and in Kena, who were strangers to them. He would not let them down.

The group fell silent as the familiar rhythm of the march settled in. For kilometer after kilometer, they trudged on. By Kena's observation, they were now deep under one of the great mountains to the north. Hramack tried not to think about the thousands of meters and many tons of rock above them.

"The mountains above us are part of the Sangre de Cristos Range, the Blood of Christ, a name derived from their red color seen at dusk," Kena said. "I read that somewhere. Denver Dome lies just beyond them to the east." His voice held a wistful catch at missing the opportunity to visit Denver Dome.

For three more days, they trudged onward. They consumed the last of the smoked meat. Only bread and dried fruit remained, light fare for marching day after day. Water, too, was running low. The tunnel had become straighter and its walls smoother as they continued northward. The tunnel was now rectangular with smoothly curving corners. It was obvious the hands of man had formed at least this part of the river tunnel system. They were finally nearing their goal.

19

PRECIOUS WATER AT LAST

SINCE MIDNIGHT, CATHI LORST AND KAL ANDERSON HAD TRAVEL NORTH-west along the floor of a broad valley. The windswept, hard-packed earth made easier travelling than the broken lands they had been crossing, yet after seven days of walking with little water and almost no rest, each step was a chore, each kilometer an eternity. The sun was just peeking over the sharp edges of the valley wall and already the heat seared her skin. Their supplies were exhausted. The overworked portable water generator finally had failed the day before. They had devoured the last morsels of the two lizards Anderson had snared two days earlier. They were both weak from hunger and thirst.

The previous day she had spied snow on several of the nearby peaks through her field glasses. Even if there was water there, she was certain neither of them had the strength to climb a mountain to find it. She observed with a growing sense of inexorable gloom that no water had rushed down the parched valley floor in many years, and it seemed likely none would in the foreseeable future. They could survive several days longer without nourishment, but they must find water soon or die.

The full disk of the sun broke over the valley rim and fell upon them with all its fury, but they could not stop, for stopping would mean their deaths. Only her stubborn determination not to lose another crewmember lent her strength to place one bone-tired foot in front of the other, a single agonizing step at a time. She thought about unzipping her suffocating flight suit to cool off, but it was her only protection against the sun's brutal rays. Her blisters had long ago broken open and drained, leaving bloody sores that chafed with each step. The pack on her back weighed heavily on her. It now contained so few useful items that she wondered why she bothered carrying it. Perhaps it was because it was one of the few things still tying her to her past aboard the *Long John Baldry*.

She knew Anderson was still with her only by the occasional slow scuffle of his feet on stone, as he plodded along wearily a few paces behind her. She did not have strength to spare to turn and look at him to judge his condition, but she knew it was no better than hers. Her decision to try to reach Denver Dome would kill them both. She felt a momentary twinge of guilt at letting Captain Moore down. She had lost a ship and three good men, friends all. She hoped he would be able to find a better First Officer than she had proven to be to replace her.

She failed to recognize it at first. The days of squinting through blistered lids had narrowed her field of vision. Centuries of weather had taken its toll on it. Slides of rock and dirt had covered most of it. If she had not looked up at precisely the moment she had trudged up a small hillock of sand, she would have missed it entirely. Yet, there it was, a huge, manmade excavation carved into the side of the valley. Barely visible inside the gargantuan opening was an expansive metal building.

"Ha," she cried through cracked lips as she began to trot towards it. Scrambling over loose rock and earth, unheeding of the scrapes and bruises as she repeatedly fell, she tottered up to the building's side. There were no markings or signs. Exposure to centuries of weather had scoured and gouged the metal sides clean. Rocks dislodged from the cavern's roof lay in piles along the building's boundary. It had no windows. A door six meters high and eighteen meters wide was set into the building's massive front. The building fit snuggly into its niche with only a little open space along one side now filled with unrecognizable rusting equipment and piles of debris. She frantically examined the building and the door for some way to gain entrance. On a small panel near the right-hand side of the door, she found an indentation for an electronic key or pass card clogged with dust and dirt baked to a cement finish. She traced the edges of the panel surrounding the slot with her fingers. She tried prying it open, first with her fingers, then with her knife, but it was no good. The fit was too tight and her hands too unsteady.

Anderson came up beside her and watched her fruitless efforts for a few minutes. In a fit of frustration and rage, he picked up a large rock and began to pound on the panel. To her astonishment, the panel popped open. Inside was a lever with two positions, ostensibly open and closed. She pulled down on the rust-covered manual override lever, but it would not budge. The rust had frozen it in place. With all her strength, she tugged on the lever again. Still nothing. *So close*, she moaned, choking back a sob.

Anderson fell to the ground, too exhausted and weak to help. She beat at the lever mindlessly with her fist until her pounding dislodged a large flake of rust below it , revealing a second, smaller access panel. Using the tip of the blade of her knife, she forced the panel open. Inside, she found a crystalline wafer dotted with tiny ceramic diodes and resistors. Solid-state circuit boards blended so seamlessly with the crystal matrix they appeared to have been manufactured as one unit. An empty slot beside the wafer had once held the power cell controlling the door. She grabbed the damaged laser, which Anderson had been unable to repair, from her backpack.

Feverishly, she fumbled at the clips holding the damaged laser's power cell in place, dropping the laser in her haste.

"Okay, calm down, Cathi," she chided herself. Taking a deep breath, she carefully removed the power pack from the laser and attempted to fit it in the empty space. It was too large. "Damn!" she yelled aloud.

Think. Think. Again using her knife, she pried open the transponder in her pack and snipped two short pieces of wire from its connections. "There goes our signal," she muttered under her breath.

After securing the wires to the power cell terminals, she inserted one end of the positive wire into the slot's positive connection. The other, the ground wire, she held above the metal box.

"Here goes nothing," she said to Anderson and smiled, then winced from the pain it brought to her parched, swollen lips. She touched the wire to the slot's ground connection. Sparks flew as a jolt of electricity traveled up her arm to her shoulder, knocking her to the ground. Still, the door did not budge. She marveled at the numbness in her arm and at her own stupidity for failing to ground herself properly. She was ready to give in to her failure. She could do no more.

"The transponder power cell," Anderson gasped out through swollen lips. "More power."

"Yes," she answered as she grasped his meaning. Why had she not thought of that? If her mind was too numb to figure out a simple door mechanism, how could she hope to contact the *Baldry*? The laser's nearly depleted power cell was not strong enough, and she did not want to dismantle their only working laser. She removed the transponder's power cell, added it to that of the laser's, and tried again. More sparks flew, but this time she avoided touching the naked end of the wire with her bare hand. Instead, she used the plasticized waterproof backpack as a glove. She juggled the rapidly heating power cells in her unprotected hand until they became too hot to hold. Just as she was ready to drop them, a loud click came from within the door, and it began to slide aside. It shuddered as hydraulic servos forced it from its centuries-long rest. The low rumble reverberated throughout the large cavern revealed within. Rust and dirt fell from the door and clouded the air around them. The screeching of metal against metal became a shrill cry.

As the door slid open, a rush of cooler air washed over them like a balm to their aching, scorched bodies. It rattled to a halt after moving only a few feet, but that was enough. Summoning a reserve of strength that she did not know she possessed, she helped Anderson to his feet and, with pains shooting through her slowly reawakening arm, half-dragged him into the cool relief of the building.

At first, she could see very little of the building's cavernous interior, but slowly, as her sunburned eyes grew accustomed to the faint light, she began to make out the familiar hulks of great throbbing machines standing in rows along the walls. "Pumps!" she exclaimed, recognizing them as enormous versions of the water pumps in the *Baldry's* hydroponics section. Her jubilant echoing voice bounded down the length of the building – "Pumps-umps-mps!" As her voice faded away into the depths of the building, another sound broke the silence: the slow, steady drip of water. Excited, she cupped her ear to pinpoint its source over the throbbing of the pumps and the pounding of her heart. She located the drip beneath one of the pumps along the wall. Letting Anderson slump gently to the floor, she forced her feet to carry her the thirty meters to the pump. It felt like thirty kilometers.

She watched a small drop of precious water gather on a pipe above her head and fall to the floor. A small splash brought her attention to a water-filled depression in the concrete floor. Over the centuries, the relentless force of dripping water had carved out a small bowl. In another million years, it might carve out a canyon. In spite of her tremendous thirst, she removed a chemical test strip from her pack and placed a drop of water on it. *Almost pure. Just a little dirt.* She laughed at the thought. She would be more than willing to squeeze water from mud and be thankful for every drop. She wet her hand in the small pool and touched it to her dry lips. The pain was sharp, but it still felt wonderful. Carefully, she filled her canteen and carried the water back to Anderson. She poured some over his brow and slowly dribbled it down his throat. After a few minutes, he was able to sit up and hold the canteen himself, if with somewhat unsteady hands.

"Drink slowly, or you'll throw up," she advised him.

He laughed softly. "My throat is so swollen I can barely manage a dribble," he squeaked out. He took another small swallow and handed the canteen back to her.

She took one small gulp, then another. Heeding her advice for moderation, she poured a little water over her face before replacing the canteen's cap.

"First we sleep. Then we look for food." She looked over at Anderson, who was already fast asleep. She lay down beside him, and soon she, too, was in heavy slumber.

By her chronometer, they had slept only four hours when a noise awakened her, but she felt as if she had been asleep for days. Her back ached horribly, and all of her muscles quivered as she tried to stand. The days of walking through the desolate lands torn asunder by the hand of both man and nature had taken a terrible toll on her body. She glanced over at Anderson, still sleeping. He was emaciated and frail. *I probably look just as bad,* she thought. He had never been in great physical shape, preferring to remain aboard ship most landfalls. She owed him a lot. In spite of the deaths of Whitehall and Pegari and the loss of the shuttle, he had followed her lead without complaint.

The noise, a low whirring sound farther down the line of pumps, repeated. She hobbled toward it on aching legs. As she came even with one massive pump, she spied a repair drone at work on it. A multi-task tool on the end of one of its appendages removed the bolts securing a gasket frame. Then, it deftly removed the torn gasket and replaced it with one it pulled from a drawer in its belly. It re-secured the frame and moved the body of the pump, where it inserted a tele-scoping rod into a receptacle and turned it. The pump switched on and began throbbing as water coursed through its impellers. Its task completed, it rolled past her without noticing her and disappeared through a maintenance opening in the wall. The automated repair drones had kept the pumps working for centuries. She assumed the leak that had saved her life had not reached the critical point of needing repairs.

She returned to the door opening mechanism and retrieved her power packs. The power cell for the transponder was fried and melted, useless. The pack for the laser had only a small charge remaining. She noticed a sign above the inside lintel of the door she had missed earlier – Mount Thunder Pumping Facility# 2. The build-ers of Denver Dome designed the facility to bring water from the mountains to the dome. The station had stood untouched by human hand for centuries, lasting longer than the dome it supplied. If there was power for the pumps, there should be sufficient power to boost her communicator. First, though, they needed food. She began to explore.

The pumping station was half a kilometer in length and two hundred meters across. The ceiling was almost invisible in the shadows thirty meters above her head. A system of rails for lifting the heavy pumps for repair created a spider web lattice across the ceiling. Ladders provided access to catwalks above the pumps. She noticed openings in the floor at intervals, stairways to lower levels. The building contained no other rooms.

She rummaged through her pack and found one small package of dehydrated fruit she had set aside for an emergency. Their weakened condition constituted such an emergency. She poured in a little water and allowed it to rehydrate. She and Anderson would need the energy to explore the station. She gently awakened Anderson and spoon-fed him the fruit, leaving herself only a small portion. Anderson's condition was worse than hers. They quenched their thirst and filled their canteens. The flashlight had died days earlier. Using only the feeble glow of the flashlight function of her wrist chronometer, they marched in single file into the blackness of one of the stairwells.

She counted one-hundred-fifty winding steps before they reached a level floor. The faint sound of a pump throbbed far off in the distance. She used the sound to guide them. Ten paces along the corridor, she spied a faintly glowing pad on the wall. She waved her hand over it. Very dim at first, but then quickly increasing in intensity, a row of lights burst into life overhead. She shielded her eyes at the sudden burst of radiance. Several banks of light were out, but enough remained to illuminate the corridor. She decided to let Anderson rest while she scouted ahead, first checking that their communicators still worked.

She located the pump five hundred meters down the corridor. It switched on and off twice during her journey, cycling water through the massive pipes above her head to prevent stagnation. It had been operating for centuries without human maintenance, a remarkable feat of engineering by her ancestors. It was evident that not all the best of Earth's people had left during the Great Migration. She felt a great kinship with the people who had designed the pumping station. They would have felt at home in the engine room of the *Long John Baldry*.

A small alcove held tables and chairs, or rather the remains of them, as if once a break area. Now, the contents were piles of dust and rust. A row of corroded metal lockers lined one wall of the alcove. Most of the lockers were empty or contained only rusted parts or other unidentifiable objects, but upon opening one locker, she hit the jackpot. Inside were half a dozen vacuum-sealed jars constructed from a type of ceramic-metal alloy that had endured the passage of centuries unscathed. Curious, she broke the seal of one. It produced a slight hiss as the lid peeled back, revealing its freeze-dried contents. Moisture oozed from the sides of the container and mixed with the desiccated mixture. After a few seconds, the jar began to warm in her hands, producing the tantalizing aroma of vegetable soup. The smell sent her empty stomach rumbling, and her smile broke open a couple of blisters on her chapped lips. She tested the jar's contents with her bio-kit.

Two or three hundred years old and still edible, she marveled. *These Earthers were wonderful.* By comparison, her people had stagnated for centuries during the middle part of the Scattering. Freed from the period of enforced cooperation during the Great Migration outward, cultures had once again splintered, and the inevitable wars over habitable planets, trade, and religious differences had decimated populations wasted valuable resources. It had taken them centuries to regain what they had lost. Earthers had adapted to their harsh environment and advanced until their downfall. Even the survivors on Mars barely maintained the level of technology they had brought from Earth. Earth could become a source of wonderful finds for her people, if she ever got back to them to announce her discoveries.

She hurried back to Anderson with her precious find. They feasted on the soup, a medley of vegetables, many she did not recognize, in a light broth. It was delicious, made even more so by their desperate hunger. Still famished, she opened a second jar, revolted by its contents.

"This one is meat," she complained. She was not a strict vegetarian, but she preferred the cultured protein available on the *Baldry*, not the chopped up muscles of slaughtered animals.

Anderson was not as picky as she was. He used two fingers to pull a chunk of hot stewed meat from the jar and placed it in his mouth. "Not bad. A little tough, but it is protein."

"It's meat from some hapless animal," she said, squeamish at watching him eat.

"Protein is protein," he countered, "like from our culture vats."

"That's different. It ... it was never a living creature."

Anderson licked his fingers. "We're starving. You can either eat this or take your squeamishness to your grave."

He handed her the jar and waited until she took it. He watched as she placed a small piece of meat in her mouth and swallowed, fighting the reflex to regurgitate. In spite of her revulsion, it tasted remarkably like the cultured protein from the *Long John Baldry* she was used to. In fact, she admitted to herself, it was delicious. She chose a larger piece.

"See. Not so bad after all." Anderson grinned and joined her in finishing the jar's contents.

After eating, Anderson handed her the laser. "I used parts from the other laser to repair it while you were gone. I won't guarantee more than two or three shots before the circuits fry."

She was satisfied. At least they had a means to protect themselves should they encounter more of Toothless's people. They had water, food, shelter, and weapons. Now, she needed only to find some way to communicate with the *Baldry*. Overlooked in their earlier descent, she now noticed a small doorway set in the wall behind the stairwell. It was rusted shut and took both of them to force it open enough for entry. A bank of lights along the ceiling illuminated the room and the various pieces of electronic equipment lining its walls. Some looked inoperable, but a couple still had rows of dim lights blinking on their panels. Their purpose was a mystery, but further search failed to locate any type of communication equipment or power source. Curious, she removed a lighted sconce from the wall. The light did not connect to any type of circuitry or contain an independent power source. She suspected that microwaves broadcast from some central source powered it, another marvel of Earth engineering – broadcast energy.

The room provided more sealed jars of food and dehydrated packages in a small cupboard. It appeared that workers ate at their stations rather than make the long journey to some central cafeteria. They added their find to their growing larder and moved down the opposite end of the corridor from the pump. It proved to be much longer and devoid of any lockers or rooms. By her estimation, the corridor headed straight into the heart of the mountain. They walked for over a hour before stopping to rest.

"I feel like we may get out of this now, lieutenant," Anderson confided to Cathi. "My stomach's full, and it's only slightly a cheerful roasting temperature in here, much better than outside."

Cathi marveled that Anderson still could maintain a sense of humor after all they had been through. She had also noticed the drop in temperature as they progressed down the corridor. In addition, she noticed an appreciable rise in humidity the deeper they traveled into the pumping facility. Her limp, dry hair was beginning to curl at the ends. That meant water ahead. The corridor gradually began curving to their left, limiting their vision. Worse than that, many of the lights were no longer functioning, forcing them to rely on the feeble light provided by her chronometer, which slowly grew dimmer as they exhausted the power from its tiny solar battery. If they did not find the end of the seemingly endless corridor soon, it would be necessary to turn back and retrace their steps in the dark.

The temperature had dropped by nearly ten degrees during the last kilometer. She detected a slight, moist breeze blowing down the corridor, carrying with it the unmistakable smell of water. She licked her dry lips at the prospect of a bath, or at least enough water to rinse her face. A week's worth of dirt and perspiration made her feel as grubby as the creatures who had captured her. A patch of light ahead of them grew brighter as they approached. Soon, they had to shield their eyes against the glare.

The corridor ended abruptly at a wide causeway carved from the solid stone of a mountain overlooking a massive lake several hundred meters below. A massive concrete dam over a hundred meters high and spanning the entire valley held the water in place. Tall, snow-capped peaks enclosed the valley. Openings identical to the one in which they stood dotted the length of the causeway. Higher up the peaks, a series of terraces designed to collect snow-melt before it evaporated channeled it through giant pipes to the lake below. They had located the source of water for Denver Dome. The reservoir, when full, could have held enough water to supply ten Denver Domes. Properly functioning, the entire region around the ruins could once again become a garden supporting millions of people, returning life to a decimated wasteland.

First things first, though, she thought. They still needed rescue. After marveling at the view of the lake from their high perch, they continued along the broad causeway. At one time, it must have been beautiful with rows of trees, beds of flowers, benches, and statues, a regular pedestrian boulevard. Now, once smooth surface had succumbed to the weather with pits and cracks in which weeds flourished. Weeds had also taken over the gardens, but to Cathi they were beautiful after days of marching through a land seared of almost all life. The stone statues were weather worn and barely recognizable as manmade objects.

The vast area surrounding the lake had its own thriving ecosystem, an oasis in a planet-sized desert. Species of birds and mammals had migrated from many kilometers to reach this haven from desolation outside the valley. Small trees and plants had taken root along the shoreline, creating habitat and food for a myriad of creatures. She stood mesmerized by the sight so reminiscent of the home she had left many years earlier. Birds flew overhead, and fish splashed in the clear, blue waters. She spotted a family of small mammals playing in the water near a copse of trees and recognized them as otters.

A few low clouds drifted by overhead, creating shade from the sun. To her utter amazement and delight, a brief rain began to fall as they strolled along the causeway. She turned her face toward the downpour and luxuriated in the feel of cold water caressing her parched skin, ignoring the pain of her blisters. The rain lasted only a few minutes, but it had revitalized her body and her soul. She badly wanted to find a way down to the lake, to submerge her filthy body in the refreshing water, and wash away the layers of accumulated stench.

Why not?

She ignored Anderson's questioning stare, as she stripped off her jumpsuit and walked to the edge of the causeway.

"It must be fifteen meters to the water," he warned. "You'll break your neck."

She smiled. "Maybe so, but you can bury a clean corpse."

She raised her arms into the air and left the ground. She knew she was taking a risk. She didn't know how deep the water was or if a dangerous predator lurked just beneath the surface. She felt a few seconds of invigorating freedom as she soared through the air, and then a moment of resistance as she sliced cleanly into the water. She could feel her body soaking up the moisture. She wished she had soap, but she made do by briskly rubbing her skin with her hands, reopening her cuts and blisters. The pain brought tears to her eyes, but it was momentary to the joy of swimming and floating. The water washed the weariness from her muscles and buoyed her spirit.

Anderson waited patiently while she found a place where she could crawl back up to the causeway. The sun hammered her tender flesh, but she felt ten kilos lighter. Anderson handed her her clothes. She dressed, wishing she had clean clothing to don, and said, "Okay. We can go now."

Behind a partially collapsed metal door, an open bay carved into the solid rock of the cliff contained several wheel-less platforms that had served as a means of conveyance, but time and the elements had rendered most of them useless. Creeping vines, drawing moisture from the humid air, grew in the thick layer of dirt burying several of the platforms. The moisture had corroded some so badly that the metal crumbled in Anderson's hand as he examined one.

"Antigravity sleds," he said with a look of surprise, "a technology we lost five hundred years ago."

Most of the antigrav units were no longer functioning, but by cannibalizing parts from the others, Anderson managed to get one sled operational. The seats and seat frames had rotted away, so they had to stand, and it was slow, moving barely faster than a slow trot, but it was preferable to walking, especially after the many kilometers they had covered on foot. Many of the openings they passed were unremarkable, similar to the one by which they had entered;

however, one corridor was much broader and lined with numerous small rooms and banks of machinery. Cathi pulled her laser when a small, spidery automated device shot out of a panel in the wall, but relaxed when it ignored her and rolled down the corridor picking up debris with its many arms and vacuuming the dust with two wide nozzles, still housekeeping after hundreds of years.

Just a small portion of the technology they discovered would have made a real difference during the Trade Wars two centuries earlier – antigravity, broadcast energy, long-term storage of food, self-repairing automated machinery. Some planets, such as hers, had returned to simple agrarian economies in order to survive. Many hundreds of thousands of people had died from starvation caused by lack of trade. Cultures had stagnated. Rebuilding a network of trade routes had been long and costly. The wars had led the way for ships like the *Long John Baldry* to operate as private trading vessels, members of the Trader's Guild.

Once again, she thought of her captain and hoped he would forgive her for letting him down.

20

THE GLASS PLAIN

H RAMACK NOTICED THAT THE WALLS OF THE TUNNEL HAD BECOME MORE regular as they progressed. The machined stone lining had given way to a hard casing of a hard ceramic-like material. The closer they got to their destination, the warier Grey Eagle became of ambush. He insisted they stop often to quiet their footsteps and listen for any sign of threat. The beams of their lights picked out gleaming metal in the darkness. As they drew closer, Hramack recognized it as a ladder leading upward through a smaller circular tunnel. At its end was a circular metal hatch with a round wheel in its center. Hramack was curious, but no one suggested climbing the ladder to see where it led. Like him, fear tempered their curiosity. Finally, he stepped forward and began climbing.

"Be careful, son," Kena called to him from below. He heard several chuckles from the others at his father's warning. His cheeks reddened with embarrassment. He was too old to be treated like a child. Some of the men from Pueblo Nuevo had fought battles when younger than he was.

He could not budge the massive wheel. One of Grey Eagle's men joined him on the ladder. Together, they were able to turn the recalcitrant wheel and push open the heavy metal door. He emerged into what had once been a large building, now merely two crumbling walls and piles of debris open to the sky. The metal door set in the floor of the building had withstood the ravages of time and weather without rusting, but the building had fared poorly. Once more, they climbed into the open sky. A feeling of relief swept over the men. Some hoped it was the end of their journey, but Hramack knew it was not. By Kena's estimate, they were still well south of their destination. Still, after days in the close confines of the tunnel, a sortie into the Empty Lands would be a welcome relief.

"We must keep an eye out for Marauders. No fires," Grey Eagle warned his men as they emerged. "We are in the heart of their territory. They will have patrols about."

After picking his way through the rusted and demolished artifacts in the building, Hramack climbed atop a partially tumbled stone wall and gazed out onto the countryside. Around him stretched a broad, shallow valley broken only by spires of rock and the occasional low shrub. Kena handed him a pair of binoculars. He scanned the still horizon. No creature stirred as far as the eye could see. A jagged line of mountain peaks, perhaps the very ones they sought, thrust above the valley rim to the west and northwest. To the north and the south along the length of the valley, he saw nothing. The valley seemed to continue forever, featureless and desolate. To the east, the valley's gentle slope climbed toward an uneven row of sentinels carved by the wind from an up thrust finger of rock.

"It seems safe," he called back down and handed the binoculars to Kena.

He began walking toward the sloping fan of rock.

"Be careful, Hramack," his father called out to him. "Don't show a silhouette on the valley rim. The Marauders may spot you."

Hramack swallowed a retort about children and fathers began to ascend the slope. His father's constant concern for him annoyed him. The farther they went, the more his anxiety increased. Could not his father see that he was a grown man? Grey Eagle did not treat him like a child. With the Pueblo Nuevo leader, he was an equal to his own warriors. He admired Kena's knowledge of medicine and desert lore, but here in this strange land, he was making it up as he went along.

The ridge proved farther away than it first appeared. He had thought it perhaps half a kilometer distant. It proved closer to one and a half. He glanced back at the others and considered waiting for them, but, still fuming from his father's chiding, he continued to climb. At first, he could distinguish little of the flat, featureless plain beyond the valley rim. The sun was a mere smudge on the horizon, and the plain was a vast sea of darkness.

"There's nothing here," he yelled to the others.

To his shock, the entire horizon behind him burst into a blaze of light, illuminating his startled companions and the building ruins as if in full sun. He fell to the ground cowering in fear. When nothing more happened, he summoned his courage, rose to his feet, and looked toward the plain. He donned his sunshades against the dazzling glare, but even so, he had to squint to see.

The rising sun revealed a vista beyond his comprehension. The entire plain was cracked and frozen, covered with hundreds of square kilometers of what appeared to be ice. He knew ice could not exist in such heat. What, then, could it be? He reached down to pick up the binoculars he had dropped. Sunlight glared from the lens and stabbed his eyes. The answer dawned on him. It had to be a sea of glass. Some monstrous unleashing of power had melted and fused the sand and earth of the entire plain into a cauldron of glass.

A sound behind him startled him. Spinning around, he saw it was only his father. Kena shielded his eyes from the glare of the plain of glass, as well, immediately surmising the source of the power.

"If my calculations are correct, we are north of Pueblo. The tunnel must have veered eastward from a direct north-south direction. This area was once the launch site of many of the great space vessels that depopulated Earth. During the wars, it would have been a threat to space-based weapons. Yarah help anyone or anything that had been beneath the touch of such a weapon. It is little wonder Arun Kane did not anticipate the destructive power of the lasers he unleashed on Denver Dome. How could anyone of sane mind envision such a destructive force? Our ancestors were madmen."

He turned to Hramack. "A major supply base for the construction of the dome was located just north of here, maybe only a few kilometers. I think we should investigate it."

Hramack eyed the cracked glass plain and wondered if the base had suffered a similar fate. "Won't the Marauders be there?" he asked.

"I doubt it. Grey Eagle thinks they fear such places as haunted. As nomads, they have little use for what they may find there. We, on the other hand, could find many useful things there. I'll talk to Grey Eagle." He scanned the plain and sighed. "Such power and still they could not rise above their petty problems. Can we do better?" He walked back down the slope to the men gathered there.

Hramack took one last look at the frozen earth shining like a mirror and followed Kena back to the building. The opening through which they had emerged had been a maintenance entrance for repairs on the waterway below. The building, partially shielded from the plain by the valley rim, had suffered damage during the destruction of the launch site. Time had completed the decay.

After a lengthy discussion, Grey Eagle called a council, in which he voiced his objections but left it to the others to decide what course to take. Kena, ever persuasive, convinced the group that a side trip to the supply base was in their best interest. Exploring it now and cataloguing its contents would save time. If a second expedition was warranted, they could return with the proper tools and equipment needed for salvage. Grey Eagle reluctantly conceded.

"We will avoid the glass plain. I do not like it. We would be too exposed should Marauders be about."

"I agree," Kena said. "It would save time, but the heat would be unbearable. We can travel north using the valley for cover. We can wait until nightfall if you prefer; shelter in the tunnel."

"No," Grey Eagle replied quickly, glancing back towards the maintenance shaft. "If the base is not far, we can rest there."

Hramack understood Grey Eagle's reluctance to re-enter the tunnel. He was beginning to feel like a mouse in a burrow.

They followed the valley northwards for six kilometers until they reached a side canyon veering northeast, where Kena's map showed the supply base to be located. After traveling a few kilometers farther in the sweltering morning heat, they climbed a low hill and saw in the distance, rising like a ghost from the wavering heat mist, the ruins of Colorado Springs spread out over a number of small hills and valleys.

Colorado Springs had not been a large city, but to Hramack it looked like giant's playground. Most of the tall buildings in the center of town had collapsed into an impenetrable pile of rubble. The roofs of other buildings along the city's perimeter protruded through rows of sand dunes encroaching from the southwest. The faint lines of highways and streets divided the city into blocks and neighborhoods. The dry gully of an ancient creek bed snaked through the city. It was Hramack's first glimpse of a city other than photos in books. In spite of the destruction, he was awestruck by its size.

"Most of the old city had been abandoned years before construction of the dome began. Much of the population was relocated to the construction material depot built south of the city on each side of Interstate 25."

The city bore the unmistakable aura of a dead thing. It was apparent that no living creatures, other than small desert animals, had disturbed its streets or buildings since its abandonment centuries ago.

Kena pointed to a wide ribbon of cracked and eroded asphalt running north and south. To the south, a complex of large ware-houses lay nestled between two low rows of hills. "That is our destination."

They had to bypass collapsed bridges on the old highway. In some places, multiple layers of raised roadways had collapsed onto each other, like pancakes. Massive piles of rubble like manmade mountains surrounded the complex, dirt and rock scraped away to create a flat surface for building.

"I do not like it," Grey Eagle stated flatly. "It is like disturbing a grave. It should be left alone."

Hramack winced, recalling Chu Li's similar thoughts."Your Chief gave you command of all things concerning our safety. I will not override your decision," Kena affirmed, "but it seems a shame to come so far just to look at it. Who knows what could be in those buildings?"

"That is my concern also." Grey Eagle's gaze was busily marking every possible hiding place for Marauders.

"We could wait until dark and sneak in," Hramack suggested. He was eager to examine the city from a closer viewpoint but trusted Grey eagle's Judgment.

Grey Eagle gave it some thought, and then turned to Kena. "There is no shelter here. We will do as you ask, but at the first sign of danger, we will leave. I do not know this area, and the Marauders are on their home ground. I will not allow them to trap us in some unholy building while they send for reinforcements. We must push on to our destination before dawn."

Kena was upset that Grey eagle was allowing only a few hours to explore such a large area, but Hramack was glad for any opportunity. They found shelter in the rubble of a row of collapsed buildings. Most of the men rested. Grey Eagle and two others kept watch as Kena restlessly wandered around digging into rubble piles.

"What are you looking for?" Hramack asked. He was too excited to sleep.

Kena smiled. "I don't know. Clues from the past, maybe." He reached down and picked up a brick. He showed it to Hramack. Hramack saw there were words written on its side.

"1929," he read. He looked at his father questioningly. "So?"

"That brick was made before man even reached into space," Kena said. "It has been used and reused countless times over the centuries much the way monuments of the past were destroyed and used for new monuments. It is an endless cycle. Man builds on the ruins of his past."

"Perhaps someday we can rebuild on ruins such as these," Hramack added.

Kena smiled. "That is my hope, too." His smile faded. "If we can unlock the secret of the water."

The remainder of the day passed quietly. A few hours before sunset, the group slipped into the city, carefully using piles of rubble to conceal their movements. To their great relief, they encountered no Marauders. The first buildings they explored were all empty hulks, slowly crumbling with age. Hramack began to worry that looters had stripped all of them over the centuries. One large building, less decayed than the others, sat alone in a large clearing, its westernmost wall partially buried beneath towering sand dunes.

"Let's try that one," Hramack suggested.

A row of large sliding doors, partially submerged in the sand, lined the building's outside wall. Each was sealed shut. Two Clouds discovered a smaller door behind a pile of rusted machinery. Forcing it open, Kena rushed inside before Grey Eagle could stop him. Hramack dismissed Grey Eagle's scowl of disapproval, shrugged, and followed his father.

Hramack expected the interior to be dark. Instead, large skylights in the ceiling washed the entire cavernous interior with light. A thick layer of dust covered the concrete floor. Row after row of metal storage racks reached almost to the ceiling. Their tiers of dust-coated shelves contained wooden crates and bins. Many of the wooden crates had disintegrated with dry rot, spilling their rusted or rotted contents onto the floor, but others, made of a durable plastic-like material, remained in pristine condition.

Bin after bin contained pieces of metal, bolts, nuts, and screws as shiny as the day of their manufacture. Piles of tarnished but undamaged bars of steel and other alloys were stacked higher than a man could reach. Pipes and pumps still enclosed in their greased casings littered the floor. Hramack investigated a few of the smaller containers inside the larger bins, finding small machined parts still gleaming like new: metal cogs, sprockets, and gears. The building was a gold mine of technology. *No,* Hramack realized, *more than a gold mine.* Gold held no value as great as the contents they had discovered.

"It's a warehouse," Kena shouted as he danced with glee, laughing.

Even stoic Grey Eagle broke into a broad smile at the sight of the metal. Hramack climbed high up the side of one storage rack, disturbing a cloud of dust that billowed around him. He pried loose the lid of one long, undamaged crate.

"Father, look," he cried, holding aloft a delicate three-meter length of vane for a windmill. "It is as light as a feather, yet will not bend under my full weight." He proved his point by leaning against the fragile-looking vane. "There are dozens of such boxes, enough to pump water or run generators to light a dozen villages. It's amazing!"

"This was a major distribution center. All those doors along the sides were for loading and unloading freight delivered by the truck full. Imagine a long, narrow home filled with goods. These were probably destined for the people who refused to enter the dome, or those who did not qualify." He turned to Grey Eagle. "These rightfully belong to your people."

"We will gladly share," he replied.

Grey Eagle's curiosity drew him to one heavy steel cabinet against one of the roof support beams. Large yellow letters emblazoned across its doors proclaimed, "Warning – Explosives."

"Careful," Kena warned as Grey Eagle jerked on the door handle.

Grey Eagle frowned. "It's locked."

Kena found a short, metal bar and carefully pried open the doors. It hissed as the seal broke and air rushed inside the hermetically sealed door. Inside on a shelf laid dozens of blocks of a white doughy substance carefully wrapped in plastic sheeting. A ceramic metal box held electronic timers, each resting in a fitted molded recess. He picked up one of the blocks of explosives and examined it.

"These were used in demolition," he explained to Grey Eagle. "They may have been used to destroy some of the buildings around us. The cabinet was sealed with a vacuum inside to protect the contents over the centuries."

Grey Eagle examined the package in Kena's hand carefully. "They are very small for such destruction." He picked up the ceramic box and looked at Kena in surprise. He hefted it in his hand. "It is very light for a ceramic box. He eyed the timers, noting the blank screen on some. Others looked much like the watch Kena wore. "These are used to ignite them when needed?" he asked.

"Yes, I think so," Kena replied as he examined the box. "Some are digital, using an internal power cell. The others operate on a wind up clockwork mechanism, probably used in situations near open power sources that might affect the digital timers. The batteries on the digital timers will be dead, of course, but the manual timers should function."

"They could prove very useful to us. Are they safe to carry?"

"They should be harmless until the timing device is set." Kena ran his finger along the edges of the box. "It appears to be ceramic, but I suspect it is an alloy with a stronger, lighter substance."

Grey Eagle's attention had moved on beyond the box. He stared at the block of explosive for a moment as if deciding whether to trust Kena's word of its safety. Finally, he took two of the blocks and placed them in his pack. "Show me how to set the timer. We will carry these with us. The rest we should hide." He looked around. "You were right to want to come here. There are metals and devices that will make our lives much more bearable. We will return as soon as possible with many men in case we are forced to fight. First though, we must find the source of the water."

Grey Eagle's words brought Kena back to the reality of the reason for their journey.

"Yes," Kena replied. "There is much here, but none of it will bring the water."

Hramack clambered down from his lofty perch, bringing with him another shower of dust. "I want to see more."

For the remainder of the afternoon, Kena, Hramack, and the others explored the wonders of the warehouse. It was a marvelous storeroom of ancient engineering, producing find after find of useful and often unidentifiable objects, and they had uncovered less than half of it. As the sun set and the building fell into shadows, they lit torches to explore further. One section of the building, separated from the rest by a wall and single doorway, drew Hramack's interest. Venturing inside, he discovered rows of dusty shelves that had once held tens of thousands of books. Now, they were little piles of dust touched only by the wind. Empty crates scattered across the floor yielded only more dust. A few tattered books lay scattered around the floor, missed by the library's pilferers. He picked one up, but it disintegrated dust as soon as he thumbed through the pages.

Kena joined him. He ran his hand along one of the empty shelves and examined his hand.

"Perhaps they moved the books into the dome," Hramack suggested.

"Perhaps," his father said, "but it looks as though they have been removed more recently." He pointed to a knee-high mound of sand that had pushed through the open door and spilled across the floor. "The dust on the floor is very thick except in a few oddly shaped spots. I believe more crates were once stored here and removed only recently. Only a thin layer of dust covers the area where they once rested. I would think they have been gone only a few months at most." He raised his torch and pointed to two parallel grooves in the sand near the door. "Those are the remains of a wheeled conveyance."

"Then who took them? Marauders? For what reason would they need books, fuel to burn?" Hramack could not imagine Marauders reading.

Kena shook his head. "It is curious." He walked over to a shelf against the far wall containing stacks of thin crystalline wafers partially buried in the remains of the boxes that once protected them. Picking one up, he held it between thumb and forefinger to examine it. "I believe this is some type of data storage device. The crystal lattice structure could contain more data than all the books in this library." He shook his head and placed the wafer back on the shelf. "It is a shame. If we had the reader that accompanies these wafers, we might learn so much. They could be a repository for the wisdom of our ancestors."

Seeing his father's disappointment, Hramack said, "Maybe we can find one in the warehouse."

"Perhaps, but with no list of the warehouse's contents or a means to locate them, it will be a monumental task." His expression suddenly stiffened. "We had better rejoin the others. If the Marauders have been here, they may return."

Almost as if his words had been prophetic, Two Clouds stuck his head in the door and yelled, "Quickly! Marauders come."

Hramack's pulse quickened. Their earlier battle with only five marauders had cost Grey Eagle one man. He did not want a second encounter.

They found Grey Eagle outside the building directing his men to positions among the piles of debris in front of the building. True to his word, Grey Eagle would not allow Marauders to trap him in the city. Seeing Kena and Hramack approach, he motioned them to remain out of sight.

"We are lucky the moon is but a sliver. They have not seen us yet. They march as if unaware we are here, but they will soon cross our tracks. There appear to be about twenty five of them." He spoke as if unconcerned at the odds, over two to one in the Marauders' favor. "These men seem healthier and better dressed than most Marauders we have encountered, and they move as if trained in fighting tactics."

"Perhaps they are the ones who have been raiding the buildings," Hramack suggested.

"Perhaps so," Grey Eagle conceded, "but their weapons also seem equally improved. I see two men carrying crossbows. Others have metal swords."

Hramack looked closer and saw metal tips gleaming on the spears and arrows in the pale moonlight. "These Marauders know how to work steel."

"Or trade for it," Kena chimed in. "Perhaps with items looted from the warehouse."

"Whatever their origins, they will be upon us shortly," Grey Eagle reminded them. "Do we fight or run?"

A yell from the direction of the Marauders reached their ears. With a sudden commotion, the Marauders split into two groups and began to approach the warehouse from two sides.

"Curses," Grey Eagle shouted. "They know we're here and are trying to surround us. We must make a break for it before they pin us down. We cannot endure a siege."

"There is another door," Two Clouds said. "Hramack discovered it."

Grey Eagle thought for a minute. "I have an idea." He signaled his men to fall back toward the warehouse.

"What is your plan?" Kena asked, running beside Grey Eagle.

"They will follow us into the building. We will exit by the door Hramack discovered, and I will explode one of these bombs you found." He pulled a block of *plastique* from his pack.

"How will you know how long to set the timer?"

Grey Eagle smiled. "I will wait until they are inside. Then I will pin them down with arrows. I will set the timer for a very short time. If I do not blow up myself and the Marauders, I will run as fast as I can to catch up with you."

"That doesn't sound like much of a plan to me," Hramack said, concerned at the risk Grey Eagle was taking.

"It is the best I could come up with on such short notice. Perhaps you have a better plan?" he asked, staring at Hramack.

"No," he admitted chagrined for speaking up.

"It's decided then. Kena, you will take my men through the door at the rear of the building. Leave the city and travel as quickly as possible back to the river tunnel. Do not stop. Do not wait for me. I will follow when I have delayed pursuit."

※

Grey Eagle watched his men leaving the building with Kena to make sure they were obeying his orders. When the last torch disappeared, he set fire to a pile of wooden crates near the door to provide some light. Then, he found a spot on a catwalk high above the door protected by metal girders supporting the roof. As he had expected, nine or ten of the Marauders poured through the door, immediately silhouetted by the flames. He fired an arrow and dropped one man. Wounded but not dead, he crawled away. The others quickly scattered for cover in military fashion. From his lofty vantage point, he fired arrows at anyone attempting to rush his position but he was hidden in the shadows. A second man rushed him and died, giving the others reason to pause. He wanted to delay them as long as possible, but knew he must act quickly before they split up and decided to surround the building.

He placed one of the explosives against one of the metal beams supporting the roof. If they were as powerful as Kena had claimed, it should bring the roof down on the Marauders. It would at least slow them down. Hoping that Kena knew what he was talking about and praying to *Tawa*, the sun god, that he had followed Kena's instructions correctly, he set the timer for two minutes. He judged that allowed him just enough time to climb down and reach the door at a full run. He fired one more volley of arrows just to keep the Marauders' heads down, and then pressed the timer. He turned to run and tumbled headlong to the catwalk with a bolt from a cross-bow lodged in his upper thigh. Pain shot up his leg like fire.

"Curses," he yelled.

He scrambled the length of the catwalk on hands and knees, leaving a bloody trail, knowing he would never reach the door before the explosion.

A shadow loomed over him. "Take my hand!"

He looked up to see Travin standing over him offering his hand. He extended his arm, and Travin yanked him from the floor, threw him over his shoulder, and raced down the catwalk as if Grey Eagle's great size meant nothing. Arrows sounded like birds in flight as they whizzed past him. Travin dropped down the ladder first and waited, as Grey Eagle slid down using only his hands. He ignored the friction burn and concentrated on stopping before he hit the ground. Travin grabbed him and propelled him toward the doorway, hopping on one leg.

They almost made it. The explosion lifted Grey Eagle into the air and deposited him with a bone-jarring thud on the concrete floor ten meters away. The sound of wrenching metal and the screams of men crushed by tons of falling metal and debris reached him just ahead of a cloud of dust and shower of metal roof panels. Grey Eagle rolled over expecting to see Travin beside him, ready to thank the hunter from Ningcha, but he was alone.

Kena emerged from the cloud of dust. "Are you hurt?" he asked.

"I thought I told you to not wait for me," Grey Eagle yelled.

Kena smiled. "Yes, you did, but I have never been very good at following orders."

"Lucky for me. Now move it before they gather their wits."

Kena glanced around. "Where is Travin?"

Grey Eagle shook his head slowly. "He saved my life by shoving me toward the door. He did not make it."

Kena looked at the pile of collapsed steel and started for it. "Perhaps he's ..."

"No," Grey Eagle said gently, holding Kena back. "None could survive that, I fear. Even so, we must leave, now. The explosion might not have killed all of them."

His words shook Kena from his stupor. He nodded and helped Grey Eagle to his feet and limped out the door. Two other men had remained behind with Kena and Travin to worry any pursuers and allow the others to escape. They saw the crossbow bolt protruding from Grey Eagle's thigh, grabbed him from Kena, over his loud protests, and carried him between them like a sack of grain. It was an undignified way to travel, but necessity required he suffer humiliation for speed's sake. He expected the marauders to overtake them at any moment.

By the time they had covered the dozen kilometers to the river tunnel, his head was reeling from the pain in his leg and the jostling. To his consternation, most of his men remained above ground waiting.

"I told you to leave," he shouted.

"And who would tell Chief Kosono of you absence," Two Clouds replied with a wry grin.

Willing hands accepted Grey Eagle and lowered him into the opening, where other hands received him. Before disappearing down the hatch, he watched Kena place the remaining explosive from his pack beside a wall of the building. At the bottom of the ladder, he pushed away from his helpers and stood on his own. The effort required was enormous, but he could not allow them to think him incapacitated.

"I am not crippled," he growled. "I can walk."

He limped out of the way while Kena and the others climbed down. The last man sealed the hatch behind him.

"That should bring the wall down over the entrance, burying it under tons of stone," Kena said. "It will take them a long time to dig us out."

They had gone only a couple of hundred meters along the tunnel when the shock of the explosion above reached them, reverberating down the tunnel. Satisfied they had stymied their pursuers, Grey Eagle collapsed cursing on the floor of the tunnel. Fire shot through his leg, blurring his vision.

Kena kneeled and examined the wooden bolt protruding from each side of Grey Eagle's thigh. "You are very lucky. It went cleanly through a the muscle without striking bone or any large veins or arteries."

Grey Eagle bit back on the pain and chuckled. "I feel lucky indeed. Someone bring dice, and we will roll a game or two for high stakes."

Kena carefully cut the sharp metal tip from the bolt with his knife. Grey Eagle winced at the waves of agony caused by Kena's ministrations.

"This will probably hurt," Kena warned. "I can give you something to deaden the pain, but you will not be able to walk if I do."

"Yank it out and bind the wound," he growled, impatient to be away from the Marauders.

"I will count to three. One, two ...," then Kena yanked the bolt from his thigh. "Three!"

Grey Eagle howled at the unexpected agony as fingers of fire lanced upward through his leg. "You can't count," he screamed, but then bit back on the string of curses he was about to unleash.

Kena smiled and began tending to his thigh. The wound bled only a little. After applying an antiseptic and carefully wrapping the wound, he said, "You should be able to walk, but it will cause you considerable pain. We can make a litter and carry you."

"I'll not be carried like an invalid," Grey Eagle protested. "This is not my first wound. Hawk, give me your spear."

Using Hawk's spear as a crutch, Grey Eagle pushed himself to his feet and hobbled down the tunnel. As Kena had predicted, the pain was excruciating, but he refused to give in to it. His men needed him. "Come, let us get away from this place," he called over his shoulder. Behind him, the others scurried to catch up.

※

Hramack searched the group as they passed, and then asked Kena, "Where is Travin?"

His father did not reply. Instead, he stared at the ground.

Hramack's throat tightened. "He's dead, isn't he?"

Kena nodded.

"Did he ... did he die well?"

Kena arched his eyebrows and stared at his son. "What a strange question?"

Hramack shrugged. "It was something he said."

"He saved Grey Eagle's life," Kena replied.

He nodded his head slowly. "Good. That was his desire."

The hunter's death saddened him, but he was strangely pleased that Travin died as he had wanted. Whatever darkness dwelt in Travin's heart, he hoped the hunter had finally found peace and the absolution he sought.

21

A FORCED MARRIAGE

TEELA HAD REFUSED TO ATTEND THE DAILY PRAYERS SINCE THE SACRIFICE OF the goat. She no longer looked upon her friends and fellow villagers in the same way. Now, the image of Chu Li's dagger across the goat's throat clouded their faces in a haze of spilled blood, their savage eyes looking on with eager anticipation. They had changed in dark ways, each one trying to offer the most fervent prayer to Yarah, as if the louder their voice the more Yarah would listen. She avoided them whenever possible except at the cisterns. There, she ignored the cold stares and accusatory glances they heaped upon her.

Most appalling of all, the children no longer attended school. Parents kept their children close for fear that the sacrifice of the goat was only the beginning. She suspected that more than a few would gladly nominate her for sacrifice. *Let them try*, she thought. Their ignorance would not protect them from her wrath. She carried her grandfather's dagger with her at all times at is insistence. If Yarah wanted blood, she would give it to Him.

No, she reminded herself, *they are frightened people.* The High Priest Chu Li was the real culprit. He played on their fears and emotions using the power of his office. From discord and chaos, he would step in and institute religious order. She wondered how long it would be before he withheld water rations from those who opposed him.

She had just returned from watering Kena's herbs, when Madras and Chu Li met her at the foot of the suspension bridge. She stopped and glared at the pair with her hands on her hips.

"What do you want?"

"We wish to discuss your future. Hramack is either dead or resigned to his new life as an outcast. In any event, he will not return to Ningcha to face his punishment. Therefore, I have abrogated your betrothal to him. As High Priest and Village Precept, as proscribed in our laws, you are free to marry Madras's son, Juresh. Such a marriage will bless the village."

"I will not," she yelled and tried to storm past him, amazed by the High Priest's audacity. Hramack had tried to warn her, but she had thought him overreaching Chu Li's malevolence.

Madras grabbed her arm and held her, squeezing tighter as she struggled to free herself..

"You will abide by the wishes of the Council," Chiu Li warned. "In times such as these, the harmony of the village is foremost in my mind."

"You think to repay Madras for his silence in Eithan's death, you mean."

The High Priest's eyes locked onto hers like sharp daggers, and she knew she had said too much. "You've been listening to the demented ramblings of you grandfather. Beware. Your tongue will be your undoing. Bearing false witness is a mortal sin, especially against a servant of Yarah. You will marry Juresh. In dire times such as these, I do not require you consent. The law is on my side. If you go against my wishes, the wishes of the village, you could face the same punishment as Hramack."

She had not seen Kaffa approach until his staff fell hard across Madras' arm. He stood behind Madras, his eyes filled with anger. His face was grim and his voice powerful, as he said, "Unhand my granddaughter, stone cutter. Perhaps you will fare better against an old man."

Madras whirled on Kaffa holding his injured arm, but before he could take a step toward him, Teela pressed her dagger against his kidney. "Think carefully, Madras, before you make a foolish move that could be your last."

"You threaten the High Priest and a member of the Council?" Chu Li yelled.

"If you attempt to force a marriage with Juresh, I will do more than threaten," she replied coldly, though her blood ran feverish with indignation. "When Hramack and Kena return ..."

"They will not return," Chu Li spat at her. "Travin will see to that."

"You place too much faith in Travin's loyalty to you," Kaffa said. "He is wise and knows Kena well. Perhaps he will listen to Kena and weigh his words against yours. Frightened people close their ears and minds to reason, but Travin is a hunter and does not frighten easily."

Chu Li licked his lips as he listened to Kaffa. His gaze flitted from Madras to Teela and her dagger. "You cannot defy the will of the Council and the wishes of the village. Teela cannot remain unmarried at a time when the village has too few young women. Our young are the hope and future of Ningcha. At the rising of the new moon, I will announce her marriage to Juresh. If she refuses, people will reconsider sharing precious water with someone who ignores the wishes of the village."

With that, he turned and stalked away. Madras remained motionless until Teela removed her dagger from his back; then, he too scurried away after the High Priest.

"Thank Yarah you came when you did," she told Kaffa, trying to smile to keep from breaking down in tears. Her anger had sustained her in Chu Li's presence, but now, she felt drained and foolish. The High Priest had given her less than a week to abide by his wishes, but she would never marry Juresh or any other boy in the village. Her heart belonged to Hramack or no one at all. She knew of too many loveless marriages arranged for political or social gain. Madras' own marriage to Anila was one. She gave the stone carve three sons and doted over them, but her looks for her husband were filed with many things, but love was not among them.

"I saw Chu Li bound for the bridge and suspected he would have words with you." He paused. "You should not have pulled your dagger on Madras."

"He would have attacked you."

"I hoped to provoke him. Attacking me would expose him for what he is, a frightened bully. Then people would ask the reason for his attack, and word of your accusation against him and Chu Li would spread." He smiled. "I would see to it."

"I ... I didn't know."

"No matter, granddaughter. I was not eager for bruises or broken bones."

"Oh, grandfather, they gave me less than a week to decide. What can I do? I cannot marry Juresh."

"I believe Hramack and Kena will return before then. If they do not, you will have no choice. I am too old to offer much protection. Without water, you would die quickly rather than slowly, as we all are. If all else fails, you must marry Juresh. I will not watch you die."

She felt hope slipping away. Had Kaffa given up? "Marriage to Juresh will be akin to death. Perhaps death by thirst would be better."

He placed his arm around her shoulder, as he had done many times in the past when she was afraid or confused. "Have faith, granddaughter. All is not lost yet."

As they walked back to her home, she glanced at the ridge of the canyon, praying for a glimpse of Hramack coming to her rescue, but there was nothing there.

✳

Chu Li's hand trembled with rage as he walked back to his home. His teeth ached where he had clenched his jaw tightly to endure Kaffa's insults. He stopped and slammed the heel of his staff against the rock.

"Why did you allow that fool Kaffa to best you?" he snapped at Madras.

Madras cowed at the High Priest's fury. "He caught me by surprise." He grabbed the wrist Kaffa had struck with his staff. "He almost broke my arm."

"And that snippet of a girl almost skewered you with her dagger," Chu Li replied in a snit.

"I did not see you jumping in to aid me," Madras replied.

"It would be unseemly for the High Priest to become involved in a brawl with an old man." He shook his head and continued toward his home. "It matters not. His day is coming soon. Teela cannot refuse marriage with your son. It is within the law."

"Juresh is not pleased with the match. He is afraid of her. He would prefer Betha, the miller's daughter, or Unis, daughter to Stennit the teacher."

"Fool! What he wants is of little importance. We must put her in her place and humiliate Kaffa. Then, Kena's house you so desire will be yours. Who knows, perhaps she will run away to die in the desert or take her own life and both our problems will be solved."

Madras paled. "You would not ..."

Chu Li waved his hand in annoyance. "Of course not, but she is a headstrong girl. Each act of defiance places distance between her and the people of Ningcha." He touched his heart and raised his hand into the air. "Yarah's will be done."

At his door, he stopped and turned to Madras. "Go assure your son he will be safe."

Madras turned his head aside and stared at the ground. "My family does not listen to me. First Eithan's death and now Anseer is gone as well. They think tragedy follows me like a summer sand storm. My assurances will not console their grief."

"Anseer and Travin will return, with or without our two fugitives."

"It has been over a week. Without supplies or water ..."

"Travin knows the desert. We left a water skin at the spring we found for his return journey."

"What if ... what if he brings Kena and Hramack back with him?"

"Stand strong, Madras. Even if he protests his innocence, the only two people who would have released them are Kaffa and Teela." He chuckled. "We cannot lose either way."

"I would not be in your boots if Kena returns alive, even with his hands bound."

Madras' barb stung deeply. He retaliated. "Nor would I be you if he learned the real reason his wife, Allana, was on the bridge during the sand storm."

"That was an accident. I did not ..."

"Silence. You did not kill her, but you coveted her. Your sin caused her death. Her blood is on your hands. Do not forget that."

Madras seemed to deflate, as if his fear was the only thing holding him erect. Now, his guilt overwhelmed him. He leaned one arm against the pillar of Chu Li's veranda. "How can I? Her face haunts me."

"Go now. I must think and pray."

As he watched Madras leave, he shook his head slowly. Madras was too weak to endure the machinations of politics. His large, calloused hands were gifts from Yarah for the carving of stone, but his mind was more fit for discerning the curves and angles hidden in the stone's grain than keeping secrets. If Kena did return, a dark fear he kept pushed down inside, Madras could not be trusted.

Inside his home, he shed his smothering robes of office and rinsed his body with a wet rag, badly wanting a real bath, but even a High Priest could not waste precious water. He had no doubt that the water would flow again. His faith in Yarah often conflicted with the real world, but the return of the springs did occur on the same day each year. Historical records indicated a variation of weeks. It had never been this late, but he was a patient man. When the water returned, he would be heralded as the divine conduit to Yarah's blessings.

He donned a lightweight robe over his naked body, worn unsashed to allow his flesh to breath. He often walked around in his home naked, but his confrontation with Kaffa had left him feeling too vulnerable. The robe was his concession to his fear, its thin material more a mental shield than a practical one. He desired no wife and had no housekeeper. Either would intrude too much on his privacy. His home was his sanctuary away from the office of High Priest and the politics of the Council. The smooth stone of the floor was cool against his bare feet as he flopped down in his favorite well-worn leather chair, a cool glass of kalquat in his hand. The alcohol slowly released the tension of the encounter and relaxed him.

Staring out the window of his den toward the canyon rim, he felt a sense of satisfaction settling over him. Sacrifices had been made. More might be needed, but the life of the village was more important than a single life. Herat, the former High Priest, had been old and weak. There was no place for weakness in the world they had inherited from their ancestors. Only the strong were worthy of surviving. Heart's weak heart was Yarah's punishment for his reluctance to meddle in daily village life. He was too spiritual, too impractical, too easily led by others from Yarah's true path. Kena's medicine prolonging his life conflicted with Yarah's will. He had not murdered the old High Priest; he had fulfilled Yarah's will.

A little known chapter of the *Teachings of Nuama*, re moved from the original and set aside decades ago, listed the names of the original settlers of Ningcha. It took little mastery of science or genetics to see that they were a dying people. Centuries of interbreeding was slowly weakening them. Teela and Hramack both possessed remarkably strong genes. Their offspring would strengthen the line, but creating one powerful genetic line did not help Ningcha survive. Teela had to marry another. Her marriage to Juresh served two purposes: spreading her genetic traits and forging a strong alliance with Madras. It would have been good for the village.

Kena had long been a thorn in his side, but Kena's propensity for exploration had offered a ready means to weaken him. Hramack, reduced in status to a mere herder, could not marry Teela. If he had not so foolishly fled the village, he would have eventually wed one of the weaker families' daughters, thereby adding vigor to their line. Now, the threat of losing both sets of DNA in order to retain his hold over the village was a distinct possibility.

He finished his drink, enjoying the soothing effects of the kalquat, and considered a second, but that would be giving in to his desires. One drink was sufficient to clear his mind of troubling thoughts but not enough to dull his senses. There was still much to do. He needed to go examine the old laws with clear-headed diligence before announcing the upcoming marriage. Kaffa was old but he was no fool. He had access to the old books only the Council did. He would oppose the marriage any way he could. If a loophole existed, he would find it. After that, he would prepare for the evening prayers.

It delighted him that the villagers were so pliable, as if waiting for a strong leader. Once he had planted the idea that Kena's probing of the dead past had started their troubles, they needed little persuasion to escalate their search for more causes. Kaffa and his brash granddaughter, Teela, treaded on a narrow ledge over a deep chasm by opposing him as High Priest. A frightened populace would have no compulsion about pushing him from his lofty perch to save their families.

He smiled. Amid a crisis, opportunity arises. He had worked too long, planned too carefully to allow a wisp of a girl and two fugitives to stop him. He gave a moment's thought to the threat Madras posed, but dismissed the stone carver as too frightened to worry about. His best interests and those of the office of the High Priest were too intertwined to unravel. The stone carver was bound to him body and soul.

Still, he worried that Travin had not returned.

22

MT. LINCOLN PUMPING STATION

O N THE FIFTH DAY AFTER TRAVIN'S DEATH, THE TUNNEL BEGAN TO SLOPE sharply upwards, making the journey more difficult. Hramack's muscles ached until he finally ignored their protests, but after each halt to eat or sleep, they made their overtaxed presence known anew. Injured Grey Eagle had an especially difficult time keeping up the pace, but he steadfastly refused to yield his position in the lead. Hramack marveled at the aged warrior's stamina, matched only by his stubbornness.

The sides of the tunnel gradually narrowed until Hramack could touch both sides with outstretched arms. The smooth, seamless sides shined as if polished. None of the men had ever seen such a material before. No joining marks marred its surface. At one point, one of the men attempted to scratch his initials on the wall, such as men have done for eons, leaving their mark for posterity. The tip of his hardened steel knife left no trace on the durable surface.

Hramack yearned to learn just a minutia of the lost knowledge of his ancestors. Life would become much easier on his people.

One thing bothered him. "Yarah did not intend the water for Ningcha," he said. It was meant for Albuquerque. It was just an accident that created the Pools of Yarah."

Instead of rebuking him for his lack of faith, Kena replied, "Accident? If not for the earthquake, the water would not have been there for Arun Kane's people. Do you not see Yarah's hand in this?"

"I see earthquakes. Is each quake an act of Yarah?"

"Perhaps. Did the earth tremble to provide water for Kane's people, or did Yarah move Kane to search for the water where the quake had stopped it? Is it cause and effect or effect and cause? Searching for answers that cannot be answered serves no purpose. Accept the outcome and believe it was Yarah's will, or believe it a happy accident. I prefer faith. Without faith of some kind, life becomes hollow and meaningless, moving from birth to death in a random series of events that mean nothing. Do you have faith that we will find the answer?"

Hramack did not answer, but his thoughts were troubled. He continued to study the tunnel walls as if it would provide an answer. He was so intent on it that he almost stumbled into Kena's back as he stopped suddenly and stood staring ahead. The look of utter disbelief on his father's face frightened him. Hramack glanced around and saw that the tunnel abruptly ended in a large, featureless chamber with no exit other than the one through which they had traveled for three weeks. *A dead end.* Hramack fought down the scream of bitter disappointment that crawled up his throat. The journey was over. They had failed.

Grey Eagle glared at Kena. "What do we do now, Kena?" he demanded. "Somewhere along the route, we passed the true source of the water. We will have to backtrack to find it."

The men of Pueblo Nuevo began to mutter softly. Hramack feared a mutiny brewing.

"My men are tired and are becoming restless to return to Pueblo Nuevo," Grey Eagle continued. "We must do something quickly, or I will be forced to lead them home."

"No, Grey Eagle," Kena pleaded. "Can't you see? All this must mean something." He began waving his hands frantically in the air, indicating the enigmatic chamber. "Can't you feel the moisture here? We are very close. Have your men spread out and search the walls. There must be something here, something hidden. Search everywhere."

Hramack had noticed the slight rise in humidity, too, but a jumble of frustration and disillusionment made it difficult to wonder at a reason. They had fought Marauders and natural disasters to cross the Empty Wastes. Men had died to achieve their goal. Now, their deaths would be in vain. He wanted to lash out at something, anything, but he was too tired. His gaze sought his father's eyes, expecting to see disappointment in them. Instead, Kena had begun to examine the wall with the intense concentration he had often seen in his father as he searched for an answer.

A blind panic had seized the others, though. They ran about the chamber staring at the featureless walls in a haphazard fashion, bumping into one another in their haste to discover an exit. Hramack doubted they would find anything in their disorganized frenzy. He dropped his pack to the ground, sat on it, and began to think, forcing back the dark gloom threatening to overwhelm him.

If the water originated from this point in the tunnel, there must be a way for it to enter the chamber. Hramack was certain they had not passed another opening, not since the one at Colorado Springs. He examined the ceiling more closely, using a technique his father had taught him about observations when he was young. "Observe the whole," Kena had said, "and discern the patterns. The details will become obvious." As he slowly scanned the ceiling of the chamber, he noticed a series of barely visible circular marks set at regular intervals that he at first had mistaken for random decoration. Now he realized they were neither random nor decorative. They served a function, but what function?

He expanded his view to incorporate the entire chamber, ignoring the human figures moving about breaking up the pattern. His attention focused on a slight variation in shading near one grouping on the wall. It was smoother, as if from many hands polishing its surface. He pushed and probed the area for several minutes with no results.

Kena noticed his son's actions and came over. He eyed the circular spot for a few minutes, and then pressed his palm flat against the surface in the worn spot. To Hramack's astonishment, the wall emitted a humming sound and two sharp clicks deep within the stone. The stone beneath Kena's palm began to glow. As he jerked his hand away, a faint line encircled an area two meters in diameter. Then, the outlined area began to recede into the wall. When it had sunk a few centimeters into the wall, it split in two, each half sliding into opposite sides of the opening, revealing a man-sized passageway beyond.

"Marvelous," Hramack exclaimed at the manner of the door's opening.

The passageway led sharply upward in a series of shallow steps. A pale white glowing strip in the ceiling illuminated the way. With a renewed sense of purpose, the group began their ascent. For a quarter of an hour, they moved upward, turning first one way, and then another as the passage meandered in a seemingly random manner. They had no choice but to continue upwards. No other exits appeared to them. Even Grey Eagle's keen sense of direction failed him.

At last, the passage ended in a large corridor filled with machinery and lined with small rooms. The air hummed with the sounds of pumps and the throb of equipment still operating after hundreds of years. *This is wonderful*, Hramack thought. *What will we find here?* Now Hramack felt certain they could fulfill their odyssey. His keen sense of smell detected water – a great deal of water.

Kena raced from one piece of machinery to the next examining everything in sight. Grey Eagle was more cautious and remained alert to danger. The others were subdued and bewildered. They stood huddled together near a wall, frightened of the unknown. Soon Kena's excitement faded, and he returned to the group.

"Wonderful," he cried. "I don't have any idea what most of this is. The rest I have only a vague notion." He pointed to a series of small desks with darkened screens set into their metal tops. "These seem to be panels for controlling pumps and valves for the movement of water. Can you smell it?"

"Yes, for some time now." Grey Eagle spoke quietly, as if in reverence for his surroundings. "We must move. We are too exposed here with nothing at our backs. Let's head that way, towards the smell of water." He pointed down the corridor.

"Yes, you're right, of course," Kena agreed, "we need water. Take the lead."

The corridor grew brighter as they continued. A soft breeze blew down it, bringing with it the taste of water. Hramack heard a gasp from ahead of him and walked up to stand beside his father. When he emerged from the corridor, the bright sunlight blinded him. He could see nothing until his eyes adjusted to the scintillating glow, but even so, his other senses functioned perfectly. The scent of moisture in the air was pervasive, like after a shower or bath. More animal sounds than he had ever heard except at feeding time for the village goats and sheep filled the moist air. The sun against his skin was pleasantly warm rather than unbearably hot, and he knew it was late in the day. He shaded his eyes with his hand and blinked away the tears.

Before him was more water than he had ever imagined existed outside his fantasies, a lake several kilometers long and at least two kilometers wide. A stiff breeze had ruffled the lake and waves broke noisily against the massive concrete wall containing it. As he walked farther out onto the broad walkway carved from the solid rock of the mountain, a sense of awe overpowered him.

"Just like one of the photos in the old books in the library," he remarked.

Kena fell to his knees and offered a prayed, "Great Father Yarah, thank you for delivering us to this place."

Kena said more, but Hramack paid scant attention to the words. His shock at the enormity of the manmade edifice overwhelmed him. He had seen photos of cities in books, the ruins of the Royal Gorge Bridge, even the sadly decayed city of Colorado Springs, but they paled in comparison to the vista before him. The dam and lake, like the pumping station, were remnants of an earlier age, but they had survived the centuries, had survived the destruction of the great domed cities, and were even now functioning as their builders had intended them to do.

To Hramack's surprise, Grey Eagle raised his arms to the sky and intoned in a deep voice, "Great Tawa, Sun Spirit who watches over us, protect us from harm."

"Your people have a god?" he asked.

"Tawa is the Sun God. There are others, but he is chief among them. The sun rules over all of us. My people have worshipped Tawa since long before the *biligana* came to this land with their Christian God and Jesus."

"You know of Jesus?"

"I have read the Christian Bible, but I place my faith in Tawa."

"I've never seen a Bible. I read other stories that mentioned it and Jesus, the Son of God, but the *Teachings of Nuama* has no prophets. We believe in Yarah, the One True God."

Grey Eagle nodded. "The Christian God was known by many names. One was Yahweh Yireh, meaning 'the Lord will Provide'. Perhaps Yarah derives from that name."

"You amaze me, Grey Eagle. You are a warrior, and yet you know more about my religion that I do."

"I know only what I have read and remembered, nothing of your beliefs. True, I am a warrior, but fighting is not my entire life. Like

your father, I have often wondered about our past, my peoples' past."
He glanced at Kena. "But now I am more concerned with the future."

The sun was just beginning to set as they attempted to take in
the vastness of the lake. As it slipped behind the tall western peaks,
the dancing reflection faded from the lake's surface. A soft golden
glow spread over the water. The breeze calmed, turning the water's
surface into a placid mirror reflecting the snow-capped peaks surrounding it.

Kena said to Grey Eagle, "As beautiful as the lake is, we must
search for a control room where we can learn how to re-establish the
flow of water. We will need food, though. I suggest you send out a
small hunting party."

"Yes," agreed Grey Eagle and motioned to three men. "There is
game by the lake," he said. "Remain here and secure food for our
empty bellies. We will continue our search. Follow us at dawn. I will
mark our path. Make good use of your time if we are to have breakfast."

Torn between remaining with the eager hunters to explore the
lake or joining the search for the control room his father had assured
them would solve their problem, Hramack lingered as long as he
could, but as enticing as the lake was, he could not leave his father.

With Kena leading the way, the group corridor travel along the
causeway until they found another opening with a corridor beyond.
The corridor continued for kilometers, eventually joining three
other corridors at a large junction. There they discovered a large
room filled with metal desks. A glass screen, like a window, was inset
in the top of each desk. As he ran his hand over one, he smiled. "

"It is not glass, but tightly woven, opaque, metal fibers." At
his touch, the screen burst into life. A dozen split views displayed
changing scenes of endless, empty corridors.

"Televisions," Hramack exclaimed in delight. "I have read of such
devices."

"These are monitor screens," Kena explained. "They show various
stations and corridors throughout this vast complex. It allowed the

men here to see what was happening in other parts of the building." He stared at the screens. "These show only empty rooms and corridors. Perhaps if we can get the others working, they will show us what we seek."

Hramack went to each desk activating the monitors. Many remained dark, but several screens displayed control panels with graphs, colored lights, and changing numbers. One desk, larger and more imposing than the others, held four screens labeled: Pump #1 Fill Chamber, Pump#2 Fill Chamber, Pump #3 Fill Chamber, and Overflow Relief Pump Fill Chamber. He touched a flashing light on the screen labeled Overflow Relief Pump, the closest one. The screen flickered to life, showing the very room through which they had entered the building.

"Look," he yelled, "the tunnel."

Kena ran to the desk and examined the panel. He slapped Hramack on the back. "This is it. This desk controls the flow of water into these four chambers." He quickly followed Hramack's lead and activated the other screens. All showed chambers similar to the first, except these were nearly full of water. He experimented with the controls on the panels until he discovered the one that controlled the flow of water into the chambers. Locating this same control on the Overflow panel, he used his finger to slide the control to its maximum setting.

"This should allow water into our tunnel," he said.

At first, nothing happened. Hramack was beginning to feel the bitter taste of disappointment. Then a shudder ran through the floor and slowly, almost imperceptibly at first, the circular openings in the ceiling of the chamber began to rotate and recede into the ceiling. Water poured through the openings.

"Water," Hramack yelled in triumph. His elation turned to despair as the water flow slowed to a trickle and stopped altogether. "It's not working," he cried to his father in dismay.

His father was not watching the monitor screen. Instead, his gaze focused on a bank of lights above the screen slowly changing from green to red. A piercing siren began to wail in the control room, startling everyone. The room shuddered as the pumps shut down. Holding his ears against the onslaught of noise, Kena looked up at the monitor screen, his face a mask of panic.

"No," he screamed. He hit the button beneath the blinking light to silence the siren.

"What happened?" Hramack asked with one finger firmly jammed in his ear in case the blast of noise continued.

Kena ran his hands over the controls, pounding the unresponsive screen. "The water should flow, but something is blocking it before it reaches the chamber. The pumps shut down automatically to avoid burning out. I must find the problem."

Grey Eagle clasped his shoulder. "That noise will bring every Marauder within kilometers to this spot. We must leave."

Kena looked at him in disbelief. "Leave? Now?" He waved his hand at the control panel. "Don't you understand? This device controls the flow of water to our villages. We must repair it." He began to pry open the doors beneath the console.

"Do you know how to repair it?" Grey Eagle shot at him.

Without looking up, Kena responded, "No, not yet, but I'll learn."

Grey Eagle reached down, grabbed Kena by the back of his shirt, and turned him to face him. "We have no time now for you to learn. We cannot hold this room against an attack. We must leave."

Kena was frantic, but Hramack, seeing the wisdom in Grey Eagle's words, took his father's hand. "We'll return later, father. We have no choice except to leave."

Kena nodded his head slowly, but his eyes remained focused on the monitor. "Okay, but remember where this room is."

"We must find the others," Grey Eagle shouted to his men over the wailing alarm.

As they raced back down the corridor to fetch the hunting party, the siren went silent.

"Thank Yarah," Hramack said.

They ran into the men from the lake less than a kilometer from the control room. Upon hearing the siren, they had abandoned their hunt. Reunited, Grey Eagle led them along several corridors until they came upon a large room with ceilings ten meters high. A metal staircase ascended to an enclosed room near the ceiling with a walkway running across the room to another door high in the wall.

"Up there," Grey Eagle pointed to the walkway. "It is easily defended."

Once they reached the lofty room, he set watches on doors and stairs. "We're safe for now," he said to Kena, as he rubbed his injured leg. The race to find shelter had placed a strain on it.

Kena's frustration consumed him. He paced the room wringing his hands. "We must go back. We don't even know if anyone heard the alarm."

Hramack understood his father's anguish, forced to flee just as they found the source of the water, but Grey Eagle's caution was contagious. The thought of confronting a band of Marauders in the corridors frightened him.

"I'll send a scout later," Grey Eagle said to soothe him. "If all is well, we will return."

Kena pointed to Grey Eagle's leg. "Your wound is bleeding. I must change the bandage."

"I haven't time for ..."

"If your wound festers, I will have to amputate it. Now, sit down."

Grey Eagle surrendered to Kena's logic and sat against the wall while Kena removed the bandage, examined the wound, and judged it clean of infection. He applied a salve from his pack and re-bandaged it.

Hramack watched his father, wishing his clumsy hands were as dexterous, until his fatigue drained him. He had not slept for two day except for brief naps. He chose a corner of the room, threw down his blanket, and collapsed on the floor. Around him, the others did the same. The excitement of discovery gave way to exhaustion. Soon, he was dreaming of Ningcha.

✳

Hramack woke with a start at one particularly loud outburst of snoring. He looked around at the sleeping group. All seemed in order, but he could not go back to sleep. His muscles protested the abuse he had heaped upon them over the past few days. He decided to walk off the pain. Hawk was on guard and nodded perfunctorily at Hramack as he passed while keeping a sharp eye on the stairwell below. Hramack followed the catwalk along the roof and through a door into an adjacent large room.

Movement in the corridor beyond the room caught his attention. He crouched and searched the shadows. Finally, he saw a slight woman with red hair skulking along the corridor. She stopped at the door of the room in which he cowered, peered inside, and retraced her steps back down the corridor. He was a bit mystified when she said, "Nothing here, Anderson." He could see no one near her with which to converse.

The woman was clearly not a Marauder. Her skin, though sunburned and peeling in spots, was lighter even than Teela's, a few shades darker than cream. She wore a one-piece jumpsuit and covered her short red hair with a cap. The blue jumpsuit was dirty and ill fitting, and its shimmery material was unknown to him. Could she be one of the caretakers of the pumping facility? He started to return to awaken the others, but then remembered their fatigue. He would let them sleep. He checked to see that he had his knife and began to move cautiously down the stairs and into the corridor to follow her.

He trailed the woman for twenty minutes. She methodically examined each room along the corridor. He became alarmed when he lost sight of her at a junction of two corridors. He peered down each corridor but didn't see her. At a slight noise from an open doorway, he took a cautious peek inside and saw her rummaging through a row of cabinets along one wall of the dimly lit room. Quietly, he moved towards her. Just as he reached a large machine across the room from her, a man stepped from the shadows. Hramack quickly scurried back into the shelter of the machine. He, too, wore a blue jumpsuit and cap, but his skin was much darker, almost charcoal in tone. He was slightly taller than the woman and walked with a limp.

"I haven't found anything, lieutenant," the man said. "How about you?"

"Nothing here, Anderson," she replied.

Anderson, the invisible man she had spoken to earlier.

"I guess we go hungry then," he said. "We finished our last food yesterday."

"Don't worry, Anderson, we're bound to find game outside. We can fish. First, we need to locate the control center. Maybe the communications system is still functioning. They must have had a means to communicate between domes or with the satellites. We'll find it."

Anderson replied, "I'd like to go back home and be welcomed as the man who discovered Earth." He smiled. "At least that's what I'll tell everyone who buys me a drink. I don't want to live out my life here on this dried-out planet or spend another three days wandering this dead place."

"Don't worry. I'm sure you'll be famous. Maybe the Traders Guild will name a planet after you. We have to get back first. Come on," she said.

The man who discovered Earth? Hramack's head reeled. The pair was not from Earth. They had to be Scattered Ones. The legends were true. Even their speech was different, their accents strange. Many of their words made little sense, but he understood enough to know they were Star People, descendants of the people who had fled Earth a millennium earlier. *Why are they here" What should I do? I should tell the others. Yes, I must tell the others.*

As he turned to sneak away, his foot slipped on a length of pipe. It rolled, and he fell heavily, hitting his head against the machine. As the pain swept over him like a tide of darkness, he thought, *I should be used to this by now.* The last thing he remembered was seeing an angel's face hovering above his own.

"Teela," he whispered. Then, the darkness took him.

23

FOX HUNT

I T HAD BEEN MOSTLY A MATTER OF LUCK THAT ONE OF HARDY'S SCOUTING parties had encountered the invaders from the south in the pumping station under Mt. Lincoln. Wisely, they had withdrawn unseen and reported directly to him. He was certain they were the same group that had decimated the salvage party at the warehouse complex near Colorado Springs a few days earlier. They numbered nearly a dozen, and they were cunning, like the fox, but he had more men. Like fox hunts he had read about ion the ancient texts he had collected, he would chase them to ground using his men as the hounds.

If the strangers were capable of creating the large explosions that had killed so many men in the warehouse, they could be capable of damaging the pumping station. Without water, his dream of rebuilding civilization would die. He had to stop them, yet he could not risk a battle inside the mountain. There was too much delicate equipment to place at risk. He would have to wait until the fox emerged from its den.

He camped with two hundred of his best men in a valley very familiar to him. It was in this very valley, lying in the shadow of a daunting two-mile high peak, that his mother had informed him of his destiny. Slowly, but surely, her vision – now his vision – was taking shape. He could not let outsiders bring it down.

He had named the valley after his mother, Ulantha Valley, Valley of Beginnings, in her honor. He had tapped into the underground water lines that once supplied water to Denver Dome and was converting the once barren landscape of the valley into a garden with the abundant water. Only a few people lived there now, their labor more necessary in New Denver, but soon it would become the second city of the New United States. He looked one last time around him and breathed in the aroma of new growth that pervaded the valley. It was for this he was fighting. It was for this he was willing to die, but not before his vision safe.

Even with such large problems facing him, he could not allow the petty problems to go unchallenged. He had postponed confronting Victor Juarez, his top aide, to admire his accomplishments. Now, he had to lay down the law. Juarez stood perfectly still facing him. No coward, he flinched under Hardy's intense gaze, finally averting his eyes. Though Hardy was shorter than Juarez was and slighter of build, he had not forged an alliance by being weak. Juarez understood this.

"I am extremely disappointed in you, Victor. These fields have taken us years to cultivate and to expand, not to mention the cost in water. Fresh fruit and vegetables are saving our lives. Without the excess for trade, we will have no control over the outlying tribes. Faced with starvation, they would turn their attention toward us. If I discover any more unauthorized harvesting, I'll stake you out in the sun until you shrivel up to the size of a dog. Then, I'll skewer your carcass on a spike at the edge of the fields for all the others to see when they're tempted to steal food." He paused for effect, pleased to see Juarez trembling. "You would make a fine scarecrow, Victor."

Juarez retreated at the vehemence in Hardy's voice, doubly chastised because of his failure at securing the fields and for withholding vital information from his leader. Hardy knew he had caught the man responsible for stealing the vegetables, but because the thief was his brother-in-law, he had not turned him in. Now, he was beginning to regret his decision. Juarez of all people knew him to be capable of carrying out his threat. In the twenty years he had known Juarez, he had born witness to the scope of his savagery. Hardy did not consider compassion one of his strong points. He was a hard man and demanded hardness from his subordinates.

Hardy's tone softened as he stepped forward and lightly placed a hand on Juarez's shoulder. "Victor, you are my most trusted aid. We have been together since the beginning. We have built an empire in the wilderness. We have taken tribes of cannibals and bands of starving nomads and molded them, for the most part, into an alliance. I have been harsh when necessary, cruel when required, but I long for a time when such measures are no longer required."

He sighed and turned his head to gaze out over the new green fields stretching to the foothills and the aquaculture farms higher up the slope. His gaze continued, beyond the horizon into the future.

"I grew up in one of those traveling bands of nomads, living on the edge of starvation, eating whatever we could scrounge, wherever we could find it, often receiving beatings instead of my share of food. I had one great advantage that placed me above the others. My mother was literate. She taught me to read at an early age. We searched out books, sometimes going hungry because we placed precedence on finding books over securing our next meal. She knew that someday, someone would rise to the challenge and bring civilization back to our country. She prayed that I would be the one." He turned back to Juarez with a gleam in his eye. "And I swear I will be that one, whatever the cost."

Juarez swallowed hard and nodded, afraid to trust his voice.

"Now, go tell your brother-in-law that I know he stole the food. If he were anyone else, I would have him flogged to death. Tell him he owes you his life, because it is so. I cherish loyalty, my friend. Just be sure that you place your loyalty to me above all others. When you have done this, gather fifty men to march to the pumping station just before sunset. We must greet our uninvited guests."

Hardy chuckled quietly to himself as he watched Juarez scurry away. He assumed Juarez would search out his worthless brother-in-law and give him the thrashing he so richly deserved. It had been a simple matter to find out who had been stealing vegetables. The tricky part had been not revealing what he knew until the information had been most valuable. Such tactics cultivated an air of omniscience that served to strengthen his position of leadership.

The past twenty years had been rough ones. Motivating people to think beyond simple survival had not been an easy task. By convincing his people that trading with other tribes was more profitable than fighting them, he secured a place of leadership.

First, they had traded salt mined from the salt flats far to the west for flint and obsidian from the south, and then used the flint and obsidian to fashion spears and arrows for hunting game. Trading extra hides for metal, they learned to forge it into more durable spear points and arrow tips. This had saved his people the laborious task of knapping flints. The free time they gained, he trained a dedicated force of hunters also capable of defending and expanding their territory. Reliable weapons made them more effective hunters. They smoked the surplus meat, allowing more time for the gathering of edible plants. The health of the tribe had increased, and the infant mortality rate decreased.

Searching out smaller, weaker tribes and either forcing or convincing them to join with his, his tribe had expanded the range of their hunting grounds and reduced the risks inherent to interbreeding. By utilizing the accumulated knowledge of the elders of each tribe and nurturing them instead of leaving the weak and old to fend for themselves, he had established a pool of knowledge that bene-fited all the tribes.

Still, convincing his people to settle so near the ruins of Denver Dome had required all his leadership skills. Years of mythos and superstition had labeled it an evil place and deservedly so. Upon first arriving at the ruins, they had encountered men so primitive as to have almost lost the power of reason. Reduced to cannibalism, these small bands of sub-humans infested the debris-filled streets and gutted buildings, slaughtering anyone unlucky enough to wander into the ruins in search of food or scarce metal, and murdering each other when times were especially hard. Repeated attempts at com-munication with them failed miserably and cost the lives of many of his men. Seeing no alternative, he decided that he would have to eliminate them if his people were to stand any chance of reestablish-ing civilization in the region.

He finally resorted to poisoned food, as if they were rabid animals. He was not proud of his decision, but it had saved lives. The cleanup had taken weeks, searching out the rotting corpses and burning them in piles in the streets. The stench of the burning bodies and the reek of their filthy warrens permeated the air for many weeks to follow, but the city was his. His first task was to dispatch men into the ruins to search for books – any books. They returned with hun-dreds. In a civilization that had been widely dependent on comput-ers, Hardy was amazed at the number of books they had recovered. Most were useless except for their literary or historical significance, but some were jewels, such as the plans to the city itself and books on metalworking and agriculture. With these, he had built a base of knowledge.

By following the pipes that had once conveyed water to the dome, they discovered the still-active pumping station under the moun-tain with its great reservoir of stored water. Once they repaired the pipes, the pumps automatically began pouring water into the city, washing away the accumulated filth centuries, and creating lakes in low-lying areas. Using fish netted in the reservoir, they transformed the flooded areas into the beginnings of a burgeoning aquaculture, adding dried fish to their trade goods. Another beneficial byproduct was fish waste as fertilizer for the fields.

They razed acres of buildings and removed the rubble stone by stone to make room for fields of fruit and vegetables. The metal became weapons, tools, and plows. The stone became new buildings. They began cultivating any plant that proved edible, using seed discovered in the city's still-sealed and intact seed vault. Soon, they had more than enough food for themselves. They built storehouses for the surplus. Food and fresh water became currencies to entice the outlying nomadic tribes to join his growing alliance. After a time, all tribes owed him at least partial allegiance. He discouraged cannibalism whenever he could, but such practices continued beyond his immediate reach. He encouraged the tribes to bring him herd animals, tools, books, metals – anything that might prove useful, rewarding them with food, weapons, or water.

Slowly, agonizingly slowly at first, civilization began to flourish in the region. Hardy established schools to teach reading, writing, and trades such as metalworking, farming, and stone working. From the rubble of Denver Dome, he was erecting an empire, a country, with him as the leader.

Hardy returned to the house he used when not in the city, a two-room stone building constructed on a small rise at the edge of the valley overlooking the burgeoning fields. Elisba was waiting for him. Her bright blue eyes were the only thing that could melt the hardness in him. For ten years she had tempered his rashness and urged him on when things became overbearing. Born in one of the northern nomadic tribes, she had not lost the lean, hard body that came from such a life. She had an uncommon beauty, but she was no trophy wife. She was a voracious reader, equal almost to him. While he drove his men forward, she quietly urged the women. Together, they made a formidable team.

"You frighten Victor," she purred softly as she walked behind him and began massaging his shoulders. He relaxed, letting her long, supple fingers loosen the tight knots beneath his shoulder blades. "He is your friend."

He knew she was reproaching him. She was the only one he allowed to do so. "Victor is my friend, but he is also my top aide. He sometimes forgets the difference. If I allow him privileges I do not allow others, they will become jealous and resentful."

"You allow me privileges," she said, stopping her ministrations and burying her face against his back. Her scent, clean and healthy, drifted from her. He turned and took her in his arms. As she gazed up at him, her blue eyes smiling in spite of her words, he smiled at her.

"You are special. I sleep with you because from you I do not fear a knife in my back. Perhaps I trust Victor as well, but no others. If I die, my dream of a new nation, a new America, will die with me. No other but you has my vision or my drive."

"You drive them too hard," she replied.

"I drive myself harder."

She sighed. "Your meal is ready."

He realized she was changing the subject before she angered him. She knew him well. He pulled her close and kissed her, as he ran his fingers through her long, black hair. "Food is not what I need. Come."

He took Elisba's hand and led her toward the bedroom.

As the sun began to paint the sky golden, Hardy set out for the pumping station under Mt. Lincoln with a half a hundred of his best men. On the slim possibility that the incursion could be nothing more than an elaborate ruse, he sent the remainder of his fighting men to the south and to the east to meet any challenges from those directions. As they marched, they passed field after field of vegetables and groves of fruit trees, each covered by a netting of fine mesh to shield them from the ravages of the sun. The new drip irrigation system they had painstakingly installed saved them thousands of liters of water. Finding the old plans for such a system had been a godsend. Now, the plants received exactly the amount of moisture they needed to remain healthy. Yields had increased by as much as twenty percent. Combined with the newly built greenhouses, the increased yields could spell the difference between merely surviving and expanding the amount of land under cultivation. Any surplus would allow them to increase the size of the herd animals.

Although less efficient than plants at utilizing resources, meat was necessary for growth, especially for the young ones. Smoked or dried, it transported well and stored easily. Perhaps, finally, he would be able to stamp out the occasional acts of cannibalism that persisted among the outlying tribes of nomads despite his best efforts to discourage them.

Too many years of work and too many people's lives had gone into his dream to allow a band of invaders to destroy it, even if he had to wipe out the entire population from his southern border all the way to the edge of the ancient sea. Approximately five thousand people now lived in or near the ruins of Denver Dome. Thousands more still lived in small tribal communities scattered throughout the territory, such as Ulantha Valley. Their lives were better today because of the dream his mother had instilled in him as a small boy. He had built schools and started apprentice trade schools. He had taught them to cultivate diverse crops and raise herd animals. He had sought out medicines, tools, books, and knowledge wherever he could find it. Some buildings even had electricity provided by windmills.

In another twenty years, his people would spread out across the country, seeking resources and other people, rebuilding the country as they went. If Kolkata Dome still existed, someday he would visit it, offering what they could, seeking what they needed.

If I can stop these southern invaders.

Hardy knew he could be cold and ruthless. Even Victor Juarez feared him, and he was the closest thing to a friend Hardy had. He had fostered these dark traits to control his men. In a system where tribal leaders often were chosen for their strength and prowess in battle, he could ill afford to show any sign of weakness, nor could his leaders. In the process, though, something had been lost. In matters of discipline or control, he could trust his subordinates to do their jobs well enough, but when subtlety or finesse was required, they were lost. Hardy found himself constantly resolving problems that even a competent secretary should be able to handle. He was beginning to tire. The prospects of another long war lay heavily on him.

In spite of the schools, the training, and the constant search for learning tools from the past, Hardy was alone. Unless he could find someone who understood his dreams, someone who possessed an iota of his strong will to force change, he knew his dream of a rebuilt country would die with him. Petty squabbles would tear his fragile alliance apart. His wife was capable of continuing his legacy, but centuries of custom assured the people would never seriously consider her as a leader. He needed to learn more about the outsiders before destroying them out of hand. Such knowledge could prevent future attacks. It would not be easy. His men's bloodlust was up, and they would not willingly spare any of the intruders for questioning.

Reluctantly, Hardy forced his men into a fast trot, hoping the lingering heat of the day would not kill them before they reached the mountain. He kept himself in good shape and insisted no less from his men. Still, as the kilometers fell away beneath his boots, his legs began to ache. He longed for horses. One of his most prized possessions was a painting of a herd of wild horses galloping through the high grasses with a series of high, snow-capped peaks in the distance. To him, it epitomized what Earth had lost in the Great Abandonment. He had seen snow high up on the flanks of the mountains above the pumping station, the source of the water that had fed Denver Dome, but to see such amounts of snow in one place as in his painting, blanketing the land – it was awe-inspiring.

With horses, they could travel from the mountains to the eastern plains in days instead of a weeklong march. The speed of communications would increase dramatically. Now, if a problem arose in a far off village, his solution was often too late in arriving. As his territory expanded, so would the problems. Horse-drawn wagons could carry ten times the cargo of small drays pulled by goats, and the outlying villages often stole them for food. He needed horses, but as of yet, no sign of the great, majestic creatures had been found. Perhaps they, like so many of Earth's creatures, had not coped with the drastic change in climate. If there were still horses in what had once been the United States, he would someday find them.

The nearer they got to the mountain, the more his men grumbled and complained. Most feared the great underground pumping facility. To them, holes in the earth were the homes of demons and the Great Devil himself, not meant for man. They entered and explored the pumping facility only because he drove them to do so. Even so, most of the magnificent facility yet remained unexplored.

The centuries-old automated systems still functioned, doing the tasks assigned to them long ago. Some areas had fallen into ruin, but as long as it did not interfere with the water supply, those areas could wait. The facility held a wealth of mysterious machinery and objects of unknown purpose. It could take many years to grasp the full depth of knowledge there.

He admired the intelligence and craftsmanship of his ancestors. The things they had accomplished seemed miraculous. One such was Denver Dome. The ruins of the dome that had covered the old city resembled a creation of nature, a crystal mountain. Even the buildings showed a fine symmetry and balance that mirrored nature. He knew it would be generations before his people accumulated enough knowledge to attempt such undertakings. For now, it sufficed simply to repair and rebuild.

The old world had died in fear and greed. The new would be simpler. Machinery, yes, but man could not forget the feel of the hammer in his hand or the sound of the plow turning the soil. Ignoring nature was as foolish as trying to control it. Man would have to coexist with nature, a harmony of steel and earth.

The strangers possessed weapons such as the Old Ones used. Perhaps there were more hidden in some buried cache. His army needed them. If the strangers refused to trade, he would force them to disclose the location. With such weapons, he could guard his borders. The strangers would have to be taken alive – at least some of them.

24

THE STAR PEOPLE

HRAMACK AWOKE WITH HIS HEAD THROBBING. HE CAREFULLY LOOKED around, trying not to move his head. The woman and the man were sitting together staring at him. As he tried to sit up, bringing on a sharp spasm of pain, the woman came over to him.

"Drink," she said, offering him a canteen. He took a long sip of water. He touched the back of his head with his fingers, wincing when they came away bloody. She produced a small tube and held it in her hand. "This will clear up your head."

He eyed the strange object for a moment, and then decided that if they wanted him dead, he would already be dead. He nodded his head. She pressed the tube to his arm. The sharp hiss startled him, but he felt no pain.

"What was that?" he asked.

She stared at him until he pointed to the tube, and then understanding his question, smiled and said, "A hypo." She tossed it aside. "It was the last one."

"Are you truly from the Scattered Ones?" he asked, then noticed the blank look on her face. He could see they were going to have a communication problem, even though they both spoke the same language, just separated by a thousand years of linguistic drift. "From the stars," he added, pointing skyward.

"Yes, we are from the ship *Long John Baldry* here to explore Homeworld, Earth. I am First Officer Lieutenant Cathi Lorst. He is Communications Officer Kal Anderson. Who are you?"

Hramack stared at Anderson. His eyes were emerald green with flecks of gold. His skin was darker than anyone's he had ever seen, almost the color of charcoal. He glanced at his arm in comparison. His deeply bronzed skin was darker than most in Ningcha, darker than the ruddy hues of the men of Pueblo Nuevo. The extra melanin in his darker skin gave him greater protection from the harmful rays of the sun, adaptive radiation, his father had called it, much like the mutation of the desert creatures and plants slowly evolving to the changing environment. He wondered if Anderson came from a desert world like Earth.

"I am Hramack, son of Kena of Ningcha," he answered. "What happened?"

"We heard a noise and turned just in time to see you fall. You hit your head. You've been unconscious almost an hour. How is your head?"

He rubbed his head, which was already beginning to clear from the injection she had given him. It still ached, but his thoughts weren't as fuzzy. He chuckled. "I'm getting used to it. What did you say you gave me?"

"A catecholamine," she replied. "It will help focus your thoughts. Where did you say you were from? Not Denver Dome?"

Her pronunciation was clipped and strange, but he recognized catecholamine, an organic compound that produced sedatives from amino acids in the human body. It was a painkiller and a stimulant. Was she also a Healer?

"No, Ningcha is a small village three weeks' journey from here. We came to restore the water to our village. Denver Dome is a dangerous place filled with Marauders."

"Marauders? Yes, we've met them." She shuddered. "Savage creatures. Are your people any better?" she asked coldly.

Hramack shot her an icy stare. "Of course. We are followers of Yarah, believers in peace. We farm and raise animals. The water stopped flowing, and we came here to restore it. The Marauders are scavengers and cannibals. We, too, have met them." He spat on the ground.

"You said we. Where are the others who came with you?"

Hramack remained silent, cursing himself for letting slip that he was not alone. Did he dare trust these strangers with military titles, even if they were from the stars? "I will not tell you," he replied.

"Okay, Hramack, son of Kena, if you insist, but you must come with us."

"Why should I?" he demanded.

"Because we don't know you and because I have this."

She showed him something that resembled a weapon he had seen in old books, using explosive gunpowder to propel a metal projectile at great speeds to kill at great distances. He reached for his knife, but discovered only an empty scabbard. They had taken it from him while he lay unconscious.

"Is that a weapon?"

"Yes," she said. "A laser. It projects a highly charged, coherent beam of light."

"You would use it on me?" Hramack asked, astonished that someone advanced enough to travel between the stars would lower themselves to kill another human being. Then he remembered that until recently, he had believed himself incapable of killing. No longer.

"I do not want to. We are not your enemy, but I will not allow you or your friends to harm my companion or me. I will treat your injury, and then you will come with us."

It seemed he had little choice in the matter. He might overpower one of them, but not both. He needed to learn more about these strange people and learn why they were here. He did not feel threatened by them, although he was certain she would not hesitate to kill him if he attacked them. He allowed her to dab his wound with a wet cloth and apply a small adhesive pad. He was surprised at how gentle she was after first threatening him with her weapon. Her hands were the hands of a Healer, like his. *No*, he reminded himself, *gentler than his*.

"There," she said, smiling at him. "That should stop the bleeding. The cut was superficial." She frowned. "I'm afraid I don't have any antibiotics. I used them all on Whitehall."

Hramack searched the corners of the room for the third Star Person.

Noticing his gaze, she frowned and said, "He's dead. So is Pegari."

"I am sorry for your loss. May Yarah keep them. Are you a Healer?"

"A what? Oh, a medic. No, I know a little about first aid but not enough to save Whitehall."

By her pained expression and the bitterness in her voice, he realized that she took full responsibility for her companion's death. That showed compassion. "Even good Healers lose patients," he said.

She turned away. "We must go now."

They traveled down a side corridor, continuing to search lockers and cabinets for food. Hramack was amazed they had found edible food after so many years. Such preservation techniques would help his village. If they survived, he reminded himself bitterly. He wondered if the others had noticed his absence by now. They could easily follow his tracks on the dusty floor. In the meantime, he would learn all he could about the strangers from the stars.

After hours of wandering up and down countless side corridors and examining the contents of numerous rooms, Hramack began to realize just how vast the underground facility was. Cathi explained that she and Anderson had been exploring it for three days.

"It is a wondrous facility, almost a small city, but finding what we need is frustrating."

Hramack almost told them about the control center they had found, but to lead them there would be taking them back to Kena and Grey Eagle. He needed to learn more about them first.

She paused at a junction where one corridor sloped downward and the other continued straight ahead. Hramack felt a light warm breeze blowing up the sloping one.

"That one leads outside," he said. He hoped they took it. He was tired of the underground facility, no matter how fascinating.

To his consternation, she chose to continue straight ahead. "I don't want to exit the mountain just yet.

Exploration of the straight corridor yielded nothing interesting, but to Hramack's relief, when they opened the final door at the corridor's terminus, they exited the mountain onto a large platform fifty meters above a valley floor different from the damned lake valley. Hramack decided that it was on the opposite side of the mountain from the lake, making the underground facility a vast complex of staggering proportions. He took a deep breath of fresh air, enjoying the slight dusty taste and the heat of the sun on his flesh before looking around. Flights of metal steps showing little sign of corrosion led down to ground level sixty meters below them. The outline of a vanished roadway ended at the mountain. Leaning over the rail, he saw a much larger entrance below them and slightly to one side.

"This heat is unbearable," Cathi commented, staring at the sky and wiping the sweat from her brow. "How have your people managed to survive?"

"We live in stone houses protected from the sun by the overhanging cliffs of our canyon. We do not venture into the Burning Lands during the heat of the day unless necessary." He shrugged his shoulders. "We have survived."

Far to the east, Hramack saw the shining edifice that was once man's last hope. Even broken and in ruins, Denver Dome was a great glittering jewel on the horizon. Its spires and towers, though crumbled by centuries of neglect and the ravages of nature, nevertheless dominated the horizon. It seemed such a waste that mankind could work together to build such massive structures, only to be defeated by the smallest and pettiest of emotions – greed and hate. If only human wisdom had grown as quickly as the ability to create, humanity would have survived the sun's fury, and Earth would once again have become a beautiful world.

Perhaps it was not too late. He saw in the return of the Scattered Ones the opportunity to rebuild. In spite of their distrust of him, Hramack sensed a pride and goodness in these Off-Worlders that made him welcome their return. It was time Earth's scattered offspring once again reunited to grasp their common destiny.

"There's nothing out here to help us," Anderson groaned. He leaned on the railing crestfallen, but jerked his arms back as the sun-baked metal seared his skin through his sleeves.

"We could explore the entrance below us," Hramack suggested.

Just as he spoke, a party of men strode from the entrance. He, Cathi, and Anderson backed away from the edge of the platform to avoid detection.

"Marauders," Cathi said. Her voice betrayed her hatred of Marauders. Hramack wondered about her earlier encounter with them. He was surprised she had survived it. Perhaps her advanced weapon played a part. "I think it best we backtrack and search for a control room. There is nothing out here."

Before they could reenter the mountain, loud shouts below them drew Hramack's attention. The group of men was now under attack by a second party more than twice their number. The smaller group took refuge behind a low, rocky wall, but some of the larger group was attempting to surround them. Cathi used a pair of field glasses to scan the two groups.

"Do you know any of them," she asked, handing him the binoculars.

He looked through lenses more powerful than his father's binoculars. Small numbers on the edge of his vision provided distance and elevation. By touching a button, the view zoomed until he could see their faces crisply and clearly, as if he were standing among them. They were far superior to the simple lenses of his father's crude pair. He recognized men dressed much like the ones who had attacked them at Colorado Springs, well-armed and eager for battle. Then he moved to the second, smaller group, surprised to see Grey Eagle standing tall in the middle of the melee, swinging his knife at two Marauders. Two of Nuevo Pueblans were already down, one dead and one injured, but he could not tell who they were. He searched the group frantically but could not find his father.

"They are my friends," he said. "My father is down there somewhere. I must help him. There are too many Marauders. Please, let me go," he pleaded.

He waited impatiently as Cathi and Anderson exchanged glances. Anderson looked at the struggle below and nodded his agreement. "We'll help," she said.

"Thank you," Hramack said; then, raced down the steps to aid his father and friends.

※

Kena awoke to Grey Eagle's urgent voice asking, "Where has your son gone?"

Kena's sleep-deprived mind snapped into focus upon mention of Hramack.

"I don't know," he answered, throwing off his blanket. "Perhaps he couldn't sleep," he added, though that did not seem likely given everyone's physical exhaustion. "How long has he been gone?"

"Perhaps two hours, maybe a little longer. Hawk saw him pass, but thought he was simply going to relieve himself. He did not return before the guards changed. We should search for him. I feel danger near."

Trusting Grey Eagle's instincts, Kena quickly gathered up his and Hramack's belongings and joined the others, who were already waiting for them on the catwalk. In the next room, they found evidence that Hramack had indeed gone that way. His tracks were everywhere on the dusty floor, as were a second set of boot prints.

Kena tried not to read too much into the second set of tracks. The tracks may have already been there, and Hramack had decided to follow them, but concern for his son's safety quickened his steps. To his dismay, a short distance down the corridor, both sets of tracks disappeared.

"They are trying to cover their tracks," Grey Eagle said.

Kena was not as certain. The entire floor was not only dust free, but polished as well. It seemed unlikely anyone would go to so much trouble to conceal their tracks, but he trusted Grey Eagle's judgment. It was better to be wary. Farther along, they came upon a line of doors along one side of the seemingly endless corridor. Searching each one, they discovered only empty rooms and more corridors. In one room, amid a pile of metal pipes, one of Grey Eagle's men spotted dried blood on the floor. Kena's heart twisted in his chest as he knelt beside the blood.

"There is very little blood, nor is there a body," Grey Eagle pointed out. "If it is indeed Hramack's blood, he is alive."

Kena picked up a small cylindrical object and sniffed it. "This smells of medicine."

"Strange that they would wound, and then comfort." Grey Eagle said.

"Yes," Kena agreed.

They followed the main corridor, deeming it the most likely way Hramack would have gone. As they continued, the temperature slowly increased, indicating they were nearing an outside exit. Kena hoped Hramack had merely ventured outside exploring. The alternative was too terrible to contemplate.

The corridor divided, with one branch continuing straight, and the other sloping downwards. Both were free of dust and footprints.

"We should not divide our forces," Grey Eagle said. "A slight breeze blows up this sloping corridor. Which way would Hramack have gone?"

"Alone, he would have chosen the downward slope. If captive, I don't know."

Grey Eagle decided. "We take the one leading to the outside first. If we do not find him, we will return and take the other one."

The corridor continued for nearly a kilometer. By then, dust began to reappear on the floor, and they knew Hramack had not gone that way. As eager as Kena was to continue the search for his son, he could see the urge to breathe outside air straining the men's faces. To them, the underground labyrinth was too much like the river tunnel. The temptation to see the sun once again was too strong to ignore.

The corridor ended in a cavernous room whose massive door was open to the searing heat of the day outside. A breeze carrying the familiar flinty smell of sand and dust blew through the door driven by the heat. Various pieces heavy machinery lined the walls of the room, some wheeled, and some with metal tracks. The rubber tires had long ago rotted away, and a thick layer of dust coated their surfaces, but the metal was corrosion-free, looking almost as if they would start up if supplied with a fresh power source. A few had wide metal blades on the front end. Others had buckets with metal teeth for digging. One, larger than the rest, had a rectangular front end in which hundreds of rotating blades were mounted.

"I believe these were used to construct the corridors."

Grey Eagle ignored the equipment and studied the dusty floor of the garage. "I see many tracks but none matching Hramack's or the second set of boot prints." He turned to Kena. "We should go back. There have been many men here recently, probably Marauders."

He motioned to his men, and they began to retrace their steps. Kena stopped him.

"Should we not investigate? If Marauders are nearby, we do not want them catching us unaware."

Grey Eagle reconsidered. It was obvious he did not want to risk his men. "We will reconnoiter," he said. He warily eyed the open area outside the garage door."But only for a short distance."

They exited into a wide valley formed by two mountains, broken by a series of heavily eroded low ridges ending in rows of rocky spires, many of which performed natural feats of balance with large boulders perched atop skinny stone or precarious stacks of rock.

"This must have been a monumental task," Kena said, "almost as daunting an endeavor as building the domes."

Grey Eagle glanced at the mountain towering above them and growled, "Neither dome nor mountain concern me as much as our invisible enemy. I feel their presence as an itch I cannot scratch."

Without warning, a flight of arrows erupted from the rocks a short distance away and landed among them. One man, an uncomplaining, happy-go-lucky youth named Moon Smiles Down, fell with an arrow protruding from his chest. Kena started towards him, but Grey Eagle grabbed him by the collar and half-dragged him to a nearby low wall of rocks. An arrow also struck a giant named Strong Arm and knocked him down, but he ignored the shaft protruding from his arm and quickly regained his feet.

"He is dead," he told Kena. "There is nothing we can do for Moon Smiles Down. As much as I detest the idea, we must seek the shelter of the mountain. There is no cover here." He motioned his men to make a run back into the mountain, but as they began their retreat, more Marauders appeared from inside the massive door. Now, their enemy lay between them and their goal.

"They must have been hiding in one of the smaller corridors we passed. It's a trap. Back to the wall," he screamed.

Seeing Kena safely behind the wall, Grey Eagle waded into a group of Marauders who had converged on one of his men and succeeded in carrying him to the ground with their massed weight. He grabbed one assailant by the arm, spun him across the ground, and then attacked another with a savage swipe of his knife. Unfortunately, he was too late to save Bright Eagle, who lay bleeding from numerous knife wounds to his chest. Grey Eagle swore an oath at the top of his lungs and began hacking his way through the attackers like a crazed demon.

His men were afraid to fire arrows for fear of hitting him. Out of the corner of his eye, Grey Eagle noticed several Marauders attempting to make their way behind them, encircling them.

"Behind you," he screamed. No one could hear him over the noise of battle. Just as it seemed the battle was lost, the ground nearby erupted in a great geyser of dirt and rock, scattering his attackers. This gave him the opportunity to reach his companions behind the wall.

"What was that?" Kena yelled in his ear.

Before Grey Eagle could respond, Hramack and two oddly clad strangers appeared from behind a large boulder and began running towards them. The woman in blue with Hramack carried an odd weapon in her hand. At first, Grey Eagle considered ordering one of his men to shoot her just to be safe, but Hramack appeared unconcerned. Suddenly, she raised the weapon and fired. A searing bolt of light burst from it and shattered the ground in front of a group of Marauders, bowling them over like in a game of ten pins. Using the distraction to cover their movements, Hramack and his two companions scrambled over the low wall to join them.

"Hello, Father," Hramack said, gasping for breath after his long run. "These are Star People come to help."

"Star People?" Kena asked, astonished.

"I will explain later. The Marauders are trying to surround you. The woman, Cathi Lorst, has an energy weapon. You've seen it?"

"A truly remarkable weapon," Grey Eagle said, still eyeing the two strangers with distrust.

"I'm afraid it's almost useless now," she interrupted. "The power cell is almost drained." She studied Kena closely. "You are his father, the Healer?" she asked.

"I am Kena. Welcome to Earth," he offered his hand. "Welcome home," he added. "Are all Star People as beautiful as you?" he asked.

She flushed at his compliment. "I'm flattered. I'm considered rather plain. I haven't washed my clothes in ten days. If we get the opportunity, I'll clean up, and then you can decide."

"I'm afraid we may die here, Cathi Lorst, if your weapon is truly almost useless," Grey Eagle told her. "We are greatly outnumbered."

Two Clouds doubled over as a Marauder knife found his stomach, but he managed to kill his attacker. Though many Marauders lay on the ground, there were many more pressing the attack. With their limited cover, Grey Eagle knew they could not hold out long. It was only a matter of time before they were overwhelmed behind their meager protective wall.

The group attacking them, Grey Eagle noted, as was the group at Colorado Springs, was better equipped, and better trained than most Marauders he had encountered. They wore cloth pants, sandals with leggings, and brightly colored, long-sleeved shirts. Their head coverings varied, but a thick leather skullcap was predominant. Each carried a bandolier of knives or bolts for crossbows across their chests. Many carried longbows and used them effectively from a distance as a trained unit, not the haphazard individual approach preferred by most Marauders.

Also, unlike most Marauders, they appeared well fed and unafraid. Two brave but foolhardy men tried to rush the wall, only to die under a withering hail of well-aimed arrows from the bows of Kena and White Elk, but arrows were running low. Soon, it would be hand-to-hand combat, and the defenders would have no chance against the Marauders' greater numbers.

Grey Eagle had witnessed the horrors Marauders inflicted upon their captives. It remained indelibly imprinted upon his mind: a nightmare that would not fully fade upon awakening.

"I will not let them take me alive," he swore. "I will take the fight to them."

His men nodded their agreement. He looked at Cathi and at Anderson, trying to judge their merit. The woman had joined the fight with the courage of a warrior. She bore herself proudly and determined. Of the dark-skinned man, he was unsure. He had been limping as he raced across the open ground to join them. He had heart, but he had not yet proven himself in battle. Now was as good a time as any.

"If you are truly from the stars, the Marauders will show you no mercy. They bear a deep and bitter hatred for the Scattered Ones, holding you to blame for Earth's demise. I salute your courage and welcome your strength beside me. Come."

Grey Eagle noted the look of disdain in the woman's eyes. "I've had a taste of their hospitality," she said. "I would rather die fighting than let them touch me again."

Hramack looked at his father with dismay. "We have not accomplished our mission," he said. Dying did not bother him as much as failing his people.

"Perhaps it was not Yarah's will," Kena answered, and then smiled at Hramack. "Yarah promises no one a long life. Come, my son. We will fight together." He turned to Cathi. "I am sorry you meet this end with us. I wish I had more time to learn about you and your people. I pray to Yarah only that others of the Scattered Ones will come home. It is time. You have been away too long."

She reached out and grasped Kena's hand, squeezing it tightly. "They will come, Kena of Ningcha, soon."

Kena smiled at her, laid aside his bow, and pulled his knife from his belt. He stood and yelled, "For Ningcha! For Yarah!"

Grey Eagle stood beside him. "For Pueblo Nuevo! For Tawa!"

Cathi stared at Kena. "For the *Long John Baldry*! For the Great Creator!"

Kena nodded to her. "Let us go, Cathi Lorst."

Cathi was not quite ready to die. She did not pray for assistance or guidance. Unlike Kena with his strong belief in his Yarah, most Traders held no strong religious convictions. Choosing one religion over another among the plethora of religions in Trader space could be a detriment to trade agreements. Traders held themselves above the political and religious fray that had fractured so many worlds.

Her upbringing on a small agricultural world had exposed her to her parents' God and the Holy Trinity of Father, Son, and Holy Ghost, but they had never prayed openly or attended the local church except on religious holidays. They had not forced their beliefs on her, and she had seen little use in an invisible deity. Now, like most Traders, she believed in a nebulous Great Creator of the Universe that allowed his creations to follow their own path without interference or assistance. She had never felt the need for anything more personal.

The one thing she was sure of was that she had been through too much to give up without a fight. This time, unlike the crash and the wretched journey across the wastes, she could put a face to her foe. She looked around, trying to assess the situation. It was evident the Marauders would soon overpower them. She checked her laser. It had enough charge for a single shot, not enough to make much of a difference against so many.

She searched for a means to escape. The well-guarded entrance into the mountain was out of the question; they would be dead before they reached it. If they could reach the stairs, their height would provide an easily defendable position above the enemy. However, the path to the stairs lay straight through the middle of the enemy. She glanced at her laser again.

"Kena, you must trust me. I think I have a way out."

"I don't understand what you intend to do," he told her, "but you must do it now." He grabbed at Grey Eagle's arm. He was already in a killing frenzy, his eyes glazed as he marched toward the enemy.

"Why do you stop me?" he growled at Kena.

"Because Cathi Lorst has a plan that might ensure our survival," he yelled back.

Grey Eagle shook off Kena's grip and roared like a wild animal. He did not retreat, but he did not charge. He stared at Cathi, waiting.

"If this works," she said, "be ready to run that way, toward the stairs. They won't expect that. We may have a chance."

"They will cut us down like harvesting maize," he snapped.

She feared he might be right. "Just run," she said.

She activated the laser by pulling the double-pull trigger only slightly and watched the power indicator climb. She allowed it to pass well into the red danger zone before shoving a small stone into the trigger guard to prevent the trigger from automatically disengaging. Instead of firing or shutting down, the laser continued to build power. When it began to hum loudly, she threw it into the midst of the massing Marauders.

"Run," she yelled.

To her immense relief, the others heeded her. The laser exploded a few seconds later in a great shower of rock and dirt, incinerating many of the Marauders in the sudden release of energy. The concussion knocked those not immediately vaporized to the ground, stunned and helpless. The remainder, thoroughly demoralized, retreated and scattered to the safety of the rocks. Partially hidden by the cloud of dust raised by the explosion, she led the others in a mad dash for the stairs. By the time the surviving Marauders had recovered from the initial shock of the surprise attack, the group was halfway to the stairs. However, their enemy had not given up the fight. Their lieutenants regrouped the scattered troops and renewed their pursuit.

Cathi scooped up a rock as she ran, pausing just long enough to toss it toward the nearest group of Marauders trying to cut off their escape. As she hoped, they thought the rock was another weapon and slowed, giving Grey Eagle's men enough time to reach the stairs. As they climbed, they began raining arrows down on the pursuing Marauders. Seeing Anderson limping and lagging behind, she waited for him, pushing him up the stairs ahead of her.

As she bounded up the last flight of stairs two at a time, she felt a sharp prick in her right shoulder. She gasped in pain and stumbled, but recovered to struggle up the last steps. The expression of horror on Hramack's face as he looked at her mystified her. She followed his fixed gaze to the metal tip of the Marauder arrow protruding from her chest, and then crumpled to the stairs. Her last thoughts were of the *Long John Baldry*.

25

TRAPPED

Hramack watched in horror as Cathi slumped unconscious into his arms, pierced by a Marauder's arrow. She had saved them all with her quick thinking, scattering and disorienting the attacking Marauders with the unexpected explosion. The stairs provided a secure, easily defendable position from which they could repel an attack. It was not until they were all safely inside the mountain facility and the door secured that she had given in to the pain of her wound and collapsed.

"Cathi!" he cried aloud, as he laid her gently on the floor. When he turned her limp body over, he saw that the arrow had penetrated her chest just below her left shoulder near her collarbone, lodging dangerously close to her heart. By the small amount of blood staining her clothing, it had not struck an artery, one small bit of luck, but blood continued to seep around the wooden shaft of the arrow.

"Can she be moved?" he heard someone ask. "What?" he muttered, irritated at the interruption. Of course, they couldn't move her. Couldn't they see she was severely injured? He probed the flesh around the arrow's shaft, hoping his father could remove it safely. It would be a tricky procedure.

"Can we move her?" Grey Eagle shook Hramack's shoulder to get his attention and repeated his question. "We cannot remain here. We can secure the door against those outside, but not against the ones inside the building. If they manage to surround us, they can starve us out. We must beat them to the control center or to the lake – some place we can more easily defend."

The worried Nuevo Pueblan's words finally got through to him. Hramack looked up from his examination of Cathi's wound and saw the look of concern on Grey Eagle's face. He knew Grey Eagle was right in his assessment of the situation. They were at risk here, but any rough treatment could move the arrow deeper into her body and nick an artery.

"She could die," he said.

Grey Eagle's voice was calm, but Hramack could hear the underlying fear and pain in it. "We could all die. I have lost two men already. Another two are badly wounded."

Hearing this, Hramack searched the group for his father. He had been so intent on examining Cathi's injury that he had forgotten the others. Kena was busy tending to the wounds of Strong Arm. Others lay sprawled on the floor, injured or exhausted, Two Clouds among them. They could not face another attack.

Anderson, who had been kneeling beside his stricken lieutenant, holding her hand, spoke up. "There are sleds here that travel much faster than we can walk. There should be one around here somewhere. We can place the wounded on them and beat the Marauders to the control room."

"Yes, that will work. Can you find them?" Hramack asked.

Anderson turned to Grey Eagle. "If you will let me have two of your men, I'm sure we can find them. There should be a transport bay nearby since this is a main entrance to the facility."

"Please hurry then," Hramack pleaded.

Grey Eagle nodded his assent and pointed to two of his men. Anderson led them at a trot down the long corridor. Hramack noticed the severity of Anderson's pronounced limp, but dismissed it as he focused his attention on Cathi. Kena had not noticed Cathi's collapse until he saw Hramack's stricken face. He left Strong Arm's bandage hanging loose and joined his son. He knelt beside her, pulled up her eyelids, and stared at her fixed and dilated pupils. He checked her pulse and frowned.

"She is going into shock. I must remove the arrow as quickly as possible, but she must lie quietly for some time afterwards. We must find a secure position." Hramack watched intently as his father probed the shaft with his fingertips and searched for signs of internal bleeding. "Go see to the others," Kena told him.

Hramack was reluctant to leave her, but he could do nothing more for her. Her life was now in the skilled hands of his father. He finished binding Strong Arm's wound. An arrow had penetrated completely through his bicep during the battle. True to his name, Strong Arm had simply snapped off the arrow's point, yanked the shaft of the arrow from his arm, and continued fighting. He had lost some blood, but he had the constitution of a bull and he would recover quickly. Hramack had seen him carry twice the weight of any other man during the journey and felt certain he was in no immediate danger.

Two Clouds looked up at him and grinned, holding a bandage to a wound in his side. "I moved too slowly. The knife went in deep, but he will wound no one else."

Hramack pulled up his friend's bandage, pleased to see that the wound, though deep, had struck no vital organs. "You will live," he pronounced.

"It does not feel like it. My belly burns as if I swallowed hot coals. Give me a sip of water."

"No water for a belly wound." He poured water onto a rag, wiped it over Two Clouds' face, and wet his lips, then wadded a handful of dried *pei* leaves, dampened them with water, and pushed them into the wound. Two Clouds squirmed but did not cry out. "I have nothing for the pain. The *pei* will stop the bleeding and prevent infection. It will itch like the devil's own fingers, but leave it in place."

Two Clouds lay back down and closed his eyes.

Hramack expressed his concern for Cathi to his father. "Will she live?"

Kena looked up at his son, his poignant expression conveying more than his words. "I don't know. She is very weak. She needs blood."

Kena bound her wounds carefully and applied a poultice of *pei* leaves around the arrow's shaft, but she had already lost a great deal of blood. Her breathing became shallow and rapid. The long, difficult journey from their crashed shuttle had already taken a toll on her strength. Lack of food and dehydration only exacerbated matters.

"She has a medical kit in her backpack," Hramack said. "Perhaps something in it will help."

He removed the kit and opened it. The medicine vials were empty, but the marvelous miniature devices inside fascinated him. His father picked up a flat screen and attempted to decipher its function. Switching it on, it displayed a flickering image of the bones in his hand. He pressed it to her chest. The x-ray scanner was unreliable, damaged in the crash, but it indicated the arrow had nicked a rib upon entry, probably deflecting it from the heart. The metal point lay dangerously close to the thoracoacromial artery. Removing the arrow would be a dangerous procedure. He could easily sever the artery. If so, she would bleed to death before he could repair it.

Hramack found a thermal scanner and passed it over her body. Her temperature was rising even though her skin felt clammy to the touch: sure signs of shock. Several sealed foil pouches in the kit contained freeze-dried plasma, but with no sterile water to reconstitute it or the time to boil it to sterilize it, Kena added water from the canteen.

At Hramack's disapproving look, he said, "I can worry about infection later. Without plasma and whole blood, she will die within an hour."

Hramack took the package from Kena's hand and thrust the needle into the vein of her left arm. His father could manufacture plasma in a crude manner using whole blood and a centrifuge, but it remained fresh for only a few weeks. Easily storable, freeze-dried plasma could have saved the lives of many villagers over the years. Hramack wondered how many more such wonders the newcomers possessed.

Kena managed to stop the bleeding, but the plasma could not replace the copious amount of blood she had already lost. For all he knew, she could be losing more each minute from internal injuries. Simply replacing her vital fluids was not enough. She needed fresh whole blood. Her medical kit contained a cross-match kit requiring only a drop of blood from each donor. None from Pueblo Nuevo matched her A-negative blood type. Of all those in the group, only his and Hramack's blood matched closely enough to be of any use to her, and then only by using anti-rejection suppressants he found in the med kit. Hramack allowed his father to take a half-liter of his blood, even though it left him giddy and weak. He watched the blood flowing into her veins but saw no improvement in her condition.

Kena continued to fret over her. Turning to Hramack, he said, "It is not enough. She needs more blood. Her pulse is growing weaker. You must take blood from me."

"Father," Hramack cautioned, you are very weak. We all are. The small amount of blood I gave her left me reeling, and I'm young and strong. If you give blood, what am I to do if you pass out?"

"If we do nothing, she will die. I must take the risk. You remember what I have taught you. I trust you. Trust in yourself."

Hramack's doubt about his ability rose in his throat to leave a sour taste in his mouth. Fear of failure haunted him always. Now, his father was putting him to the test. "I don't have your skills," he protested. "My hands are clumsy, and my mind is like a sieve."

Kena reached out and grabbed Hramack's hands, squeezing gently. "Nonsense, my son. These hands are capable of great wonders. They remember what your mind forgets. You are a Healer in your heart. Let your heart guide your hands."

"I'll try," Hramack whispered. As frightened as he was, he could not disappoint his father.

He carefully inserted the needle into his father's arm, found the vein, and sighed in relief as Kena's blood began to fill the empty plasma bag. Once it was full, slowly, drop-by-drop, they transferred the precious blood to the woman from the stars. Hramack prayed it would be enough.

Grey Eagle kept vigil at a small window by the barricaded door, waiting both for the return of his men and any sign of improvement from the woman. He was eager to be away. The Marauders had not yet attempted to attack up the bottleneck of the stairs, nor were they visible on the plain below. This concerned him. It was probable that they had entered the facility and were even now on their way to press the attack from behind them. He hated the idea of dividing his men, but the female could not walk and carrying her could kill her. Kena thought she was important, and he could not bring himself to sacrifice her while there was still hope. Such wounds seldom healed. He had seen strong men die from less. Kena would be a great Healer indeed, if he saved her life.

Thirty minutes passed since Anderson left in search of the sleds he had spoken of. Grey Eagle was growing impatient. At the sound of a low whine from down the corridor, he motioned his men to prepare for an attack. Then, as he recognized Anderson, White Elk, and Small Sheep's Horn each operating one of the sleds, he sighed with relief.

"We got lucky," Anderson said. "We located a small garage with several sleds in much better condition that the ones I found earlier near the lake."

Though the Star Man seemed pleased with his find, Grey Eagle eyed the strange conveyances with suspicion. Each wheel-less sled hovered a few centimeters above the floor by some means of which he could not even venture a guess. He had seen many wonders in his long life, but none could match the wondrous vehicles. Each was large enough to carry four riders. He had no time to marvel at them or examine them. He quickly directed the others to place the woman on Small Sheep's Horn's sled with Kena and Hramack. The others mounted White Elk's sled. He chose to ride with Anderson to keep an eye on him. The Star People had aided them in the battle, but he still did not trust them fully. Their goals, whatever they were, were not the same as his. Their loyalty could prove as capricious as the winds.

He held on as the sled sped away. It was smoother than he had expected, but he was concerned about the loud whine they made. The sound reverberating down the corridor revealed their position to any nearby Marauders. However, they needed the sleds. His men were exhausted. The sleds relieved them of the additional burden of carrying the woman. Riding also reduced the stress on his injured calf.

He solved the problem of ambush by directing White Elk's sled with three armed men slightly ahead of the others as an advanced guard. In the event of an attack, either group could quickly aid the other. They did not have time to check each of the rooms and side corridors they passed, any one of which could have hidden a large force of Marauders. They would have to trust to luck.

The journey to the control room took less than thirty minutes, much quicker than their outward walking journey in search of Hramack. Grey Eagle set his men about the task of erecting a barricade at the junction of the two main corridors adjacent to the control room by dragging heavy pieces of machinery to block the corridors. They removed steel doors from doorways and placed them on their sides against crates, desks, chairs – anything they could find. A few well-armed men could hold the barricade for days without exposing themselves to enemy fire, while the enemy would come under a withering fire in any foolhardy attempt to dismantle it.

Since they already knew how to operate one, he sent White Elk and Small Sheep's Horn on one of the sleds to the lake to obtain as much water and as much fish and game as they could catch. If the enemy besieged them, they might have to hold out for days, and he did not intend to starve. The Marauders knew the facility better than they did and would use the knowledge to their advantage. The question that plagued Grey Eagle's mind was why they had not attacked already.

Grey Eagle kept an eye on Anderson while Anderson examined the panels and gauges in the control room with great interest. He could barely keep his excitement from his stoic face. Kena and Hramack were both intent on the woman. He smiled. It was obvious Kena was enamored of her. It was a good thing to see. Kena had told him of his wife's death during their long journey to the mountain. A man should not be alone. He hoped, for Kena's sake, his efforts on her behalf proved effective.

He was alone, but he had enjoyed many good years with his wife, Anora. Her death had been hard at the time, almost unbearable, but his need to protect his village from Marauders had taken all his time since, leaving little time to brood about his loss. Many others had lost loved ones to disease or the Marauders. His sorrow was no different from theirs. He was an old man, even if he protested the fact. He could feel his age each morning and after each battle. His bones ached from sleeping on the hard ground. His wounds healed more slowly. His leg wound troubled him even now, though he tried not to let his pain show.

If he survived, this would be his last battle. Upon his return to Pueblo Nuevo, he would turn command over to one of the younger men and settle down in his small pueblo facing the setting sun. He would sit quietly in his favorite chair each evening and smoke his tobacco, while watching the sun drop behind the mountains west of the village. He never grew tired of watching the sky turn first a ruddy pink, and then darker purple as the shadow of the mountains raced across the great, flat plain towards him. The first stars that burst forth in the night sky reminded him of the twinkle in Anora's eyes when he had first met her at her father's house, peeking from behind a door. She had chosen him as her mate a few moons later. She had never lost that twinkle in all her fifty-five years.

The soft thud of the machinery below his feet vibrated the floor, reminding him where he was. An occasional beep as some piece of equipment switched on or off was the only other sound in the room. Though two were injured, he set all five remaining men to guard the barricades. If no attack came soon, he would allow the two injured men as much time as he could for their wounds to heal. If attacked, they, too, would have to fight. He hoped the two men he had sent to fetch food and water would not run into trouble and return soon with food. The Marauders could attack at any time, and he would need all his men. He could not count on Kena or Hramack until they had properly tended to the woman. Anderson would be of no use with a bow, and they had destroyed their explosive weapon to purchase their escape. He looked too weak to be of much use at hand-to-hand combat.

It had been forty-eight hours since he had slept. Grey Eagle could hear its sweet call each time he moved. His muscles ached and his joints were sore. The wound in his thigh ached bitterly, but he could not afford to give in to sleep's siren call until they were safely out of the mountain and well on their way back to Pueblo Nuevo, their purpose here achieved. The lives of the others were his responsibility. Already he would have to listen to the Grieving Songs of three widows. He could stand no more.

Hramack roused from a nap and saw his father slumped against a bank of machinery. "Father, wake up." He shook his father, but Kena could not raise his head. He opened his eyes, but he was groggy and weak.

"Father, wake up," he repeated. "You passed out."

"Help me up," Kena whispered weakly.

Hramack wrestled Kena to a sitting position on the floor. Kena looked over at Cathi. Her condition had not changed appreciatively. "You were right, son," he confessed. "I feel very tired."

"You should rest."

"No. I need to walk and clear my head."

Hramack lent his father his shoulder for support as Kena walked around the room. He was unsteady on his feet, stumbling often. Anderson stood over a console scanning drawings that flashed across the screen almost too fast to follow.

"How is she?" he asked without looking up.

"She's stable but still very weak," Kena replied. "I will have to remove the arrow soon."

"She's my friend and my commanding officer; therefore, I am naturally concerned for her welfare, but why are you so concerned with her well being?" He looked into Kena's eyes as if trying to judge the truth in Kena's response.

"She is in need. All life is sacred to us." In a quieter voice, Kena added, "And I must confess that I am more than a little in awe of her."

Anderson nodded, satisfied with Kena's answer. He turned his attention back to the screen. He slid his finger across the screen to change the perspective of diagrams he was viewing.

"What are you doing?" Hramack asked.

"I found schematics of this complex on the computer. I wish I had found them earlier. It would have saved a lot of walking. See, here we are."

He showed Hramack a blueprint of the control room and the adjoining corridors. He drew back on the view until the screen displayed the entire facility in three dimensions. He rotated the view to show the many levels and kilometers of corridors, each indicated by various colors. Absorbing the facility's true size made Hramack dizzy.

"And that doesn't include kilometers of service tunnels and water passages beneath the facility." He reduced the image and zeroed in on their location. "A complex this size must have a first aid station, if not a complete medical facility. If I can locate it, and if it is still functional, then we can take the lieutenant there." He continued to scroll through schematics while Hramack watched over his shoulder.

"Wait!" Hramack shouted after a few minutes. "Go back."

Anderson slowly reversed the images.

"There." Hramack pointed to the symbol he had recognized earlier, a winged staff with intertwined serpents. "A caduceus," he yelled, "a medical symbol, the sign of a Healer."

Anderson touched the symbol, and a schematic of the room appeared. "It's an infirmary." He repeatedly touched a second symbol, frowning, as he mumbled, "Huh."

"What is it?" Hramack questioned.

"The cameras aren't functioning in that area. Power is off in many of the corridors – no lights." Seeing Hramack's look of concern, he added, "That doesn't mean the equipment isn't working. As an emergency treatment center, it might have a dedicated power source."

Hramack remembered the many empty rooms he had seen, looted long ago. "If it is still there."

Kena joined them, staring at the screen. "Is it far?"

Anderson pinpointed the location relative to their present position. "It's not too far from here. Maybe a kilometer."

Grey Eagle came over, drawn by the commotion and the excitement in Hramack's voice. "What have you found?"

"Anderson has located a medical facility, an infirmary, nearby. With it, we may be able to save Cathi Lorst's life and help Strong Arm and Two Clouds."

Grey Eagle stared at the screen. He traced his finger along the corridors to the infirmary. He grunted and turned away. "This room is back toward the lake, off a small side corridor, but deeper within the mountain. There is no good place to mount a defense. If we leave this position, we could be easily overrun by the Marauders."

"But we must go," Kena said.

Hramack watched Grey Eagle closely, as he paced the room in deep thought, weighing the life of one woman against those of his men. After several minutes, the old man said, "You, Hramack, and Anderson will take the woman. Two Clouds will accompany you. He, too, needs treatment. The rest of us will remain here guarding this corridor. We must wait for the others to return from the lake."

Hramack shared his father's impatience, urging the men to return from their foraging expedition. He filled the time by redressing Two Clouds and Strong Arm's wounds. Strong Arm's arm was sore, but even at half strength he was still more powerful than most men. He squeezed Hramack's hand so hard he thought it would break. The bleeding had stopped from Two Clouds' wound, but when Hramack had him draw his bow to test his strength, he broke out in sweat and his arm trembled.

Finally, the foragers returned bearing full canteens of water and stringers of small silvery fish. Hramack wanted to take time to examine the fish, the first he had seen except in books, but Kena urged him to hurry. They carefully placed Cathi on the crowded sled, and he, Anderson, Two Clouds, and his father set off down the corridor to locate the infirmary. Following Anderson's directions, they took many smaller corridors, some dusty and filled of debris. Hramack was disappointed to see that some areas of the enormous facility had fallen into such decay. It was as if someone had defaced a monument.

Many of the overhead lights were not functioning, forcing them to rely on the lights on the sled to guide them through the darkness. Each turn carried them deeper and deeper into the twisting maze of corridors. To Hramack's bitter disappointment, the corridor ended at a collapse of the ceiling. Machinery and metal furniture from the floor had crashed through the floor above and now blocked their path. The sled could carry them no farther.

"It will take hours to clear this," he moaned.

"There is room enough to pass through on foot." Kena pointed out a narrow gap between the wall and the debris. "We can make a litter to carry Cathi from that piece of wood and walk the rest of the way." He pointed to a broken piece of wood half-embedded in the wall. When Hramack pulled the wood from the wall, he discovered that though it looked like wood, it was much lighter and harder, some kind of resin.

He and his father carried her on the makeshift stretcher, picking their way through the debris. To his relief, the door bearing the caduceus symbol and a red cross in a circle was free of rubble. A sign on the door read – ROOM MZ 1437 D – MEDICAL (PRIMARY)

"This is it," Kena called out.

Hramack looked down the dark, dilapidated corridor. Several wall panels had peeled away and hung over the corridor like tree branches in an arbor. Cobwebs draped the ceiling and dust lay deep on the floor.

"I hope everything is still working," he said.

"We'll find out in a minute." Anderson tried to force open the door, but it would not budge. Hramack and his father set down the stretcher. He and Anderson threw their combined weight into the door. The door suddenly slid back into a recess in the wall, throwing them off balance. Hramack tumbled into the room and rolled across the floor amid a cloud of dust. He waved his hand in the air to dispel the cloud of fine particles floating around his face, coughing at the musty smell the dust raised.

The room was a small office filled with rotting chairs, a desk, and cabinets full of decayed files. A second door, frozen half-open, opened into a larger room filled with rows of machinery covered with plastic tarps. A thick coating of dust covered the desks and the equipment in here as well. Disappointed in the condition of the room, Anderson strode to the wall and pressed his hand against a panel. Slowly, the overhead lights flickered to life.

"At least we have light," he said, smiling.

Hramack wrinkled his nose. "It smells of the tomb in here." He examined a bulky, plastic-draped item. "Perhaps the plastic coverings have protected the equipment."

Anderson nodded. "It looks like they neatly packed everything before they left."

Hramack noticed a panel marked Housekeeping and touched it. Small doors opened in the wall, and several types of small whirling and sucking machines raced into the room, dancing menacingly around their feet. Two Clouds leaped back with his bow ready to fire an arrow into the strange creatures. Ignoring them, the automated robots began attacking the years of accumulated dirt and debris. Dust filled the air in their wake, forcing all of them back into the corridor.

"What did you do?" Kena asked, holding his hand over his mouth and coughing from the stirred up dust.

Hramack shrugged and smiled. "It's faster than sweeping."

After several minutes, the noise subsided, and they entered a much cleaner and more sanitary room. The odor of musty air had disappeared, replaced by the stringent scent of disinfectants.

"Amazing," Hramack whispered. Two Clouds continued to look frightened and kept his bow ready.

Anderson and Kena began stripping the plastic covers off the various pieces of equipment. Most of the names emblazoned on the machines meant nothing to Hramack, although Anderson whistled appreciatively.

"Here," he said to Kena, pointing to one particular device, "a soft tissue scanner." He activated a panel and, to their delight, the screens lit up. He pointed to another device, "A computer-operated surgical table. It can remove the arrow and seal the wound unassisted."

Hramack was almost in tears with appreciation of the accumulated medical knowledge and techniques available to his ancestors.

Anderson yanked open the doors of a cold storage cabinet. "Whole blood and plasma! Frozen for centuries." He looked at the labels. "It is artificial blood – antibody and antigen free. No risk of agglutination. Remarkable. Even my people can't do that."

Kena had held up on the journey to the infirmary, but now his loss of blood took its toll on him. He turned to Hramack. "You must treat Two Clouds' wound first. I am dizzy.

Hramack's face blanched. "I cannot," he protested. "I know nothing of this strange equipment."

"Nor I, "Kena said, "but Anderson does. He will help. I must rest or I will not be fit to operate on Cathi Lorst."

Hramack knew his father would not have suggested it if he did not think Hramack capable, but Hramack was not as certain of his abilities. Half guessing at the surgical machine's operation, Hramack keyed a display listing a menu of surgical choices and chose the one he thought most appropriate. Two Clouds lay nervously on the metal surgical table, his usual ready joke or quip forgotten in face of the strange machines. The machine came alive, produced a hypodermic from a cavity within, and jabbed him in the arm, almost frightening him to death at the hiss of air injection. Next, a light shone on the wound, changing through the full spectrum of colors as it scanned the knife wound in his belly. Then, the machine directed a bright blue beam of light into the open wound. A wisp of smoke drifted from the wound along with the odor of seared flesh. Two Clouds' face paled, and he tried to rise from the table. Hramack gently pressed him back down.

"Do you feel pain?" he asked.

"No, only a tickling, but it is burning my flesh."

"It is cutting away damaged tissue and sealing broken blood vessels to aid healing much more efficiently and less invasively than I could hope to."

The light changed color, becoming dark crimson. It exited the wound and began sealing the flesh around the wound as it moved along the opening. Next, a second hypodermic jabbed the skin next to the wound, hissing as a burst of air injected its milky contents. Finally, the machine applied a small bandage.Two Clouds, who had closed his eyes at first sight of the moving beam of light, opened them when the noise subsided. He looked at the bandage on his stomach and flexed his abdominal muscles. "I feel nothing. Thank you, Hramack."

Hramack laughed. "Don't thank me. I did nothing. Thank the builders of this device." However, Hramack felt a sense of joy at his small part in the procedure. He might not have Kena's innate sense of empathy with his patients, but he now knew he was a capable Healer. With the help of my ancestor's machines, he reminded himself.

Two Clouds rose from the table. Grabbing his bow, he drew back the string, smiling when it produced no pain. "I will guard the corridor," he said and walked off.

"Amazing," Hramack said. "Our ancestors were capable of doing all this, and still they chose to destroy each other. Just think of what wonders must be left in Denver Dome."

"Let's get the lieutenant ready," Anderson suggested. His impatience made his words sound gruff.

While Cathi received a much-needed transfusion and Kena rested, Hramack toured the medical center, examining each new piece of medical equipment, writing a mental wish list. He discovered a library of digital medical texts and skimmed through them on the screen. He found a new use for a microwave autoclave sterilizer, using it to cook their fish in just a few minutes' time. He picked the flakey, white meat from the bones, savoring its delicate flavor. After one of the tiny pin bones stuck his cheek, he carefully picked through the remainder of his meal. He made Kena eat to build his strength; then, checked the medical database for a drug that would aid Kena's recovery. Finding a suitable medicine, he injected it into his father's arm. Within minutes, his color and strength had returned.

Kena, fully recovered, scanned Cathi's shoulder, as she lay on the table silent and pale. The point of the arrow was dangerously close to the artery, but the sharp edges of the flat point were oriented away from it. It would have been a risky operation for him to perform with his limited equipment at home, but its removal would be easy for the automated surgical machine.

Two Clouds burst into the room before he could begin. "Marauders! A dozen or more are moving this way. We must leave."

"We can't," Kena replied. "The woman will die."

"We can't fight them all. They are too many," Two Clouds insisted.

Hramack looked at Kena and knew his father would not leave Cathi behind. He had to buy his father, and her, more time. "I'll go with Two Clouds and try to lead them away. You and Anderson stay with her to perform the operation. When she's able to move, join Grey Eagle at the control center."

"No," Kena said. "Send Two Clouds for Grey Eagle. We can barricade the door until they arrive."

"We may draw Grey Eagle into a battle he cannot win."

"Hramack is right," Two Clouds said, grabbing him by the shoulder. "We can lead them away from here. Your machinery has made me hale again. I can fight if need be."

"I'm going with you," Anderson said. "Lieutenant Lorst does not need me here."

Hramack studied the man from the stars; saw the determination in his eyes. He was no warrior. *But then, until this journey, neither was I.*

"What about your leg?"

Anderson brushed aside Hramack's concern. "It's nothing. Sore muscles."

"All right." He turned to Kena. "We'll pile debris against the outer door. Perhaps they won't look too closely, especially if we show ourselves to them."

Kena embraced Hramack, a display of affection that normally would have embarrassed him. However, this time, with the real prospect that he would never see his father again, he cherished the moment.

"Go with Yarah, my son. Stay safe."

With a last glance at the comatose Cathi Lorst, Hramack joined Two Clouds and Anderson. The three of them began gathering overturned tables and loose trash and piling it in front of the door. Satisfied with their handiwork, Two Clouds erased all signs that anyone had entered the room by scattering dust over the area. They raced to the end of the corridor just in time to see the burning torches of Marauders approaching from a side corridor. Two Clouds let out a loud war whoop to get their attention and fired an arrow, striking one of them in the shoulder. The man howled in pain. The others growled in anger and attacked.

Two Clouds grinned at Hramack. "Good, we have their attention. Now, let us give these mongrels a good run."

The three of them retreated down the corridor just ahead of the pursuing Marauders, past the entrance to the infirmary, and into the darkness beyond.

26

A PROPOSAL OF MARRIAGE

TEELA LISTENED QUIETLY THROUGH THE PARTIALLY OPENED DOOR AS Madras spoke with her grandfather. She was ashamed at her impropriety but knew the discussion was about her.

"Kaffa," Madras said. "Hramack has been gone almost three weeks. They are not returning to Ningcha. Even if they did return, they face death for the murder of Eithan."

"Perhaps there are others to blame for your cousin's death," Kaffa suggested.

Madras' face turned pale. Teela saw his Adam's apple quivering. She knew her grandfather suspected Chu Li in Eithan's murder. Madras' nervousness verified it.

"I ... I don't know what you mean," he sputtered. His eyes darted around the room.

"The truth will come out, eventually," Kaffa told him. "Will you stand by the High Priest's side then?"

"I came to speak of Teela," Madras cried out. He settled in his chair to regain his composure. "There is no question of Teela's marrying Hramack now. It would benefit the entire village if she were to consent to marry my youngest son, Juresh, before Chu Li orders it tomorrow."

Teela gasped, and then put her hand over her mouth to avoid betraying her presence.

Kaffa smiled. "You mean it would benefit you and Chu Li. With Teela in your household, you think to silence me." He stood abruptly, grabbed his staff from its place leaning against the wall, and held it in the air. "Kena and Hramack risk their lives even now to save our village, while Chu Li seeks only to gather more power for himself. The people are beginning to question him. He sacrificed a goat and still the water has not returned. He sacrificed a cow and still the waters have not returned. What will he sacrifice next – one of us?"

Kaffa stalked across the room until he towered over Madras, the tip of his staff inches from the startled stone carver's face. "Chu Li no longer speaks for Yarah. He speaks for himself. Go! Tell your master that I will not rest until he is finished in this village. I have seen the return of the water in my dreams with Kena and Hramack riding the crest of the waves. The old ways died because the people desired it. They will not allow the harsh days of religious rule to return. I, too, was reluctant to embrace Kena's searching of the past, but we must if we are to survive."

As Kaffa spoke, Madras slowly stood and backed toward the door. He ran out without closing it behind him.

Teela burst through the door to her room and flung her arms around Kaffa. "Grandfather, thank you!"

Kaffa smiled at her. "I will not forsake your happiness, ever," he promised.

"You're wonderful."

Kaffa eased her from around him and into a chair. "There is danger still. If the waters do not return soon, we all perish. Already,

Chu Li is claiming it is our lot to perish because of Kena's delving into the past. I fear him."

"The people will not –" she began.

Kaffa cut her off. "The people are afraid. They will act but perhaps not before it is too late."

"Hramack will return," she said boldly. "You saw it yourself, in a dream."

Kaffa dropped his head. "I said that to frighten Madras. My dream ... my dream was not as bright."

Teela steeled herself for bad news. "Tell me."

"I saw Hramack bound and carried toward his enemies. I felt much hatred from them."

"Other people?" Teela gasped. "The savages of the wastes."

"No. That is the strange part. They were not savages, as we believed. They were ... like us. Perhaps that will make all the difference. Come, Teela. It grows late. You should sleep."

She knew she could not sleep. Thoughts of Hramack in danger plagued her mind. "Yes, grandfather," she answered, but when he entered his room, she quietly left the house to walk and think.

The village was quiet. Usually, the early night reeled with song or the playing of musical instruments. None had the energy now. Lack of water was taking its toll on everyone. In the distance, she heard a child crying and wondered if it was crying because it was thirsty. The Council had reduced the water ration yet again. She touched her hair. It felt limp and stringy. She had not washed it in many days. She smiled as she remembered Hramack's hand running through her hair and the way he enjoyed the smell of her shampoo.

"Oh, Hramack, where are you?" she cried into the night.

With tears in her eyes, she returned to her room, knowing morning would find her bed untouched.

27

TOP OF THE MOUNTAIN

C ATHI'S RAPID RECOVERY ASTONISHED KENA. THE REMARKABLE MEDICAL equipment had not only located the arrow point and stabilized it, but had gently removed it with minimal damage to the surrounding tissue and cauterized the wound. It had chosen a combination of drugs of which he had only a vague idea of their purpose and added them to the whole blood IV dripping into her arm. Within hours, she was conscious and able to sit up.

"I'm hungry," she complained, looking around the unfamiliar room. "Where are we?" She frowned and glanced down at her injured shoulder. Only then did she notice her nudity. She pulled the sheet up around her chest. "I remember being struck by the arrow, but I didn't think it was that bad, at least until I woke up here."

"If not for the equipment here, still functioning after all these years, you would have died." He looked sheepishly at the floor. "It was beyond my meager capabilities to save you."

She recognized Kena's anguish. "Yet you kept me alive until we reached this place. Do you think I would have lived if you had not been a Healer?"

Kena smiled at her attempt to salve his bruised ego. "Perhaps not, but you are a strong woman and very much alive now. The color has returned to your cheeks and your eyes – well, they look as alive as they did when I first saw you fighting back the Marauders." He blushed, and then stammered, "Well, I will prepare you some food."

"Did you undress me?" she asked, holding out the sheet.

Kena's face reddened. "It was necessary. I am, after all, a Healer. It was either me or my son."

"It's okay. Nudity is more acceptable in my culture. Sometimes I wear no clothing at all," she added, and then began to lower the sheet.

"It is unseemly," Kena protested. "You are my patient, but ..."

"Did you like what you saw?"

Kena sputtered uncomfortably. "Your food is ready."

He noticed her grin and realized that she had been jesting with him. He returned her smile and handed her a bowl of hot soup filled with fish and vegetables. Its hearty aroma filled the room. She inhaled deeply, wrapped the sheet around her body, and sat on the edge of the table. The thin material of the sheet could not hide the curves of her body or her pert breasts. The need to prepare her for surgery had tempered his earlier brief glimpse at her naked body. He had been in healer mode. Now, he found himself drawn to her, both for her physical beauty and for her strength of character.

Utterly famished, she practically poured the soup down her throat in her haste to eat. She smiled and handed Kena the empty bowl.

"Thank you, Kena. That was great. I feel as if I haven't eaten in days."

Kena looked at the empty bowl and smiled. "It appears your appetite has recovered. Would you like more?"

"No, thank you. Where are the others?"

Kena wondered the same thing. It had been almost four hours since they had led the Marauders away from the infirmary. He had heard nothing of them since. "Grey Eagle is guarding the control center. Hramack and Anderson are ... away."

"Which one is Grey Eagle?" she asked.

To help take her mind from the dangers around them, he filled her in on his and Hramack's journey from Ningcha and their meeting with Grey Eagle at Pueblo Nuevo. Hramack had told her a little about their journey when he had been her prisoner, but he had mentioned no names.

"This Grey Eagle seems to be quite a man. I remember seeing him in action during the fight. He was quite an imposing figure for an old man."

"Yes, and a strong leader also," Kena added.

Cathi looked at him. "I think you are an imposing character as well. The others followed you here, far away from their homes, in a quest you proposed. Your son braved the threats of the Burning Lands, as you call them, to find you. I think you will become a great leader after this adventure." She looked directly into Kena's eyes. "I would follow you."

Kena blustered and fumbled with the equipment on the table. He had not thought too much about women since the death of his wife, but this strange woman from the stars stirred something in his blood that went beyond the fact of her exotic origin or even her honest beauty. Her fiery red hair was unknown to his people. Her hair and the paleness of her skin gave her the appearance of a goddess. She seemed a match with him in both personality and intellect. His heart fluttered. It was silly of him to think that such a woman, who knew the stars of hundreds of worlds, would find him anything but a provincial savage.

"How long have they been gone?"

"Several hours."

She touched a finger to her throat above her sternum and spoke. "Anderson? Do you read me?" She paused, and then repeated it.

Kena stared at her, mystified by her actions. "What are you doing?"

"I have a comm unit embedded in my throat and a receiver in my mastoid bone. It's mainly used for shipboard communication, but we've used it here." She frowned. "No response. He could be out of range."

"Perhaps the metal in the building blocks the radio waves."

"You know about radios?"

Slightly miffed by her remark, he replied, perhaps more sharply than he needed, "We are not backwards primitives in spite of our appearance. I have constructed a crude radio in my village, but I have never contacted anyone else."

Chagrined, she said, "I did not mean to imply . . ."

At a sudden noise outside the door, he cautioned her to silence."

Cathi had heard it too. "Have your friends returned?" she asked.

"Perhaps," he answered, but it sounded as if many men were scuffling about the corridor. He went to the door to listen more closely.

"Check each door! Find them!" he heard an unfamiliar voice yell.

"Marauders," he whispered to her.

She looked around the room. "What do we do, fight them?"

"No, they are too many." He rolled a large piece of equipment in front of the door and blocked its wheels. "That should slow them down," he said.

He tossed her the jumpsuit he had removed for her surgery. She dropped the sheet and pulled it on, stopping briefly to stare at the bloody hole in the shoulder, allowing him time to confirm that his first impression about the perfection of her body was correct. *No time for this*, he chided himself.

He hurriedly began to throw open cabinets and doors he had not yet opened. He found more machinery and medical supplies but no exit. She pointed to a smaller panel on one wall near the pint where the cleaning robots had emerged.

"That looks like a service duct."

"A what?" Kena asked.

"A passageway allowing maintenance personnel access to plumbing, electrical, or ventilation systems." She had begun to pry the panel away from the wall as she spoke. Inside, a narrow tunnel disappeared into the darkness. "It will be a tight fit, but we can make it."

Kena eyed the narrow opening with doubt. "It is too small to turn around in. We could become trapped," he said.

"It should lead to a larger, central passage," she said. The Marauders began to pound on the door loudly. "We don't have much choice."

"I suppose not," Kena reluctantly agreed. He gathered their supplies and weapons and tied one end of a short leather thong around them. He then secured the other end to his leg. "To drag them behind me," he replied to her questioning look. "If I push them ahead of me, I will be unable to see where I'm going." He held his flashlight in one hand and knife in the other. "I will lead," he said. "Try to close the panel behind us. It may buy us some time."

Before entering through the panel, he activated the cleaning robots, hoping their activity would mimic the sound of humans and confuse the Marauders. The confines of the river tunnel had not affected him, but the narrow service duct made him nervous. His shoulders brushed the sides, and he kept bumping his head on the low ceiling. He feared he would become stuck and die trapped in a square tube of dark metal. He glanced back to see that Cathi had managed to close the panel and followed close behind him. He knew the duct would place a strain on her shoulder. Even the wonders of technology could not quickly heal bruised and damaged flesh. He only hoped the effort would not reopen her wound.

Kena heard a crash behind him as the Marauders forced open the door. They began overturning equipment and smashing glass in their frenzied search of the room. He hoped they did no serious damage to the medical equipment. He had hopes of salvaging and studying it. If he could get it back to Ningcha, it would save many lives.

The sounds died away behind them. They crawled for what seemed like hours, but in reality was less than twenty minutes before reaching a T-junction in the tiny tunnel. *Left or right?* It did not seem to matter. He chose right. Another fifteen minutes passed before the tunnel intersected a larger corridor in which they were able to stand. It felt good to stretch cramped muscles. He checked her wound. She was sore and in pain, but otherwise looked very well. There was no bleeding. They rested for a few minutes, Kena carefully listening for sounds of pursuit. None came. The Marauders either had missed the access duct in their search and attributed their escape to magic, or were afraid to enter it.

The larger passageway accommodated rows of large pipes over-head and boxes filled with electronic equipment along the walls. There was a definite hum in the air, like the buzz of angry insects. Lights placed at intervals in the ceiling illuminated the passageway. Tunnels similar to the one through which they had traveled entered the corridor at several spots along the wall. A procession of small mobile machines came and went, ignoring the two intruders, bent on their preprogrammed tasks.

"Repair drones and automated cleaning machinery," she suggested. "They won't bother us."

Kena looked unsure when he saw one small machine festooned with numerous cutting devices. "If you say so."

She was busy examining recessed boxes in the ceiling from which the hum emanated. "These seem to be power relays of some type, receiving microwaves from a central source and broadcasting it to the lighting and various pieces of machinery: power without wires. This would reduce power loss due to resistance and distance. Remarkable."

She had lost him with her explanations, but Kena sensed her excitement. "Could this power be broadcast a very great distance?" he asked.

"I'm sure it could," she answered, still examining the emitters.

"Then it could be broadcast to Ningcha."

She followed Kena's reasoning. "I see what you mean. Yes, it could broadcast anywhere on the planet if the source was powerful enough. With a receiver in your village, you would have unlimited power."

Kena envisioned his village lighted and powered by such a source independent of the uncertainty of sun and wind. Pumps for water and power for machinery, even such equipment as they had seen in the infirmary, would ease their labor considerably. More time could be devoted to living than to simple survival. With a constant source of water and power, the people would be more reluctant to let a tyrant such as Chu Li control their destiny. There would be no reason to abandon Yarah, only Yarah's self-appointed, power-hungry priest.

The corridor continued for several kilometers with service ducts and smaller corridors at intervals along the way. Cathi attempted to contact Anderson several more times with no results. He could see the worry on her face. He tried to fathom the markings at the junctions, but without a point of reference, they meant nothing. They wandered for hours until they came upon yet another intersection.

"You decide this time," he told Cathi. He was tired of making perhaps the wrong choices. Perhaps it was time to let her lead. It would also serve to take her mind off her companion.

She pointed to a door a few meters down one of the branches. "That one."

By the desperation in her voice, Kena knew her wound was aching horribly, and he had no way to relieve her pain. With her agony and her inability to contact Anderson, she was becoming more irritable and cranky as time wore on. Other than its larger size, he saw no difference between that particular door and any other of the hundreds of doorways they had passed in the last several hours. Most of the doors opened only onto small rooms filled with tools or electronic equipment or were empty. He shrugged. Anything would be a change from the constant sameness of the endless service corridors.

As they approached, he noticed what she had spotted: an illuminated panel beside the door. Above the door, engraved on a metal plaque, were the words – Level 7, Section C.

"It's a service elevator," she said, the smile returning to her face for the first time in hours.

She touched the panel, and the door slid open. Beyond lay only a small room. Before Kena could put voice to his frustration, she pressed the top position on a panel inside the room. He lurched backwards as the room began moving upwards. His weight increased as the elevator picked up speed. Numbers flashed on the panel in rapid succession – 7, 15, 21. When the elevator stopped suddenly, his weight lessened, threatening to bring his stomach up into his throat. The panel indicated 65. The door opened, revealing a short corridor with a single door set in a metal wall. Still reeling from his rapid ascent, he allowed her to exit first.

The door was different from any other door they had encountered. It was oval in shape set in the wall a few centimeters above the floor. A metal wheel in the middle connected to a series of metal bars extending to the edges of the door. A heavy flexible gasket filled the gap between door and bulkhead. Kena placed his hand on a small screen beside the door, but nothing happened. He tried to turn the wheel, but it would not budge.

"Is it rusted shut?" Kena asked.

She examined it closely. "It's an air-tight security door, meant to give only certain people access to whatever lies beyond it."

Kena sighed. "Then we must retrace our steps." It was a prospect he did not relish, especially the elevator ride back down.

"Wait," she said. "Help me pry off this panel. Maybe we can short it out."

Kena took his knife and wedged it under the edge of the panel, twisting the blade until the cover popped off, exposing a shallow cavity with hundreds of tiny metallic nodes embedded in a crystalline surface. Within the clear crystal, a web of lines finer than human hair radiated from the node. Cathi took his knife, pried away one of the nodes, and slid the tip of the blade into the vacated slot. Sparks flew, but the door clicked and opened slightly.

She looked at Kena's questioning smile. "I've had some practice."

This time, the heavy door opened easily when he pushed it. A wave of refreshing cooler air washed over them. It took several moments for his eyes to adjust to the glaring light. He took a deep breath of air and realized that they were much higher up the mountain, where the air was cooler and thinner. They had emerged onto a terrace carved into the face of the mountain. He walked to a low parapet and gingerly looked down. The lake lay over three thousand meters below, looking no larger than a puddle in the distance. The concrete of the retaining dam shone like a white line in the sun. The mountain peak rose another thousand meters above them. A thin layer of snow still clung to the nooks and crannies of the gray rock. Along the face of the mountain above and around them were a series of stone barricades whose function was the collection of water from the melting snow and channeling it into the lake below.

She pointed to a cluster of parabolic antennae at one edge of the terrace. "This one is a power emitter, perhaps to other facilities or even Denver Dome. The larger antennae are for communications with orbiting satellites. That would allow this facility to communicate with other domes around the planet or even Mars. I can call my ship." Her pain forgotten in her glee, she wrapped her arms around Kena, and began to dance around the terrace. "I can call the *Baldry*. We're saved." She suddenly stopped dancing, grabbed Kena's face with both hands, said, "Thank you," and kissed him on the lips.

Surprised, Kena returned her kiss, lightly at first, then, as her lips continued to smash against his, with more passion. Slowly, she broke her kiss and looked him in the eyes. The look of elation on her face changed to one of passion. She kissed him again and, as he wrapped his arms tightly around her gave in to the moment. Their kiss lasted several minutes. Kena attributed her passion as elation at surviving danger, but how would he classify his reaction?

Reluctantly breaking apart, she said, "Well, that was nice. I'm glad to see you Earthers haven't changed too much."

Confused both by her sudden change in behavior and by his eagerness to give in to the urges he felt, he muttered, somewhat clumsily, "The sun will set soon. We should eat and rest. It would be best if we spend the night here. I do not relish the thought of those endless corridors again."

"Nor do I." She rubbed her shoulder. Kena wished he had something with which to ease her pain. "Tell me about your people, Kena. Are they all like you?"

Kena laughed. "It would seem not. My son and I are condemned to death on our return for leaving them with no Healer. Perhaps if we had accomplished our goal, they would have been more lenient. With all I have seen in the past few weeks, I don't know if I can return to such a life, in spite of my duty to them as Healer."

She touched his hand gently. "Perhaps you were meant for something greater than Healer. Perhaps your fate is to unite your people, rebuild Earth. We can help, the Traders Guild, I mean. We can offer knowledge and supplies. You have kin on Mars also. They have terra-formed their world. With their help and ours, we could replace Earth's depleted seas with ice asteroids and rebuild the atmosphere to filter out UV and X-rays, as they have. The sun is more stable than it was centuries ago and seems to be cooling. Earth's environment would recover in time. In return, we would ask only free trade with your world. As soon as we return with word that Homeworld has been located, your name will be known throughout the universe."

Kena laughed. "My name. Only those I touch will remember my name. The name of Lt. Cathi Lorst of the Merchant Ship *Long John Baldry* will ring down the centuries throughout the known worlds. You will have your pick of worlds and of men. What will you do with such fame?"

She laid her head on his shoulder and whispered into his ear, "We'll see. We'll see." She then fell fast asleep.

Kena smiled and made himself more comfortable against the wall. A cool breeze blew across the platform and the stone was cool on his back. He liked the sensation of her head nestled into his shoulder. He had not felt such peace in many years, not since the death of his wife. It was easy to forget the problems they faced and his concerns for his son and his village. There, on the high terrace jutting into space where only the mountain peaks were visible, it was easy for him to stare into the future and see an end to all problems. He closed his eyes and fell asleep feeling only the warm gentle beat of a woman's heart next to him.

Hramack, Two Clouds, and Anderson had managed successfully to lead the Marauders away from his father, becoming involved in only one minor skirmish in which they killed two of the Marauders. They lost their pursuers in a maze of narrow, twisting, darkened corridors. Now, they rested in a room that had once served as a conference room. Metal chairs with disintegrating plastic cushions were positioned around a long metal table with darkened screens inset in the tabletop in front of each chair. Anderson sat in one of the chairs, his face across his folded arms resting on the table. He was bravely trying to keep pace with the others, but with his limp, he lagged farther and farther behind. Hramack doubted that he had recovered from his long trek across the Empty Lands to the east. The Star Man's condition concerned him.

"Are you all right?" Hramack asked.

Without looking up, Anderson replied, "Just a few minutes and I'll be fine. I just need to rest my feet."

Hramack looked down at Anderson's worn and shredded boots and noticed spots of blood staining the leather. "Let me look at them."

Anderson loosened the bindings and slipped the boots off. Hramack gasped at what they revealed. Bloody blisters covered both feet. Clotted blood filled his boots, soaking his socks, and causing them to adhere to his anguished feet. Hramack winced when he thought how Anderson had managed to run on two such pieces of such bruised and damaged flesh, yet he had offered no complaint in all the time they had been running.

Two Clouds looked down at Anderson's feet and sadly shook his head. "He is a brave man," he said with respect.

"Why didn't you say something?" Hramack asked Anderson.

Anderson shrugged. "We've had enough problems as it is. Lieutenant Lorst's safety came first. There hasn't been time."

Hramack took his water bottle and began to wash Anderson's feet as gently as he could, knowing each movement caused him extreme pain. Anderson sucked in his breath in agony. He wiped away most of the dried blood and rubbed a soothing salve on the wounds. He then wound his feet in clean bandages.

"There. That should help a little," Hramack said. "The salve will ease the pain, but nothing except time will heal the wounds. If they become infected there is little I can for them with what medical supplies I carry. When we get back to the infirmary, my father will do a more thorough job."

Anderson grinned. "That feels great. Thanks. I watched you work on the lieutenant and just now on my feet. It's easy to see you learned much from your father."

"He is a great Healer. With what he has learned here, he will be even greater."

"Don't sell yourself short. You have the touch. You just need the confidence."

Anderson's praise embarrassed him. He held out his hands. "I am clumsy. My hands are too large."

Anderson smiled. "My captain is a bigger man than you, and yet he can set the *Baldry* down as gentle as a feather on top of eggs without cracking them."

"I think you jest."

Anderson's chuckle was the first sound of mirth Hramack had heard from hum. "Maybe a little."

He glared at his boots, knowing it was necessary to fit his feet back into them. As Hramack help him slip them back onto his feet, it was all he could do to keep from crying out. Hramack knew he was only putting on a brave façade. The pain must have been excruciating, but they had no time to linger. They had to keep moving to stay ahead of the Marauders. He doubted Anderson had much effort left in him. They had to change plans.

"Two Clouds. Go find Grey Eagle and warn him about the Marauders. I'll help Anderson back to the infirmary and see to his feet."

Two Clouds looked dubious of Hramack's decision, but he trotted down the corridor. They had seen no other signs of the Marauders for hours. He considered the risk of going back was less than that of trying to stay ahead of the Marauders with Anderson's crippled feet.

"The way you found the medical room with the computer," he asked Anderson. "Could you find a way to get the pumps to operate?" Hramack asked.

"Perhaps. The schematics are on the computer. There should be a maintenance program."

"We managed to get the water started, but a siren sounded and it stopped flowing," he explained.

"Sounds like a blocked pipe or valve. It would shut down the system automatically. We would have to locate the damaged section and repair it."

Hramack smiled. "Then it can be done?"

"If the damage is not too severe."

Hramack nodded his head. "That is good."

Slowly, with Hramack lending his shoulder for support, he and Anderson retraced their steps back to the infirmary. Hramack was dismayed to see that the Marauders had been there before them. They had battered in the door, and the room was in shambles. They had attacked the room with a savagery bordering on psychotic, strewing equipment about the room, breaking glassware, and ripping charts and pictures from the wall. Most of the medical equipment was too sturdy to damage too severely, but they had shattered the computer screens, rendering them useless, and ripped wiring from the walls. To Hramack's relief, there was no blood and no bodies. He prayed his father and Cathi had escaped. At Anderson's look of defeat, he said, "If the Marauders had taken my father and Cathi, I don't think they would have bothered smashing all this. They did this in rage at not finding them."

Searching through the debris, Hramack managed to find fresh bandages and a pneumatic hypo containing a painkiller. He stripped off the bloody bandages and rewrapped Anderson's feet with fresh ones. This time the ordeal was less painful. Some of the blisters bled anew, but the salve was helping to form healthy scabs. When time allowed, he would repair Anderson's useless boots with the deerskin he had brought back from Royal Gorge. He allowed Anderson to rest while he searched up and down the corridors for some sign of his father's passing. He found nothing. Knowing Anderson would never make it back to the control center, he settled down to wait on Grey Eagle.

A short while later, noises in the corridor outside roused him. He glanced over at Anderson, who was fast asleep. The noises grew closer. He hoped it was Two Clouds with Grey Eagle's men, but he doubted the battle wise leader would allow his men to make so much racket. Alarmed, he awakened Anderson.

"What"? Anderson began before Hramack silenced him. Then Anderson heard the noise. "Marauders?" he mouthed.

Hramack nodded. They looked around for a place to hide, but the room was too open and the closets too small. Two armed Marauders walked into the room, saw them, and let out a loud, piercing whistle. Before either Hramack or Anderson could act, two more men hurried into the room to join them, bows drawn with arrows notched and pointed at them.

The leader looked them over. His eyes came to rest on Anderson and his tattered but easily recognizable jumpsuit.

"Hardy will be pleased we have caught you," he said. He then turned to Hramack. "You are a southerner, one of the pueblo dwellers. Why have you invaded our territory? Where are the others?"

Hramack said nothing.

The leader leaned down until his face was a hand's width from Hramack's. His breath was sour. "Do not think us stupid, southerner. You will tell us what we wish to know. You cannot invade our territory at your whim. We will deal with you and your friends harshly." He glanced at Anderson. "Where is the woman who accompanied you across the eastern plains?"

Anderson shook his head. "I don't know who you're talking about."

The Marauder leader scowled. "Hardy wishes you brought to him unharmed, but later we will torture you until you talk. Talk now. Better a quick death than a long, slow, painful one."

Hramack was proud when instead of flinching, Anderson growled, "Who the hell are you?"

The man tapped his chest. "I am Victor Juarez, Hardy's Second-in-Command." He looked at the bandages on Anderson's feet. "Can you walk?"

Hramack quickly realized that this group had not been in contact with the men they had earlier led on a merry chase through the building, or they would have killed him outright for lying to them. He spoke up quickly, seeking to delay them until Grey Eagle arrived with the others.

"No, his feet are too badly injured. You will have to carry him."

Anderson, recognizing Hramack's ploy played along, wincing as he moved his leg. "I think my ankle's broken."

While Juarez's men constructed a litter from spears and strips of the plastic that had covered the equipment, one of the Marauders guarded him and Anderson, but his gaze scanned the room, clearly uncomfortable around so much strange machinery.

Anderson nudged Hramack when he noticed Hramack's subtle movements. "What are you doing?"

Hramack continued moving his hands behind his back. "Trying to save our lives," he whispered.

He had no time to explain further. The litter completed, they placed Anderson on it. They none too gently searched Hramack's pack, strewing its contents on the floor. One of the men smiled when he noticed the silver and turquoise bracelet he had used to scratch the message, Aseara's gift for Teela. He snatched it off the floor.

"Give that back!" he yelled at the pilferer.

The man slapped him across the face with the back of his hand, laughed, and shoved his plunder into his pocket. Then, he tied Hramack's hands behind his back, slipped a noose around his neck, and dragged him from the room and down the corridor.

Hramack prayed Grey Eagle would discover the sign he had left for them.

28

CONTACT!

KENA AWOKE WITH THE MORNING SUN SHINING IN HIS FACE. IT POURED onto the platform above the lake. Mists rising from the lake hid it from view. The mountains around them blazed as the first rays of the sun touched the snow-capped peaks turning them golden. Cathi was not beside him. He stood up too quickly and almost fell as his numb legs buckled. The hours of prowling the corridors had taken its toll on his muscles. After a moment of panic, he spotted her crouched beside one of the many antennae that sprouted from the terrace. She had managed to open a metal box at the foot of one of the antenna and was busily working inside it.

"Good morning, Cathi," he said.

Cathi looked up from her work, and with a piece of metal in her mouth, answered, "Good morning, Kena."

She smiled at him, making his arms tingle with goose bumps, like a child. He realized something had changed in their relationship. It was no longer simply Healer-patient. He liked the change.

"What are you doing?"

She removed the metal from her mouth and stared at him. "I'm trying to utilize the local signal of this array to bounce a message off one of the satellites overhead and contact my ship using my ship's communicator. I've managed to boost the output by piggy-backing the power from one of the receivers. Then, I filtered the signal through a series of buffers and modified the frequencies to a narrower spectrum. If I can only compress it sufficiently to squirt it through any interference caused by the localized ionization of the atmosphere, my people may be able to pick it up and trace it back to here."

Kena laughed at her reply. "You are speaking a foreign tongue to me. Your words have no meaning. Your people are so much more advanced than us. You must think us awful savages."

"No, we are more technologically advanced, but my people are but a poor shadow of what we once were. We have lost much since we left Earth, both materially and spiritually. You believe deeply in your god, Yarah. Some planets have gods or deities, but most of us believe mankind is alone in the universe."

"We are never alone," Kena countered. The idea of not having faith mystified him. "Faith is personal, but everyone believes in something more than themselves. It is why men strive. But enough of this. I am no priest to convert you to my beliefs. I gather you have managed to come up with a way to contact your people."

"That's right." She sat back and drew a deep breath. "Well, here goes." She adjusted a digital slider on one of the many pieces of elec-tronics in the opened box and touched the microphone in her throat. Kena watched on puzzled.

"Lieutenant Lorst to the *Long John Baldry*. Come in *Baldry*."

There was only silence. She moved the slider a little more and jumped when the speaker in her ear emitted a shrill squeal of static loud enough for Kena to hear.

"Lieutenant Lorst to Captain Moore. Lorst to Captain Moore. Come in *Baldry*."

Faintly at first, but then, as she fine-tuned the controls, more clearly, she heard a voice through the static. She repeated the message for Kena's bebefit. "This is the Merchant ship *Long John Baldry*. I read you faintly Lieutenant Lorst. Can you boost your signal?"

Cathi cried out in glee, "Mims, is that you? Get Captain Moore." She turned to Kena. "I've got them. They heard me."

"Captain Moore is busy now, Lieutenant Lorst. We are under attack. I've marked your position, but your signal is weak."

Cathi frowned. "Under attack? By whom?"

Mims had left the microphone keyed. She heard the commotion in the control room. "The laser is firing, sir ... Damage report". The last voice, she recognized as Captain Moore's. Then the signal went dead. She tried repeatedly, almost frantically to raise the ship. Finally, the makeshift connections of her jury-rigged transmitter began to smoke.

Nearly in tears, she said, "They're dead. They're all dead, and it's my fault. They came to rescue us, and the satellites got them, too. All my friends are dead, and I killed them."

"Ridiculous. Anderson said you did everything you could possibly do to land the ship safely. You saved his life. If this Captain Moore is as good as you say he is he would not have blindly followed your ship to Earth without anticipating the possible dangers. There must be dozens of reasons you lost contact with your ship. Perhaps their antenna was damaged, or your receiver failed before we saw the smoke. None of this is your fault. You are a very brave and courageous woman. You cannot give up hope. I need you."

She brushed away a tear and said, "Because of me, you and your son are separated. We don't know where he is. We don't even know where we are."

"Come. If there is nothing more you can accomplish here, we should find the others." He was afraid for his son, though he did not let on to her. Hramack had led the Marauders away, yet the Marauders had returned. *What did that mean for Hramack and*

Anderson? Were they dead? Somehow, they had to find Grey Eagle and the others. It was time to leave the mountain.

They took the elevator back down, and then prowled the maintenance corridors before locating a door that led back into the main corridors. Carefully and quietly, they tried to find their way back to the control room corridor. They inspected several rooms as they went, finding rooms filled with pipes and tubing, boxes and bundles, and electronic equipment both large and small. They witnessed small mobile machines picking and choosing items from the warehoused material and disappearing into the walls with it.

"The automated maintenance robots are continuously repairing the facility using the spare parts and equipment from these storerooms." Cathi had recovered most of her composure during the long walk. She picked through the boxes and examined some of the contents. "There are many items than might be useful in your village – pumps, generators, computers, and metal rods and pipes."

"Perhaps someday I will return for it. Now though, we must find the others."

Kena was becoming edgy and nervous. They had seen no signs of the others since yesterday. He had lost all sense of direction in the maze of corridors in the gigantic facility under the mountain. They passed room after room, all bare. The centuries of repairs had emptied the storage rooms with no replacements coming in. Someday, maybe centuries from now, when the last spare part was gone, the pumping station would shut down.

One large room caught their attention. A large object covered with a tattered tarp sat in the center of the room. The opposite end of the room was a massive sliding door. Driven by curiosity, they removed the tarp. Underneath, they discovered a vehicle obviously designed for flight. It was triangular-shaped with flattened sides flaring out to form thin, curved wings. Two indented steps led to a hatch just forward of the wings. The vehicle rested on three retractable struts.

"It's a plane," Cathi cried out, "or at least some kind of aircraft." She began examining their discovery. "It looks large enough to carry a dozen people or an equally heavy load. I'm not sure what powers it. I see no obvious engine or exhaust nozzles. Your ancestors might have figured out a way to use antigravity for propulsion as well as lift."

She placed her palm on a raised circular spot beside the door, and it whispered open, revealing the plane's interior illuminated by light entering through a transparent canopy.

"The material of the canopy is polarized against the glare of the sun, making it indistinguishable from the rest of the plane."

Two seats sat on a slight raised platform at the front of the craft directly beneath the canopy. Other seats in the open rear cargo area popped up from the floor when needed for passengers or remained secured for cargo. A simple joystick controlled the plane, and a panel in front of the two forward seats indicated the status of various functions of the plane. Cathi sat in one of the seats. It moved to wrap around her, securing her in place. She reached out and touched a spot on one of the screens and it brightened at her touch. She examined the various screens, experimenting to determine their function.

"I'm certain this craft operates on a combination of antigravity for lift and magnetic propulsion for drive, but the power levels are almost on zero. It needs an exterior source of power to charge the magnetic propulsion system. I think it will fly if we can manage to power it up and open the hangar doors. It's big enough to fly everyone out of here and back to your village."

Kena was dumbfounded. "Fly us back. I've never flown before."

She laughed at Kena's hesitation. "I've never flown one of these planes either. We'll both be starting even."

While Kena tried to quell his concerns about flying through the air, Cathi exited the plane and attached a long power cable from a box on the wall. "There," she said, wiping her dirty hands on her even dirtier jumpsuit. "That should do it." She seemed happy to be once again in her element, smiling, as she watched the numbers on the power panel slowly move into the green.

29

A SLIGHT DETOUR

"They're alive," Mims called out. Captain Moore nodded but could spare no time to celebrate. They had managed to destroy one of the defense satellites with the help of the Martian asteroid miners, but others would quickly replace it.

"Nothing on the scope yet," Secord reported. Moore walked over to his station and placed his hands on Secord's shoulders. "Good job. Your invention worked well."

"It kept the satellite busy for your little surprise. Keeping the ship in front of the incoming asteroid until the last possible minute fooled the satellite's tracking system."

"We were lucky."

"Uh oh. Here come two more satellites." Secord pointed to two blips approaching from the opposite side of the globe.

Moore had hoped that only one satellite would replace the one they had destroyed. Two were beyond their ability to outmaneuver, and he had no more asteroid surprises left.

"What's their ETA?" he asked.

"Twelve minutes," came the reply.

He shook his head. Even if they ran the risk of a steep reentry, twelve minutes would still place them within range of the satellites' lasers.

"What do we do, captain?" Secord asked. The bridge crew stopped what they were doing and waited for his answer. Moore was known for taking chances to edge out the competition. The hazardous journey to Homeworld proved that. Now, they wondered if he would take a similar risk to save crew. His silence contrasted sharply to the raucous barking of orders just a few minutes prior. Everyone wanted to rescue their downed comrades, but knew they could never destroy or disable two defense satellites. The *Baldry* was a merchant ship, not an armed escort.

Captain Moore stood silent and toyed with his beard. He had removed the braids and clipped its length upon his return from Mars, much to the surprise of the crew.

"Bring us about, Mr. Secord," he ordered. "We'll come back another day."

The relief of the crew was evident.

"Captain! I'm getting another message from the planet," Mims yelled across the bridge.

"Is it Lieutenant Lorst again?"

"No, sir. It's someone identifying themselves as Kolkata Dome. They demand to know who we are and why we have destroyed one of their satellites."

"Kolkata Dome? By damn, someone is still alive on Earth. Tell them who we are and what we are attempting to do."

He turned to the helm crew. "Put us in a steep glide path for Lieutenant Lorst's last signal."

He waited tensely as Mims relayed the message. It boded well that Kolkata Dome had never tried to contact a Mars ship in all these many centuries but were contacting them, but then, Mars had never knocked out one of their satellites. Maybe they were a bit concerned the *Baldry* was an invader. By heading into Earth's atmosphere, he had limited their choices. If Kolkata Dome wanted them destroyed, they did not have much of a chance.

Minutes ticked by as the two satellites drew closer. The satellites' targeting radars began to home in on them. They would be within range in three minutes. Still, no reply came from Kolkata Dome.

"Three minutes, sir," Secord dutifully reported over his shoulder.

"I can read, Mr. Secord," he said a bit too sharply. He began fingering his beard. It was beginning to look as if he had blundered badly. He made a decision. "Target the nearest satellite and prepare to fire all missiles on my command."

There was a very slim chance one missile would get through and damage the satellite, leaving a gap wide enough to slip through.

"They are deactivating the defense grid for us," Mims relayed excitedly. Cheers went up over the ship. Moore let them celebrate for a few seconds before motioning them to silence. "They advise us to land outside their dome and wait for an envoy."

"Satellites just went dead and are moving off, Sir," Secord called out. "But they're not returning to their original positions," he added. "They're lingering in the area."

Moore wiped the nervous sweat from his brow. Kolkata Dome was giving them an opening but on their terms. "Perhaps it would be a wise thing to meet these Kolkatans before mounting a rescue for Lieutenant Lorst," he said. He had ignored Mars' help, and it had cost him a shuttle. He would not ignore possible help again. "Tell them to relay landing coordinates and then set a low, cruising course for us. I want to see this planet. We've been a thousand years getting here."

Kolkata Dome glinted brightly in the early morning sun as the *Baldry* approached over some of the highest and most majestic mountains Captain Moore had ever seen on more than fifty planets he had visited during his career. They marched on, row after row, for thousands of kilometers. Two or three of the largest were nearly ten kilometers high. Snow glistened on their peaks like a dusting of diamonds. Rivers of banded, dirty ice flowed down the valleys between them to form lakes in the high valleys. Earth was far from a dead world. She was slowly recovering from her long ordeal.

The dome was large – nearly a kilometer high and over sixty kilometers in diameter. Hundreds of smaller buildings of various sizes and shapes butted up against the dome's flanks and dotted the vast, open plain surrounding it. A small river, its water crystal clear, meandered across the plain. White, long-legged white wading birds dotted the marshy banks. Enormous flocks of other birds swirled and danced in the sky above the river. Herds of animals wheeled and turned as the ship approached. He recognized horses, cattle, sheep, and magnificent gray beasts with long white tusks and large floppy ears. Many more he could not identify.

Scores of small boats plied the river, some fishing and others carting freight upriver to small villages along the banks. Hundreds of people plowed large, green fields nearby using teams of oxen. He could not help noticing the armed men along the edges of the fields. He did not know if they were there to protect the workers or to keep them from running away. The dome was large to house a million people, but thousands more lived in the small villages and the collection of buildings surrounding the dome. There was no spaceport proper. A small area of level concrete designed for smaller aircraft would have to do. They landed in the middle of the pad, expecting an official delegation to arrive. Instead, a crowd of over one hundred thousand eager people swarmed the ship, yelling and singing. They stood swaying and clapping hands to the accompaniment of drums and horns. The cacophony was audible over the sound of the ship's engines winding down.

"It looks as if they're glad to see us," Secord commented as he surveyed the crowd.

"Aye, break out some of that brandy we got on Mars and a couple hundred of those metal tags we got printed up on Mars just for this occasion. We'll toss out some of the tags and make them happy."

"What about the brandy?"

"That's for us. We're the second group of Traders to set foot on Earth in a millennium. That calls for a celebration. The *Long John Baldry* will go down in history."

A roar went up from the crowd as Secord opened the hatch and started tossing out metal tags. Moore had ordered printed tags that read, "Peoples of Earth – We have returned." The crowd scrambled for them as if they were 100-credit chips. Eventually, the crowd parted as a long black automobile slowly made its way to the pad.

Several men and a woman wearing long, flowing robes exited the vehicle and passed through the crowd to the ship. The people in the crowd bowed and backed away deferentially as they approached. Captain Moore, bedecked in his finest uniform, strode to the end of the gangway and stood waiting with Secord. One of the dignitaries, a tall, thin woman wearing a white robe glittering with gold embroidery along the cuffs of the sleeves, the hem, and the high collar, broke away and approached. She moved gracefully with deceivingly short steps that brought her to stand before them quickly.

"Captain Moore?" she asked in a soft, musical voice. Her accent was as fluid as her voice, but her pronunciation was meticulously exact, as if Standard English was not her native tongue.

Moore swaggered forward. "I'm Captain Moore."

"We are honored to greet your arrival. My name is Inaya Pachmarudhi, the Chancellor of Kolkata Dome. Our Esteemed Lord, Vinjay Alahambra Khan, could not leave his palace. It would not be seemly to mingle with the masses. He has sent me to do you honors in his name." She bowed deeply. He noticed the others made certain to bow lower than she did.

Moore took an instant dislike to the chancellor but tried to hide his feelings. He had met similar dignitaries on dozens of worlds, a perfunctory diplomat who deemed all others below her station. Her broad smile barely hid the contempt in her cold eyes. Her skin was alabaster, almost as white as the cranes wading in the river. She was too thin for Moore's taste. She appeared to be in her mid-forties. She would have been pretty, but the dark lines around her cold, dark eyes and her ruby-red lips looked more sinister than inviting. She wore her long black hair in a tight bun on the back of her head, held in place with two delicately carved ebony pins."You do us honor. We are here seeking comrades that crashed on a large continent to the west near Denver Dome."

Pachmarudhi consulted one of her companions. "We have not heard from our brothers in Denver Dome in the many years since it was destroyed by rebels and religious zealots. Some survivors fled here. We had assumed all others had perished long ago. The land there is extremely harsh, unlike our own lovely valley." She raised her hand and extended it toward the plains.

"Our comrades are still alive. They signaled us just a short time ago, informing us that an armed party of men is pursuing them. We must rescue them. We came here first to meet with you because you seem to be the last remaining population center. Thank you for disarming your defensive satellites. We desire to show you we mean your people no harm. Our primary purpose is to discuss trade with your world."

Again, Chancellor Pachmarudhi consulted her assistant. "My Lord Khan would never forgive me if I did not present your group to him. I must insist you do us this small honor."

She lifted her hand, and twenty uniformed men stepped from the crowd, armed with rifles. Moore recognized an armed escort when he saw one. He briefly considered resisting, but then noticed triangular-shaped planes rolling out of their hidden hangars at the edge of the landing field. He couldn't mistake the large pods mounted beneath the stubby airfoils as anything other than weapons. Even if the *Baldry* managed to take off, the planes would probably shoot them down before they had a chance to defend themselves.

"Secord, come with me. Mr. Desmond, take command until we return. Follow Plan B in twelve hours."

Desmond frowned. "Yes, Sir, Plan B." He was not happy. Plan B ordered him to get the ship away on the assumption the captain was either dead or a prisoner.

Moore and Secord followed Pachmarudhi as the armed guards shoved the people out of their path, sometimes brutally. As they reached the vehicle, Moore noted with a trader's eye that it floated above the ground using antigravity motors. If they could reach a trade agreement on antigravity, the voyage would pay for itself. Four heavily fortified bunkers flanked the dome's massive doors. He spotted the barrels of large bore cannons and heavy machineguns protruding through narrow slits in the bunkers. More troubling was the fact that all four weapons emplacements could fire either outward toward the landing field or inward through the doors, keeping people either out or in.

The dome was clean and neat, but cosmetics alone could not disguise its age. Its buildings may have once been the peak of architectural perfection, but over the centuries, the occupants had converted them into simple utilitarian buildings. The only statues visible were of a tall man wearing flowing robes with his arms outstretched benevolently, as though embracing the entire dome's population.

"My Lord Khan," Pachmarudhi intoned with respect, noticing the direction of Moore's gaze.

Moore simply nodded. Royalty did not impress him. He had seen too many worlds ravaged by petty warlords and despots. The car entered an underground garage and dropped them off at a regal staircase protected by six heavily armed guards. The guards eyed Moore and Secord with suspicion as they ascended the stairs behind Pachmarudhi. He had no doubt the guards would have shot them down instantly if not for her presence. Two lavishly dressed servants opened the polished brass doors for them. He stepped into a spectacular circular room. Three sets of three-tiered balconies lined three-quarters of the room's perimeter, each separated by wide double doors. The fourth quadrant held a massive holovid screen.

As soon as they reached the center of the room, the holovid came to life, displaying a ten-meter tall likeness of Lord Khan. He looked down at them with a smile and spoke softly in his language. When he had finished, Pachmarudhi translated.

"My Lord Khan wishes to welcome you to Earth and to our city. He looks forward to enterprises that will be beneficial to both our peoples. He bade me make you welcome in his name."

"Be sure to thank him for me," More told Pachmarudhi. He suspected the image was merely a recording and doubted the message said any such thing.

With the servants leading the way, they were shown to a suite of rooms that made his quarters on the *Baldry* look like a storage closet. Three enormous bedrooms, each with its own bath, opened onto a central lounge as large as the *Baldry's* aft storage hangar. Soft, luxurious couches and low tables laden with bowls of fruit and bottles of wine were scattered about the room. A pool with an elaborate carved stone fountain in its center covered one entire end of the central room.

"Very nice," Secord muttered under his breath. He had to agree.

"I hope you will be comfortable, gentlemen," Pachmarudhi bubbled. "The servant will return shortly to escort you to the dining room."

She abruptly turned and left. Secord started for the door. Moore stopped him.

"Don't bother. It's probably locked."

"Are we ...?"

"Prisoners?" he finished Secord's question. "I don't know. We'll have to wait and see."

Secord looked around, picked up a crystal goblet, and poured a glass of wine. He tasted it cautiously, and then smiled broadly. "Still, if we have to be imprisoned ..."

Moore nodded. "I know what you mean."

With a more serious voice, Secord asked, "All this seems somewhat above and beyond, if you know what I mean."

"Yes, but I doubt that many of the people here have access to such luxury. It's as Earth was in the twenty-first century, if I remember my history. There were two classes of people, the Haves and the Have Nots." He waved his hands around the room. "This definitely belongs to the Haves."

"What do they want with us, the ship?"

Moore cocked his head. "Aye, but I doubt they really think they can take it from us, not with what I've seen. No, it seems more like a delaying tactic of some sort."

"For what purpose?"

"That, Mr. Secord, is the question of the day."

Moore had been mulling it over in his mind, but damned if he could think of a reason to hold them. The Kolkatans were surely aware that any attempt to harm them would incur a response from the *Baldry*. Even as small as she was, she could still do a lot of damage to a place like this. There had to be another reason, something to do with Denver Dome. He snapped his fingers.

"That's it." He looked at Secord. "Chancellor Pachmarudhi said they had lost contact with Denver Dome during a rebellion. They thought the city was dead. I told them there were armed men there. Damn my big mouth."

"What is it?"

"They're going to send men to Denver Dome. They want it back."

"What can we do?"

Moore kicked a small table and sent its contents careening across the room to splash in the pool. "Not a damn thing," he groaned.

By avoiding a direct fight with the people of Kolkata Dome, he had placed himself in an untenable situation. If they did not release him in twelve hours, Desmond would take the *Baldry* and search for Cathi and her crew. If so, his life and Secord's was probably forfeit. He checked his chronometer. He had eleven hours to come up with a plan. He certainly did not trust that female weasel, Pachmarudhi.

If they were honored guests at a state banquet, as Pachmarudhi said, then all was well and good. However, he had seen the expression on the diplomat's face as she eyed the *Baldry*. She was almost drooling. She wanted the ship and would no doubt do anything to get it. Moore wondered briefly if that would include torture. He certainly would not put it past them.

"We're probably under surveillance even now," he told Secord. He looked around the room but saw no sign of cameras, not that he would know a spy camera if he saw it. Pachmarudhi's people probably had a long history of spying on the populace. It was just one more way to keep them under control.

Moore had managed to settle down by the time a servant arrived to announce dinner. They followed him, flanked by two guards, down a series of lavishly appointed corridors until they arrived in the largest room he had ever seen. He knew it must be near the center of the dome, for the ceiling was invisible above them. He searched for but failed to find the source of the soft, pervasive light filling the room. It was almost as if the walls themselves glowed. The walls were at least two hundred meters apart and lined with recessed balconies.

Tables filled the immense room and servants scurried about like ants bearing trays of fruit and meat. The room could hold thousands, maybe ten thousand, but certainly not the entire population of the dome. From what little he had seen before they had whisked him into the dome, most of the populace did not eat like this. These, then, were the elite, the ruling class of Kolkata Dome. In spite of the large number of people gathered there, there was surprisingly little conversation. It was as if they were afraid what they said might be overheard. Better to say nothing.

The guards escorted him and Secord to an immense table near one wall, separated from the others by a high glass wall and resting on a raised dais. Moore assumed the glass was bulletproof. Twenty men and women sat at the table, including Pachmarudhi, grinning ear-to-ear as she wooed a young man half her age. The young man refilled his glass constantly and wore the dazed expression of a lamb led to slaughter. Perhaps he had heard frightened whispers of

Pachmarudhi's conquests and their eventual fate when she tired of them.

A seat at the head of the table was empty, the Khan's, he presumed. Pachmarudhi jumped up and took Moore by the hand, patting it gently while slightly caressing it with her thumb, making him uncomfortable.

"Ah, Captain Moore, please be seated. You as well, Mr. Secord. Food will be brought immediately." She cast a withering glance at a servant and waved her hand, and he immediately broke into a trot toward the kitchen. Moore imagined, with such a large room, the servants did an awful lot of running. "Wine?" she asked, producing a crystal decanter.

He accepted the wine graciously and took a tentative sip. The wine was surprisingly good with a delicate, dry aftertaste. He set the glass down. "Where is Lord Khan?" he asked casually.

Pachmarudhi frowned, and then smiled broadly. "My Lord Khan is extremely busy seeing to the many and constant needs of his people. He will surely make an appearance to greet you but just a short one."

The food arrived hot and steaming and was set before them. Some things he recognized – rice, carrots, beans, some of the fruit, and the roast duck. Other meats were unknown. He sampled a few and found their tastes to be delicate but rich. "What is this?" he asked with his mouth full.

Pachmarudhi ignored his deliberate poor table manners and said, "Pork is the first. It comes from pigs, a porcine animal. The second is veal. It is the meat of newborn calves taken from their mother's womb."

Moore coughed as he almost choked on his meal. He reached for a napkin and spit his food into it. Pork he had heard of but never tasted since he was of Jewish descent. Few Jews still worshipped God in the same manner as their ancestors, but followed many of the dietary restrictions. Veal, however, was another matter. It was a barbaric practice. He was ashamed he had thought the taste pleasing. Still, as trade goods, they might offer a tidy profit in spite of his personal revulsion.

"Are you all right, Captain ?" she asked, feigning distress at Moore's bout of coughing.

"Fine, fine. Merely went down the wrong way," he explained as he took another sip of wine to rinse his palate.

Pachmarudhi smiled. "Once my people disdained the meat of cows and held them to be sacred creatures. That, of course, was foolish. Protein is protein, and times were very difficult for many centuries." She dropped his smile and stared into Moore's eyes. "We are no longer a foolish people."

Before he could reply, a flurry of trumpets and drums filled the room from some unseen source, and everyone in the room suddenly rose to their feet. He and Secord followed suit. A floating platform surrounded by half a dozen guards entered the room from a hidden doorway behind them. Atop the platform, sitting on a golden throne, sat an extremely old man dressed in red silk robes inset with diamonds and jewels. The wealth of a small world was riding on the platform.

"My Lord Khan," Pachmarudhi whispered with bowed head.

Moore did not bow but watched intently as the wizened old man approached. He was a good thirty years older than the image on the screen. As the leader of Kolkata Dome got closer, Moore saw just how old he was. The Khan could not be a day under 120 years old. He was merely leathery skin draped over a skeletal frame. His eyes, probably once blue and full of vigor, were now almost closed and dulled with age. The platform stopped beside their table.

"My Lord Khan, these are the men of which I spoke. They are returned from the stars."

The Khan said nothing as he carefully examined his guests. He crooked one finger, and Pachmarudhi leaned forward and whispered something in his leader's ear. Then his platform slowly floated away and exited the room through another cleverly constructed hidden doorway.

After he had left and everyone resumed the meal, Pachmarudhi spoke. "My Lord Khan wishes you to help us repair our defense satellites. They are our protection against Mars. You, after all, did destroy one in your attempt to land here."

Moore knew the defense satellites protected larger weapons platforms trained on the planet and had served just such a purpose in the past. He guessed Pachmarudhi did not know that he knew. "If we assist you in their repair, what assurance do I have they will not be used against us?" he asked carefully.

By Pachmarudhi's frown, Moore suspected that few refused her requests. "We seek only to protect our precious resources from Mars. They have tried to conquer Earth for centuries." She smiled broadly. "We have no reason to wish harm to our new friends from the stars."

Her smile was so big that Moore thought he could have piloted the *Baldry* through it. He nodded his head as if considering the idea. If he refused, he suspected Pachmarudhi would order their immediate execution.

"It can be done. My engineers should be able to make the necessary repairs."

"We are most grateful but, in reality, it is better to teach a man to fish than to feed him. Our engineers have studied the plans for the satellites carefully and thoroughly understand them, but alas, we have no way with which to reach them."

There's the kicker, Moore thought to himself. *They want the Baldry. If they ever get aboard, they'll take her for sure.* "My ship is too large and cumbersome for such an operation," he lied. "Perhaps I can contact Mars. They should be more than willing to trade one or two smaller ships perfect for the job in exchange for, say, food. Animal life is still rare on Mars. Meat is a luxury item."

He saw that Pachmarudhi was considering the option. "We would have to control the trade," she said warily.

"No problem. You could meet outside the defense satellite screen and exchange goods. No one would land on Earth." It sounded good to him. He hoped Pachmarudhi was buying into it. In reality, Mars had plenty of meat, though they were mostly vegetarians. What Mars wanted from Earth was technology they suspected still existed there. If there was technology on Earth, then the Traders Guild got first crack. He had not come all this way for nothing.

Pachmarudhi's look of contemplation suddenly turned into a cold calculated grin. "You had me going, Captain Moore. I almost believed you. Your ship will suffice. I am sure we can learn to operate it in time. We are a resourceful people. We must defend ourselves from Mars and from your brethren returned from the stars." She almost spit the words as she said them. "You left us here to fend for ourselves and are surprised to find us still here after such a long time. This is our world and we will keep it," she screamed. "Earth is no longer yours." She raised her hand and a dozen armed guards surrounded them. "You will call your ship and order them to surrender, or we will attack it with our planes and rebuild it after your men are dead. You may remain here in luxury, but the ship must be ours."

She handed Moore a small radio. "It is set to the frequency you used to contact us. Call them."

Calmly, he took the communicator and called his ship.

"Mr. Desmond. This is Captain Moore. You will surrender the ship immediately, or they will kill Mr. Secord and myself. I will give you two minutes to inform the crew and call me back." He handed the radio back to Pachmarudhi.

"Very wise, Captain Moore. You will see that we are a reasonable people. Too long have our brothers in North America been away from our fold. I am a descendant of those who fled Denver Dome during the murderous rebellion centuries ago. It is time we become one people once again."

Another way of saying slavery, Moore thought. Slowly, pretending to wipe away nonexistent perspiration from his neck, he pressed the comm unit to activate it.

"So, we're your prisoners," he said to Pachmarudhi.

"Hostage is a more proper term."

Ten minutes passed. Pachmarudhi was visibly growing impatient. "Is it not time for your ship to call you back?"

"Any minute now, I hope."

A guard ran into the room yelling at Pachmarudhi. Moore watched as Pachmarudhi's eyes turned to ice. They knew.

She leaped to her feet. "You think to trick us while your ship escapes," she yelled. "Our planes will follow and shoot it down. You disappoint me, Captain."

The room began to shake. Bits of ceiling cascaded to the floor. People panicked and threw themselves beneath the tables. Pachmarudhi stared in disbelief at the ceiling, and then leveled her gaze at Moore.

"You did this," she accused.

Suddenly, the roof caved in, sending large pieces of metal and glass to the floor, scattering the diners. Moore smiled as the *Baldry* slowly settled on her landing jets. She looked small in the enormous cavern of a room, but she was big enough for him.

Before the guards could react, he grabbed a knife from the table and wrapped his arm around Chancellor Pachmarudhi's neck. "You will escort us to my ship or you will die slowly," he whispered in the frightened ambassador's ear. Pachmarudhi nodded, keenly aware of the knife at her throat. Using his whimpering hostage as a shield, he and Secord backed up the lowered ramp. The guards were too frightened to fire and risk hitting the chancellor. Once inside, he tossed Pachmarudhi aside and told an armed guard to watch him; then, rushed to the bridge.

"Good job, Mr. Desmond. I had hoped you would have the wherewithal to trace my signal. The banquet room was a readymade landing bay."

Desmond smiled. "Yes, sir. I just set her down through the center of the dome. They'll have to fix that leak before the next rain." He laughed. "The planes tried to intercept us, but we fooled them by hopping straight to the dome. I don't think we can fool them again."

"We have a hostage to keep their weapons silent. Even so, take her straight up hard and fast till we're well out of their range."

He resumed his command chair. He had not proved much of a diplomat, but he did not care. The Guild had dealt with small-minded windbags like the Khan before. If, as he suspected, Pachmarudhi was the true power behind the throne, he was now in an extremely good bargaining position.

Now, to find Lieutenant Lorst and the rest of my crew.

30

PRISONERS

A FTER TWO CLOUDS MADE IT BACK TO GREY EAGLE WITH THE STORY OF their ruse, Grey Eagle realized the Marauders were able to move at will through the labyrinth of corridors, making it only a matter of time before they managed to flank his position. He decided to abandon the control center and locate Kena, Hramack, and the others. Then, they would find a way out of the mountain.

"Come. Let's leave this place. It's time to go home."

Two Clouds led them to the infirmary. Grey Eagle's heart sank when he saw the carnage left by the Marauders. "There is no blood, no sign of a struggle. I cannot believe the Marauders could have taken them without a fight." Then he noticed a small discoloration on the surface of one of the otherwise pristine walls. He bent over to examine it more closely and discovered an A and an H scratched within a circle, and a K and a C, outside it.

He smiled. "Hramack managed to leave us a message. The Marauders have captured him and Anderson, but Kena and Cathi Lorst are still free. The Marauders do not have them."

"What do we do?" Two Clouds asked.

"We find and rescue Hramack," he answered. "He would do no less for us."

"What of Kena and the woman?"

"Kena is resourceful. He will find a place safe for the injured woman. We will search for Hramack. He is in the greatest danger."

The Marauders had not bothered to hide their trail. In addition, small discrete signs left by Hramack marked the way and indicated the band consisted of ten men. Not too many to take on once they caught up to them, Grey Eagle thought, but they must hurry before they joined with a larger party. Hramack had left one more sign for Grey Eagle, the sign for carelessness. With it, he communicated that the group had thrown caution to the wind as they marched through the corridors with their captives. They were not expecting trouble. Grey Eagle was certain that when he caught up with them, he could overpower them.

Another kilometer farther, he changed his mind. They had come once again to the main entrance to the underground facility. Outside, another twenty Marauders sat in the shade of the mountain, resting. Such a large group would be too much for Grey Eagle's small band to take on. There was no way around them. They would have to wait until they left before following Hramack. Their future looked bleak once again.

✳

The group bearing Anderson and Hramack marched for hours through the heat of the afternoon. Their urgency in getting their prisoners to their leader, Hardy, drove them to suffer the scorching heat. Neither Anderson nor he was given water. The sun beat down upon them with a fury he had not felt in weeks. His raging thirst became a demon to conquer. Each time he stumbled or slowed down, a sharp tug on the rope about his neck sent an urgent choking reminder to quicken his pace. He had hoped Grey Eagle would catch up, but perhaps it was too late. They had passed many groups of men since leaving the mountain, part of a well-trained army.

After dusk, the group halted. Hramack, exhausted, collapsed immediately. This time there was no jerk on his rope. Anderson had passed out on his litter either from the heat. They made camp beneath a series of spires of red rock that seemed to pierce the sky, *hoodoos*, one of the men called them. Hramack watched them as they methodically set up camp and post guards. He no longer thought of them as Marauders. They were distinctly different from the Marauders that had attacked them before they reached Pueblo Nuevo, the savages that constantly attacked the village. Those Marauders were dirty, ragged, and poorly fed.

This group was well armed, healthy, disciplined, and well organized. They wore clothing made from soft vegetable fibers dyed to match the colors of the desert – khaki, rust, brown, and buff. Their weapons were sharp and forged from good quality steel. A complex, organized society of weavers, metal smiths, farmers, and engineers were necessary to maintain such an army, a thriving society, not bands of wandering nomads.

They finally brought water, but no food. He took a few sips and handed the canteen to Anderson, who drank deeply. Just after moonrise, one of his captors kicked him to arouse him for another forced march. He and Anderson received a meager meal of stale bread, dried fruit, and a few sips of water.

By dawn, they had traveled several kilometers and had reached an area planted in groves of fruit-bearing trees and fields of plants irrigated by small pipes carrying water from much larger pipes buried underground. Thousands of square hectares of shading material suspended above the crops supported by thin metal rods protected the plants from the full fury of the sun. He saw groups of people working the fields and tending to cattle, sheep, and goats.

Ponds, covered by thick membranes to prevent evaporation, dotted the slopes.

"What are those?" he asked Juarez.

Juarez seemed proud of the work. He answered, "Fish ponds. We raise many kinds of fish there. When we harvest a pond, we drain it and use the waste and mud from the bottom to fertilize our crops. Hardy taught us this."

"Who is Hardy?"

"He is the man you will tell why you are here," he answered in a threatening voice.

The day wore on savagely. The heat pressed down on him like a heavy stone weight, forcing air almost too hot to breathe from his lungs. This time, even the soldiers grew weary from the forced march. A few hours before nightfall, Victor called a halt. Hramack felt certain they were nearing their destination. It was time he tried to escape. He knew Anderson would never make it far on his injured feet. It was clear Hardy wanted Anderson delivered in good health, but Hramack was not as sure of his status. Victor implied torture and death. Dying in the desert seemed a better alternative to that.

He waited until the moon had risen before working his bonds loose. His captors did not expect him to try to escape and had not tied his hands too tightly. Twenty minutes of rubbing them on a sharp rock, and he was free. He had seen many soldiers along the way. It would be senseless to try to return to the mountain by the route they had taken. If he could retrieve his pack, he could use his compass to find his way. He knew in which direction the pumping facility lay, and he had tried to recognize landmarks along the way. With luck, he would be able to find his way back and avoid recapture along the way.

The road was in a valley sandwiched between two high ridges. One was very steep and ended against the flanks of a high mountain. The other rose at a manageable slope and dropped off into a series of washes and arroyos: a perfect place to avoid pursuit. It was also the first place they would search.

He did not wake Anderson for fear he would demand to go with him. If he could find the others, they could free Anderson later. He found his pack stacked with several others. His canteen was still inside, but it held only a few mouthfuls of water. Only two guards patrolled the perimeter of the camp. It was a simple deed to reach the steep talus slope of loose dirt and rock covered the slope undetected. Ascending it silently proved difficult. He made small movements and searched for each handhold carefully to avoid either sliding back down the loose slope or precipitating a small landslide that would alert the guards.

Near the top of the slope, a narrow goat path clung to the steep, rocky cliff. He followed it into the deep shadows. It was a difficult climb in his condition, but he hoped to avoid detection. Two days' forced march in the heat of the day with little food or water had weakened him, but his determination to reach the others drove him upward. Centimeter by centimeter, from one precarious handhold to the next, he climbed. An hour had passed before he heard a commotion in the camp below. They had finally discovered his absence.

If they first searched the obvious route, it would give him time to make good his escape. In the moonlight, following his tracks would not be easy. Kena had taught him the art of hiding his tracks when he was much younger. Such skills seem forgotten until called upon in times of need. His need was now great. He rested several times on small ledges to catch his breath and ease the cramp in his bleeding fingers. Too soon, he heard men climbing below him. They had discovered his ruse. He fought his growing despair. He would have to work hard keep ahead of them. If any of the soldiers had ropes and skills at rock climbing, he would be in trouble.

Dawn burst upon him with the fury of an enraged beast. He had no food and no more water. The open cliff face offered no shelter from the sun's fierce heat. He was certain he stood out against the side of the mountain like a black tick on a white goat. If his pursuers had spotted him, they were too involved in their own climbing to waste energy shouting.

He estimated that he had climbed a thousand meters, but the top was another 500 meters above him, and the path had petered out, offering few handholds. He would have to traverse laterally across naked rock to find a better way up.

Small ledges and cracks in the rock barely large enough for his fingers allowed him to go another 200 meters before suddenly ending in a sheer blank wall. A section of rock had broken free and slid down the face of the mountain, scouring it like sandpaper. He was trapped.

He faced two choices, neither of which pleased him – return and give up, or try to climb back down and search for another path. He was trying to decide when the first arrow bounced off the stone less than an arm's length from his head. He looked down and saw a man armed with a bow leaning backwards into space secured by a rope around his waist held by two other men. If he did not descend, eventually an arrow would find him.

"Aai!" he yelled to those below. "I give up. I'm coming down."

Descending took less time than climbing up had. When he reached the ridge top, several angry soldiers began to beat and kick him. A shout from below stopped them. They tied his feet and wrists securely and lowered him like a pack to the valley floor by rope. Sharp rocks sliced into his back, and judging from the laughter coming from below, it seemed that they purposefully banged his head and limbs into large boulders for pleasure.

When he finally reached the bottom, Victor Juarez stood over him rubbing his finger along the edge of the blade of his knife. "I think I should kill you now and save time."

With one eye bruised and swollen shut and his lips bleeding from his rough handling, Hramack summoned his courage and answered defiantly, "If you wanted me dead, you would have simply fired arrows until one struck the mark. No, you want me alive for Hardy. Now, give me water, or I'll die before we reach your den of vipers." He grinned to show his disdain for his captors.

Juarez cursed but sent a man to fetch water.

After Hramack had drunk his fill, Juarez ordered, "Make a litter for this one and tie him to it. We must be off."

He remained bound hand and foot as they marched. At night, a guard remained beside him and Anderson. They were not allowed to speak to one another. They received no food and only a few sips of water. After two more days of uncomfortable swaying in the litter, they rounded a large hill and came upon the ruins of Denver Dome spread out across a vast, flat plain. From Arun Kane's journal, he knew that the dome once was home to two million people, an unimaginable number. It towered almost a thousand meters into the sky and covered an area over sixty kilometers in diameter. People from as far north as Canada, as far south as Mexico, as far east as Missouri, and as far west as Washington state had come to the dome when Earth had become almost uninhabitable because of the ever increasing heat and solar radiation. Six of the Great Domes were in America – L.A. Dome, New York-Boston Dome, Atlanta Dome, Chicago Dome, Juneau-British Columbian Dome, and Denver Dome. Only Denver Dome had come through the wars and the Upheaval intact. Arun Kane had unleashed the terrible fury of the orbiting defense satellite on the dome in hopes of forcing the Elite rulers to allow man to walk once again on the land and to repair the damage caused by both man and nature.

In the shadow of the rubble of Denver Dome, Hramack saw new buildings under construction. These were simple two and three-story buildings built of salvaged brick and stone, but they had a beauty and symmetry of their own. Many bore paints of bright colors that reminded Hramack of wildflowers or the sky. He saw windmill generators, streetlights, and fountains of water. If Hardy was responsible for the revitalization of the area, perhaps he was a man with whom Hramack could reason.

A crowd gathered as the group approached. By their looks, they were as afraid of him as he was of them. He must try to overcome the mistrust and the misunderstanding. They each had what the other needed and now, with the return of the Scattered Ones, they would need to work together to ensure that they, not men from the stars, retained possession of the Earth.

At last, they came upon a group of stolid-looking men standing outside a large building. The men carrying Anderson's litter lowered him gently to the ground. With Hramack, they simply dropped his litter.

"Give them water," a voice said. A jug of water was produced and someone poured water down his throat, almost choking him. "Release him," the voice ordered.

Hramack leaned onto his side as someone cut his bonds. He fought back the urge to scream as the circulation in his arms and legs returned. He stood, but his legs were still wobbly from heat exhaustion and lack of water. He reeled and almost fainted. A man in his early forties stood before him. He was slightly shorter than Hramack, but carried himself with an aloof presence that made him seem taller. Hramack surmised that he must be Hardy, the leader.

As if the stranger had heard his thoughts, he announced, "I am George Washington Hardy, leader of this Alliance. You," he pointed to Anderson, "you are one of the Scattered Ones returned to us?" Anderson nodded. He turned to Hramack. "You are one of the southern invaders. Why have you brought war to our country? Where are the others who came with you?"

Hramack ignored the pain in his legs, stood straight, and faced Hardy. As he spoke, he massaged his cut and swollen lip. "We are not invaders. We came to find the source of the water that feeds our villages and return its flow. Your people attacked us without warning. We simply fought back."

Hardy smiled. "Rather successfully from what I hear."

"Grey Eagle's people have learned to fight from decades of attacks by Marauders." He paused and stared at Hardy. "But you aren't Marauders, are you?"

"Marauders? Ah, yes, our southern and eastern allies can be somewhat . . . overzealous, at times. They protect our borders and owe loose allegiance to me, but they still cling to their old ways."

"We are not your enemy. I see you have knowledge of electricity and irrigation. You grow food and raise animals. You try to survive, as do we. Together, our two peoples could do much to rebuild the Earth. It's a pity we are fighting."

"Your words make sense, young one, but your actions speak louder. I have lost many men to you and your companions."

"We fought only to defend ourselves."

Anderson spoke up. "What he says is true. From what I have learned of these people, they are not bloodthirsty, but decent, honorable men. They have committed themselves to me and to my companion's protection. Your men attacked from ambush without warning. My companion came in peace, and we wish to leave in peace, but I will not allow you to kill this man."

Hardy walked over to Anderson. He stood above him and said, "Very bravely spoken, but you are in no position to dictate to me. Just why have you come here, Star Man? To rescue us? I think not." He waved his hand in the air. "You want something from Earth and think to take it from us." Hardy clenched his fist and narrowed his eyes. "Be warned. I have more in common with this southerner than I do with you. Your people abandoned our world after stripping it of its resources before fleeing to the stars, leaving those of us who remained to fight over the scraps you left behind, like starving dogs over a bone. Once, our people soared through the skies and made wondrous machines that supplied us with light, food, and water at the touch of a finger. Now, we scratch at the earth and pick through the garbage heaps of our world like beggars. Do not come here and expect us to greet you like gods or even as long lost brothers. You have long ago forfeited your right to this world."

He turned to the men assembled around them. "Take these two to the common square. Tomorrow we will execute them both, the Scattered One for what his people did to our ancestors and as a message to others who may come; the southerner, as an example to others who sneak into our country and try to steal what is ours."

Hramack's dismay overwhelmed him. He staggered backwards into the waiting arms of Hardy's men.

31

CHU LI'S WRATH

MADRAS RELAYED KAFFA'S MESSAGE TO THE HIGH PRIEST. TO SAY THAT Chu Li was angry would have been an insult to the depths of his loathing. He could not understand how one old man could pose such a problem. Forcing the marriage of Teela to Juresh was within the law. None could fault him for that, and yet, the villagers continued to resist his edicts, inspired by Kaffa's opposition. The animal sacrifices had not worked, and people were growing restless. Without the springs, they would be out of water in a few short weeks. *If the remaining supply had to serve the entire population,* he mused, somewhat surprised by the audacity of his thoughts. It was cruel, but should not a few die to assure the life of the village? By sacrificing the elderly, the sick, and the discontented, they could extend the water rationing for weeks longer.

He comforted himself by considering it one of Yarah's tests to weed out the unbelievers among them. Whatever the outcome, he would insist that Kaffa be one of the sacrificed to quell his private rebellion.

Madras was no longer trustworthy. He grew more distressed with each passing day. He avoided his family whenever possible, spending his days besotted with kalquat. He stood before Chu Li now trembling in fright.

"Teela will marry your son. Kaffa, for all his bluster, is an old man. He cannot stop it. However, his quiet insinuations against me have created ripples in our community at a time when we have troubles enough to endure. His actions can no longer he tolerated." He smiled. "Let him grumble and shake in rage tonight. Tomorrow, the Council shall send for him for questioning. We will pull his teeth before we announce your son's upcoming marriage."

Madras' face became ashen and his brow erupted in perspiration. "What if the people protest? Kaffa, though no longer Village Precept, still has many loyal to him."

"The Council will declare him a troublemaker and sanction him. As High Priest, I will declare him a heretic. Siding publicly with him places his followers treading dangerous ground. Public humiliation might soften his rhetoric."

Madras shook his head rapidly. "Not Kaffa. He is old, but he retains the vigor of someone half his age. You will simply invite him to redouble his efforts."

Chu Li smiled at Madras and closed his hand into a fist. "That is precisely what I intend. Let him languish in the silo prison while we continue with our plans."

Chu Li considered letting Madras in on his decision to reduce the village's population, but then decided he could not trust him. Besides, one of Madras' nieces was ill with the strange fever that affected several in the village. She would be included in the culling. It would best not to allow Madras time to reconsider his allegiance.

"Go. Inform the other members of the Council of my intentions. Tomorrow, we end this constant bickering."

As Madras slunk away into the darkness, Chu Li shook his head in wonder. "I offer him everything, and still his heart is not in it. He is a weak man and weakness cannot be tolerated." He sighed. "His time has almost come."

✳

Morning came with a renewed fury of heat blasting the village, baking the stone beneath their feet. The sun rose angry and red from dust in the air, but many saw it as a sign. Centuries of watching the sun burn away the past had created an aura of malevolence around it. Now, it was an angry red eye staring down at them in celestial fury.

To Chu Li, it created the perfect backdrop for his latest announcement. After the Morning Prayer, he would inform Kaffa of the Council's decision to question him. Kaffa, as usual, would protest loudly, offering Chu Li the opportunity to have Kaffa led away under Council arrest. His public humiliation might earn him the sympathy of a few, but most would welcome the show of power as a sign the Council had a plan.

He stood at the edge of the canyon, facing the empty Pools of Yarah, as he intoned his prayer, roasting beneath the heavy robes of office in the unusually oppressive heat.

"Yarah, we beseech you to bring harmony to our village. We abide your testing of our faith, but those among us who falter create ripples that become waves. It is a time for a Cleansing. We must –"

"She is dying!" someone shouted.

Chu Li whirled to see Alton the furniture maker standing in front of the crowd, his hands bunched by his side. The veins of his neck stood out as he yelled.

"My daughter is dying, and you do nothing."

"Our Healer, Kena, had abandoned us," Chu Li responded. "He has incited Yarah's anger."

"She is burning with fever. She needs water, but you ration it." He raised his arm and pointed his finger at Chu Li, shaking it. "You promised the waters would return, but it has not. Must we all die, must my Denora die, to prove we are worthy of Yarah's grace?"

"Give her water," someone in the crowd shouted.

Chu Li stared at them, his gaze moving along the line of faces. "Which of you will give up their water ration? Alton's daughter has the dust fever. Without a Healer, she will die. You know this. Yarah will accept her pure soul, but it is not Yarah's doing. The fault lies with Kena and Hramack. They murdered Eithan and invoked Yarah's wrath down on our village. The sacrifice of a few lives are the penitence we must perform to purge the village of sin."

Kaffa stepped from the crowd. "Do you, Chu Li, decide who to sacrifice?"

Chu Li frowned at Kaffa's use of his name instead of his title of High Priest. "Yarah decides all things. As High Priest, he speaks through me. Do you question Yarah's will?"

"I question Chu Li's will.

"They are one and the same."

"Yes, and that frightens me."

"You have opposed me for years. Your actions border on blasphemy. Yarah –"

"You sacrifice my daughter," Alton yelled. "I will not allow it."

Many in the crowd gasped, as the rail-thin furniture maker, a man so meek he paled when he saw blood, drew a knife used for shaping wood from his robe and rushed at Chu Li.

"I will not allow it," he repeated.

Chu Li looked into Alton's eyes and saw not the furniture maker, but a madman driven to a killing rage by grief, dismay, and the heat. He knew he could not reason with him. With the odd realization that he was not afraid, Chu Li pulled his dagger from his robes, the one he had used on Eithan and the sacrificed animals, and held it out in front of him. He did not strike out, but Alton's awkward charge propelled him onto the dagger's blade. He felt the blade push into the furniture maker's stomach until it hit his spine. Alton's eyes went wide with surprise. Whatever rage had taken him, faded with the realization of his death. He dropped his knife and slid down Chu Li's body.

"Denora," he gasped and died.

The gathered crowd was silent. What was to be a prayer for their survival had escalated into a bloodbath. One of their own was dead, driven insane by lack of water and the heat. They knew any of them could be next.

As Chu Li stared down at Alton's body, blood dripping from his dagger, Kaffa said, "Now you have your sacrifice," and strode off.

Chu Li fought to recover his composure. Showing just the right amount of surprise and regret, he said, "Our brother Alton was not in control of his actions." He pointed to the sun, now looking even more red and swollen, as if the furniture maker's blood had strengthened it. "That is our enemy. It has scoured our world of everything. We cling to life by our faith. If we abandon Yarah, who among you can assure our survival? We must stand together or die. We must all make sacrifices." He pointed to Alton's body lying at his feet. "He has made his sacrifice. Now, his stricken daughter can have his extra share of our dwindling water supply. Or, with the knowledge that she will not survive, we can leave it in the cisterns for all to partake. You must decide. This is a village matter, not one of faith. You must each look into your hearts and decide who is worthy and who is not."

He motioned for men to remove Alton's body. "he had made his prayer. There is no need for another."

He walked away from the silent crowd. The furniture maker had accomplished what the High Priest would have had trouble doing. Now, he was an example. He stared at his hands as he walked away. *More blood. My hands attract blood like sweat attracts gnats.* He sighed. Before it was all over, he knew he would have to spill more blood.

Yarah wills it.

32

Soaring Like an Eagle

A FTER WORKING ON THE PLANE FOR HOURS, CATHI FINALLY DECIDED TO
stop and rest. Her arms ached and her head throbbed where
she had banged it repeatedly on the engine cowling. Kena
helped when he could, but he knew nothing about planes. Since he
was good with tools, she put him to work tightening or loosening
bolts where she indicated and pulling wires that she pointed out.

"I need a break," she told Kena. He looked up and nodded; then
he smiled.

"What?" she asked. He touched his nose. She took a rag, wiped
her nose, and then saw that her nose had been covered in grease.
"Thanks. Almost ready," she said. "In a few minutes we'll find out if
this thing still works after a few hundred years."

"You are doing nothing to instill confidence in me," Kena jested.

"Don't worry, Kena. If it quits working while in the air and we
crash, you will still become the first Earth man to fly in over three
hundred years."

"An honor I had rather live without, I assure you."

She laughed. It felt good to laugh again after so long. For a brief moment, she forgot about Whitehall and Pegari, but only a brief moment. "It's time to give it a try. Are you ready?"

"I had rather die in the sky than under this mountain. Let's go."

Kena chose the seat beside her, the one she called the co-pilot's seat. He was a little uncomfortable as the seat curved around him, leaving only his arms and legs mobile. A cushion inflated behind his head, allowing him to turn his head but little else. Cathi took her seat, her right hand gripping the joystick controlling pitch, yaw, and speed. Another lever beside her left hand controlled power.

"Here goes."

She touched an illuminated tab marked Hangar Door, and the plane jerked as it lifted into the air, then settled down, as she pushed the controls forward. When they were within ten meters of the door, Kena wriggled anxiously in his seat. He relaxed when the doors began to slide open, revealing a tunnel perhaps a hundred meters long. Bands of colored lights raced down the sides of the tunnel toward the opposite end. When they reached the end of the tunnel, another door slid aside.

She powered up the plane. With a high-pitched whine, it lifted several meters into the air. She edged the joystick a little more forward, and the plane shot into the air and over the side of the mountain, dropping slightly until the wings caught air. Kena's stomach protested. She tested the controls, smiling at Kena's groans of discomfort, as the plane pitched left, then right. She pushed the stick to its maximum and felt a surge of power. The mountains flew by at an alarming speed. They were travelling at 1200 kph, faster than the speed of sound, and she felt no wind resistance at all. She nosed the plane higher to avoid the mountain peaks and headed east. An urge rose in her to fly over the tortured lands through which only days before she and Anderson had wearily trudged. She turned back toward the mountain. She did not want to see the ruins of her crashed shuttle or the graves of Pegari or Whitehall.

She noticed a great deal of activity below them. She turned to Kena. "We were told these people were cannibals and savages. I see signs of agriculture, aquaculture, and herds of domesticated animals. They have irrigation. These people are at least as advanced as your people, maybe more so."

"We've had only contact with small bands of Marauders on our journey," stammered Kena defensively. "My people did not know any humans were left alive until we met the men of Pueblo Nuevo. Grey Eagle's people would not lie. Perhaps not all of the tribes in this territory are as advanced as these seem to be, as your encounter on your journey here would seem to indicate. Maybe we can reason with them. We have no need to fight each other. It is a large planet, and we who remain are few."

As they neared the mountain, they saw a familiar sight below them. Less than a kilometer from the entrance, sight of their first battle with the Marauders, the unmistakable form of Grey Eagle and his men marched determinedly down the valley toward Denver Dome.

"Let's land," he said.

She slowed the craft and turned in a tight arc above the group. As he noticed the plane's approach, Grey Eagle signaled his men to scatter for cover in the surrounding rocks while he stood defiantly alone facing the unknown threat. It was only until the plane had landed and Kena had come running out of the doorway, that Grey Eagle recognized his old friend and threw up his arms to embrace him.

"Kena, my friend," he said, as he squeezed Kena in his strong arms. "We thought you lost, swallowed up by the mountain."

"Good to see you again," Kena said, prying himself from Grey Eagle's embrace. He searched the faces of the group of men. "Where are Hramack and Anderson?"

Grey Eagle lowered his head and was silent for a few seconds before replying, "Taken, captured by the Marauders. They are alive and unharmed. Your son has left signs that we are following." Grey

Eagle examined the plane in which his friends had just arrived. "What thing is this that flies like a great eagle? A device of the old ones no doubt." He walked around the plane and stuck his head inside the door. "Will its belly carry all of us and still fly? If so, it will aid our cause greatly."

"Yes, it will hold all of us," Cathi answered. "But we cannot just attack them. There has been a great misunderstanding."

She and Kena began to describe the things they had seen flying over the nearby valley. Grey Eagle listened intently, frowning often.

"They are not all cannibals and looters, as you have thought," Kena concluded. "They have developed a thriving culture here."

Grey Eagle was unconvinced. "It is true these Marauders seem better fed and more organized than those along our border, but I still would not dine with them until I first knew the menu. Nevertheless, if what you say is true, then we can perhaps make a treaty with them and end this bloodshed." His gaze became stern as he asked Kena, "What do you propose?"

"Tomorrow, at first light, we will land in their city in this plane. It will show them we are not savages. I will go alone and speak with their leader to secure the release of Anderson and my son. You and the others will remain in the safety of the plane. If the talks go well, we will make a treaty." Kena's expression hardened. "If they kill me, you will return to the mountain with Cathi, find any weapons you can, and return to free my son."

"You are a brave man, Kena of Ningcha. I hope you are not a stupid one. We will go with you to their city, but if they attempt to detain you, we will pour from this craft and kill all we can. Honor demands we protect your life as you have protected ours."

Kena smiled. "You do me great honor, Grey Eagle, but if we continue to kill one another, we will never rebuild this planet. We must talk with them. We must win their trust."

"If we must die to win their trust, so be it." Grey Eagle said. "We will rest and eat. Tomorrow we will meet these Marauders face-to-face in their own city. We will leave as friends, or we will not leave."

To Kena's consternation, he added quietly, "If they do not kill your son tonight while we sleep."

Anderson and Hramack lay chained to the flagpole outside the main meeting hall of the Marauders, fully exposed to the harsh sun. He doubted they would live to see another. His father and friends were in the mountain still searching for them. With no hope of rescue, their future looked bleak. Throughout the day, passersby gathered to hurl insults or something worse – feces, rotten vegetables, even stones – at them. Hramack's body sported several new bruises from well-tossed stones. Anderson was in worse shape. His ordeal and now his impending death had drained his will to live. He lay motionless, curled in a fetal position. Hramack tried to rouse him.

"Anderson." No reply. He called again. "Anderson!"

Finally, Anderson moaned. "What do you want?" he barked. "Let me die in peace."

"You cannot give up hope. We are still alive. My father and Grey Eagle will come."

Anderson laughed. "Look around you, Hramack. There are thousands of people here. Do you think your father can just walk in here and free us? We're dead, and if they try to free us, they're dead as well. Lieutenant Lorst knows better than to attempt something that foolish. She will remain in that facility until she contacts our ship, and they come and get her off this miserable planet. I wish I had never come here."

"There is always hope, my father says. Yarah will protect us."

He surprised himself in his faith in Yarah, but in such times, man did need hope in something greater than himself. Even the Scattered Ones, as great as their accomplishments, still had an empty spot that yearned for fulfillment, or else why would they come many light years in search of a myth, a legend? Man's existence has always been a fine balance between the need of religion and its rejection. Each stride in science and technology made man less dependent on a god or God, while each setback sent him in search of his spiritual roots.

When man tamed lightning, or the atom, or space, he felt god-like and all-powerful. Each new insight into knowledge heretofore unknown gave him a feeling of omniscience. Yet, each cataclysm, natural or as a result of man's own folly, sent the masses scurrying back into the empty churches and mosques, searching for someone to watch over and protect them. Only when man walked side-by-side with the knowledge of a Supreme Being and the knowledge of the atom would true progress take place, a deeply profound progress of the mind and of the soul.

Now was such a time of a new beginning. If only he could reach his captors.

Throughout the rest of the day and into the night, they lay chained to the pole. Only once did someone bring food to them, poor as it was. They received no water as they languished beneath the harsh sun. Instead, the crowds taunted them by drinking water and pouring it on the ground just out of reach. Hramack stretched as far as his chains would allow, but could not reach any of the small, tantalizing pools of water. He watched them evaporate, taking his last hopes with them.

It was well after midnight when someone approached them. Anderson was asleep. Hramack waited for another savage kick or stone flung from the darkness.

"So, Southerner, how do you like our hospitality?" a voice asked.

He squinted to try to identify the voice but could see nothing. "Not very well," he answered. "If you free us, we'll be on our way."

The man laughed and came closer. Hramack saw it was Hardy.

"Why do you want to kill us?" Hramack asked. "We have acted only in self defense."

Hardy leaned over Hramack and whispered, "I have spoken to my men, and I'm beginning to suspect that is true. Is it coincidence, or providence, that the Scattered Ones arrived just as you did? The future of my people is a great weight on my shoulders. I sense that we now walk a sharp path no man has traveled with our eyes shut. If we stumble, if I stumble, we will all fall into a great abyss. Great changes come." Hardy surprised Hramack by squatting beside him. "Sometimes our allies along the borders and, I'm sad to say, my own men, act hastily, without thought. It's not easy holding together a nation of people who less than ten years ago were eating one another." He laughed, then stared into Hramack's eyes, as if he could dig out the information he wanted. "Why are you here?"

Hramack sighed. He knew his response might be the key to his and Anderson's survival. "Until a few weeks ago, my people thought we were the only ones to survive the falling of the Denver Dome, other than a few scattered bands of nomads slowly dying out. Then we met Grey Eagle's people, who did not enter the dome and have lived free for centuries. Marauders attacked us, the same ones who have been attacking his people for years. We came here only to return the life-giving flow of water to our villages. In that, we have failed. We mean you no harm. It is easy to see that we have much to learn about your people, just as you have much to learn about ours."

"What of him?" Hardy pointed to Anderson, still sleeping on the ground.

"He is one of four who crashed their ship many days east of here. Only he and a woman survived. They, too, had to fight off attacks on their journey here. They are from the Scattered Ones searching for their Homeworld. They say there are men on the next planet, Mars, who would come here to plunder our world but for the defense satellites circling our world. If we do not band together, soon others will claim this world for their own, and we will have nothing.

"There is much here they want, great machines that even the Scattered Ones do not possess. We can trade technology for their help in teaching us its use. If they wish to come here to live, we can trade land useless to us in exchange for the chance to rebuild our cities in peace. There is no need for our people to fight each other. We are the last people on Earth, and we have the responsibility of stewardship of this planet. If we do not cooperate, we may soon cease to exist."

Hardy had said nothing as Hramack spoke. When he finished, Hardy nodded his head slowly. "Much of what you say rings true, but I cannot control all the people in this land. I don't have the resources. I have forged an alliance of these tribes your people call Marauders, but many more exist beyond my reach, far to the north and to the east."

"With the help of the Scattered Ones, we can teach them new ways."

Hardy narrowed his eyes, and Hramack saw a bit of the cold, hard determination that Hardy's men feared. "If the Scattered Ones are so powerful, they could easily rule us. What if we grow too dependent on their help?"

"They need us as much as we need them."

Hardy laughed in derision. "What do we have that they so desperately need?"

"Their history." Hramack smiled. "We are Homeworld to them; their Center and their Origin. They need to connect the threads of their history backwards to their beginnings. We are their forefathers."

Hardy nodded. Hramack hoped he had begun to see the tapestry that his poor words were attempting to weave. "I think I understand." He laughed. "We are Eden." He pulled a key from his pocket and removed the chains from Hramack and Anderson.

Anderson, awakened by the laughter, rolled over. "What's going on?"

"History is going on, my friend, history," Hardy answered. "Come, we will see that you have the opportunity to bathe and eat and find a proper place for you to sleep. Tomorrow we will find your friends."

The three walked to the Meeting Hall through Hardy's bewildered guards. Hardy turned to Hramack. "Can we talk more? There is much I need to know."

"First, your men must return something they took from me."

Hardy nodded. "I will see to it."

For the first time in many weeks, Hramack felt hope.

Just as dawn broke over the eastern hills, the plane carrying Grey Eagle, Kena, Cathi, and the men of Pueblo Nuevo winged its way towards the city of the Marauders. Either today would bring about a new alliance of the remnants of man, or they would all die. Kena's heart was light even at the thought of death. The previous night, he had made his peace with Yarah. They had failed in their mission. They had not returned the waters to the villages, but he had faith in Yarah's will. If it were possible, someone would do it. If not he, perhaps the Star People would.

The mood aboard the plane was quiet and somber. No one spoke. Each man was deep in his own thoughts. As they approached the new city in the ruins of the old, they saw a great crowd of people gathered around the central structure.

"If we have to fight, we will die," Two Clouds said looking out the window.

"At least we will not have to walk home through that cursed tunnel," Grey Eagle chimed in. A few men laughed, but it quickly faded.

"Land in the middle of them," Kena told Cathi. "They will move."

The crowd below panicked when they saw the plane overhead. As it hovered above their heads, they began to shove each other in their hurry to get out of the way.

Grey Eagle laughed. "At least we frightened them." Then he saw the throngs of armed men on the edges of the crowd. "Tawa, protect us."

Anderson and Hramack stood beside Hardy as he spoke to his people gathered in front of the Meeting Hall. The crowd had come to witness an execution. Instead, Hardy told them of his plan to unite the scattered tribes of the west with Hramack and Grey Eagle's people and form a new alliance to rebuild the country. He introduced Anderson, who drew jeers and taunts from the crowd. Hardy silenced them and stood beside Anderson as Anderson explained what the Scattered Ones would do to aid them through the efforts of the Trade Guild. Just as Anderson finished speaking, a flying machine appeared overhead.

"Your ship?" Hramack asked him.

"No. This ship is not capable of space flight. It is one of yours."

"Whose?" he asked.

"We will soon see," Hardy said excitedly.

The crowd scattered in panic as the plane gently settled in the square. As the high-pitched whine faded away, a door opened in its side. Hramack instantly recognized the man emerging through the doorway.

"Father!" he yelled, running toward the plane.

Kena stopped and stared at the crowd in bewilderment. Hramack understood his father's confusion. He had come expecting to free his son. Instead, his son now rushed to greet him.

"Don't worry, father. We have found new friends."

Kena looked skeptical, but smiled as he embraced Hramack. "Yarah works wonders," he said.

As Cathi descended from the plane, Anderson greeted her. "I see you've found transportation."

"We may be here for a while," she answered. She told him about her contact with their ship and that it, too, had become a victim of the satellite lasers.

"They may have gotten through," Anderson said. "We did."

She nodded, wiping a tear from her eye.

Kena motioned Grey Eagle to join them. He cautiously exited the plane, eyeing the crowd, wary of a trap. His men followed his example and formed a protective semi-circle around their leader.

Hardy walked over to stand before Grey Eagle. "There has been much bloodshed between your people and those that ally themselves with me. I cannot undo this wrong. Let us therefore endeavor to prevent the spilling of more blood." He removed a knife from his belt and thrust it into the ground at his feet. "Here my knife stays forever."

Hramack held his breath as Grey Eagle studied the man standing in front of him. Finally, he said, "I am only a warrior and cannot speak for my people, but I see the wisdom in your words. There is no need for further bloodshed between our two peoples. It is as Kena has said a time for rebuilding." He removed his own knife and drove it into the ground beside Hardy's blade. "Forever," he said. He offered his empty hand to Hardy.

Great whoops of joy erupted throughout the square as old enemies grasped hands and set aside weapons. Hardy proclaimed a day of thanksgiving and called all the people from the fields and farms into the city for a day of celebration. After days on short rations, the idea of a feast sounded good to Hramack.

33

LONG JOHN BALDRY'S
RELUCTANT PASSENGER

APTAIN MOORE SAT ACROSS FROM CHANCELLOR INAYA PACHMARUDHI, smiling as she drummed her long fingers on the table in irritation. Her long, red-lacquered nails made a pecking sound on the hard surface. She returned his smile with a scathing scowl. He had locked her in an empty cabin during their hurried lift off. She had not been happy at her ill treatment. Two armed guards had escorted her to the officer's mess, which he had deliberately ordered off-bounds so she would not see the women and children. If the Chancellor thought the *Baldry* was a military vessel, she might have a greater respect for her capabilities.

Her short confinement had not quelled her anger. "You have damaged our dome and taken me prisoner. Do you think we will allow this violation to go unpunished?"

"You tried to steal my ship, Madame Chancellor. In my mind, that makes you and your people thieves. The Trader's Guild frowns on theft or attempted theft of Guild property. You're lucky I don't level your dome as an example." He suppressed a chuckle, as a look of disbelief and fear crept across her face. She was not certain he was lying, and that small amount of uncertainty was all he needed. "I needed you as a hostage to get free of your city safely." He looked at her squarely in the eyes and said, "Now, I have no further need for you." As he had hoped, she misinterpreted his meaning. "If you want, I can drop you off here."

She peered at the view screen above the table displaying the terrain over which they passed. The dry, cracked, quilt-work bottom of the Bay of Bengal, abandoned by a retreating Indian Ocean that had left the island of Ceylon attached to the Indian Subcontinent, gave way to Southeast Asia, once a land of long, lazy rivers and impenetrable jungles. Now, it was a seared brown plain devoid of life. Ancient stone cities, once swallowed by the dense green growth, now sat alone, naked reminders of the region's more grandiose times. The rusting bones of modern cities had fared no better, dotting the sunken lines of dried rivers or clinging to the dirty, white, salt encrusted coasts. Where forests once stood, only a few tenacious scattered plants clung precariously to life, and only the hardiest wildlife had adapted to the harsh environment, eking out a meager sustenance existence.

They passed over a large, deep crater surrounded by broken, fused earth that had once been Bangkok, Thailand, one of the many cities destroyed during the wars. Her already wan complexion paled to shy white. She had never strayed far from the dome, and the vista of desolation frightened her. Her rigid pose relaxed and she sat back in her seat.

She sighed heavily. "I will remain your hostage. What do you intend to do with me?"

Moore was pleased to see he had spilled a little wind from the Chancellor's sails. "I intend to find my crew. You wanted to see Denver Dome, so you'll get your chance. Maybe they will prove more amiable toward a trading agreement than your people did."

The Chancellor's eyes narrowed and for a moment, she resembled the bird of prey Moore suspected she was. "Do not be hasty, Captain Moore. The Khan is an old man. His mind wanders the corridors of the past. He sometimes becomes enamored of grandiose things. It is my duty as Chancellor to steer him back onto the realities of the present. You have shown him your power. I am certain an acceptable trade agreement can be reached that would benefit both our peoples."

Moore doubted the Khan had even been aware of his presence in Kolkata Dome. He was the titular head of state, but the true power behind the throne sat across the table from him in the guise of a pleading, repentant woman.

"Perhaps. I will speak with my people and see if they think a deal is worth the effort."

"Please do. I am surprised you do not simply take what you wish. We do not have the means stop you."

"Except for your weapons satellites," he reminded her. "Don't think I've forgotten about them. We don't operate that way, Chancellor. If you don't want to trade, we'll leave you in peace, but that doesn't mean some other planet might see things differently. As a Trade Guild partner, Earth will have certain privileges. Protection from pirates is one."

"I see," she said with a sneer. "We will be dependent upon your good will."

He ignored her jibe. "As trading partners, we will not interfere with your internal forms of government; however, we will require a certain amount of cooperation between your separate governments. Wars are bad for business, and slaves make poor workers."

"Our people are not slaves. They seek our steady guidance in a changing world. Dissention is allowed until it interferes with our ability to govern. Kolkata Dome is the last surviving dome because of our benevolence and our foresight, but if you wish to remove us from power ..."

"We have no wish to take over. If your citizens desire to over-throw you, that is between you and them. The Guide will make certain no liberties are taken with or reprisals enacted upon other trading partners."

"That borders heavily on interference."

Moore shrugged. "We will make a substantial monetary invest-ment in your planet. We only want to see that we do not lose it due to petty squabbles."

The Chancellor folded her arms across her chest and smiled. "Do you think we will allow your ship to leave Earth, Captain Moore? Even now, our satellites are tracking you. My life will be forfeit, but you will not return to reveal our location."

"Oh, about that. When you relayed the disarm codes to the defense grid, we intercepted the transmission. It was small matter to decipher the numerical sequence. I think you will find that the satellites no longer obey your signal."

This last insult was more than the Chancellor could take. She yanked one of the ebony pins from her hair, and launched herself across the table at him. She was strong for her size, doubled by her outrage, but the slightly, lower gravity aboard ship altered her trajec-tory. The deadly pin slid harmlessly past his shoulder. He pressed his elbow into her back, pinning her to the table.

"That's not very lady like, Chancellor, nor is it very diplomatic. If you persist on such tactics, I'll return to Kolkata Dome and drop you off, from orbit. You'll have plenty of time to ponder the error of your ways as your city grows inexorably closer second by second."

She ceased struggling. "You win, Captain Moor. I will meet with the leaders of these other survivors. It is apparent to me that our differences are nothing compared to our need to unite against you."

Moore shrugged. "As I said, Chancellor, we will leave your world if you ask us to, but you are not likely to get a better offer from other interested parties. Your technology is too tempting for some worlds to ignore."

She sat back and tried to regain her lost poise. "The carrot and the stick, I see. You hide the stick with neutral words, but it is still there."

Moore did not understand her reference, but her meaning was not lost on him. He would be glad to drop her off and pick up his crew. He had remained a bachelor because of women like the Chancellor.

34

REUNION

NEAR DUSK ON THE SECOND DAY OF CELEBRATION, DANCING AND FEASTING had given way to quiet conversation. Kena, freshly scrubbed and dressed in new clothing provided by Hardy, was eager to return to the pumping facility beneath Mount Lincoln. He still hoped to discover a way to direct the flow of water to Ningcha. Hardy's invitation to join him took him by surprise.

As they walked, Hardy said, "It is a full-time job keeping this Alliance together. I never get to go into the ruins around us anymore. There is much I have not seen, many things we can use."

Kena described some of the devices and machines he had found. "We can trade. I will help find them and learn to use them, and then teach others to use them. In return, you will expand the lands under cultivation and irrigation. We must grow enough food for ourselves and for trade. From what Cathi has told me, the outer worlds have an endless desire for exotic foods. It will be a good trade item."

"Perhaps," Hardy conceded. "We must build together, though I fear the return of the Scattered Ones."

"Why?"

"They are many, and we are few. What is to prevent their simply taking what they want?"

"They are traders, not conquerors. United, we present a strong front against them. When settlers come, we allow them in, but on our terms."

Hardy considered Kena's words. "Earth should be for Earthmen," he stated.

Kena slowly shook his head. "Left on our own, it would take hundreds of years to rebuild, perhaps longer. The other worlds will not wait that long. With the Trade Guild's help, we can do it in ten. They can help protect us until we are ready to protect ourselves. If we disregard them now, who can say who will follow them here intent on conquest. No, we must accept their aid and agree to some of their terms. This includes settlers."

"Then we will do it," Hardy said and reached out his hand to Kena's. "I want to be alive when we rebuild our country, our new world."

"We have much to learn from each other," Kena told him. "First thing, do you know how to get the water flowing to my village again?"

Hardy hung his head. "We know little about the pumping station under the mountain. My people fear to go there. It was a simple thing to restore our water, but yours, I do not know."

"I can." They turned to see Anderson smiling. Two days of rest and food and Kena's ministrations had wrought wonders in him. His limp was barely noticeable. Cathi stood beside him. "I believe I know what the problem is. We just need to find the damaged section of pipe and repair or replace it. It must be located beneath the pumping facility. The necessary tools and equipment to do the job should not be that difficult to locate."

Kena raised his eyes to the heavens. "Thank you, Yarah," he whispered.

While Kena was whispering his silent prayer of thanks to Yarah, a bright light filled the sky overhead. Startled that it was in response to his prayer, he averted his eyes. Only when he heard Cathi's joyous laughter, did he glance up. The light was smaller now but moving swiftly across the horizon and descending.

"It's my ship," she began screaming. "It's the *Baldry!*" She grabbed Kena and kissed him. "You were right," she told him softly; then she danced away and screamed, "They're alive!"

He turned to an equally startled Hardy. "We shall soon have the opportunity to meet the Trade Guild. You can judge for yourself if they are worthy of our trust."

The ship landed in a clearing less than a kilometer from the town. At first frightened, people's curiosity soon overcame their fear, and they began to gather around the ship. As the landing ramp descended, Cathi led the way, running. Less than a dozen meters from the ship, she suddenly stopped running and began walking slowly as she brushed off her threadbare uniform. Like her, it was now clean, but the journey had reduced it to tatters.

"She's an officer," Anderson whispered to Kena in explanation. "It wouldn't look good for her to be seen running up to the ship yelling like a castaway." He winked.

Kena wasn't certain he understood, but nodded. A rotund man with a beard stood at the foot of the ramp. Cathi saluted as she approached. To her surprise, the red-bearded captain grabbed her in a big hug, lifted her from the ramp, and then set her back down.

Cathi's voice trembled in anguish, as she reported the deaths of Whitehall and Pegari.

"It is a sad loss," the captain said in a booming voice. "We shall miss them, but you're alive, and I see you and Mr. Anderson have made friends. That's good. We seem to have disturbed the natives." He crooked his finger, and Chancellor Pachmarudhi walked out of the ship looking downcast and frightened.

"This is Chancellor Inaya Pachmarudhi, a high-echelon windbag from Kolkata Dome." He looked Pachmarudhi in the eye. "He can't be trusted, but we've had time to talk a bit on the journey here. I believe she now sees the mutual benefit of allying herself and her people with yours."

Pachmarudhi shot Moore a withering glance that could have singed his beard, but he smiled and nodded. "It will please me to learn more about your people. Captain Moore," she said with undisguised hatred, "has told me that we can all benefit greatly by presenting one face to the Scattered Ones as they return to their Homeworld."

Kena immediately distrusted her, but knew the Chancellor, as a representative of Kolkata Dome, would have to be included in any negotiations with the Trader's Guild. If Earth were to survive the coming years of contact, they would need the help of Kolkata Dome. He supposed this was his first lesson in politics.

Moore spoke up. "I believe Pachmarudhi here fears your people. It seems her ancestors were once the rulers of Denver Dome, before your people threw them out." His loud guffaw made Pachmarudhi wince. Kena would have known Captain Moore was a good man even if Cathi had not assured him so.

Kena laughed. "We will be too busy rebuilding our own country to worry with them, though we will accept any help they wish to offer or trade for. And you, Captain Moore. What do you want of us?"

"I am a merchant, sir. I come to trade. Politics bore me. My people will make no claim to Homeworld, though many will wish to come as settlers, I'm sure. Earth will be a balm for their souls and an ointment for their hearts." He cocked his head to one side. "What do you want, Kena?"

Kena sighed. "I want to go home. It has been a long journey. But first, I must ask a favor."

"Ask."

"I have failed to bring the water back to my village from the pumping facility under the mountain. Anderson says you may be able to help us."

"Well, for starters, I think I can get you back there much quicker than your trip here. Come. Let's talk."

Hardy turned to Pachmarudhi. "Are there many people left on Earth?"

Pachmarudhi drew closer, as if in hardy she had spotted a kindred spirit. "From what we have managed to observe from our satellites, there are scattered bands of people here in the southwest and southeast, as well as near a series of small lakes far to the north. A few small villages remain in northern Europe but no cities. Perhaps there is a scattering of people on small islands in the salt oceans, but sadly we few are all that remain."

Kena noticed Pachmarudhi carefully did not reveal how many people remained in Kolkata Dome. Hardy missed this omission. "We should talk, you and I," he said.

"Indeed. That is my wish also."

To Kena, it had felt like pulling teeth, but finally they had reached an agreement concerning possible settlement and trade with the Traders Guild and had agreed to form an Earth Council to meet later to finalize details. Kena had concerns about both Pachmarudhi and Hardy. Both appeared overly ambitious and eager to lead the Council. He feared trouble later, a conflict of wills, but he knew they could not achieve perfection in one meeting. Over time, as each realized the needs of Earth, he was hopeful they could arrive at a position that would benefit all.

Captain Moore had told him of the plight of the people of Kolkata Dome and of their great numbers. He wished there was something he could do about it, but it was beyond his ability. The Guild could take no active part in change, but Cathi had told him that the Guild could initiate subtle changes through trade agreements. Certainly, they could accomplish nothing from New Denver, as Hardy was calling his new city rising from the ashes of Denver Dome. They had problems enough. He regretted that they would be cooperating with a power with so little regard for its citizens. All peoples deserved to live in freedom. After all, it was that very desire for freedom that had prevented his ancestors from abandoning Earth ten millennia earlier.

Using the *Baldry*, Moore transported them to the underground pumping facility under Mount Lincoln, named, he learned, after a past U.S. president who had presided over America during a great civil war. It had taken Anderson less than ten minutes to locate the proper diagnostic screen on the computer in the control room.

He pointed to a long corridor on one of the video monitors. "This corridor contains the overflow pipes that control water flow to your villages. They operate only when the lake becomes too full from melting snow. The damage has to be there." He touched a point on the screen to enlarge it, revealing a darkened section of the corridor and a pool of water. "We should be able to repair the damage and reset the overflow parameters to assure a constant flow of water to your villages."

"Remarkable," Hramack said.

Kena's words were more humble. "Praise Yarah."

The four of them – Cathi, Kena, Anderson, and Hramack – rode an antigravity sled down the long corridor, following a large pipe running the corridor's length. After half a kilometer, the tunnel grew darker as they neared the damaged area.

"The corridor is blocked," Hramack said, pointing to a pile of stone and masonry filling the corridor from floor to ceiling. A section of pipe lay crushed beneath the heavy fall. A pool of water lapped against the rocks, leakage from their earlier attempt to start the pump.

"Now we know what stopped the water," Anderson said.

"Perhaps an earthquake caused this," Kena suggested. "I have felt tremors many times in the past." He got out of the sled and waded through waist-high water to examine the landslide. "It will take weeks to clear this rubble and repair the pipe."

Hramack's heart thundered in his chest. "Everyone will be dead by then." *Teela!*

Anderson spoke up. "I don't think so, Hramack. With the heavy machinery we found in the garage and some additional manpower, we can have this cleared and the water on its way to your village in a day or two."

"This is true?" Hramack asked.

"For a fact," Anderson told him.

Hramack's burden lifted. "Then we did not fail." He was overjoyed that he would soon return to Teela.

"Let's return to the *Baldry* and set things up," Anderson suggested.

✳

"We can help you rebuild your world," Captain Moore told Kena as they drank coffee on his ship.

Hramack lounged beside his father on a low couch, sipping the beverage that had once been so ubiquitous on Earth but now grew only on a few of the outer worlds. He found the taste slightly bitter, even with the added sugar, but his heart raced from the caffeine it contained. He suspected that coffee would soon become a cherished trade item for the captain, especially as water became more available.

They had cleared away the rockslide using the heavy earth-moving equipment in the garage. Hardy's men had supplied the labor. After replacing the damaged section of pipe, with a simple touch of his finger, Kena had sent water flooding the chamber and rushing toward Ningcha. It had seemed to Hramack a decidedly anticlimactic ending for such a dramatic adventure.

"In exchange for what?" Kena asked the captain.

Moore laughed. "There is technology far beyond what we have. We will study it and teach your people to use it. We would both learn from the exchange."

"A fair exchange," he agreed. "I'll bring it before the Earth Council when we next meet," Kena said.

Hramack smiled at his father. He had taken on the mantle of leadership. He thought it fit his father well.

More laughed. "You're quickly becoming a good politician, Kena."

"Earth will need politicians as well as Healers."

"Well, gentlemen, I promised you a quick ride home. I think it's time to go."

"How long will it take the water to reach Ningcha?" Hramack asked.

Moore gave the question a moment's thought, then smiled broadly. "I'm not sure, a few days. We can track its progress underground with our scanners if you wish." He cocked his head. "Why?"

Kena was beginning to suspect what was on Hramack's mind. "I think my son believes our people need a miracle."

"I can't wait to see the look on Chu Li's face when we return," Hramack said.

"Yes, Chu Li," Kena said absently, as he thought about the reason for their leaving. "There will be a reckoning." He turned to Moore. "Yes, Captain, it is well indeed time to go home. We've been away far too long and there are changes we must make."

Moore saw the grim look on Kena's face. "I wouldn't want to be the man deserving of that look."

Hramack was concerned for his father. He had no doubt that he could best Chu Li in any fight, but wondered how the High Priest's death would affect him as a Healer. It was true that his father had taken lives on their journey, but that had been in battle against an enemy that showed no quarter. To kill someone you knew face-to-face, however dangerous, would be a difficult thing to do. It would be an even harder deed to live with.

35

HOMECOMING

TEELA SAT ON A ROCK BY THE EDGE OF THE CLIFF AND CONTEMPLATED THE darkest thoughts she had ever felt. It had been weeks since Hramack and his father had left the village. The cisterns were almost dry. Earlier that morning an argument had erupted at one of the cisterns between two women over a broken jug of water. One of the women had broken down in hysterical tears.

Chu Li had announced her marriage to Juresh, Madras' youngest son. Though Kaffa was adamantly against it, his health was failing. The pressure of resisting Chu Li and his refusal to drink more than a few mouthfuls of water each day had taken their toll on him. Teela feared the worst. If anything happened to her grandfather, she would have no choice in the matter. She had felt things could get no worse when they had sacrificed a goat to Yarah. She had been wrong.

People were afraid to leave their homes for fear of becoming targets of accusations as the source of the ills that the village faced. The crying of fevered children had replaced the sounds of people singing. The dust fever now affected many. *If only Kena would return,* she thought. Oh, Hramack!

There was no water for the animals. They had brought all of them up from the canyon bottom to the pens in preparation for their eventual slaughter. The village was nearing its end. If Hramack did not return soon, she would fling herself over the precipice and onto the rocks below. She would never marry another and could not bear to face life without him.

She heard Kaffa's cough as he walked up to her. It sounded like a death rattle.

"Why do you sit here alone, child?" he asked. He sat beside her, using his staff to lower his frail body to the stone. She noticed the dark circles around his eyes and the slight tremor in his hands.

"Grandfather, you look ill. Have you had your water ration today?"

He did not answer.

"You cannot continue to do this," she said, chiding him. "You will die."

"Death will be welcome, my dear. I am too old to watch others die."

"Nonsense. The village needs you. I need you."

"I am useless. I fear I can no longer protect you from Chu Li. The people avoid me now for fear of Chu Li's wrath."

"I will kill him," she said quietly. She didn't really know if she was capable of murder, but her loathing for the High Priest might just push her to such an extreme measure.

Kaffa patted her hand and smiled weakly. "Now, Teela. You cannot do such a thing. Chu Li will get what he deserves."

"He deserves death," she cried, thinking of Hramack. "He has robbed me of my future."

Kaffa was distracted. He raised his head and stared at the sky. "Funny. I thought I heard thunder, but that is impossible." He shook his head. "I am getting too old."

"No, grandfather," Teela said, listening. "I heard it too." She scanned the sky for the sound she had heard. "There are no clouds.

Perhaps it was merely a rockslide down the valley." She glanced at the rim of the canyon once more, as she had many times over the past three weeks, hoping to see Hramack walking down the path. Since her nightmare, she held a secret fear that she would never see him again. To her disappointment, all she saw was shimmering waves of heat rising from the rock.

Chu Li, more pompous than ever since the departure of Kena and Hramack, slowly made his way to the edge of the cliff for the Morning Prayers. Slowly, the villagers gathered around him. *Like sheep*, she thought bitterly. Since Alton's attack and death, the prayers had become more fervent, almost frantic.

"We will pray to Yarah together to ask his forgiveness," Chu Li commanded. "The blasphemers are dead. I have seen it in a vision. The waters will come." He raised his staff above his head and waved it in the air.

Teela gasped at his announcement of Hramack's death. Kaffa touched her shoulder and shook his head. "Be strong," he said. He faced the crowd and raised his voice. "I do not think so, Chu Li," he challenged, his voice sounding once again strong and loud. "Behold."

He raised his staff and pointed to the path leading from the canyon rim. Five mirage figures marched toward them, angels floating above the ground on waves of shimmering heat. One of the figures broke away from the others, flying down the path toward the village. As the illusion broke, it became a man running, one Teela recognized.

"Hramack," she yelled. Her heart pounded with relief and delight.

"It is the blasphemer," Chu Li cried. "Seize them!"

A few men moved to intercept Kena and Hramack, but most remained where they were, curious about the strangers accompanying them. Teela raced ahead of them, intent on begging Hramack to run away, intent on fleeing with him if necessary, anything to be with him again. Two of the figures wore curious blue one-piece jumpsuits. One was a redheaded woman whose skin was so pale it almost glowed, the other darker than anyone she had ever seen.

Before Teela could wonder where they had come from, the woman produced a device from her belt and pointed it at the opposite canyon cliff. A beam of light shot from the device and struck the cliff. A shower of rocks erupted from the cliff wall and cascaded down into the canyon. Teela froze at the display of power, afraid that the woman would mistake her headlong rush to save Hramack as an attack.

"Chu Li, people of Ningcha," Kena cried out as he approached, "Kaffa. I want you to meet Grey Eagle of Pueblo Nuevo, my new friend."

A towering, broad-shouldered man with his long grayish hair tied into a ponytail unlimbered his bow, but rested one end of the bow on the ground in front of him. His eyes narrowed as he stared at Chu Li.

"These are also new friends." Kena lifted his hand and pointed at the two figures in blue. "They are of the Scattered Ones returned from the stars. They have sought us out after a thousand years. We are no longer alone. With their help, we will bring back the waters to the Pools of Yarah. With their help, we can rebuild the Earth to its former glory."

Teela opened her arms as Hramack rushed to her. She held him close, her eyes filled with tears of joy as he lifted her into the air. Hramack held her face to his and kissed her on her lips. "I will never again leave your side," he promised.

Chu Li yelled, "Seize them! They have forfeited their lives by returning here. Have you forgotten Eithan's murder?"

Several men once again started towards Kena and Hramack. The woman raised her weapon, but Kena placed his hand on it to stop her.

"Devils! You have brought devils to our village," Chu Li screamed at Kena. "You are in league with evil. I am the High Priest. Yarah demands your death."

Kena stood his ground. "Like he demanded the death of the old High Priest, Herat? Did Yarah tell you to murder him, Chu Li, or was that your idea?"

"It was my right! I should have been chosen." Chu Li suddenly realized what he had admitted to and shook his head. "You confuse the issue. You are on trial here, not I."

"No. You murdered Herat in the name of Yarah to become High Priest. You compounded your crime when Eithan released us." He heard gasps of surprise from the crowd. "Yarah does not need men such as you to speak for Him. He speaks to our hearts and to our souls. You would corrupt His words for your benefit and your unholy desire for power. No more. We are not alone in this world. There are millions of men and women willing to rebuild our world that we may greet our returned brethren as equals. We are not the Chosen of Yarah, nor special in His eyes. He does not choose us. We, each of us, must choose Him. In my travels, I have learned Yarah has many names and lives in many hearts, and He does not need you to speak for Him, Chu Li. We can all hear His words if we listen with our hearts."

"Murderer!" Chu Li screamed as he shook his staff at Kena.

Madras stepped forward and pointed his finger at Chu Li. "No. It is as Kena has said. Chu Li killed my cousin and blamed Kena for the foul deed. I kept quiet for my own selfish reasons. Kena is innocent."

As one, the crowd turned to face their High Priest. They stood unsure of what to do, their faith shaken to its core by the High Priest's exposure.

"No! Yarah demands their blood if He is to bring back the waters." Chu Li ran toward Kena. As he ran, he produced a knife from the sash of his robe.

Teela watched terrified as Kena stood his ground. "Run," she yelled, but he remained rooted to the spot. Her hatred and anger rose to the surface. She would not allow the High Priest to harm Hramack or his father. She grabbed her grandfather's staff and rushed at Chu Li. "Leave him alone," she warned.

Chu Li glared at her, as he shifted the knife in his hand. Too late, she realized she had entered into a fight for which she was ill equipped, but she did not back away. Chu Li tried to step around her, but she positioned herself between the High Priest and Kena and Hramack.

"If you want water," Kena shouted, "then water you shall have. Behold!"

Ignoring Chu Li, Kena stretched out his hand toward the Pools of Yarah. A distant rumble shook the ground beneath Teela's feet, as if some giant entombed creature were clawing its way to the surface. Childhood stories of underground demons flashed through her mind. She looked to Hramack for reassurance and saw that he no longer stood beside his father. He stood only a few meters away, his knife in his hand ready to defend her from Chu Li. He smiled at her, unperturbed by the quaking ground. She moved to him and took his hand, felt his strength flowing into her. Chu Li looked puzzled. As the ground continued to shake harder, he fell to his knees.

Across the valley, a geyser of muddy water shot from the mouth of the springs and cascaded into the Pools of Yarah. A cloud of mist rose from the canyon and filled the air, washing over the crowd. When it touched Teela, she felt her parched skin soaking up the precious moisture. The end of a rainbow shimmered at her feet, an omen of good fortune. Within minutes, the pools had filled to overflowing. A deluge of muddy water rushed down the canyon in a roar of thunder.

Chu Li, seeing the water, yelled, "No, Yarah demands blood." Climbing to his feet, he launched himself at Kena. Kena easily sidestepped the frenzied attack and threw Chu Li to the ground, then kicked away his knife.

"Your day is done, murderer," Kena said to him.

Chu Li attacked again, this time with his staff. He swung it above his head to gain the momentum to crack Kena's skull. Without thinking, she rushed at Chu Li and grabbed the staff. A look of madness came over his face. His eyes glazed and spittle ran down his chin. He slung her aside. She hit the ground hard.

Madras, seeking to atone for his sins, attacked Chu Li. The High Priest saw him at the last second and turned aside. Madras' knife scored his shoulder and sent Chu Li into a rage. He screamed, grabbed Madras in a bear hug, and began slamming his head into Madras' chin. The stunned man stumbled backwards toward the edge of the cliff. Chu Li saw the cliff and lashed out, sending Madras into the raging flood below.

He turned to face Kena, looking more like a rabid animal than High Priest. He was beyond words. Animal grunts and growls erupted from his throat as he rushed at Kena with his hands outstretched, his fingers thrust out like claws. Teela covered her mouth with her hand and wondered why Hramack did not rush forward to protect his father. She soon learned the reason. Kena met Chu Li's mad rush by grabbing one of his arms and pinning it behind his back.

"Surrender, Chu Li. Your power is gone."

With a yell of rage, the High priest broke free. He backed away from Kena, stared at the people around him. His eyes fell upon the two Star People and a change came over him, as if his reasoning had returned. He lowered his arms. Then, before anyone could react, her aced to the edge of the cliff and threw himself over. By the time Kena reached the edge of the cliff, Chu Li's body was gone, washed down the canyon by the rushing waters.

"It is as Yarah willed it," Kaffa said. "Chu Li made his last sacrifice." He stamped his staff on the ground. It rang solidly against the stone, echoing down the canyon even over the roar of water. "Once again, the Pools of Yarah are full."

"And the water will run continuously Kaffa, my old friend," Kena said, taking Kaffa's hand. "These are our new friends." He presented Grey Eagle and Anderson. Then he introduced Cathi.

"Your father's eyes twinkle when he speaks of her," Teela whispered to Hramack as Kena made his introductions. "It is good."

Hramack smiled and hugged her closer. "I believe she feels for him also."

"Perhaps we could have a double wedding," she suggested and watched the startled expression on Hramack's face slowly give way to a broad smile.

Hramack reached into his pocket. "Then perhaps you should wear this," he said. He took her arm and placed a silver bracelet set with large blue turquoise stones.

"It's beautiful," she exclaimed.

"It was a gift to me for you."

She looked into his eyes and saw there was more to the story but did not ask. She knew he would explain someday when he wished her to know. For now, she was too happy to have him back safe to care.

Hramack and Teela stood side by side, watching the water spill from the crevice and plummet into the pools below. Clouds of mist rose to caress their faces. It had been a long journey with many surprises, but now it was over.

Teela snuggled up to Hramack. "How did you summon the water?"

Hramack smiled. "The water has been on its way here for many days. We followed its progress using the ship. We simply timed our arrival to intimidate Chu Li and frighten everyone else."

She pulled away. "Ship? What ship?"

A long silver shape shot across the sky above them. Hramack laughed at Teela's astonishment. "The *Long John Baldry*," he said. "Captain Moore dropped us off over the ridge. When he lands, I will be glad to show it to you. It is a truly wondrous thing."

"Then Yarah did not send the water?" she asked.

Her beliefs had suffered deeply during the past few weeks. Would Hramack pull them out and toss them aside? He drew her closer.

"Yarah watched over our every move," he said. "As my father said, 'Yarah helps those who help themselves'. I believe it was Yarah's will that my father did not have to stain his hands with Chu Li's blood."

Teela looked at the water. It was muddy now, but it would soon turn clear. The filters of the pumps would remove any remaining dirt. They could soon refill the cisterns. The village would live. Hramack had returned safe, and her long ordeal was over. She was content.

She looked at Hramack. "What now?"

"Someone will be needed to speak for our people in the Great Council that is soon to be held at New Denver. I think the people will choose my father. Then, who knows? Cathi Lorst says there are many beautiful worlds out among her stars. Perhaps she and my father will see a few before they return here."

"What of us?" Teela asked, fearing Hramack's answer.

Hramack took her hand and held it tightly. She squeezed back with all her strength. He looked into her eyes. She could see her reflection in them and willed it to remain there forever. "I will stay here with you," he said quietly, resolutely. "I will become the Healer of Ningcha. I know now that it is my destiny. I have been tested by fire and by water. My love for you has taught me to divine the feelings of others. I am no longer afraid of failure. With the devices from the mountain and the books Hardy has recovered, I can serve our people well." He sighed. "I have seen enough of our world for a while."

"You do not wish to also visit these other stars?" she asked, turning her head slightly away from his gaze, afraid he would see the tears in her eyes as she spoke.

"I have no need for other stars when I have the ones in your eyes."

Her heart pounded beneath her breasts as if a drum heralding his return. Teela smiled as he leaned over to kiss her. It was a perfect day.

※

Kaffa walked up the path that led to the brimming full Pools of Yarah. His footsteps felt lighter than they had in many weeks. The world Arun Kane had hoped to build would soon come to fruition.

With help from the Scattered Ones, Earth would become a garden again. The Scattered Ones would find their Center, their thread of history. The men of Earth would regain their legacy and their heritage. All that had once belonged to mankind would come into being. Together, the children of the stars and the children of Earth would reunite and march forward into a brighter future. Now was the time to lay out a great banquet for mankind. The Prodigal Son had returned.